MIST OF LIES

Once Upon A Tilted Rock

Matthew Kevan Zimmer

A publication of Akimbo Creative

Copyright © 2024 Matthew Kevan Zimmer

All rights reserved. No part of this publication may be reproduced, stored or transmitted in any form or by any means, electronic, mechanical, photocopying, recording, scanning, or otherwise without written permission from the publisher. It is illegal to copy this book, post it to a website, or distribute it by any other means without permission.

This novel is entirely a work of fiction. The names, characters and incidents portrayed in it are the work of the author's imagination. Any resemblance to actual persons, living or dead, events or localities is entirely coincidental.

Matthew Kevan Zimmer has no responsibility for the persistence or accuracy of URLs for external or third-party Internet Websites referred to in this publication and does not guarantee that any content on such Websites is, or will remain, accurate or appropriate.

Designations used by companies to distinguish their products are often claimed as trademarks. All brand names and product names used in this book and on its cover are trade names, service marks, trademarks and registered trademarks of their respective owners. The publishers and the book are not associated with any product or vendor mentioned in this book. None of the companies referenced within the book have endorsed the book.　　　　　　　　　　　　　First edition

CONTENTS

Title Page
Copyright

Epigraph
Prologue
What happened first — 1
What happened next — 296
What happened after that — 557
What happened in between — 577
About The Author — 579
Stay in touch — 581
Also By The Author — 583

A novel based on reality

content created 100% by a human being.

```
Books, Music,

Emotions
```

Acknowledgements and thanks

It takes a village idiot to start writing a book. It takes a village to finish it. This is my village.

Agnes Zimmer

Jim and Randi Mrvos

Justin Zimmer

Susan Helsel

Jane Scott

Karen Petley

Lisa Morris

Betsy Lang

Cheri Kiesler

Live every day as if what you do matters and one day it will.

ARTHUR MARKOVICH

PROLOGUE

Once upon a tilted rock

Was built a beautiful world

It was the most precious world of all

Perfect, but for one flaw

The universe tried again and again to fix the flaw.

This is the story of its latest attempt.

WHAT HAPPENED FIRST

The slow death of his soul was getting harder to ignore. An unpleasant annoyance, not enough to cause pain. Brody Markovich leaned on the quartz vanity in the master suite of his upscale condo. "Dammit, this is pissing me off. Tired. I'm just..."

Brody started most mornings greeting another grand and glorious day of opportunity. After a quick workout, shower, and a healthy smoothie, he would bound out the door by seven. Other days he ate cold pizza waiting for the shower to heat up, barely making it out the door by eight. Today was a cold pizza kind of day. He had been up most of the night reviewing the details of his work project.

He looked again at the mirror. "More sleep, man. That's all you need."

The year 2015 had been a very good year and he had no intention of slowing down.

—ε-ε-ε-ε-ε-ε—

Augustine Chalamet walked up the stone path in the courtyard outside her flat, studying an envelope she pulled from her post box. She sat down on a bench under a large tree, setting the envelope on the bench. It was October, 1905 and the world of science was exploding. Einstein, Planck, Bohr and others were starting their long reign as kings of intuitive thought. A half century before, Darwin charted out how things naturally get better and smarter as time goes by. They spent the twentieth century scrambling to create a unified theory of the inner workings of the universe. No one could crack that nut.

Until Augustine.

From the outside, it appeared Mlle Chalamet led a sad life. She was orphaned at a young age and her only contact with people was with her students at a prep school. She never traveled beyond the cobblestone streets of her small hometown of Meaux, France. Yet, you could say she went farther than anyone. With her mind, she had traveled to the deepest recesses of the cosmos.

And, oh, the things she discovered.

With mild detachment, she watched leaves dance across the courtyard. In her younger days, she would have ripped the envelope open in excited anticipation. But the decades of countless rejections had worn her down. She couldn't bear the thought of reading yet another tersely worded rejection. She pulled her shoulder wrap tighter as the autumn wind served up a chill. The wind rustled the envelope.

Go ahead, blow it away. I already know what's in there.

A strong, well-timed gust would save her from "We have determined your work is not fitting with our publication standards. Your conclusions are not based on any known supporting information." Every publication was the same. The rejections became a mirror in which she viewed herself. The paper she wrote that had driven her to skin and bones was something the world needed to see. She was tired of being treated like a foolish woman. "Femme folle" in her native French.

With a resigned sigh, she opened the envelope.

—ε-ε-ε-ε-ε-ε—

Saronda Mia Jackson shuffled sideways as a teenager half her age pushed past her on the escalator. She glanced at her phone and saw that the Metro train was two minutes away. *Slow down, dude. Plenty of time.* She watched as he jumped the gate and trotted to the platform. Her name was Saronda, but everyone called her

Roni. She hated it but could never find the assertiveness to push back. To her, the pain of confrontation outweighed the annoyance. Even her mom called her Roni when she wanted to get under her skin, which was often. She found her usual spot on the train, standing near the door, facing away from the crowd. Her face fell into the dull, downward stare of a commuter, and her day began.

Her phone lit up. "What does she want now?" She surveyed the train to see if anyone took notice.

"Hey Mom. What's up? I'm on the train."

"Are you coming this weekend? I didn't hear from you."

Roni pulled up her calendar. Crap, she had totally forgotten. Her mom wants her to come over to celebrate her sister Shay's Black Achievers Award. To Roni, this was an opportunity for her mom to continue the evergreen discussion of Roni's failures and dead-ends compared to her sister. She knew there would be so many unspoken questions: "Have you looked for a better job? Are you going to enroll full time at Trinity U? I forget, how far did you make it with your degree? Was it two years or just the one?" The words wouldn't always be spoken but they would hang over the room, crowding out everything else.

She played out her mom's words. "Shay, how many black achievers are there? It sounds very impressive. It shows what you can do when you work hard and focus."

The script changed but the message never did.

Roni started college ten years ago. It fizzled out. Then she got the idea to be a French translator but never applied for the certification. Her Army dad was stationed in France when Roni was young. She knew the language well, but science was her jam. Carl Sagan was her idol, digging deep into the cosmos. Roni didn't have a plan. She drifted, throwing her fate to the universe.

She arrived at Union Station and rushed across the street to The Corner Bakery, one step ahead of the crowd. Every day the same.

—ε-ε-ε-ε-ε-ε—

Mlle Chalamet bolted up from the bench and put her hand to her mouth to stifle a gasp. She raised the letter above her head as far as her eighty-six year old shoulders would allow. A journal agreed to publish her science paper! She hugged the acceptance letter against her frail body. She may have even done a little hip swivel. This was a big deal. She was getting published, under her real name, as a woman. A French woman getting published in a scientific journal in 1905 was unheard of. Mme Marie Curie had to discover two new elements and receive a Nobel Prize before being considered legitimate. Augustine used her real name, not a male pseudonym, because she wanted that to be the name to go down in history. Truth be told, even a respected male scientist would have had trouble getting the paper published. It went against current thinking. It was outlandish, silly almost. To Augustine, her theories were perfectly obvious, common sense. Silly to a fool maybe. But, for now, no more rejections. The world would learn what a beautifully coherent place the universe is. Mlle Augustine Chalamet, with the twentieth century emerging, was going to be a published scientist and the world would learn how the universe "works." She tilted her face up and felt the sun as it broke through. She chuckled. What version was this? Twenty? Thirty?

She was open and ready to discuss. And what a grand conversation it would be.

—ε-ε-ε-ε-ε-ε—

Brody stepped into the October sun, nodding to the doorman. "Hey big man, how 'bout them Stillers? Gotta beat the Bengals though." The doorman replied, "Here we go." It was the way to greet people in Pittsburgh, especially during football season.

He bought the condo after a recent promotion. His father told him, "Not bad for a guy in his thirties, but what you got so far is just a ticket to ride. You're not flying the rocket yet."

The crunch of his footsteps added to the chorus of autumn, scattering the leaves that had fallen from the trees that lined the Allegheny River waterfront. His purposeful gait and cocksure demeanor gave cover for a lack of confidence. As he walked, he mentally reviewed his charts for an upcoming meeting. It was a simple update meeting but any missed detail could be seized upon by rivals derailing his carefully planned trajectory.

Brody was a rising star at ExpoLytics. The

company was top heavy with founders and early-joiners who got rich from stock options, sitting in positions of authority with little skill except watching the stock price grow. They lived life large and in full view of the young guns yearning to climb the ranks. Brody took a look at that and said, "yes please, more if you got it."

It was a strange world where being the smartest in the room didn't matter. Sarcasm was revered. Snark and asking stupid questions in high profile meetings were a bonus. Brody fit right in. The formula was simple: ride a high horse, color inside the lines and don't mess up.

He had the tools: ambition, street smarts, and really nice hair. Once in a while he had a good idea.

—ε-ε-ε-ε-ε-ε—

Roni started working at the National Postal Museum in 2005. Ten years sitting at the information desk. It was supposed to be three, just until she got a degree. That never happened. One year melted into the next in a cozy job that paid the rent. The years weren't entirely wasted. She had plenty of free time to pursue her passion; absorbing knowledge. Learning new things was the inner flame she imagined when singing "This little light of mine" at Ebenezer Baptist in northeast D.C. She spent her days reading and scrolling Twitter, mostly science, but she wandered into all areas. One day it could be French poetry, the next, the life cycle of a sheep parasite. She interacted online through her Twitter handle @MathRonda. She named it before she realized she hated math. Math didn't cut it for her. They would teach "pi is an infinite number," but what she really wanted to know is why the universe made it that way. She wanted to know how things worked.

She would spend hours diving deep into something, considering it from every angle. The next moment, she would be on to something else. Her bedroom was a minefield of old books, dusty and worn. Some she had read, most she had not. She would start reading a book and then abandon it.

It greatly mirrored her direction in life.

—ε-ε-ε-ε-ε-ε—

Brody pushed through the revolving doors of the large glass monolith overlooking the Roberto Clemente Bridge. He high-fived the security guard standing beneath the large company logo ExpoLytics, The Future of Deep Analysis, and held his badge to the reader. The display lit up: B. Markovich 16. His promotion bumped him to the 16th floor, known simply as "the 16", where the movers and shakers are. Everyone on the lower floors were basically anonymous. Six months ago, Brody was one of the anonymous ones. He was an entry level software tester. It was a job a trained aardvark could do.

He didn't work his way up to the 16 step by step. It was more of a leap. Brody had one big idea and up he went. His old workmates gave him a nice send-off but there was clearly a jealous tension. He knew they thought he was an imposter. He wasn't so sure they were wrong, but he never let on. His father's words stayed with him:

"Wrap yourself in confidence until you figure out how to be useful."

Truth be told, he didn't have a complete idea, but he used enough of the right words so Wayne Drakauer could sketch it out. Wayne was a wunderkind if ever there was one, at least when it came to computer code. He listened to Brody's tangled words and fleshed out the idea. It was nothing short of a breakthrough for ExpoLytics. Major. Groundbreaking. Huge. It was Wayne's skill that made it work, but somehow, it became known as "Brody's Code." Wayne and Brody didn't exactly become friends after that. Brody treaded softly. His father's words guided him:

"Don't burn a bridge. You may have to use it someday."

Brody stepped onto the elevator. *Crap, Drew Waltham standing ramrod straight.* Drew was "the guy." He wasn't the head of the company, but he was well on his way. Always in control. Buttoned up, yet somehow able to pull off the "I'm your best bud" routine. His shirts didn't wrinkle. He was coming up from the parking garage. He had one of the precious few reserved parking spaces. Brody heard that Drew drove a Maserati Ghibli. *Geebly? Jeeblee? How do you even pronounce that? Such a pretentious ass.*

Brody was about to deliver an offhand remark full of self-promotion but Drew spoke first.

"How was your weekend? Do anything fun?"

Brody deadpanned, "Well, I was here pretty much the whole time. You see I'm working on that… "

"Oh that's cool. Man, I took my boat out on Lake Erie. Great weather. Stayed out overnight. Had to, I've been trying these cocktails from this book my wife gave me. You met my wife, right?"

Brody gave a muffled, "No."

He knew this was Drew's way of reminding everyone that his wife was a well-known local news anchor. She had big white teeth and wore tight dresses.

"Anyhoo, got a few pages into this recipe book for cocktails and then didn't know what I was mixing. Grapefruit, bitters, hell I don't know what all was in there, vodka of course. Lots of vodka. Kinda got away from me, if you know what I mean," Drew said, winking. "No way I could dock the boat after that. Gotta have your senses sharp with such a big boat."

Brody didn't know people overnighted on Lake Erie but figured he must have a nice boat if he could sleep in it.

"Sounds like fun, Mr. Waltham."

"Yeah, Brady, you'll need to come out sometime. Great fun."

Brody's sharp reply was only in his head. *Yeah, well maybe when you learn my name, ya jagoff.*

His real reply. "That would certainly be an experience."

Mercifully, the doors opened. Drew turned left toward the executive suites. Brody turned right. Brody walked past rows of cubicles and headed straight to the break room. Yes, break room. Coffee. Now.

—ε-ε-ε-ε-ε-ε—

Roni pulled a tattered folder from her bag. It held two versions of a half-filled enrollment form for Trinity Washington University. Emblazoned on the letterhead was "Discover <u>Your</u> Strength." *Dang, I know my strength, what I need is an elective.* She vacillated between Psych and Econ. Her phone lit up. It was a text from her roommate. *Hey roomie girl, new bookstore opening near us. Knew you liked those geeky things. XoXo*

Roni clicked the link. A used bookstore was opening half a block from her apartment. This ranked up there with the opening of the all night pho place. Suddenly the day could not go fast enough. She pulled up the Metro app and timed the redline trains so she could get to the bookstore before closing.

—ε-ε-ε-ε-ε-ε—

It happened… again. Brody didn't know what to make of it. This time it was more persistent, clearer. Another annoying episode where things seem to change.

He glanced at his coffee. There was cream in it. Brody never puts cream in his coffee. It was little things like that. Time and again, stupid, distorted observations. He stared at his cup. The coffee was black the way he always drank it.

A strong voice jolted Brody. "I really wished you'd have come in earlier."

It was Brody's boss.

Hank "Brooster" Drucker, the head of the entire analytics division, including being in charge of "Brody's Code." Over seventy percent of ExpoLytics' revenue came from analytics. That made Brooster quite the big deal.

As the acid rose up from his stomach, Brody deflected with a deadpan snark. "Why? Is something up?"

"Jeezus, Brody. You know you gotta lotta eyes lookin' at you. This is a trial balloon. A test. And nobody knows if you got this handled. People are comin' in today to look at *your* stuff. You know, the stuff that I haven't seen in what, two weeks? The stuff you haven't reviewed with me. They'll be crawling through your shorts with a spyglass and a blowtorch. I thought you cudda used a little extra time this morning to button things up."

Brody replied, "Any more buttoned up and it couldn't breathe. We got this."

It was a little strong, but brashness was like a union card around the 16. He spoke with way more confidence than the situation deserved. In truth, Brody's project was not buttoned up. One could say it was mildly under control. But, as his father taught him:

"Never let them know you got no money until the bill comes due. You just might win the lottery."

They stared at each other awkwardly and then Brody said, "Well, I best get at it. See you in there."

Brody walked away. He could feel Brooster's eyes burning a hole through his back. Blustering about not seeing Brody's pitch was a sad joke. Hank Drucker, or Brooster as he insisted, never wanted to review anything prior to meetings. It was because he didn't understand any of it. Brooster joined ExpoLytics as a clueless intern when the company was young. He ended up with a sizable stock package. He's still clueless but now he's rich. He runs the entire Financial Analysis division.

Like Drew Waltham, they gave him his own parking spot. No telling what kind of car he parked there. Brody really wanted Brooster's job. He wanted his lifestyle.

Brooster's agitating and the unexplained episode with the coffee left Brody anxious as he returned to his office. He stared at his computer, nervously toying with a squishy rubber duck, bobbing it back and forth. This was his first big project. He was doing analysis for FinCen, the powerful Financial Crimes unit of the United States Government. The work had to be precise. A small screw up can be disastrous. He already delivered a preliminary report. Today was supposed to be a simple update.

Brody leaned back in his chair. People were already

filling the meeting room across the hall. It was odd to see so many early arrivals. He crossed the hallway and felt a more intense energy than usual as he got to the door, what the — no way. Two of the five SEC commissioners were sitting in the front row. Brody recognized them from pictures he had seen. Brooster was already there too.

He saw Brody and jumped up and came into the hallway. "Holy Jeezus alive. Do you see who's in there?" Brooster fidgeted back and forth, his short arms resting akimbo.

"Well, yeah, I see the SEC commissioners and some other suits. Who are they?"

"The guy to the right is the head of FinCen. The guy beside him, I don't know his name, but someone said he's FBI."

"FBI? What the hell?"

Brooster hunched his shoulders and threw up his hands. He scurried back in and sat down. Brody silently thanked him for his brilliant insight. He grabbed his thumb drive from his office and hurried into the meeting, taking his place at the front. The room was eerily quiet. The company's C-Suite was there, live and in person. It was like they sensed something was up and "had to be there to be seen." Drew Waltham was front and center. *Why was a sales guy here? Why were any of these people here?* He glanced at his contact at FinCen and she gave the same hunched shoulder guidance he got from Brooster.

Brody said, "OK, welcome, let's get… "

"Excuse me, I'd like to say a word before you start."

Brody turned toward the intrusion. It was one of the SEC commissioners. That's when it happened again. Another episode. The commissioner's tie was blue but as he stood, Brody saw that it was a maize color.

"Thank you, Mr. Markovich. And thank you to the ExpoLytics team for allowing me to take a few moments to reset this important project."

Brody barely recovered from his episode when the word "reset" sucked the oxygen from the room. He stiffened as the commissioner continued.

"What I'm about to say can't leave this room. All of you have been vetted to be read in. In fact, if someone can please close the door, and pull the blinds to the hallway. Also, please, everyone turn off your cell phones and place them in front of you where they can be seen. No outside comms. Thank you."

Brody's mind clouded over as the commissioner described how they had taken Brody's preliminary report to a secret grand jury. The blood drained from Brody's face. His report was now the basis for a criminal investigation into GeneraCur. The SEC and DoJ were taking over from FinCen. Brody assessed the ramifications. *The investigation is for the previous ten years. Every line item of every transaction, loan, payment, paycheck, etc. would need to be analyzed for every shell* company. *This is likely the biggest case ExpoLytics has had in some time. Do well and my name will be on one of those parking spaces someday.*

"Brody's code" is the reason the government chose ExpoLytics. It's the only company that can handle such complex cases. The concept of "Brody's Code" was simple. ExpoLytics connects thousands of desktop computers together over the web and "steals" computing cycles from each one. The result is thousands of processors working together to amass the computational power of a supercomputer. ExpoLytics tapped into the desktop computers of their clients. This was a huge boon for ExpoLytics. The stock price notched up when they announced the new capability. GeneraCur will be a big test.

Maybe too big. Brody worried they would assign the case to someone more senior.

—ε-ε-ε-ε-ε-ε—

Mlle Augustine Chalamet's work was genius. She unraveled mysteries about the universe others hadn't even considered.

It wasn't only the physical universe. Her theories covered the spiritual universe too.

Her paper was published in an obscure French journal, Science de la Planète. It was more a magazine than a journal. The editors did very little vetting and probably didn't even read her submission. Pay the 35 franc "reviewer's fee" and you're in. That was more than a week's salary but Augustine had no choice. Other, respected journals didn't want to hurt their reputation with such "théories folles" from this "femme folles."

She spun a mesmerizing tale of how the universe creates reality, a story of wrestling with truth and discarding wayward theories. One day, when she was young, she hurried home from teaching school, eager to continue her thoughts from the night before. It was early spring, one of those days when she felt like she could live forever. The air was light and fresh. She skipped up the gravel path to her flat. In mid-skip, she stopped cold. An intuition hit her. She sat under the large oak, her eyes straight ahead, unfocused, as she thought through her new insight. Above her, on each tree branch were new buds with young leaves coiled tightly inside, biding their time until they would become fully formed leaves, taking in air and sunshine, creating the beautiful medley of shape and texture that was the tree. It was the process Augustine used to create beautiful mosaics of thought and logic out of thin air, sorting them, arranging them, forming patterns. Patterns. Her supple mind saw the universe as a place full of beautiful interconnected patterns. She pictured the trillions of collisions between energy and matter that make up each moment in time. Each moment in time has its own pattern, unique from the moment before and the moment after. *Energy and matter are woven together to make a pattern. They're woven together in such a way. In such a way that reality is created...*

That was the thought that stopped her cold.

Reality is a pattern woven from energy and matter.

What does the weaving? What magic hand exists that could do such a thing?

Afternoon gave way to evening. The birds quieted and the sky became dark. It would be a decade before Augustine knew the answer.

Physicists of the late nineteenth century were grappling with how forces and energy interact with matter but Augustine discovered what the universe uses to create reality. It wasn't a force. It wasn't energy. Not a single person walking the earth today knows anything about it.

Saronda "Roni" Jackson was about to find out.

—ε-ε-ε-ε-ε-ε—

A pleasant-sounding bell rang as Roni took three tentative steps into the cluttered room.

She hesitated. "Hello?"

Boxes were everywhere. Some opened, some closed. The place reeked of old books. It reminded her of her room.

"We're not open yet, please come back."

The gentle male voice came from a backroom even more cluttered than up front. Roni took a small step forward. Every ounce of her wanted to turn on her heel and leave. Instead, the allure of old books, the prospect of discovering new truths, drew her in.

"Oh I'm sorry. My name is Roni. I live down the street. I'm so excited to have a new bookstore. This place is like heaven to me."

Alex Maillon came out from the backroom, rubbing his hands together like they were cold. "Well it's not heaven for me. I'm here helping out my wife. This is her dream. She's downtown signing some papers. I'm just unpacking boxes."

"That's so nice of you. Great team effort."

Alex walked toward the back. "Well I'm not making much progress. Damn achy hands."

"Maybe I could help." said Roni, her boldness catching her by surprise.

Alex turned back toward Roni. His face gave a look.

"If you're looking for a job, we don't—"

"Oh no. I was just saying if you need someone to help unpack, like I said I love old books, might even see something I like and be your first customer," Roni said with a lift in her voice.

"OK, start on that side of the room. Stack them on those trays. I'm Alex by the way."

They both went quiet. Roni was elated, it gave her a chance to rummage. She was drawn to a box that was different from the rest. It was covered in dust, the sticky kind that builds up from sitting for years in the back of a fry kitchen.

She found a box cutter. Slitting the aged cardboard released the stale air and dusty smell of old books. She pulled one out. French poetry. Pieces of thought from the mind of a long-passed author, freed from the confines of a grimy cardboard box. She shivered.

She pulled out two more books. A magazine that had been stuffed between them tumbled to the ground. Reaching down to pick it up she saw that it was a yellowed science magazine. It felt electric in her hands. The title caught her eye, Science de la Planète. Octobre 1905.

"Does your wife order books from France?"

Alex poked his head out of the backroom. "Oh I don't think so."

"I found a French magazine in this box."

Alex gruffed, "Magazine? I don't think she has any plans to sell magazines."

"I'll buy it from you. It's in French. I don't think anyone else will want it."

"Tell you what, take it. You've been a big help."

"No, I want to be your first customer."

Alex's face lightened some. "OK, how about a

dollar? We'll frame it and hang it on the wall."

"Deal."

Roni turned on her heel to leave and glanced back over her shoulder. "When do you open?"

Alex was back to being knee deep in boxes and didn't answer.

—ε-ε-ε-ε-ε-ε—

Augustine didn't stop at theory. She derived equations for her intuitions. That was the only way to know if her thoughts made sense. Equations reveal new truths if you study them, scrutinize them, consider them from all angles, no matter how extreme. As she dug into them, she concluded one undeniable fact; there was more than one reality. In fact, there are many.

Not only are there many realities, they're moving, vibrating, undulating. We can't see them, but they are out there. Augustine loved thinking about these things, solving riddles, thinking of consequences.

One of the consequences, realities can collide.

—ε-ε-ε-ε-ε-ε—

Roni bounced into her apartment. She, who would rather be covered with fire ants than talk to a stranger, entered a yet-to-open bookstore, and made herself at home. Buying a magazine that wasn't even for sale put a bow on her red-letter afternoon. It would most likely join her collection of forgotten books. She tossed the magazine on the kitchen counter and pulled on some sweats and a loose T-shirt, planning for some quick aerobics at the workout room. As she was leaving her apartment, she paused. Maybe a better idea would be to make a frozen pizza. Zeal for fitness: zero, doing something else: one. She sat at the counter while waiting for the pizza to bake, mindlessly leafing through the one-hundred and ten-year-old science magazine. It was nothing special other than being old and in French. There was an article on the wonders of the carbon atom, and another on nitrogen in chlorophyll. A minute before the timer dinged on the oven, Roni turned to the last article.

The abstract for the article hit her like lightning.

"L'auteur montre le lien Universel entre les propriétés physiques et spirituelles de l'Univers."

"The author shows the universal connection between the physical and spiritual properties of the universe."

Turning the pages, there were hundreds of math equations filling page after page but it was the words that grabbed her, sweeping her into a world where our spiritual reality and physical reality mix. Roni was captivated. She only stopped reading when she smelled the smoke from a burning pizza. She raced across the kitchen to retrieve the pizza from the oven, as if saving three seconds of travel time would make a difference, and then did a frantic dance waving a dish towel at the howling smoke alarm, cussing it out for doing its job.

She took the still smoking pizza into her room, along with the article.

—ε-ε-ε-ε-ε-ε—

The office was quiet now. The big guns from the government had left. Brody reflected on the whirlwind of changes as he stared out at the darkening skyline across the river. The yellow-gold color of the Roberto Clemente bridge seemed to brighten as the sun set.

"Sure hope you're buckling up." Brooster's irritating voice shattered the scene.

Brody spun around in his chair. "Yeah, but you know… "

He was about to launch into a rant about how the massive data dump would break the system. He was distracted instead.

Brody nodded. "Did you change your shirt today?"

"No, what are you talkin' abaht?"

"Weren't you wearing light yellow? Ahh never mind."

The episodes were getting more annoying. They were like someone sitting behind you at a movie and constantly flicking your ears. Trivial but distracting.

Brody continued, "Well I'm sitting here trying to figure out how we're going to handle the huge amount of data that's about to hit."

Brooster barked over his shoulder as he turned to leave, "I'm sure you'll figure it out, you're Mr. Data after all. Catch you tomorrow."

Being called Mr. Data made Brody shudder and feel very alone. It was all on his shoulders to figure this out. Words from his father rang in his head. *It's great to be a star but space is cold as hell.*

The stars outside his window, pushing through the twilight, were his only companions. And they were a million miles away.

—ε-ε-ε-ε-ε-ε—

Roni lay on her bed. She reached to turn on a bedside light, jostling the plate with the burned parts of her pizza. She couldn't pull herself away from the article in the science magazine. The audacity of the assertions drew her in. Intellectual confidence oozed from the pages, convincing her it was real and correct. Paragraphs of prose were peppered with complex differential equations. Roni drilled in, pausing only to re-read sections.

It was heady stuff. She jotted notes.

There is one universe. There are many realities.

Realities are like 'balls' that move. We exist in one of them.

Reality is an ever-changing pattern.

Whispers???

She wrote those notes, but she didn't understand them.

She pulled her blanket over her legs. *Why am I cold?* She then remembered she had opened all the windows to air out the smoke of burned pizza. She laughed. The article had so monopolized her attention. She navigated the small apartment closing each window. In the waning daylight, she caught a glimpse of a faraway star. It was brighter than the others.

Augustine Chalamet wrote, "Tout ce qui est proche et lointain fait partie d'un modèle étonnant."

Everything that is nearby and far away is part of an amazing pattern.

—ε-ε-ε-ε-ε-ε—

Brody got in early the next day, skipping his workout, eager to get started. He was laser focused on upgrading the system to handle the large data load. He dreaded setting up a meeting with Wayne Drakauer but he knew Wayne was the only one who could get it done. Meeting with him promised to be pure anguish. Brody thought of Wayne as a loutish cynical malcontent and he suspected Wayne thought of him as an undeserving clown.

As Brody set out for the meeting, Brooster called with some breaking news, "GeneraCur is going to be handled from the Bethesda office. It's closer to the SEC."

"I'll head to your office now."

He canceled his meeting with Wayne. He mentally ticked off a list of concerns. *Who would he be working with in D.C.? Were they competent? Did they know about Brody's Code?*

Number one on his mind: *Will I still own the project?*

He settled into a chair in Brooster's office. "So, give me all the deets. How's this going to work?"

Brooster picked up on Brody's anxiety. "Slow down rocketman. Take in the moment. Breathe. Do you feel that? That's you suddenly becoming a really big deal. This is a big step for you."

"So it's still my project?"

"Yes, of course. Should it be otherwise?"

Brody's elation gave way to a feeling of inadequacy. "I'm not sure our system can handle this much analysis, not with this short schedule."

Brooster turned in his chair. "Oh there you go again about data and schedule. But I don't think you're talking about the system. You're afraid *you* can't handle it."

His boss continued, "I know you can. That's why I fought to keep it with you. But, look around, Mr. Myopic, our system isn't your biggest problem. Your biggest problem is all the sharks looking at this. You're going to have to fight to keep ownership. There's plenty of people in the Bethesda office who would love to put this feather in their cap. Don't keep droning on about how your code can't handle this. You'll figure it out."

Brody's hyperactive mind was not convinced. "OK, you may be right but ten years of transactions of a multinational behemoth plus the hundreds of offshore shells they run. I don't think we'll be able to—"

Brooster snarled, "Brody, fix the problem, don't keep whining about it, and listen, this is your chance to shine. Don't mess it up."

Brody was face to face with the fact that "fake it 'til you make it" wasn't as easy as it looked. He had a deep-seated sense that he wasn't good enough. He would bring home test scores from school. "I got 98 out of 100." Instead of praise he would hear, "So you missed 2, maybe you can do better next time." It was always the same. The words were front and center in his head. This was a huge project. Ninety-eight out of a hundred wouldn't cut it. And then there were those unexplained episodes: the coffee, the commissioner's tie, Brooster's shirt, and dozens more.

Brody trotted to his condo, packed a couple weeks' worth of clothes, and jumped in his car for the four hour drive from Pittsburgh to D.C. He was heavy on the gas pedal, pumped full of feelings of elation mixed with inadequacy. He called his father and described his new project. He listened for pride in his father's voice.

"Well, son, you know what I always say, when you're the one flying the rocket, don't screw up."

—ε-ε-ε-ε-ε-ε—

He spent the entire drive from Pittsburgh to D.C. thinking through how to start the project. *Can't fly the rocket if it never leaves the launchpad.* He checked into "The George", a boutique hotel close to the SEC HQ. He went to sleep with his brain still spinning. He awoke the next day swimming in a mix of endorphins and stress hormones leaving him in a twisted mood. He needed caffeine.

He stepped out of the lobby into the crisp fall air. The doorman nodded. "Sleep well, young man?"

Brody glanced at the doorman's name tag. "Yessir indeed, Ed." It was as if the doorman was a longtime acquaintance.

Ed said, "Well you have a good day."

"Oh I will, but not if I don't get a cup."

Ed motioned. "Forty-seven steps that way."

Forty-seven steps later, Brody skipped up the two short steps into The Corner Bakery. *Ahh, fresh coffee.* Behind him was the U.S. Capitol. Not far away, the White House. He shook his head. Never in a million years did he think he would be working on such a big project in the nation's capital, interfacing with two government agencies.

"Saronda," barked the barista.

Brody thought it strange that she had a name tag that said "Roni" but guessed it could be short for Saronda.

"Brady."

What was it about the name Brody? Brody crossed the street. Union Station was on his left as he made his way to SEC HQ. He took his first sip of coffee as he pushed through the glass doors off F Street and into the large lobby area. Upon checking in with the guard, Brody texted his SEC contact, Irene Gentz.

He said to the guard, "It's like surround sound in here. All those echoey footsteps. Kinda cool. People on their way to do important business I guess." The guard nodded.

A set of footsteps headed in his direction. He turned to see a smartly dressed woman in maybe her late thirties or early forties.

"Brody, I assume. I'm Irene Gentz."

Brody nodded and extended his hand. Irene gave a firm but short handshake. She pulled a multi-page document from a folder and handed it to Brody.

"Please fill this out and sign it. Then I'll let you into the office area. Please read every line closely."

Brody felt the weight of the document, at least fifteen pages. He communicated his displeasure with his face.

He looked around. "Fill out? Here?"

"I'll wait. You can sit there." Irene motioned to a

marble bench.

"OK then." He resigned himself to the bench.

After a beat, Brody said, "This could take a while, won't we be late for the nine o'clock?"

No response.

Three pages later. "No really, don't you think we're going to be late for the meeting?"

"The meeting's at ten o'clock. Plenty of time."

Brody said, "I was told nine."

She motioned to the document. The questions were endless. Brody flipped ahead several pages to see how many more questions.

Four more pages done.

He stretched his neck and looked up at Irene. The angle was perfect for puppy eyes. "These are quite detailed questions." He studied Irene for any hope of getting released from this loathsome time-waste.

"They will be used as a basis to start your background check."

"Background check?"

"Yes, you'll be doing work related to the U.S.government. Everyone must submit to a background check. Did no one tell you?"

Brody turned to the last page of the hellish form. "Upon penalty of perjury I hereby declare… "

Irene said, "It's for the government, we have to be sure."

They walked to the elevator and took it to the 6th floor. The doors open to a hushed, library-like hum.

"I'll take you to the meeting room so you can set up."

"Set up? Am I expected to present something?"

"Did no one tell you? Did you not discuss this with Ian?"

"Never heard of Ian but I have my updated files on a thumb drive. Is there a computer with an overhead I can plug into so I can— ?"

"Of course there is. We've leaped into the 21st century."

He took that as Irene humor so he chuckled.

—ε-ε-ε-ε-ε-ε—

A new day meant new learning. Roni crossed Massachusetts Avenue carrying her coffee in one hand and her canvas bag in the other. She had two granola bars and a yogurt, along with the October 1905 edition of Science de la Planète. She entered the marbled lobby of the Postal Museum.

Reading Augustine's paper the night before gave her a burning desire to continue. She propped up the magazine behind the counter of the information booth where she worked and spent all day reading and re-reading sections of the paper. She took "thought journeys" to sit back and puzzle out what Augustine wrote. She looked around the large, high ceiling museum and took in the "reality" around her: the sounds of tourists echoing off the cold marble walls, large brass framed doors opening and closing causing a wave of cathedral-like echoes. She tried to visualize reality as Augustine had described it. Roni felt the oak desk. She ran her fingers over the varnished slab, the product of countless leaves turning air into wood. Reality is both physical and spiritual. It made no sense. *How could a physical desk be made of something spiritual?*

—ε-ε-ε-ε-ε-ε—

Irene dropped off Brody at the ten o'clock meeting at 10:23, subjecting him to a project owner's worst nightmare, losing control. He pushed aside the panicky feeling and took a seat. Everyone across the table was backlit by a wall of windows. The sun was blinding. This violated what his father told him.

"Always sit where you can see their faces. That's where the message is."

He thought about moving but that would be awkward. Brody scanned the agenda displayed on the flat panel screen. Apparently, the SEC assigned a case number, an important detail Brody didn't know. The assembled team were already into the weeds on how to proceed. Clearly, Brody needed to reign this in if he was to be regarded as team lead.

At a break in the action, Brody blurted, "Excuse me, I'm Brody Markovich."

The team looked up from their notebooks and phones.

"I'm from the Pittsburgh office of ExpoLytics. I'm the team lead for the GeneraCur project, uh, case."

Brody noticed some uncomfortable shifts in body language but couldn't see their faces.

"Hi Brody, welcome. I'm Ian Richards, Vice President in charge of Case Management at ExpoLytics, Bethesda." Ian emphasized the words vice president and case management. He stood at the front of the room, hands on hips, dripping with authority vibes. Brody wondered if they teach that somewhere.

Brody turned toward Ian. "Oh hi, so you're Ian. Nice to meet you. Irene said you wanted me to brief everyone on the case?"

"Well, I don't think that will be necessary. We're all read up on the details and think we know where we're headed."

Control is slipping away.

"So you already have a plan?"

"Yes, we fleshed it out this morning, pretty standard stuff."

Brody felt his face get hot and was hoping he wasn't flushed.

"I would like to review it."

Ian turned toward the agenda on the screen and glanced back over his shoulder.

"Oh you can, you'll be included on an email with all the details."

Brody spoke to Ian's back, "No, I mean I would like to review it with the team and then ultimately approve it."

The air left the room. Brody stood up. Mercifully, the window blinds blocked the sun.

Ian turned back toward Brody. "Do you mean approve it with the Pittsburgh office?"

"No, with the team here, this is my case. I'm the team lead, and I need to ensure we're going in the right direction. Now, I'm sorry I was late, but I spent the morning filling out a personal history that literally went back to pre-birth. Why they need to know how my parents met, uh, look, I need to have a chance to review the plan and— "

Ian dismissed the threat to his alpha status. "I

think we know what we're doing. We handle these kinds of cases all the time."

"Do you though? Have you ever handled one with this complexity and data load? Not to mention the schedule. Does your plan lay out where you'll get the bandwidth and processor time? Or working with Pittsburgh to schedule computer time? Have you factored that into the timeline?"

The look on Ian's face indicated those things hadn't been discussed.

"Do you even know if Pittsburgh has given us access to Brody's Code?"

Brody really wished it was called something else. People around the meeting table gave each other sided-eyed glances. Some smiled. He paused from his rant to try to read the room. It looked like some may be siding with him. Most looked like they were in abject fear of what Ian would say next.

Ian said, "Look, the team will work those things out as we go along."

Brody retorted, "But that's not how this works. Listen, I believe this team put together an excellent plan of how to file a case, with a staged communication plan to the SEC. But here's the deal, we're going to need to apply huge computational resources to complete the analytics. Without that, we won't be able to ferret out evidence of wrongdoing. GeneraCur uses a multitude of offshore accounts. Does anyone here know how many?"

A voice said, "Three-seventy-eight."

Brody looked around the room. "Did anyone else know that?"

There were no takers. He refocused on Ian. "So, I have to ask, how much have you looked at the details?"

Ian said, "Look, we know this case is a little more complicated than—"

"It's not a *little* more complicated." Brody tried to calm himself but his voice raised in pitch. "It's *way* more complicated, not just the number of accounts, but the methods they used to funnel money around." He was talking faster now. His breathing was shallow. He caught a hint of understanding from a woman across the table.

He continued, "As I look at it, this is the future of corporate fraud and corrupt accounting. Except it's not the future, it's now. If GeneraCur gets away with what they are... what they are allegedly doing. If we can't figure this out, other companies will use these same techniques to swizzle their books. And stock price."

Brody could feel his heart beating. He felt awkward standing.

He took a breath. "OK, this isn't how I wanted to introduce myself. I'm sorry. I know it looks like I'm pulling the team backwards but we need to consider all the factors at play."

As he sat down, a strong female voice came from

across the table. "Uh guys, Brody is right, that's why we hired ExpoLytics."

Damn sun. He couldn't see her face. He thought about standing again.

The woman continued, "This case is complex. It's also why Brody was asked to come down here. ExpoLytics needs to get this right and apply the needed resources."

The woman extended her hand to Brody. "I'm sorry, we haven't met, I'm Rebecca Standiford, special case leader at the SEC."

Brody stood, reached over, and shook her hand. His father would be proud.

"Never shake hands sitting down."

Ian smoothed his tie and chimed in. "I think this would be a good time to take a break."

He motioned to Brody and Rebecca to meet out in the hallway.

"I don't want this to turn into a turf battle." Ian said. Brody raised both eyebrows.

Ian continued, "We've handled dozens of cases out of this office. I appreciate the outside help from Brody but we don't need to overthink how to —"

Rebecca cut him off. "Ian, you don't understand. This one is different. If you use your normal methods, GeneraCur will skate. Brody's work in Pittsburgh shows this case is very complex. We don't know GeneraCur's motives, but we suspect they're not good."

Ian looked incredulous but yielded some. "What do you suggest?"

"I suggest we let Brody take the team through what we know, as we discussed last night."

Brody brazenly presumed Ian would agree and pulled out his thumb drive. "Let's get started!"

He strode back into the meeting room, not waiting for Ian to reply.

—Ɛ-Ɛ-Ɛ-Ɛ-Ɛ-Ɛ—

Roni's day raced by. She spent it immersed, unlocking secrets of the universe. Her sponge-like mind soaked up concepts from a paper that had been trapped in a claustrophobic cardboard box in the musty storage room of a bar. It painted a picture of how reality is spun by mysterious Whispers. Her Metro app chirped that her train was on its way to Union Station. She left the Postal Museum, her mind filled.

—Ɛ-Ɛ-Ɛ-Ɛ-Ɛ-Ɛ—

Brody spent the afternoon showing the team of ExpoLytics and SEC analysts the details of the case. Ian was nowhere to be seen. After several hours, the team had taken in as much as they could. Brody exhibited a bit of authority and declared the meeting adjourned. Rebecca gave a slight nod from across the table. They hadn't assigned Brody an office yet, so he decided to return to his hotel and work from there. He headed out into the late afternoon sun. The sidewalks were filled with people rushing to Union Station. Brody felt like a salmon swimming upstream. It was then he realized he hadn't had an episode the whole day, or at least any he knew about. That bit of pleasantness on an otherwise taxing day didn't last long. As he waited to cross 1st, he noticed a guy on the other side. He had a backpack slung over his left shoulder. Then, the backpack was on his right shoulder. Brody tried to shake it off. As he crossed the street, he noticed the girl from the coffee shop that morning. *What was her name? Sharonni? No, that's not it.*

His thoughts were interrupted when he heard a commotion. He turned and saw that the girl had fallen. She looked to be OK, and people were helping her, so Brody continued to the hotel. His thoughts turned back to how to wrestle his project to the ground while taming Ian. It was a challenge but he viewed coming to D.C. as an inflection point. A point where everything is going as planned, and then everything changes.

—ε-ε-ε-ε-ε-ε—

Roni had an inflection point with a concrete curb. She was enraptured with the brassy boldness of Augustine, the way she laid out her theories. It was a window into an insightful and sensitive mind, a mind that could turn complex concepts into rigorous mathematical equations. To her core, Roni felt Augustine weighing the nuance of human emotion, connecting it to the physical universe. She had never read anything like it. Emotion, that unseen part of us that drives behavior connecting to the physical universe. The connection creates reality. Roni had assumed reality was just "there." But Augustine had the audacity to declare that it's created. Roni was starting to view everything and everybody through the lens of Augustine's theories. It was a spiritual awakening. It filled her conscious thoughts. She misjudged the curb and it was concrete meets leg.

Embarrassing.

The next morning, she lay in bed praying her swollen foot hadn't gotten worse. She sat up, and gingerly dropped it to the floor. *That's a relief. Not bad.*

She shuffled to the kitchen.

"Hey Danielle, you're up early." Danielle is Roni's roommate.

"O.M.G Roni girl, you grew a cankle."

"Shut up. Did not. I tripped over a curb yesterday."

"You should probably wrap it up or something."

Danielle Sközy was in college but it wasn't clear to what end. She and Roni had little in common other than a need to share expenses. Danielle was ten years younger. Her parents moved from Fáro, Gotland, a small town on an island east of Sweden. It consisted of a church and pastures separated by stone walls. Her only memory was that it was cold. She became a U.S. citizen when she was eight and perfected her English by writing song lyrics in a notebook. Roni was born in Sierra Leone but she came from everywhere, moving often as an Army brat.

—ε-ε-ε-ε-ε-ε—

Brody grabbed a granola bar and an apple from the front desk and trotted toward the workout room. He never made it. The walls, the floor, everything, twisted into a distorted vertigo. Around him, nothing but a misty landscape devoid of context.

This episode was different. More intense. More extreme. And with it, pain. Visceral pain. One that reached deep. To his soul.

It lasted less than a minute. He made his way back to his room, trying to shake it off.

I have a project to run. OK, game face.

He got dressed and headed out.

The doorman said, "Lookin' good young man. Big day?"

"World by the tail, Ed. World by the tail."

—ε-ε-ε-ε-ε-ε—

Roni limped from the train and willed herself in the direction of the coffee shop. As she started up the two steps, the door swung open.

"That curb sure didn't treat you nice." A guy with nice hair held the door for her. "Come on in, foot looks bad."

Roni laughed at herself as she labored up the steps. "Oh, uh, it's bruised but not broken."

"Sounds like my day at work yesterday. You must work around here. I saw you here yesterday, in the morning. And then you were walking to Union Station late afternoon so…"

Roni stiffened. She turned toward the counter. "Uh huh."

"I'm Brody, I saw you fall." She could hear that he was close behind her.

Roni stared at the menu board like she had never seen it before.

"They must not let you wear your blue shoes at work."

Roni turned around. "Excuse me?" She purposefully acted annoyed.

He plowed on. "Well, I noticed you were wearing bright blue shoes in the morning, but in the afternoon you had on —"

Roni cut off his forwardness. "I don't own blue shoes. For your information."

He persisted. "No really, the other day, they were very cool, and very blue, almost electric. Of course it could have been an episode."

Roni turned back to the menu.

He said, "OK, my bad. Can I pay for your coffee?"

Cringe. She took a step toward the counter. Roni had planned to get a pastry and rest her foot before heading over to work. New plan, coffee and bolt. She gave the barista a fake name and drifted towards the door. After an eternity, the barista announced "Sharon." Roni grabbed the coffee and left.

She made her way to the Postal Museum and set up the information desk with a few snacks and the science magazine. She texted her sister: *You would not believe the dude I met this morning.*

Shay answered: *Dish*

He thought I was wearing some crazy ass shoes.

Shay texted back: *Some old guy creepin?*

Roni texted. *Not old, about my age.*

Cute?

He had his good points. But sis, he had stalker vibes.

Nice body? Eyes?

Shay stop. I gotta work.

—ε-ε-ε-ε-ε-ε—

Brody spent the next few days working with the team in D.C. Ian was nowhere to be seen but Brody suspected he would make his life hell at some point. Brody worked with each team member refining the plan while waiting for the subpoenaed materials to arrive. He convinced the team they needed to tap the resources of the Pittsburgh office because of the daunting analysis ahead of them. He liked the team. They worked together well but Brody sensed something was off.

As he headed back to his hotel, Ian called, "HR at the Bethesda office is there for you if you feel you need help with anything. They have information on stress management. Might be best to make an appointment, you know, just to see… "

Ian's voice faded into the background as Brody tried to process what he was saying.

Brody said, "Hmm, thanks for the tip. I'll think about it." He added a silent *jagoff*.

—ε-ε-ε-ε-ε-ε—

Augustine often regaled her students with her theories. She would carve out a few minutes at the end of class to talk about the shortcomings of current theories, going so far as discounting the work of giants. Most students would sit, bored, and willing the clock to go faster. Paul Appell was different. He was fascinated by Augustine's wild ideas. Her fierce rantings left a lasting impression.

He became a prominent mathematician in France in the late 1800s and early 1900s earning him a seat as the Rector at the University of Paris, but it was a random conversation in a pub and a letter he wrote that would change the fate of the world.

Professor Appell was asked to serve on a military commission to clear the name of Alfred Dreyfus. Dreyfus was a Jewish military officer who had his life ruined by lies. The scandal ripped apart late-19th century France and moved antisemitism from a festering boil to a country-dividing open wound. His mission: slow the rampant lies that fed the rising hate tearing apart his beloved country.

By chance, he met a physicist one evening at the inn where he was staying. The early 1900s were a particularly exciting time in physics and math. Great minds were penning papers and letters that nudged along our understanding of the physical laws of the universe. He and the physicist shared a bottle of wine and had a lively discussion about one paper in particular, published by a young man in Switzerland. The paper put forward some provocative ideas about space and time, challenging the heralded Maxwell's equations. They laughed that someone would be so bold as to challenge the completeness of Maxwell's equations, which were the bedrock for understanding how different forms of energy interacted in the universe. They found it equally amusing that the paper was written by an unknown patent office clerk, a young German named Albert Einstein. The crazy theories reminded him of Augustine.

The next morning, he arose early, dashed off a letter and put it in the post before returning to the work of the commission.

—ε-ε-ε-ε-ε-ε—

For Roni, the morning held no promise of something new. Her days were rinse and repeat. Catch the Metro, grab a coffee, then spend all day wandering through the mind of a genius. She decided to have the pastry she skipped when she had the weird encounter with "that guy." She sat near the window. The sun felt warm as it washed sideways across her face. She wore little makeup.

A shadow fell across the table. *Oh crap, him again.*

He said, "Listen, I want to apologize for a couple days ago. I know I made you uncomfortable and I just want you to know I'm not stalking you."

Roni stared straight ahead and deadpanned. "Well that's comforting."

"But I really thought you were wearing blue shoes, you know, the other day. Sometimes my mind plays these tricks and I see things and it's like they're different than what they should be."

He paused for a reply. He got none. "Anyhow, so maybe I'm going crazy. But I'm not a creep."

Roni wanted him to leave. "Equally comforting. Did you need anything else?"

"No, just that, ya know, I'm sorry."

Roni raised her hand. "I gotta go."

She shoved the rest of the pastry into the waxed paper bag, stood, turned on her heel, and left. As she made her way to the museum, she texted Shay: *Dude's back.*

Creepn on u?

He's got issues.

She opened the magazine and re-engaged with the world of physics. Her mind dwelled on each new concept, trying to piece it together. She tuned out the reverberating sounds of the museum. She imagined stars, planets, living and nonliving things as patterns created by Whispers. The patterns moved, evolving moment to moment. Everything had a different pattern. Even a lowly rock. The concepts flowed over her, not all of them sinking in. Then, frustration. *What is reality? What's it made of?*

It's the patterns. Dangit, you knew this.

She focused.

All right, what makes the pattern?

She remembered her notes.

"The patterns are woven by Whispers," blurting it out loud.

She glanced around to see if anyone noticed. *It's the Whispers!*

She pulled her notebook from her bag. There it was.

Our Whispers use the raw material of physical and spiritual energy to weave an ever-changing pattern of emotions, reactions, beliefs, what we call reality.

It all came together as a full body blow.

Roni bolted out of her chair. The force caused the chair to roll backward and careen off the railing launching itself down the two stairs of the booth's platform. The sound echoed off the hard walls for what seemed to Roni a very long time. This escaped no one's notice. Patrons and co-workers rushed over to see if everything was OK.

She held up her hands. "Oh yeah, nobody hurt. But wow, I just discovered what ties each and every one of us to the stars and rocks and... We're connected to the universe! Spiritually, physically. Uh, I can't believe I said that out loud. Sorry, can I help anyone? Pamphlets? Brief history of the museum?"

The attention was like death to an introvert like Roni. Her skin took on a slight rosiness. An elderly woman turned to her husband and told him to help Roni with the chair. He obliged and everyone shuffled away.

She wrote in her notebook:

The pattern of reality is created by "Whispers"!!!

A privileged lightness fell over her. She had been permitted a peek at the inner workings of the universe. When quitting time came, she didn't walk to Union Station, she skipped. Her sore foot would have to zip it. She needed to get home and bury herself in the magazine.

She rode three stops north from Union Station and walked from the Metro platform to her apartment.

Danielle was headed from the kitchen to the living room. "Hey, you're just in time. I'm firing up the DVR to watch last night's Bachelorette. The suspense is heating up."

Roni said, "I'll bet it is, you'll have to tell me all about it sometime." *Probably never.*

Then eyeing the counter. "What's this?"

"Oh, that's some leftover meatloaf from Carolina Kitchen. Jacob and I went there last night. Take it, it's yours. I'm stuffed."

"You lovely, wonderful roommate." She took the meatloaf to her room, not bothering to heat it up.

—ε-ε-ε-ε-ε-ε—

Brody pressed the keycard to his door and waited for the little green light. The distinctive aroma of a hotel room hit him as he set his bag down on the desk. He sighed. The mints on his pillow seemed to shift from the left bed to the right bed, just annoying enough to notice. The episodes had become a constant companion. He prayed he wouldn't have another bad one like this morning's.

He wanted a quiet evening to forget the madness. He got a phone call instead.

"Brody, it's Rebecca."

"I knew that because my phone said Rebecca SEC. So, Rebecca SEC, what's up? I really should put in your full name because I've already forgotten your last name."

"Standiford. We need to meet, there's an issue."

Taking note of her business-like tenor, Brody became serious. "OK, when would you —"

"Now. Walk to Hamilton's."

"Wait, I don't know —"

"The front desk will know where it is, see you in a bit." Just like that she disconnected.

It was a chilly eight-minute walk to Hamilton's Grill. Brody opened the painted door and stepped into the warm embrace of fried foods and varnished wood. *Oh nice, my kind of place.*

He started to take in the huge variety of beer when he felt the chilly blast of the door opening behind him. It was Rebecca.

"Ah, you beat me," Rebecca said, taking a scarf off her head and putting it in the pocket of her long Burberry coat. She did the same with her slender leather gloves.

Brody wanted to say something light like "I like your coat," but thought that was inappropriate and "That's a nice coat" also seemed inappropriate. His brain detected that his silence was growing too long so he said, "You look nice," which was clearly not appropriate so he added, "in that coat."

He looked away. *You look nice… in that coat? Really? That's what your brain came up with?*

He re-made eye contact.

Rebecca said, "OK, thanks, let's get a booth. We need to talk."

—ε-ε-ε-ε-ε-ε—

It was the autumn of her life and Augustine spent her days wondering why no one had responded to her paper and why the world was so incurious. She craved a discussion with someone, anyone, who would dive deep into her work.

She sat at the small table in front of the solitary

window in her one room flat. It was her quiet place where her brilliant intuitive mind roamed the universe. It was now small and airless. The bright sunflower drapes were now the color of sad faded nicotine. The table's shellac was uneven and worn from the hours of Augustine's thin fingers pensively drumming as she contemplated deep mysteries, acrid smoke trailing thinly upward from home rolled cigarettes. It was in this place, decade after decade, Augustine would fall into prolonged periods of deep concentration, her "la transe productive." Trance was an apt description. The only visceral cues she had of the outside world were the feel of the wood table and the stinging draws on her cigarettes. She didn't pause to take notes until she had come to a full conclusion on something, not wanting to break the glorious flow. The intense quiet and lack of distraction allowed Augustine to delve deeply into her thoughts of the cosmos and the interaction of energy and matter. She went down dead-ends, sometimes discarding months of work. Her pursuit of truth was exacting and relentless. Those were the good days.

Her flat was now a place to sit and wait in a cloud of melancholy. Her window was angled such that she could see to the end of the alley. The leaves were off the large Sycamore tree, no longer hiding the foot traffic on Rue du Général Leclerc. Nothing much was down that way other than a cheese shop and a sad park. All the action was at the other end of town, on the other side of Cathédrale Saint-Étienne.

It was "la Toussaint." All Saints' Day. While others walked to the cemetery to place flowers on the graves of loved ones, she expected that there would be no one to place flowers on hers.

—ε-ε-ε-ε-ε-ε—

Rebecca took off her coat and hung it on the hook near their booth. Brody waited for her to sit and then slid into the other side of the booth.

Brody asked, "Should we order food or is this thing too important to wait?"

"Brody, I'm going to tell you straight up. Ian thinks you're a half-baked casserole."

"Well that's a picture. But hey, I may not have a lot of experience but I'm competent."

"That's not what this is about. He thinks you're going crazy. Coo Coo for cocoa puffs. Other people think so too."

"Crazy? Why?"

"C'mon, Brody. You have to know. All that crazy, weird stuff you see and then don't see. Like the other day you commented on my yellow umbrella. Nice. Except I didn't have a yellow umbrella. And it was a sunny day. Who owns a yellow umbrella anyway?"

Brody studied the napkin-wrapped silverware, picking at the paper band holding it together. He knew exactly what she was talking about. Episodes.

She said, "Look, it's not just Ian, others are saying

things as well."

"And you?"

Rebecca paused.

"I think you need to figure out what's going on. Is it stress? New surroundings?"

She tried to lighten the moment. "Bad diet?"

Brody forced a chuckle.

He tried to brush away the awkwardness. "I think you're saying I should order a salad."

It came out stilted.

"Well, they're known for their Buffalo Chicken Salad here, guaranteed to light you up. And you can say you ate healthy 'cuz you had a salad."

"Thank you, Rebecca."

"For what?"

"For being straight with me. Ian suggested I meet with HR to discuss my, well, I guess, to discuss this issue."

Rebecca stiffened. "Be careful, HR is there to protect the company. Not you."

—ε-ε-ε-ε-ε-ε—

Roni picked at the last of the meatloaf as she sorted through what she had read. She visualized Whispers weaving energy, picturing ethereal strands.

Whispers reach out into the universe beyond the bounds of our body and weave a pattern unique to us. Emotions. Desires. Passions.

—ε-ε-ε-ε-ε-ε—

Brody did not sleep well that night. Rebecca's revelation rattled him. *Why is this happening to me?* He flipped through the TV channels looking for something, anything, that wasn't an infomercial or a fifty-year-old movie. It was two a.m. The hotel room felt like a crypt.

He found the hotel notepad and started writing:

Working with new team — STRESS

They are trained forensic accountants, I am not — STRESS

Turf battle with Ian — STRESS

Told me to go to HR??? Corp speak for can't handle STRESS

And the episodes. They were frequent and intrusive. Giving up on sleep, he pulled out his notebook computer. Surely, a little time with Google would help him figure out what was going on. He found a list of possibilities. Most were scary: schizophrenia, schizoaffective disorder, schizophreniform disorder, the list went on.

His sleepless brain muddled through whether to visit HR. He knew HR would be assessing him as a resource rather than helping him. After all, it was right there in their name, Human Resources. He looked at what he had written and tore it into pieces.

He mentally flipped a coin and decided to go to HR.

—ε-ε-ε-ε-ε-ε—

Roni carried the plate with remnants of meatloaf to the kitchen.

Danielle paused the DVR. "Roomie! You're missing some good shit. This one bachelor, who's dumb as rocks, thinks he can fake it by quoting words from books. How's the meatloaf?"

Roni replied, "Gone."

"Good, wasn't it? So, what's new with you?"

"Not much. I have a stalker. He's got issues. He sees things that aren't there."

"Maybe wanna stay away from that one. You don't want someone haunted by a different reality." Danielle went back to her show.

Different reality. A week before and those words would have been nothing more than idle chatter. As it was, they sparked a thought. *Was that dude seeing a different reality?* Her week-long immersion in Augustine's paper led her mind in a new direction. Augustine wrote about multiple realities. *Maybe there's a reality where I wear blue shoes.* The thoughts were coming into focus. They combined with the thoughts filling her head on the day she crossed that intersection and tripped and made a commotion noticed by a guy with nice hair, who turned around and saw her shoes. Her *brown*, certainly not *blue* shoes.

—ε-ε-ε-ε-ε-ε—

Augustine cursed under her breath and rested after walking down the gravel path from her flat. It got harder each day for her body to lean across a small strip of a weedy garden to reach her post box. Compared to when she was younger and working on her theories, her thoughts now were trivial and inconsequential. She filled her days mostly fretting about the lack of response to her paper. Was it that many of the pet theories of the day were challenged, completely uprooted by a woman?

The twentieth century was off to a roaring start, an all-out revolution in travel and communication that made the world a smaller place. But there was no understanding of how physical and spiritual energy were connected. As the world got smaller, people grew further apart. Augustine ached, wanting to tell the world how our Whispers can tap into the full energy of the universe. She received not a single sign of curiosity. It was the feeling of rejection all over again. It weakened her.

Augustine stared woodenly down the weathered cobblestone alley. The metal box screeched as she wrestled open the rusted door.

There was a letter.

—ε-ε-ε-ε-ε-ε—

Brody walked into the office of Helen Ramsey, Director of Human Resources ExpoLytics. He stopped mid stride. Everything on her desk was in perfect alignment. Her shirt, perfect alignment with her jacket. The colors were straight out of the corporate climber's handbook. *She'll no doubt have her own parking spot someday. Let's see, what did Father say about HR? "Never let an employee's problem become your employer's problem." Apparently, I'm a problem. Handled improperly and she'd have to find a place to park on the street every day. That can be a real hassle. I hope I don't ruin her life.*

Brody sat. "I love the way all your pictures line up perfectly."

"How often do you have these episodes?" Helen Ramsey perched behind her well-ordered desk, hands placed symmetrically in front of her.

"They're kinda random, but maybe twice a week, maybe more, maybe less," Brody lied. They were happening almost hourly.

"You haven't been tracking them? Writing them down? Time of day? Severity? Keeping notes?" Helen interrogated.

Brody sat silently. This felt like an ambush.

Helen continued to scold, "These things need to be measured, analyzed, observed by a professional."

Brody could already tell he made a big mistake

taking the forty-five minute Metro ride to the ExpoLytics office in Bethesda.

Helen leaned forward, casting a shadow on a perfectly aligned stapler. "Did you take any notes? Any tracking at all?"

Brody took a breath and then didn't say, *"Dang Helen Ramsey, HR maven, have you been tracking how many times that bug crawled up your ass?"*

Instead, he answered, "Uh, no."

"It sounds like you need help, professional help. I would advise that you see a therapist. I'll give you the name of two approved therapists. You need to pick one of them. I'll put a note in your personnel file about this visit."

Oh this was a 'visit'? Wasn't exactly a weekend at grandpa's farm but I did get to meet an ass.

He wasn't sure why he held this woman in such contempt. It was just a feeling.

He left. *What kind of jagoff keeps every friggin' thing on their desk lined up like that?*

A note in his personnel folder sounded ominous. He left in a fog wondering what was going to happen to him next. As Brody boarded the Metro, he found out. He received an email from HR. They were putting him on indefinite leave. He felt flush and needed to clear his head. Instead of returning all the way to Union Station, he got off at Dupont Circle and started walking. Brody was in no hurry. He suddenly didn't need to be anywhere. A rage buzzed just below the surface. Helen *"Judge Judy"* Ramsey with a wave of her hand took away his ticket to ride and banished him to a shrink. Did she even believe the episodes were real? This made him look weak. He could hear it now, "He can't handle the big cases." He wondered what they were telling the team. "Brody will be taking some time off. Carry on." Things like this happened to other coworkers. They'd go through a rough patch and even their manager wasn't allowed to know why they weren't there. The rumors would fly: terminal disease, going crazy, caught with porn at work. People get very creative with these things. He continued walking, took a detour at Farragut Square and wandered down to Duke's Grocery, a boutique lunch place. He had heard they have the best burgers in D.C. He sat down at a table outside and ordered.

As the waitress brought his order, he realized how uninterested he was in food. He took a small bite of his wagyu burger and set it on the plate. *God, the humiliation.* Hotshot upstart sent to D.C. to wrestle a complex case. And now he sits eating a hamburger in the middle of the day. One quick discussion with HR and bam, he's out on his ass.

He called Brooster, his biggest fan. "I can't believe you picked up. You must not be busy."

"Brody! Hi." Brooster did the thing where he acted like caller ID hadn't been invented yet. Brody considered it an age thing, like past a certain age that's what you're supposed to do.

"So, have you heard? They kicked me out."

"Whaddya mean? I haven't heard anything other than you're duking it out with Ian. Nice job."

"I'm off the team."

"What? No, only I can pull you off."

"Not if HR thinks your bird has left the cage."

"Brody, what's going on?"

Brody sat up and snapped at Brooster, "I don't know, maybe you can find out. Ehh, I don't mean it like that. Look, this is upsetting. Can you sniff around and see what this is about? HR thinks I'm crazy, wants me to see a therapist."

"Jumpin Jeezus, thinking you're crazy. But are you?"

"What? Crazy? Hell no. But I'm told that's what all crazy people say."

They disconnected. Brody leaned back and took out the cards Helen gave him. He twirled them around his fingers as he stared at the two names. He decided to call the one with the friendliest sounding name.

Marci Matthews, PsyD MD, Psychiatrist

"Yes, Dr. Matthews can see you this afternoon," said Kim, the pleasant-sounding receptionist.

"That was quick, I thought I would have to wait."

"Oh no, we were expecting your call."

His mind was reeling. A psychiatrist was put on high alert that a crazy person was going to call. Confiding in HR was a big mistake. He pushed his uneaten burger aside and headed south, which served nicely as a metaphor for his career. As he passed behind the White House, he saw a protester on a unicycle holding a cardboard sign that read "this space available for protests, $20/hr." You gotta love capitalism. He thought about throwing the guy a twenty for an hour's worth of "Brody Markovich is not insane," but he wasn't sure the tourists cared, and he didn't want to possibly add to the disinformation already on display. Checking the time, he'd need to hustle to get to his therapy appointment on time. It's bad to be crazy *and* late. He got on the Metro at McPherson Square. Walking up 2nd Street, he saw people eating inside Pete's Diner and realized one bite of burger was not enough. Walking farther, he saw a liquor store. He pondered which was worse, drinking on an empty stomach or going to a psychiatrist on an empty stomach.

Here's to finding out. Brody walked into the small waiting area of Dr. Marci Matthews.

—ε-ε-ε-ε-ε-ε—

The letter felt electric in her hand. Augustine's heart skipped as she read the name in the return address: Professor Paul Appell, one of her prized students.

Paul Appell was a giant. He was known for Appell's Equation of Motion. He shared an office suite with the likes of Henri Poincarre, another giant of mathematics. Oh, how she would enjoy discussing her paper with him. She ripped open the letter, not bothering to remove her coat.

Dearest Augustine,

How many years has it been? I trust this finds you in good health. Are you still teaching at the academy? I think of my years there as the best of memories. I am writing to you with something that may be of interest. I recall fondly the theories you would share with us at the end of class. I thought deeply about what you were saying and still do to this day. Are you still working on your theories?

The letter fell from Augustine's hand. He wasn't writing to her about her paper. He doesn't even know about it. After a time, she retrieved the letter, composed herself, and read on.

I happened upon a paper published in a German journal by a young patent clerk in Switzerland. A patent clerk of all things! Can you imagine? This sentence from his paper made me think of you:

Daß die Elektrodynamik Maxwells - wie dieselbe gegen- wärtig aufgefaßt zu werden pflegt - in ihrer Anwendung auf bewegte Körper zu Asymmetrien führt, welche den Phänomenen nicht anzuhaften scheinen, ist bekannt.

I remember you were adamant that Maxwell's equations didn't describe reality.

Augustine stopped reading.

She wished she had taken the time to learn German. This man wrote that Maxwell's equations do not describe reality. *Of course they don't, because they are incomplete.* Augustine had known for years that Maxwell's Equations didn't accurately describe reality because he didn't account for spiritual energy. And now, someone else is saying the same thing.

Augustine mumbled, "Has this author also discovered Murmures de l'univers?"

If you are interested in this young man's paper, I can have the university loan you the journal. It was published in "Annalen der Physik." 17 1905.

Zur Elektrodynamik bewegter Körper; von A. Einstein.

If it pleases, at your convenience allow me to arrange sending the journal.

Wishing you the best of health.

Your lifelong student,
Paul

She so wanted to meet this young man named Einstein.

—ε-ε-ε-ε-ε-ε—

Another crisp fall day, the leaves were beginning to change. Roni pushed through the doors of the coffee shop, and there he was sitting by the window. She took a breath. *Fate won't take you anywhere your feet are unwilling to go.*

"Did you really think I was wearing blue shoes?"

"Oh hey, uh, yeah. Blue shoes. Yeah, that was embarrassing."

Brody paused. "Clear as day but you see —"

"I just might believe you," Roni blurted, a little too quickly.

"Believe me, why? 'Cuz you really do have a pair of blue —"

"No, because you saw a different reality. Your Whisper crossed over into a different reality."

It was a line Roni had memorized and it came out robotic. Brody was silent for a long time.

Roni stood behind a chair, using it as a shield. "At least I *think* that's what's going on. I've been reading about it in a magazine, but I'm not done yet and there are things I don't understand, and maybe I'm wrong but... "

She was mortified. It was not how she had practiced. She would have paid rent money for confidence at that point.

Brody leaned forward and said in a hush, "If this is a spy meetup, you've got the wrong guy." He surveyed the room. "Or are you creeping on me now?"

Roni stayed serious. "No, you said your mind was playing tricks on you."

"Yeah, I may have said that. In fact, it's more than…" Brody pulled back.

"More than what?" Roni leaned in, expecting an answer.

She hoped she was communicating moxie but feared only her nervousness was showing.

He sighed and dropped his shoulders. "What the hell. You wanna sit?"

"It's not exactly tricks. I went to see a therapist." Brody paused.

Roni sat. "And?"

"Prodromal episodes."

"Say what?"

"Prodromal episodes, that's what the therapist called them."

"Dude, what the? I'd google that if I were you."

"Oh, I did. It means pre-psychotic."

Roni leaned back and in a voice louder than she intended, "Pre-psychotic! Just how *pre* are you? I'd kinda like to know if you're about to go into an uncontrollable rage." Roni made a stabbing motion and screeched like "Psycho."

Roni wished she hadn't tried humor. Brody stiffened.

He was abrupt. "Ouch. That felt mean, whoever you are, 'Roni' from your name tag who I don't know anything about except you work around here and you don't own blue shoes."

"Sorry, first, my name is Roni Jackson and second your therapist is wrong." She wished she had added more contrition.

"Oh good, my therapist is wrong. Speaking of my therapist, I have another appointment in like, soon, so…"

"Look, I think I know what's happening to you." Roni realized she overstepped.

Brody stared out the window. "I gotta go. I come here most mornings if you've got any more insight from whatever screwy pop-psych rag you're reading. Maybe we can figure out who's crazier, you or I."

"You or me."

Brody looked straight at her. "Whuut?"

"It's you or me, not you or I."

With that, Brody stood and shifted awkwardly on his feet. He didn't say "nice to meet you" or "gotta go". He just left.

Roni was unfazed. It was no "screwy pop-psych rag" she was reading.

—ε-ε-ε-ε-ε-ε—

Augustine was elated. A guy named Einstein questioned the completeness of Maxwell's equations. She sat at her table and thought about how important this was. James Clerk Maxwell showed how different forms of energy interact. But his equations did nothing to explain spiritual energy. It took her more than a decade, but Augustine expanded Maxwell's equations to show how physical energy interacts with spiritual energy. She showed how physical things interact with spiritual energy to create reality. Heady stuff, not easily understood, but truly seminal. And now, someone else, this A. Einstein, had maybe done the same thing. Oh to talk to this fresh new explorer of the universe. She wrote a letter to her dear former student Professor Paul Appell.

Dearest Prof. Appell,

Your recent letter to me was such a delightful surprise. Your thoughtful suggestion that I read the paper by A. Einstein comes at a very good time. I have kept up my work on my theories. How kind it was of you to remember they are my passion. I am proud to say they have been published! I enclose to you the journal in which they are published. Please read my paper. I would so dearly love to discuss it with you.

Thank you,

Madame Augustine Chalamet

She dropped the magazine and her letter in the post.

The following day she set out to get a replacement copy. She settled into her seat on the 7:27 a.m. train to Saint-Denis, north of Paris. She separated 1 franc fifty and placed it securely in her inside coat pocket. It was the exact sum for a copy of the October 1905 edition of the Science de la Planète. She stepped out of the Gare du Nord train station into a cold Parisian drizzle and walked two blocks down Rue LaFayette to a nondescript office in a three-story building. She pushed through a door with stenciled letters "Éditions Dominion Compagnie." The small anteroom smelled of dusty paper and wood. She shuffled across a worn wooden floor.

"Bonjour, I wish to purchase a copy of the October issue of Science de la Planète."

A sad-looking woman sitting at a desk answered, "Oui, you will need to speak to our back issues manager. I will get him."

After a short wait, Augustine stated her request to a stoic, detached man in a ragged sweater. He disappeared for a time and returned with the issue. Augustine paid the one franc fifty, thanked the clerk, and turned to leave. As she moved toward the door, she opened the issue and stopped dead in her tracks. She could feel the skin tighten around her temples. It wasn't there. Her paper was not in the magazine. She checked the issue stamp, yes, the correct issue. She frantically ruffled through the pages, dropping the magazine at one point. Her paper simply wasn't there.

"Excusez-moi, monsieur, madame, there is a mistake. This must be a different issue."

After a flurry of discussion, Augustine was quite lathered. The stoic clerk remained emotionless and unhelpful. He didn't share Augustine's distress. The editor was summoned.

"Yes, I recall your name, Mlle Chalamet. It was months ago you sent us an article as I recall."

"Yes, and it was published in the October issue," Augustine insisted. "I had a copy. My paper was in there. October. I had a copy."

"No, Madame. You must be thinking of the author's review we sent you. We did not hear back."

Augustine became disoriented. Her breath was failing her, she leaned on the counter. "I don't understand."

"Madame Chalamet, we send a copy for review to each author. We do not publish until we receive approval back, along with an additional publishing fee. Your article was replaced with another. I am so sorry. We can review your article again for a future issue. Maybe sometime next year. Kindly resubmit. That is all. Thank you for coming in today."

The man took off his pince-nez and rubbed them with a cloth he pulled from his vest. His condescending look indicated to Augustine that she had been dismissed. The others went back to their passionless duties. It was a long walk to the train station. The ride home was eternal.

—ɛ-ɛ-ɛ-ɛ-ɛ-ɛ—

Brody left his therapist's office with his mind spinning.

God, what a morning. Hang a little long getting coffee and it's "Miss read-it-in-a-magazine" and then... whatever the hell the therapist was spouting.

The session was a flop. Incomprehensible psychobabble with tons of probing questions.

A voice interrupted his thoughts. "Going down?"

"What? Oh."

It was Kim, the young receptionist from the therapist office.

She said, "The doors. They're open."

"Oh yes, sorry I kinda zoned for a second. After you."

"I assume you want L?" Kim asked.

Brody, the morning still haunting him, said, "L. Yes. Please... and thanks."

She pressed the 2nd floor button after pressing L.

Her voice crashed his thoughts. "You're not the only one."

"Excuse me?"

"You're not the only one seeing Dr. Matthews about these weird episodes."

Wait, how did she know about my episodes? How does she know that there are others?

"What others? How many?"

"Oh I can't tell you that, HIPAA, ya know."

"But you somehow knew about me."

The elevator doors opened. Kim exited, glancing back at Brody.

Great, more weirdness.

—ε-ε-ε-ε-ε-ε—

Augustine exited the train. The cold misty rain had followed her all the way from Saint-Denis to Meaux. The train was crowded but Augustine was alone. Her life work that had finally been accepted was shelved, cast aside, discarded. It wasn't out there being absorbed by great minds. It wasn't being debated somewhere in the rarified halls of academia. It was just one printed copy in a ragtag publication. The sole version was making its way through the post to a former student. "We can review your article again for a future issue. Maybe sometime next year. That is all." Dismissed.

She tried to imagine where she would get the strength or energy to once again submit her paper. Her spirit was breaking. The streets of the town where she had spent her whole life were now cold and foreign. She made her way up the gravel path and through the courtyard to her flat and stepped out of the cold. It would take a while for the wood burning stove to heat up as she sat at her one small table. She had a thought to pull out her notes and start to reassemble her paper, but the trip had worn her down. The world had worn her down. Her gift to the world had slipped from her fingers and she was tired.

All the elation she felt when she thought her paper was published was gone.

She decided to regroup her energy and meet her old student Professor Paul Appell at the University of Paris.

—ε-ε-ε-ε-ε-ε—

"Dammit."

Brody yanked the curtains closed.

"I want these... these fucking things to stop."

The episodes were getting more frequent. And real. They were no longer as if in a dream. These were like he was actually there. Wherever there was. This morning, the view out his window was pasture, no cows, just pasture.

He leaned backwards on the window. His knees gave out partly due to being disoriented but mostly due to the pain. It was the soul pain again. He swore it was more intense, if that could even be possible. It made him weak.

He sat on the bed holding his head in his hands. He wanted to scream.

Why is this happening to me? And why now?

Brody felt rudderless. He was stalled. He wasn't working his plan. He wasn't progressing. He sat in his hotel room with the curtains drawn, in the afternoon. Brody Markovich, who carries a life-plan in his wallet that he created when he was twenty years old, with detailed goals including when he would get his first boat, is sitting in a hotel room, in the afternoon.

He walked to the bathroom and looked in the mirror.

His voice was rough. "So, Dr. Matthews, what's the verdict? Am I crazy? Oh, Mr. Markovich, we don't call crazy people that anymore. Let's get back to what you were feeling just before your last episode."

What a load of crap. My emotional core is being ripped out. Does she think this is all in my head?

He probably knew more than Dr. Matthews. He googled prodromal episodes to the point where he typed "P" on his computer and the search page filled with Prodromal Psychosis, Prodromal Schizophrenia, Prodromal signs of mental illness. He could teach a course on delusions with what he learned. His were not normal delusions. People usually have the same delusion over and over. Brody's were never the same.

And there was this woman, Roni, at the coffee shop. "Your therapist is wrong" and "I know what's happening with you."

Friggin' modern-day Madam Lenormand thinks I'm looking into a different reality.

But her dark eyes were so intense.

So, what's it gonna be? Coffee shop or therapy?

Maybe it was stress. But he was Brody Markovich, born to take it.

*"Stress sharpens the knife that
cuts out the weak parts of us."*

He felt like he was all weak parts.

Dusk arrived and the day had gone by, wasted, a picked over room service tray the only thing of value he had created. He needed air. He walked out into a cold November rain. He didn't bother going back in to get an umbrella. He needed to get out. He walked past the lit-up Capitol on his right where the power-hungry puffed out their chests and proclaimed nothing of worth. Odd to think that they probably got more done that day than he did. He continued down D Street past a nail salon and a Pho place. He found Union Pub. Happy Hour five until close. Five-dollar drinks. Sold. He sat at the bar, his hair matted from the rain. He looked like hell. Being around other people perked him up.

"Can I get you a beer?" The young female bartender was the first person he had talked to all day.

"No, maybe something a little quicker... er, different. What's that in the round bottle?"

"This?" She pointed at a bottle on the shelf.

"No no, the brown one right above it. Yes, there."

"Hendricks, it's a gin."

"Nice. What do people make with that?"

"Oh, just about anything. Tonics, basic martini. Tell you what, I've heard people put a pickle in it and make a martini."

"Sounds interesting. OK, put a pickle in it."

It felt good to be out in the land of the living. He made quick work of the pickle martini and was nearly done with his second when he glanced to his left and saw Donny Davino.

"Donny! Donny Davino! Paisano, Mr. Get Things

Done at good ole' ExpoLytics." He was starting to feel the gin.

"Hey Brody. You look —. How have you been?" There was tension in Donny's voice.

"Oh good, trying to adjust the dosage."

"Dosage?"

"Uh, I was trying to make a joke, big man. I figured everyone probably thinks I'm going crazy. So you know, dosage. Meds. Never mind."

"No, no one thinks you're crazy," Brody sensed that may be a lie.

"Well that's good, keep 'em guessing. I guess. So how's the ol' case?"

"GeneraCur?" Donny lowered his voice, "Sensitive subject. The case is struggling. We don't have the resources to handle the data."

"Computer resources?" Brody downed the rest of his drink.

Donny nodded. "It's bad."

"Man, who could've seen that coming?" Brody waved his hands around dripping with sarcasm.

"Is Pixburgh helping?" Brody held back a belch.

"Pfft, you kidding? We don't even exist down here. Probably need to drop the case."

"Drop the —?" Brody itched to jump in and figure out how to get things on track.

"Listen Brody, I gotta scoot. I'm waiting for someone. Good luck with — I mean take care."

Brody stared at the floor. "Yeah, nice seeing you."

Brody had a third pickle martini and headed out. The rain had let up, but it was cold. Brody shoved his hands in his pockets and hustled toward his hotel thinking about what Donny had said. The brisk air and the aromatic gin made for delightful companions. So delightful that Brody got an idea. By the time he got back to his room, he was convinced the idea would work. Free of inhibitions, he picked up his phone and typed a text: *checksum the diffs.*

He pressed send and fell asleep still in his street clothes.

—ε-ε-ε-ε-ε-ε—

Wayne Drakauer got out of bed and headed to the shower. He turned on his phone and saw he had a text. His blood boiled when he saw who it was from: Brody M.

Wayne mumbled to no one. "Why the hell was he texting me at two a.m.?"

checksum the diffs

"Oh good, more gibberish from the mighty Brody, self-branded king of bright ideas."

—ε-ε-ε-ε-ε-ε—

Brody's phone rang. He sat up in bed trying to get his bearings. The gin was still with him.

"Whoa. Wayne, dude, what's up?" Brody's voice was all cotton mouth and roughness.

"What do you mean what's up? I'm calling about this bogus text."

"Text?"

Brody's brain was playing catch up. "Oh yeah, the text. It's an idea I had to help the GeneraCur case."

"GeneraCur? Bro that ship has sailed. Drew's about to torpedo the whole thing."

"Drew? Drew Waltham? What's he have to do with GeneraCur?"

"Drew is now in charge of software, and software drives everything, so he's the guy calling the shots."

Brody's alcohol-soaked brain was spinning. Why was Drew Waltham, a sales guy, suddenly in charge of software?

Wayne continued, not giving Brody time to process, "I hate to break it to you, but Brody's Code ain't so great at handling large multi-threaded differential data loads. Drew says 'don't improve the software' so we don't improve the software. Bye bye GeneraCur."

"But that's what my text is about. To speed up the code and let it work on multiple threads at a time."

"Multiple threads? Man, you'd have to speed it up by four to five times, and free up processors. That would have to be a helluva big idea. And why are you working on this anyhow? I thought you had a brain tumor or something."

"Oh is that the current rumor?"

"Is it true?"

"Yeah, I'll be dead soon, so we need to talk fast."

Wayne answered weakly. "Really?"

Brody paused for effect. "No, I'm not dying."

"Well, a man can dream."

"What about my idea? Does it suck? Crazy? Ooh, need to be careful with that word."

"Look, I'm running late. I don't have time for this. What does this even mean?"

"Well, I noticed during my testing days that you checksum the entire stack when the code makes a certain number of calls."

Wayne confirmed. "Yes, to catch math errors. So?"

"Yeah, if I remember like every 10k calcs or so. It's like you cycle through all the code over and over again, checking it line by line."

Wayne hurried the discussion along. "Something like that. But I see where you're headed. Well listen we already increased it to more than 10k calcs to speed things up, but we started getting errors."

"No, that's not where I'm headed. My idea is, instead of doing a checksum on the entire stack… "

Brody paused, hoping Wayne would see it for himself, but nothing.

Brody continued, "How about if you check just the code that has changed? The diffs. Put a flag on everything that changes and then check that. Don't check the code that hasn't changed. It's already been checked."

Brody realized he was starting to lecture Wayne. So he waited.

Brody took Wayne's silence as agreement.

"And Wayne, take credit for this one, wouldja? Like it came out of thin air and this call never happened."

"What call?"

—ε-ε-ε-ε-ε-ε—

Augustine steadied herself with the handrail to pull herself up the steep steps of the train. It was early morning and impatient commuters rushed her along. She silently cursed every one of them. Traveling on trains wasn't part of her plan for her remaining years. She wished to be sitting in her flat reviewing numerous notes and letters about her groundbreaking paper. Instead, she was using this late November day to retrieve the only existing copy of her paper.

Paris was a bewildering place to Augustine. She had only imagined how big and chaotic it was. Now she was right in the middle of it. Carriages rattled along, passed by bicycles. Pedestrians in Edwardian clothes, women in ankle length dresses and immaculate hats, and men in their bowlers, crossed streets at their peril. She managed to find a trolley and rode it to Le Jardin du Luxembourg in the Latin Quarter. A friendly stranger gave her directions to the university. "Go to the Pantheon and turn north, toward the river." It was her first contact with a human since that awful, patronizing man at the publisher. Her heart sank every time she thought of it. How could she not know she needed to send back an approval? And with more money!

The walk was short. She marveled at the large buildings and how they made the streets look like canyons. She found the university and had to ask no fewer than five people how to get to Professor Paul Appell's office. He was a dean! Why does no one know where his office is? Her short, clickety footsteps echoed off the walls and high ceiling of the long corridor.

"Puis-je vous aider, madame?"

"Oui, s'il vous plaît. Je suis ici pour rencontrer le professeur Paul Appell"

"Je suis désolé, madame… "

"As I say, Professor Paul Appell is not present. He is serving on a very important commission concerning 'L'Affaire Dreyfus.' It is important he not be disturbed. We need to rid the streets of these rioters and haters. Liars, every one of them! But, please, madame, come back in the future. An appointment perhaps?"

The rest of the assistant's response overwhelmed Augustine in a slow-moving gelatinous ooze. The woman's voice became muddled and distant.

Fading. "No, he cannot be reached. He must not be disturbed."

Fading. "No, I do not have permission to enter his office to look for your manuscript."

Fading. "I do not know if he received it. I don't recall it at all."

Fading. "Hello, madame, are you OK?"

Augustine awoke in an oak paneled office.

A man with a diminutive mustache was seated behind a desk. "You fainted. You should drink. We brought you some water. It's there on the table."

"Oh dear. I didn't wish to cause trouble." Augustine sat quietly sipping the water.

"They tell me you are looking for Paul."

"Yes sir. He was a student of mine. I taught professor Appell at prep school."

"And your name?"

"I am so sorry. I am Madame Chalamet."

"My name is Dr. Henri Poincaré."

Augustine's jaw went slack. Dr. Poincaré was one of France's leading mathematicians.

"What is your purpose for visiting Paul?"

He shuffled papers as she told her story, showing little interest. He took a drink of water as she talked and licked his rubbery lips somehow missing the drops of water that hung from his greasy mustache like tinsel on a sad discarded Christmas tree.

As if to establish his status. "I will beckon one of the girls to find out if they've seen your paper."

The word "papier" shot little drops of water across the desk, ridding his mustache of half its load. Augustine's mind filled with a response which a woman in the early 1900s would not ever dare speak. *Haughty, disdainful little man, I've already asked them. Perhaps you could use your emperor status to ask the 'girls' to open Paul's office so maybe we could have a look and find my manuscript. Or would that be too taxing for a man of such great import?*

Instead, she addressed the great scholar with an undeserved respect, "Perhaps you could ask Paul to contact me when he returns?"

"But of course."

He made a show of checking his watch and huffed, "Is there anything else you need?" not wanting an answer.

He gave no more thought to Mlle Chalamet and her juvenile paper.

—ε-ε-ε-ε-ε-ε—

Brody dragged himself through the morning routine of getting showered and dressed. *Drew Waltham. In charge of software. Something's up.* He grabbed a coffee from the free cart in the hotel lounge. He went into Union Station through the east doors. It added a few minutes, but it avoided Roni. He rode the Metro to his therapist feeling like a gin-soaked rug.

"Dr. Matthews will see you now."

"Thank you, Kim Dire." Brody held eye contact and drew out her name, reading it off her nameplate.

Kim was really the one he wanted to see. He wanted to know what she meant when she said, "There are others."

Dr. Matthews started the session. "So, what have you been up to since our last visit?"

"Well, last night, drinking."

"Do you think that's healthy?"

"No. Is it? What'd they teach you in psych school?"

"How did it make you feel to take those drinks?"

"Drunk."

You wanna know what I've been up to? Hmm let's see, not working for one thing, only because you think I'm looney as limburger. What else have I been up to? Well, I sit around googling psychotic episodes to see if I can relate. And you know what? Some of that crap feels familiar. So maybe I am a bit ginger nuts.

He didn't say any of that. Instead, he sat, hands on knees. Dr. Marci Matthews babbled on with what apparently counts as two hundred dollars worth of psychiatry.

He cut her off in the middle of some meaningless sentence. "But how does that get rid of these diabolical episodes so I can get my job back?"

She gave no answer, because there was no answer. Dr. Matthews was striking out.

As he passed by the reception desk, he discreetly handed Kim a note: *text me 412-555-8102.*

—ε-ε-ε-ε-ε-ε—

Brody went to bed at eight. After last night's battle with the pickle drinks, he needed to sleep. His next moment of coherent brain activity was when the sunrise pierced the gap in the curtains and laser-beamed him into consciousness. Sunrise had shifted fourteen degrees to the south since he first checked into The George. Seasons were changing and Brody felt the unnerving desperation of time slipping away. He was in a pit with no way out. He couldn't fathom the thought of the GeneraCur case crumbling, taking his career with it. He was convinced Dr. Marci Matthews was going to throw him in a soft room and lock the door. His only hope was finding the coffee shop lady. Maybe she could exorcize his demons. He rushed to the coffee shop so he could get there before she did.

He stood off to the side as she walked in and spoke from a distance, "Why do you think you know what's happening with me?" He wished he had shaved.

Roni turned, the light from the new sun played on her distinctive jawline and tawny skin.

She said, "You look like you've been hit by a bus."

"It's been a bad couple days. I'm debating how much to tell you. Do you have time to sit?"

Roni maintained eye contact. "I might."

She went to a table near the door.

Brody stared out the window, sullen, not at ease. "Look, I'm not doing well. There's nights I don't sleep. I can't stop thinking about what you said. My therapist thinks I'm crazy, which can't be right because I'm not crazy, but maybe I am which means she's right, but you say she's wrong,"

He took a breath and continued his run-on sentence. "because you've read this thing in a book or something —."

Roni stopped him. "She *is* wrong."

Brody paused.

"Yes. *Wrong*." Roni continued, "I found an article written in 1905. It's in French but luckily I know French so —"

"Wait a minute, you've been reading something written like a million years ago, and that's going to help me?"

"A hundred-and-ten."

He sputtered, "What?"

"It was written a hundred and ten years ago. And yes, it explains your so-called prodromal episodes. And everything else."

"Everything else?"

Her pace quickened. She talked fast, spitting out facts, "We are all connected. We interact with the universe to create reality. Reality, our conscious mind, what it is and where it comes from. The stars, the planets, the eggs you had for breakfast, the chicken that —"

"Stop. That sounds great but how does it help me?"

Roni thought for a beat. "I have to keep reading."

Brody ran his fingers through his uncombed hair. "Cuz, that's all I really need right now."

She softened her eye contact. "I get it. I do. And I want to help you. I think I can. I need to go to work now but there's one thing I need to know about you before I do."

Great, more questions. More probing.

Brody asked sharply, "Fire away, what is it? I can hardly wait."

"What is your name?"

Brody's face loosened and he laughed for the first time in days. "Wow, I laid bare to you that I'm seeing things and am going to a shrink, but I never told you my name? Actually, I think I did, but anyhow it's Brody Markovich."

He extended his hand.

"Saronda Jackson." Roni thrust her hand out awkwardly.

"I thought it was Roni."

"It was. It's Saronda now, the way it should be, and I think we're about to go on quite a journey together."

They agreed to meet the next morning. Trying to put his cheese back on the cracker had taken a new twist.

He went to his hotel and took a nap.

—ε-ε-ε-ε-ε-ε—

The train ride back to Meaux was interminable. It felt twice as long as the morning's ride. Every bump and jostle sent pains through Augustine's weakening bones. She was vacant, not seeing the soft light of the moon on the moving landscape.

She was numb. Her paper, her song to the world, was trapped, maybe discarded. Her heart weighed heavily. She hunched over, not from fatigue, but from having her soul ripped out. She stepped off the train feeling older than when she left, pulling her shoulder wrap tighter as she shuffled past ancient stone walls. Lanterns flickered in the flats with shadowy glimpses of families gathering for dinner. She wondered for the millionth time what it was like to have a stable family. She never knew her mother or father. There were no records of what happened to them. Augustine was orphaned before she could remember. She was passed around from temporary home to temporary home. She considered the house on Rue Saint-Feron as her only true home. She had half a thought to turn left and walk past the old place. She was placed there with an upper-class couple when she was seventeen. They had lost their only child during the cholera outbreak of 1832 in Paris. Cholera spread so fast that grave diggers and casket makers couldn't keep up. The last they saw of their daughter was when she was placed on a cart and taken away. They fled to Meaux and took in Augustine, treating her as their own. She felt rich living there. They paid for secondary school for Augustine. She earned her teaching certificate and taught for over fifty years. And, she poured everything she had into a set of theories that explained reality. Theories the world may never see.

The wind hurried her along to her flat, up the gravel path. She sat on the wooden bench. The courtyard of her building swirled with an autumn wind as the moon cast muted shadows of the large oak onto the waning garden. The cold air gave her a lift, but it couldn't erase the helpless claustrophobic feeling of losing her paper. Henri Poincare had shown no interest in helping the "femme folle" that happened into his office. She tried to remember if they even wrote down her name or details. She felt a palpable grip on her heart.

She was defeated. The wind rustled the oak leaves still clinging to their branches. They were brown and dry and stood like sentinels against the wind. Augustine often wondered why the old oak clung so tightly to leaves long past their usefulness. The other trees had dropped their leaves weeks earlier while they were still ablaze, supple and glorious.

She was empty. Her song may never be heard. It wasn't just gone. To the world, it never existed. She had reached into her soul and with singular insight, created a beautiful gift to the world. It was a gift now in the hands of fate. A fate hinging on the actions of an indifferent derisive man. She felt smaller now, sitting on the bench, than that glorious spring day when thoughts came to her like life-giving rain. The air that once felt fresh now served only to chill. It was a bone deep chill. The oak leaves rustled in dissonance to Augustine's shallow breathing. She knew it was all about fate now and fate could be cruel.

She also knew our spirit cannot be extinguished. It is, and always has been, and always will be. She had the equations to prove it. Our spirit has always been part of the universe, waiting. Waiting to be woven into a magnificent reality. With that in her heart, she went inside.

She was cold. Augustine pulled the blankets of her well-worn bed to her chin. The light from the moon shone through the window, casting shadows on the sum total of her material goods.

Augustine laid her head on the thin pillow and died.

With a gust of wind, the oak tree released a single solitary leaf which fell to the ground away from the moon's light, unnoticed.

—ε-ε-ε-ε-ε-ε—

The sun reached through the opening in the curtains, striking the side of Brody's face. He rolled over, dwelling on the suffocating grip the episodes had on his life. Each one tore another piece out of him. He entered the bathroom, catching a glimpse of his naked body in the mirror, trying to convince himself his swimmer's body was still in there. He stood long in the shower wishing for the warm water to give him clarity.

Deep down, he knew the idea of an alternate reality ruining his life was crazy, but Saronda had an intoxicating passion. He looked forward to seeing her again. Maybe because he felt she could help him or maybe he liked seeing her again. She had an energy about her that was never on display but always there, front and center.

He dressed nicely and combed his hair.

He walked through the lobby and Ed, the bellhop, greeted him with, "You're looking good today, my man. Meeting someone special, perhaps?"

"Oh no, thanks for asking. I got a good night's sleep, that's all. Works wonders." *Why did I say that? I slept like shit.*

Ed held the door. "Well, enjoy your day."

"Thanks, Ed, you do the same."

Saronda was already at the coffee shop.

"Oh man, am I late?" Brody said as he sat down. He noticed she looked different. *Was her hair straight before? Is that make-up?*

He thought about saying she looked nice but was murky on what was appropriate.

Saronda smiled. "No, get your coffee. Then let's get started."

Brody nodded toward the notebook and papers scattered on the table. "Are we going to have enough time to go through all that?"

"Unless you've got someplace to be. It's Wednesday, my day off."

"Nice." He got in line for coffee.

Wow. Wednesday already. Thanksgiving is tomorrow.

He told his parents he would visit them and stay overnight. He realized he hadn't decided what to tell them, which details to leave in, especially which ones to leave out. Details like he wasn't working and his brain was short-circuiting. Delicate issues at best.

The barista called, "Brody."

Saronda said, "I'm going to start by telling you about 'Murmures de l'univers', Whispers of the universe."

"Whoa. I haven't even sat down."

"We're connected to the cosmos. It's through our Whispers. They weave our perfect reality. It's all part of destiny."

Brody sat. "Ooh, deep. Sounds mysterious. I'm in."

"Glad to hear it. Now, Whispers —"

"Can we hear them?"

"Augustine doesn't say but I haven't read everything."

"Augustine?"

"Yes, she's the one who wrote all this."

"A woman? Like a million years ago?"

"Yes, is there a problem?"

"No, it's just that, I didn't think that, nothing." *Sheesh, where am I going with this?*

Saronda held eye contact for a beat and then continued, "We had women back then. You know, you come off as a bit of a jackass sometimes."

"I've been told. Can I ask a question? Why are you so into this?"

"Because a hundred and ten years ago, a woman wrote about the destiny of the universe and no one's ever heard of her. That's why. Now, do you understand what a Whisper is?"

Brody wanted to say yes. "No."

"OK. Listen this time. Whispers are things we can't see. They are inside us. They reach out into the universe and create our reality. They weave physical and spiritual energy into everything we see."

Brody gave a smirk. "Color me incredulous. Why

should I believe this?"

"What else you got going?"

Brody thought of his therapist. "OK. Keep going."

"Augustine wrote with such passion. She wrote how we fit in with the universe. We think of ourselves as small inconsequential specks. But if you look at how much spiritual energy we have, we dwarf even the biggest stars. Stars, rocks, trees don't have nearly as much spiritual energy as we do. It permeates the universe."

Saronda was a woman transformed from when they first met.

He said, "That's mind blowing. More energy than stars."

The excitement in her voice drew him in as she continued. The next hour went quickly.

"The next part is what's important to you. There's more than one reality."

Brody's eyes drifted.

Saronda leaned forward. "It's important to know that because *your* Whisper is different. Your Whisper is energetic enough that it reaches into another reality sometimes. Hello. Anyone home? Knock Knock."

She leaned back. "C'mon. Let's take a break."

He took a deep breath. "No, I want to keep going. You said there were equations. Is that what will fix me?"

Saronda replied, "Yes. Probably. But, we would have to use a computer. There are hundreds of equations. It would take months. The calculations are complex."

Complex calculations. That rolled it right into his wheelhouse, being the inventor of Brody's code.

Saronda said, "There are trillions of Whispers. Remember, everything has a Whisper, rocks, stars —."

"Rock stars." Brody added unhelpfully.

Saronda's duet of stern eyebrows and intense eye contact sent a message. "You're drifting. Stay on track."

"Just trying a little levity. If you can't have fun while going insane, what's the point?"

"Brody, this is serious. Focus. Technically, you're correct. Rock stars are people and people have Whispers. Let's move on. The problem is, reality takes millions, trillions of Whispers moving, twisting, evolving, creating patterns of their own. Each Whisper has many spikes of energy shooting out that weave that interact. Imagine all that happening—"

Brody interjected, "Totally random."

"It's not random. It's complex. But not random."

"OK, Miss Nuance. You science people can be so

pedantic."

"And non-science people can be so polysemous."

"My mom has an English degree from an ivy league school. You'd think I'd know what that meant."

Saronda said, "Well I hate to be all nerdy and stuff but there is a very important difference between complex and random. Random things can't be calculated. But complex things —"

"—are calculated all the time," Brody said with insight, his voice lifting.

Saronda raised an eyebrow.

Brody became useful. "If you have all the equations, making the calculations would be easy."

Saronda said, "If we had a very powerful computer, maybe."

Brody stared out the window. "I have an idea. But we need to talk first."

After a second, he said, "I'm going to go sit in that park across the street for a while."

"Can I join you or are you tired of me?"

"Come. We'll enjoy the nice weather."

They sat on a bench and blankly watched an oak leaf dance across the sidewalk.

Brody said, "I had another episode last night. They're getting worse. Each time, it takes longer to bounce back. They're ripping me up. It's not only about getting my job back."

He turned to Saronda. "I'm following what you're saying. I understand what a Whisper is. I understand it's this magical thing and mine is too magical and it sees another reality. But, these patterns and equations. How are they going to stop the terror? Just plug some numbers in, snap our fingers, and bye bye demons, I'm fixed?"

"All I can say is, Augustine's paper is a work of genius."

"So are the Brandenburg Concertos but I don't see how they'll keep me off lithium."

"How's that therapist working out for you? Brody, I don't know how this works. Every day, I open this paper. It's like turning on a fire hose. There has got to be something in there that can help you."

He listened to the flag flapping in the breeze. "There are others. I'm not the only one."

Saronda's face fell.

"We need to fix this, Saronda. Not just for me. Because, if it can happen to others…"

—ε-ε-ε-ε-ε-ε—

Months had gone by since Augustine died. Paul Appell settled behind his desk. It felt good to once again be back in his office at the University of Paris. He had been away for months bringing the long painful saga of Alfred Dreyfus to a close. Piles of papers and letters covered his desk and extended to every horizontal surface of his well-appointed office. He was determined to read the many letters and requests that had accumulated. It wasn't until a dreadfully hot day in August 1906 that he came upon a large envelope. The return address of Augustine Chalamet filled him with a melancholy sadness. He had forgotten his letter to her. Augustine's article in the magazine drew him in. He retreated to a cool stone-walled walkway and sat on a marble bench under the shade of a large tree, each glossy leaf shielding the other from the relentless sun. He was enraptured. Returning to his office to get some notepaper, he asked his assistant if she remembered the envelope being delivered. It was insignificant, like the incident of the fainting woman who had sent it. No memory, it was long ago. He sat outside again, scribbling notes. "Possible to change reality." "Can alter history." He wished he had the time to review each equation but thought it would be best if Augustine could review it with him and some of the other minds at the university. If her equations were sound, then what she had postulated would be truly astounding. He wrote a letter to Augustine.

Dearest Augustine,

Please allow me to express my deepest apologies for

not responding to the thoughtful gift of your fine paper. It is most captivating, and I would greatly cherish the opportunity to discuss it in detail with you. Please do not think by my long-delayed response that I lack interest. I have been away serving on a commission to rid our beloved country of the riots caused by lies and distortion. Please accept my apologies. At your earliest convenience, let me know if you would care to visit me and discuss your splendid work.

In deepest regards, your student,

Paul

He dropped it in the post and put the magazine on a shelf. It soon fell from his attention.

—ε-ε-ε-ε-ε-ε—

"OK, let's talk about these calculations." Brody said to the air in front of him with Saronda close behind as they headed back to the coffee shop.

Saronda upped her stride. "It won't be easy. There are countless equations. Hundreds. It will take a long time to make all the calculations, even on a high zoot desktop computer."

Brody chuckled. "Ha Ha zoot. That's how we measured computing power."

"What are you talking about?"

As they came to the intersection, he said, "We

called them zoots. Like, hey we're clocking 1.3 megazoots today." He paused. "Oh it's what I worked on when I, you know, worked."

Saronda plowed on. "Augustine models the entire universe. That's a lot of zoots."

Brody said, "The place I worked at... Oh sorry, I shouldn't interrupt."

"You also shouldn't stop in the middle of the street either. Keep walking."

Saronda continued, "I was saying there are other realities out there. Wait. Tell me about these zoots."

"It's a playful term we used for computing power. We ran complex models and analysis. Financial analysis. We used desktop computers."

Saronda responded, "Augustine's stuff would blow up even the most powerful desktop computer. We'd need a supercomputer."

As they got to the other side of the street, Brody stopped and said, "Yes, yes I know. What I was getting at when you were so rudely interrupted, was, we essentially built a supercomputer using desktop computers."

Brody made full eye contact. "We string them together, the desktops, string them together and have them all work in tandem. They calculate in parallel, each one feeding off the other. That's what I worked on."

"You strung them together? How many?"

Brody started walking and looked back over his shoulder. "Thousands, sometimes even tens of thousands."

Saronda trotted to catch up. "Seriously? Slow down. You had some giant cable and hooked them together?"

Brody stopped. "Ever heard of the Internet and a high-speed connection?"

"Right, they communicate through the web." Saronda smacked her forehead as if to punish herself for being so dense.

They both became quiet. Brody let her absorb what he was saying, watching the flag across the street wave in the wind.

She said, "Do you think we could —"

Brody read her thoughts. "Yes, use them to model the universe."

"What do you call this thing?"

"Brody's Code."

—ε-ε-ε-ε-ε-ε—

Brody set out early Thanksgiving morning. The local news was all about how bad the holiday traffic was on I495 and I270. He took a more rural route up US15 before heading west to Pittsburgh. The highway snaked across soil created by the erosion of Everest-sized mountains.

The drive provided a backdrop for Brody to think. Nothing made sense. A dream project that would launch his career into overdrive: crumbling. The software, "Brody's Code," his big idea: not up to the task. Wayne Drakauer: afraid of Drew. Drew Waltham, Mr. "I have a boat on Lake Erie that I sleep in": in charge of software. WTF?

But it was the episodes that dominated his thoughts. And the almond-eyed girl with a fierce inner fire just below the surface, waiting to be released.

He pulled into his parent's driveway at noon. They lived in a tony part of Pittsburgh called Shadyside. Brody's father, Arthur, was a big deal at Dynamic Business Partners, LLC. DBP was a consulting firm that helped other companies negotiate complex business deals. Arthur was the best. He was all about control. Mind over matter. He once closed a business deal while passing kidney stones. No one knew. He kept everything close. He was Brody's mentor and biggest cheerleader. For now, Brody wanted to step into the warm embrace of Thanksgiving aromas, leaving D.C. miles behind him.

A very energetic Australian Shepherd was the first to greet him, pushing past Brody's mom, Sylvie. The excited barking obscured Sylvie's voice. "Come in. Oh, we've looked forward to this. Take off your jacket. Where are your things? Your father will be down in a minute."

The sounds were a welcome chorus to Brody as

they group-hugged on the massive porch with carved columns and bluestone steps.

"Uh, my stuff's in the car. I'll go get it."

"Oh, let your father help."

"No, it's OK. It's not much," Brody said with a short tone.

"Is everything OK?"

"Yeah, no, we'll talk. Let me get my stuff." His goal of hiding everything from his parents got off to a bad start.

Brody took his overnight bag upstairs to his room. It wasn't the room he grew up in. His parents bought this house when he was sixteen, after his father closed a huge business deal. He looked out the window at the large street trees and the small park across the way. He could see himself buying a nice place like this someday. It was a mansion by any standard, a symbol of his father's success. The last time he slept here was unplanned. His father insisted on celebrating Brody's promotion so he picked Brody up at the new condo. Brody was so jazzed that his father was acknowledging his accomplishment that he celebrated a little too much. They had to carry Brody into the house. This time, it wasn't a celebration. Brody thought it may be more an inquisition.

He heard his father's voice downstairs and decided to face the parents.

"Hey champ, you're looking good."

"So are you but I guess this cold weather keeps you off the links."

"Hell no, been golfing all the way up to last weekend. Probably go again tomorrow, want me to see if I can fit you in?"

"Oh no, not me. I've got things to keep me busy..."

Getting my sanity back is a full time job.

Sylvie interrupted, "The meal is served."

He could tell his father was staring at him as they walked to the dining room.

"Wow, Mom, you must have gotten up in the middle of the night to get all this ready."

"I enjoy it, now eat. And what's this you want to talk about."

Arthur turned his full focus to Brody.

Brody said, "Let's get some food in us first. And wine."

And it started. Arthur immediately went fishing. "How's the project you were sent to D.C. to work on? When you get back to work, what are you stepping into?"

Brody was happy to talk about the case. "My project, which is now a Federal case with the SEC, is struggling because we can't get the computing resources we need. The Pittsburgh office is like radio silence. Not helping. We're simply not getting what we need. But the strange thing is, they were turned upside down because of a strange re-org."

"What kind of re-org?" His father was all about the inside politics at corporations.

"Well, this guy, high level guy, Drew Waltham, took over software; development, deployment, everything with software."

"So?"

"He's a sales guy. Knows nothing about software. Wouldn't recognize it if it came to his office and shook his hand. Clueless. Software is everything at ExpoLytics, the crown jewels. And they gave it all to this guy? Nonsense. And the thing is, he's slow-walking everything that could get my case back on track. He's stalling."

"Does he have it in for you?"

"That would be crazy, this jeopardizes the whole company. Not to brag, but my case is a really big deal. I don't know why he wants to stall," Brody hesitated. "and there's something else I need to tell you."

Brody set down his fork. "I'm having these episodes where I see things, little things. They change and then they change back."

Arthur and Sylvie looked at each other.

"I'm seeing a therapist, one recommended by HR. She thinks it's some light delusions. They don't want me working until I get rid of them."

His father coughed. "Don't want you worki—."

"I've been placed on leave."

The air in the room got thick. No one spoke. Brody could feel his pulse in his ears. Hell, he could feel his parents' pulse in his ears.

Sylvie asked the obvious, "Were you... ?"

"Fired? No Mom, it's just a leave."

They continued eating. Brody silently counted down, 3... 2... 1... Go.

Slyvie said, "Maybe you're not ready for such a high-level position. You were promoted very quickly. Maybe this job isn't right for you. Can they get you one with less stress?"

Brody bristled. "Why do you always do that? Why do you always sell me short?"

"I'm not, it's just that we all have limits."

"I wasn't failing, that's not why. It's the delusions."

Delusions. The word had probably never been said in this house with these people.

Arthur set his fork down. "Ya mean like voices?"

"No, I see things. Well, I hear things too, not voices. The therapist isn't sure what they are."

Brody waited an eternity. Finally, his father said, "Listen, I can make some calls and get you a good therapist, one who can —"

"Father, you can't jump in every time I have a problem."

"This is no small matter. You've been put on leave for chrissakes."

"Yes, I noticed," Brody snarked.

Sylvie jumped in. "Let's talk about something else."

The trio sat and the tension increased.

Arthur said, "You know, I think you're right. This move by that sales guy is strange."

It was a welcome shift but Brody knew they were processing.

Sylvie scooted her chair back. "Who wants pie?"

She retreated to the kitchen and returned with three pieces of pumpkin pie.

They ate in silence.

Brody said softly, "It's really good pie, Mom."

He thought he saw his mom's eyes welling up. He

walked to his room and watched the sun set. It was a great house in a great location. He desperately wanted this. *Why is everything so hard?*

Arthur knocked on Brody's door. "Why don't you come downstairs? We should talk."

They settled into the twin Italian leather chairs of Arthur's den. They were the kind with the shiny burgundy leather and dozens of brass buttons making deep indentations. They had hand-carved legs and feet. Their provenance was storied but Brody didn't remember the details.

"OK, first, you're not going crazy. We'd be able to notice if you were."

Brody's first thought was that he was getting better at hiding the episodes. The day had been riddled with them, even during dinner. Small ones.

"Second, you need to convince them you're OK to go back. Get your game on track."

The chair leather squeaked as he leaned forward, "And third, this move by the sales guy to take over software does not compute. Sorry, bad pun."

Brody countered, "All puns are bad, that's what makes them good."

"So you do listen to my wisdom."

"Every word."

His father mused, "So, he's kind of an empty shirt. Why would they give him software? The crown jewels?"

Brody waited for one of his father's time-tested idioms. Arthur Markovich had a million of them. He leaned forward trying to guess which one he would apply to this mess.

Arthur sat with his elbows on his knees and stared at Brody. "It's strange Brody, and when people do strange things —"

"There's always a reason." Brody finished the sentence.

They both smiled.

Brody said, "Maybe they didn't give it to him. I was thinking on the drive up that —"

Arthur finished the sentence. "Maybe he took it. A pure power play."

"Or he knows something."

"I've got decaf." Sylvie walked into the den with two coffees. "But you'll have to come out and sit with me if you want another piece of pie. No hoggin' the kid. He's only here one night."

He followed Arthur and the smell of fresh coffee to the kitchen. He thought of Saronda.

"You know, I didn't tell you the bizarre side of all this." Brody was feeling much more at ease.

Sylvie said it all, "What could be more bizarre than losing your job because you're seeing things?" The words caught in her throat a little.

"First, Mom, I didn't lose my job. It's a leave. They are still paying me. And second, I'm going to figure out these episodes, these delusions. I'm working with someone who thinks they know what's happening to me and—"

"Are you talking about your therapist?" Having a therapist was not a Markovich thing. Neither Sylvie nor Arthur ever entertained the idea. Brody squelched the thought of telling her it's a full-blown psychiatrist.

"No, I'm talking about someone I met that has an article, a manuscript."

His father jumped in. "OK, go on, so you met a guy who—"

"It's not a guy, it's a girl. We met at a coffee shop."

The awkwardness was off the charts. Brody's voice quavered.

Sylvie probed. "What's her name? This girl you met. What's she like?"

"Roni. I mean Saronda."

Arthur pounced. "Is it Roni or Saronda? Or don't you know?"

"Well, it *was* Roni, but now she wants it to be

Saronda."

Arthur opened his mouth and was about to pile on when, "Arthur please, leave him alone. Brody, what's she like?"

"She's quiet and studies a lot. She's a very serious person. And she works at a museum. Not sure where she lives or where she's from."

Arthur couldn't resist. "Well, you sound close."

Sylvie glared. "Shush. Now Brody, tell me more about this girl."

"She's not a 'this girl'. It's not like that. I met her in a coffee shop after making a fool of myself and now she thinks she can fix me. I mean, not fix me, but help me with my delusions. At first she thought I was a creep and I thought she was stuck up."

Arthur couldn't resist. "It's something, finding a girl who immediately wants to fix you. I can see it working out."

"Arthur, stop." Sylvie put her hand on Arthur's forearm and turned toward Brody, "Do you really think she can help you?"

"I don't have any other choice. My therapist is a dud."

His parents watched as he walked up to his room.

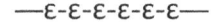

—ε-ε-ε-ε-ε-ε—

He slept well at his parents' house. He walked into the hallway and was hit with a cloud of breakfast aromas; bacon, eggs, hash browns. They all played their part in a symphony of delight.

Sylvie said, "I can tell *you* slept well. Your hair, dear. It's asymmetrical."

Brody ran his fingers through his hair. "You cooked up a storm again."

"So this girl, Brody. What is she trying to do again?"

"She's trying to help me with these episodes."

"Yes, but how?" It was his father.

Brody told them about the article in the old magazine and about the girl "his same age."

Sylvie said, "It's nice that you've met someone."

Arthur said, "Even if she is a nutjob."

Sylvie glared. Brody dug into his now cold bacon and eggs.

—ε-ε-ε-ε-ε-ε—

Brody carried his overnight bag to his car. He and his parents had said all the usual "goodbyes" and "come back soons" and "yes I wills."

As he was closing his trunk, his father walked up, dressed for golf.

They shook hands with one hand, reached around and patted each other's back with the other.

"Brody, get through this. Think it through. If you need help with anything, you know, we're here. Oh, and about this girl —"

"Don't try to be Mom. It doesn't look good on you."

"OK, but, sometimes cosmic bullshit is just cosmic bullshit."

It was a lonely drive to his condo.

—ε-ε-ε-ε-ε-ε—

Saronda watched the seconds tick off the microwave in the mid-century kitchen in the walk-up her mom shared with no one. Her mom lived alone ever since her husband was killed in the line of duty.

Her dad's death hit Saronda hard. They were close. He was a shield against her mom. He softened things, made everything OK. "Oh, she didn't mean it that way." Saronda believed him. It was too painful to think otherwise.

BEEP! "Cornbread stuffing's ready." It was the first words her mom said all morning.

Saronda dished some to her sister Shay and sat down.

"Roni, that was a wild tale you told us last night."

"Mom, stop it. You're doing that because you're mad at me."

"Doing what?"

"Calling me Roni. You only call me that when... Oh never mind. I want everyone to call me Saronda."

Shay said, "Wait a minute. I'm confused. Everybody? What am I supposed to call you?"

"Saronda. I never liked Roni."

Shay said, "After all these years."

"Anyhow, it's more than a tale. It's science and it's genius."

Her mom measured her words. "I think it's great that you have a new interest. Maybe you can write about it and get your story published. How you found this magazine from a long time ago. How you know French because your dad was stationed in France when you were young. Maybe you could track down the origins of this magazine and who this lady was who wrote it."

"Mom, it's more than just finding a magazine. This is deep. It's laws of physics mixed with spirituality and even theology. It contains the answers to a lot of stuff. It's revolutionary."

Shay said, "It sounded looney toon to me"

"Stop it. It's not crazy. It's real. I've read it. I've studied it. It all makes sense, and I'm going to prove it."

Shay chuckled. "How? Catch a whisper in a jar? Transport to another reality?"

Saronda shuddered. "No, I'm going to prove it by fixing this guy."

"A guy?" Shay leaned in. "You didn't tell us about a guy. And you need to fix him? Good luck with that."

Shay is three years older than Saronda and her dating life is a revolving door.

"No, it's not like that. He has episodes. He sees things. I'm going to —"

Shay cut in. "This dude sounds destined for a psycho ward and you're going to fix him with the help of a hundred-year-old woman who sounds as whack as he does?"

"She's not a hundred-year-old woman. She wrote an article a hundred years ago. Let's not talk about this right now."

Her mom said, "Well Roni —"

"It's Saronda. I want to be called Saronda."

Her mom smoothed her apron and summed things up. "Sometimes when something looks crazy, it's probably because it's crazy."

Shay covered her mouth to stifle a laugh. "Ooh Mom, burn it to the ground."

Her mom left. Saronda felt her face flush.

Shay said, "Hey, Sis, you OK? You're taking this kinda hard. You're always talking about crazy stuff, we're fujoking, messin' with ya."

Saronda looked down at her food. "I believe in this woman."

Shay sat, "Sis, what do you want from all this crazy shit?"

"I want it to matter. I read, I learn, but it's like an afternoon's entertainment. I want it to mean something."

"Girl, not everything changes the world."

—ε-ε-ε-ε-ε-ε—

Brody walked from the cold parking structure and opened the door to his condo. Cold. He pulled out his phone and cranked the heat.

"What do my eyes behold?"

On the counter was an opened box of Sarris Chocolates. He let each Almond Meltaway languish on his tongue as he looked out the floor-to-ceiling windows at the Allegheny, a river that carried the raw material that rocketed the wealth of the nation into the stratosphere, making many people rich. He wondered what demons *they* had to battle.

I need a plan. He had none. He found a pen.

Step 1, Stress eat a box of old chocolate.

He crossed it out and threw down the pen.

Come on jagoff, get serious.

He leaned back for a minute. Then, picked up the pen.

Sweet talk Wayne to write some code
Run the calculations
Use ExpoLytics computers
Step 1: Call Wayne

God this is stupid. What do I say? Hi Wayne, I know you're a cynical bastard but could you do this tiny thing for me? Get unauthorized access to the system and do some sorcery so I can be sane again?

"OK, here we go."

Wayne answered, "Bro, it's the day after Thanksgiving. What the hell?"

"Hey it's always the day after something. I thought you'd be free to talk about how the code improvement was going. You know, the checksum thing."

"*Actually, I was hoping to be free to live my life today.*"

Brody gave Wayne a friendly verbal punch in the

shoulder. "Am I interrupting something? I don't picture you as a big Black Friday guy."

Wayne wasn't playing.

He sniffed. "We haven't done much with the code improvement you mentioned. I've architected it but —"

"But what, why not run a test? If you need someone to come in and test it, I bet I still remember how."

"Brody, you're on leave. Anyhow, a lot has changed. Drew Waltham, who is fresh off reading 'Code Stuff for Dummies' wants to review everything."

"So you guys are sitting around doing nothing?" *Nice! He has lots of free time.*

"Hell no we're not sitting around. The dipshit's got us running around looking at all sorts of crap."

"I would think improving the code to salvage the GeneraCur case would be top of the list."

"Bodacious thought but it's just the opposite. Drew wants nothing to do with GeneraCur. He wishes it would go away..."

"Go away? That's downright silly."

"Yeah, it's not a priority, OK."

"GeneraCur is not a priority! That's the biggest thing going —"

"Brody, I gotta go. I'm online shopping for socks

but between you and me, I think it's a really good idea you had. The checksum thing."

Wayne disconnected.

Brody's heart sank. He had made no progress.

—ε-ε-ε-ε-ε-ε—

It was five blocks from her mom's place to Saronda's apartment. The leaves were off the trees, sitting in piles along the gutter waiting to be vacuumed up. Saronda dwelled on her mom's comment.

"Sometimes when something looks crazy, it's probably because it's crazy."

It resonated like a jingle defining their relationship. Taken by itself, the words were trivial. To most they were an aside. But, in truth, they could serve as the cover notes of a book written by a mother and her daughter, a story arc defiled by sharp comments, unspoken thoughts, innuendos, piercing glares, and long awkward silences. But mostly, total, complete dismissals of anything Saronda felt passionate about. Her mom was not informing, she was judging. "This is more of your dead-end silliness. You get all excited about something and then poof, you're onto something else. You never finish anything." But there was more to it. There was always more. "Other people figure out what they want. They go get it. You need to decide what you want to do and do it. Do something sensible for a change." And then the closer, "Look at your sister Shay. She has a steady job as a nurse. She has her own place. She has a… "

The words were never spoken all at once. They were doled out over time. Most times they weren't words at all, just a well-timed, "mmm hmm", a turned back, or a sub-surface disappointed sigh. There was no point arguing. How can you argue with an eye roll or an aggressive lean on a kitchen counter, or maybe a cabinet door closed with a bit too much force? Her sister Shay wasn't immune either. Hers was a different set of slights from her mother. They were all woven into the jacquard pattern of the family quilt. All subtle. All effective. All infuriatingly exempt from pushback. "Oh no honey, that's not what I meant. Don't be so sensitive."

It was a quilt that smothered. Saronda lived with this shadow, a quiet status quo, and muddled on. The article by Augustine had given her confidence. It *was* her confidence. It was a gift that had been given to her by fate. Ten words from her mom and doubt crept in. How could she have been taken by an old magazine not much above a comic book? It probably came with a stick of bubble gum. It was silly to think a woman could, over a hundred years ago, explain things that have eluded the greatest minds. A woman whose name is never mentioned anywhere in history. Certainly, if this article had merit, it would have long ago become common knowledge.

Walking across the street, she saw a car waiting to turn right. A rush of inadequacy swept over her. She felt like she was in the way, blocking the car, interrupting its path. *Settle, you have the crossing light, it's your turn to cross.* Still, the thoughts crept in. The thoughts that made her feel like Roni, not Saronda. Because of her, this car now had to sit for an outrageous 5 seconds. She hated the feeling. It was a part of her that filled a whole chapter of the book. When she reached the curb, the car gunned its engine making its precious turn and going on its way. She turned and almost apologized for the delay she caused. It was a hole she couldn't escape.

—Ɛ-Ɛ-Ɛ-Ɛ-Ɛ-Ɛ—

Brody's plan didn't have many details but he knew he needed to get started. He pulled out of the parking garage, turned right onto Stanwix St.and headed back to D.C. The drive was a good time to sort things out. Sweet-talking Wayne was a bust. "It's all Drew Waltham's fault." Brody kicked himself for not making progress with Wayne.

*"An open-ended question is the
sauce that makes the meal."*

Don't ask yes and no questions. Let people talk, idiot.

He tightened his grip on the steering wheel, Drew putting GeneraCur on ice made no sense. And Wayne not fighting it made even less sense, Wayne was all about working on cool edgy stuff, discovering the limits of massive computing power. His passion cut through the sarcasm. Brody was tired of thinking about this and pulled over for gas, as his father's words continued to filter in.

*"When people do strange things
there's always a reason."*

He decided to meet with Saronda. Google maps said he could be to his hotel and the coffee shop in an hour.

—ε-ε-ε-ε-ε-ε—

Saronda made her way to the coffee shop, buoyed by the fact he wanted to meet. She anticipated the lightness of talking to someone who didn't judge her every word. Confidence, she needed confidence.

Brody bounded up the two steps into the coffee shop and pulled up a chair. "Wow, place is deserted. Black Friday must not be big for this place. Oooh. You don't look happy. Was Thanksgiving a drag?"

"Yes, my mom just... but that's not everything."

Brody leaned forward and Saronda confided, "I got notice that my job has been eliminated."

Brody slumped back in his chair. "Wow, that's nuts. What's with that? Are they replacing you?"

There was sincerity in his voice. It raised her mood a notch.

"Yes, with a sign. And some arrows. It seems all they think I do is point people to the restroom and show them where the exhibits are."

Brody snarked, "Well at least your replacement sounds capable of getting the job done. I'm not so sure about mine."

Saronda bristled, "This is no joking matter. I did a lot more than that. I provided a friendly face and explained the history and... " She lightened, "Oh you were trying to be cute. How quaint, but the real problem is, I may need to move in with my mom."

"Would that be bad?"

"Only in that it would destroy me. Losing my job. Ehh, it was always a temporary thing in my mind. But now I have to explain it to my mom and she'll want to know what I'm going to do. She'll lay a lot of grief on me."

"Grief?"

Her mood plummeted. "She has a way."

Her voice had none of the confidence from before. "She'll start with observations like, 'Well that was a dead-end job anyhow, I don't know why you stayed there so long' and 'You need to find something that leads to something' then she'll move to my age or lack of degree and she'll finish it all off with a comparison to my sister."

Oh my God, I can't believe I shared something so personal with... it's not like he's a complete stranger.

There was a long silence. It wasn't an awkward silence. It was two people reflecting on each other's situations, neither of which was so hot.

"But I shouldn't lay all that on you. You've got these episodes."

Brody said, "Well aren't we just two unemployed hapless souls down on our luck. I know a place we can drink."

"Day drinking?"

"Yeah, what do you suppose your mom would think about that?"

"She'd be mortified. *Very* judgmental. She would wag her finger but good. I say we do it!"

"Should we invite her?"

"Jackass."

"Alright then, just us, prepare to have your first pickle martini."

They walked to Union Pub and sat at a table close to the bar. Brody saw the female bartender from before and gave her a wave. She smiled.

"Do you know her?" Saronda pushed her hair behind her ear.

"Yeah, she's the one who told me to put a pickle in it."

He ordered two drinks. The bartender brought two pickle martinis with Hendricks Gin.

"So, that's really cool that you bring the drinks over to the table. You didn't when I was here before."

"Well, it's early. Not much going on. Keep it open?"

Saronda was surprised he kept the tab open.

He watched as she took her first sip. "Whaddya think? Good huh?"

She set down her glass. "Uh, if that's what you wanted, it certainly is a good one, I guess. Brody, there's something I want to talk about."

Brody had made a sizable dent in his martini. "Is it about your mom? Let me say, I think you are very impressive, the way you figured out this article and all the stuff that's going on."

Saronda took in the kind words and then, "Thanks, but I don't want to talk about my mom anymore. The more I study this article, the more I understand. And the more I'm, frankly, Brody, I'm scared. You said there are others."

Brody downed the last of his martini and motioned for another to the bartender. "Ooh, that reminds me, I gotta talk to Kim."

"Kim?"

"I'll tell you later, keep going."

"You're having these episodes because your Whisper is reaching into another reality. This means another reality is getting closer to our reality. It could get close enough to collide."

Her mood was dark now. Brody broke eye contact. He appeared to study the dartboard across the room. Late morning gin was new to him.

After a beat, he said, "We all have our own reality. You have yours, I have mine."

"That's not it. You're not getting it. Think of the big picture. *Reality.* With a capital R. The reality we all live in. It's a big ball. Inside is everything we can see, hear, touch, feel. That's reality, our reality, yours, mine, everyone's. It's all in the ball."

"Yeah…" Brody was distant.

"Brody, there are other balls out there! Other realities. Not just the one we live in." She said it kinda loud and the bartender looked over.

Brody leaned back. "And these other balls are bouncing around out there? You learned all this from that magazine?"

"Yep."

He leaned in. "You believe it? It's real. No joke."

"Damn straight."

Brody rubbed his eyes as if weighing what he heard. "And this has to do with me, how?"

Saronda drew in a breath. "People like you can see into another reality. It's because you have a highly energetic Whisper. Whispers have these little spikes on them that weave energy, making reality. You have very energetic spikes."

His second martini arrived. Brody said, "Look, it might be the gin, but can we take this step by step? So, let's say there's two realities, the one we live in and another one we can't see but it's out there somewhere. Two balls of reality, one of them is this reality... " He waved his arms around the room.

Saronda brightened. "Yes! And sometimes *you* can see into the other reality, the other ball. Not everybody, you. When you do that, you have episodes. Things change because you're looking at a different reality."

Brody said, "It's no pleasure cruise. I never told you this, but I don't fully recover. It's like a little piece of me is destroyed each time."

Saronda slid to the front of her chair. "Brody, that other reality is getting close to ours. We're on a collision course."

He tried to reason it out. "So if our ball collides with another ball. How does any of this help fix me?"

As he said that, the bartender appeared at their table and set down his third martini.

Saronda touched Brody's arm. "We will fix you, but first, you need to understand the two balls. Second, you need to figure out how to get the computers and the code."

The bartender looked at them. "Did you want to close out?" She paused. "Yeah, I think I'll close you out."

Brody took a large draw of his third drink.

He turned his attention to Saronda. "I can't remember what we were talking about."

He leaned on the table with both elbows and put his head in hands. "Do you have a boyfriend?"

She looked at the now empty martini glass.

"Brody, really?"

"Do you date much?"

"Oh come on. OK, I used to date more but, guys are strange."

"They sure are. Some even see things that aren't there. Woo hoo. Like me. Ever been serious about a guy?"

Saronda nodded at the martini glass. "If you make that your last one, I'll tell you my sad tale."

Brody leaned in with full attention.

"I was getting serious with this one guy. It was a while back. He was nice. Dressed well. Had a good job. But we went back to his place, and he had post-it notes all over, everywhere, the walls, the counter, chairs. They were his to-do list."

"So?"

"One of the to-do's was 'Get a girlfriend by end of May'. And it was like May 25th!"

"Sounds like he was gonna make the deadline. Good for him."

"Bullshit. I left, never saw him again."

Brody shook his head. "Wow, that's rough."

"It sure was."

"Yeah, I mean you left the guy with less than a week to find a girlfriend."

Saronda threw a napkin at him. "Thanks for the sensitivity. And for proving my point."

"There's two realities?"

"No, that you're a jackass. Alright, look, we need to move along."

Brody displayed a brief moment of clarity. "You said we need to do some things. What?"

"OK, welcome back. We need to use Augustine's equations to change the path of an entire ball of reality."

"Nice, let's do it!"

Saronda stared at him. He pulled out the crumpled hotel notepad with his notes. "All we need is a large number of computers and someone to write some code."

"Sounds good. Can you get that from where you

work—worked?"

"Yes! Don't despair, Brody has a plan." And then put his head on the table.

Saronda thought about how to tell her mother she had lost her job and went day drinking with a guy. "Yes Mother, it's the guy I talked about. Yes, the one I'm trying to fix, and he's kind of… fun."

—ε-ε-ε-ε-ε-ε—

"Always make sure you know what motivates someone before adding them to the team." —Arthur Markovich

Brody needed a programmer, a warm body to bang out some code. Wayne Drakauer was a brick wall. But when you're three martinis deep and it's not even five o'clock, sometimes pushing through a brick wall doesn't seem like such a reach. Brody punched in Wayne's number.

He was halfway through his third sentence when Wayne cut in. "Have you been drinking?"

"Is that important?"

"Well it's like, four twenty in the afternoon."

"Ooh getting close to five, happy hour!"

"Really though, why are you calling? You're rambling, and drunk. If this is about checksum again, I told you—"

Brody cut him off. "I need someone to port Brody's Code and make some changes, run some calculations, it's really, really important, I need to fix me."

In his trademark cynical tone, Wayne answered, "I must say, your yearning for help and heartfelt plea is truly touching but you know that's not gonna happen right?"

"I do not know that, for a fact. I suspected that but I do not know that. But if that's what you're saying then…" Brody's words technically made sense, but the gin was showing.

"Hey, rambling man, slow down. Listen, if you want work done on the code go hire someone."

"I don't know anyone."

"Start looking, guys like me are everywhere. You need to find someone who knows Erlang."

"Who's he? Or she?"

"Idiot, catch up. Erlang is the language Brody's Code is written in."

"Erlang, right. I'm taking notes." Brody tried to find the note app on his phone and almost hung up on Wayne. "Is that with a U or an I?"

"OK, actually, that's not going to work. You can search all you want but Erlang is pretty obscure these days. I use it because there aren't a ton of experts in it. Nobody is going to hack my Erlang code. Kinda like stealing an Oldsmobile. Not much to brag about. Plus, it allowed us to handle the thousands of computers and bring on additional ones easily. It's pretty slick. But finding someone..."

Brody almost nodded off. "Not exactly in the yellow pages?" Brody laughed at his non-joke. "Maybe you could teach me. Kinda sketch it out. A little diagram."

"You? Bro, there's not enough crayons in the world. But I know a guy from when I interned at Ericsson. The guy is a colossal freak, but he knows Erlang in and out."

Wayne paused. "Oh my God, you and that fastidious little bastard working together. That would be one for the ages. The guy is weird. Says weird shit, like, we were at a company picnic and he never talked, just stared at one of those bug zappers, watching bugs get zapped. All day. As he was leaving, he said, 'if we all had one of those, we'd stand a chance.'"

Brody asked, "Where is he?"

"Hell, I don't know. Last I heard, he's living in a bunker out west somewhere. Said he wanted a place that could withstand mortar fire."

Brody said, "A little strange. Vibe de' Koresh. But can he do the code for me?"

"Yeah, all you need is for him to shave the yak."

"Excuse me?"

"Shave the yak. Get things set up so you can mess with your calculations. He'll be able to do that. Don't count on him for much more. He gets in over his head pretty quick. I don't think he finished college. Smart, but doesn't know a lot about programming."

Brody said, "I'll give him a call."

"Oh, he won't answer, you need to text him, see if he'll call you back. I'll dig up his number and send it to you."

"Thanks. What's his name?"

"Kelso, Kelso Radovic. God, it'll be a hoot, I'm sure. You, working with him. His little words of wisdom for everyone. Oh to be a fly on the wall. One more thing, sober up before you talk to him, you might have a fighting chance at making sense. Goodbye Brody, good luck with your hangover."

They disconnected.

Brody saved Kelso's number into his phone and noticed he had a text. It was Kim.

"Kim!" He said out loud, "Kim Dire from the psychiatrist!"

He pulled up her text: *meet at Ebenezers. Now or never closes at 6.*

It was almost five. He googled Ebenezer's. Nice, it's close.

He texted Kelso: *call me.*

He rushed to Ebenezer's and walked in.

She was in the back. "You made it with not a moment to spare."

Brody said, "Yeah, it's been a busy day."

"How does someone on leave have a busy day?"

How did she know I'm on leave. He let it slide.

"How does someone like you know I'm 'not the only one'. You must have broken some HIPAA rules to know that."

Brody noted that her eyelashes were longer than when he last saw her.

She countered, "I said there are more people with your condition."

"Yeah, but you knew I had a 'condition' as you call it. That means you've been nosing around my file."

"Everyone has a condition."

"You called them episodes in the elevator, that's a pretty specific 'condition'. You know exactly what I'm being treated for. In fact, you probably know more about me than I do. So, c'mon stop playing games. Why are we here?"

"Hey, you're the one who wanted to talk." She

twirled a long strand of her hair.

"You tracked me down in the elevator. You didn't have to do that. You want to talk about this, it's obvious."

Kim leaned forward, sending a small wave of perfume Brody's way. She lowered her voice. "Look, I could lose my job, maybe be in legal trouble but I have to tell someone. Yes, I've looked through some files, but only new patients'."

"Why only new patients'? What's so special about them, us, me?"

She picked at the bright red fingernail polish on her left index finger as she spoke. A bright sparkly dot came free and fell onto her black mid-thigh dress.

She continued talking softly. "Marci— Dr. Matthews has had a huge increase in patients the past few months. Usually we go in at nine out by two or three. But now, I'm scheduling people through late afternoon, sometimes evenings. Dr. Matthews has me prioritizing the new patients over ones she's had for years. I've canceled appointments for some of the old."

"Yeah yeah, you've got a lot of new patients. So what."

"That's the thing. I looked through their files and yours. Every one of them is being treated for the same thing, 'unexplained psychotic episodes.' Every last one of them."

"Did you read the doctor's notes?"

"Oh heck no, she keeps those locked away."

Brody sat for a beat. He began to speak. Then he stopped. His mind was trying to make sense of this. Something was nagging at him, obscured by a pickle martini haze.

The silence had gone past awkward. Kim said, "I mean don't you think that's odd? Every new patient, the same thing. And there's a lot of them."

Ah! That's it. Brody blurted, "So why me? If she has all these new patients, why me? Why is it me you wanted to tell?"

"Because you seem the most stable."

Brody blinked.

She continued, "The other ones. Most are really stressed. Marci has them on drugs. She hardly ever prescribes. She's not a pill mill. But she's writing scripts now."

Brody noticed the crew was cleaning up, stacking chairs for closing.

"And you don't know what drug?"

"No."

Brody got everything he was going to get and thanked her for her courage. His walk to the hotel was filled with plenty to think about. Back in his room, the events of the day swirled in his head. He couldn't sleep so he figured he would get a head start on what to say to Kelso.

But Kelso wasn't his only issue. He also needed computers, lots of them. He thought about Rebecca Standiford. She works for the government. Maybe they have computers.

Drowsy from drinking, he went to bed.

—ε-ε-ε-ε-ε-ε—

Marguerite Borel wrote award-winning novels, created a scientific journal and founded a hospital to help victims of World War I. She headed a group that found employment for women. She was the daughter of Professor Paul Appell, Augustine's former student. With all her accomplishments, it was a simple act of kindness that changed the course of history. Paul Appell gave Augustine's paper to Marguerite and asked that she and her husband, a mathematician, review it. They gave it scant attention. They thought maybe it was written in jest. They laughed about Paul Appell's scribbled note, "Possible to change reality," dismissing it as nothing more than an evening's entertainment and set it aside. That was, until Marguerite used it as a prop to cheer up a friend..

The friend was Marie Curie. It was Nov 1911 and Mme Curie needed a place to stay. "Yes, I insist you stay with me, at least until this subsides," Marguerite said firmly.

"But it's not fair, all these threats they throw at me,

these things they say, yet Paul receives nothing, no pain for him." It wasn't Paul Appell Mme Curie was referring to. It was Paul Langevin, Marie Curie's former student, and lover. Yes, lover, a fact that had gone unnoticed for a long time until letters between the two lovers were leaked to the press revealing the ongoing affair.

Marie Curie came home one night to find a raging mob at her house yelling anti-semitic, misogynist epithets. They branded her a loose Jewish woman. She wasn't Jewish, but facts didn't matter. The story played well to the twisted minds filled with xenophobia and hate. It built on a base of underlying misogyny.

"Yes, it is not fair, but it is what it is. We can't change that." Marguerite poured glasses of milk for Marie's two daughters.

Marie mused. "I wish I could change things. Make things different. Women would be respected, people wouldn't throw hate at the Jews, fascists would go away. Poof! I could love who I want to."

Marguerite set down the milk and made a whimsical look. "Marie, you're going to love me. I've got exactly what you need."

Marguerite scanned the bookcase crowded with books and old journals.

An intrigued Marie looked on as Marguerite thumbed through years of abandoned journals. "Ah, here it is!" Marguerite said as she pulled the science magazine from the pile.

She opened it to Augustine's paper and pointed at her father's notes. "Here, try this. It says right there, 'Possible to alter reality.'"

Marie showed no understanding and then, noticing Marguerite's broad grin, knew it was a joke. "Oh my, change reality indeed, but oh, for it to be true. I must show Paul. That's if I can ever see him again." Her voice fell.

"C'mon, let's have wine." Marguerite declared.

They spent the evening talking and laughing about everything and anything, except, "L'affaire Paul Langevin et Marie Curie." She received her second Nobel Prize that year and though the prize committee sent her a letter dis-inviting her to the ceremony citing "questionable moral standing," she showed up anyhow, and proudly. She was, after all, a woman who moved to France penniless, became the first woman in France to earn a PhD, discovered two new elements, suffered the death of her husband five years prior, was raising two children while inventing portable life-saving X-ray machines, and was not only the first woman to win a Nobel Prize but the first person to win two Nobel Prizes. Adding to all that, she publicly chastised Albert Einstein when he insulted her. A letter from a committee of faraway men didn't stand a chance.

The press continued the furor over her affair. Newspapers repeated lies and distortions that fueled an ugly narrative. Marie Curie tried to ignore it, but small lies were fashioned, one by one, slowly and imperceptibly, into a Big Lie. Fashioned and repeated. It was a cycle no one could fight. The lies were plausible enough so people believed them and the brushfire grew and soon the story became "Marie Curie is a foreign homewrecking Jew who sullied the great name of her husband, who killed himself when he found out about the affair." None of it was true. She was not Jewish. Her husband had long been dead when he supposedly killed himself. None of that mattered. The scandal became a rallying cry feeding anti-semitic outrage. Jew haters now had a new manufactured scandal with which to divide the country, a country that just five years prior, suffered through the Alfred Dreyfus scandal, which was also based on lies. The lies were so widespread, and the constant questions so vicious, that Mme Curie moved to England for a time to elude the press. As a parting gift to Paul Langevin, she gave him the science magazine, telling him "Here is a gift. I wish we could use this to change reality," and pointed to Paul Appell's notes. They both laughed, brightening an otherwise sad moment.

—ε-ε-ε-ε-ε-ε—

"Other people's desperation can be a powerful tool." —Arthur Markovich

Rebecca's phone lit up. Brody M. *Again?*

A cold December rain sent streaks down the brutalist architecture of the concrete parking structure across the Metro tracks. Rain in December in D.C. is usually a misty drizzle, but this was a driving rain that erased all sense that Christmas was a little over three weeks away.

She waited to see if he left a message. *Deedoot!* He did. She turned back to the charts she was working on.

Summary: GeneraCur case on hold.

Translation: I am screwed and don't know how to fix it. Nothing's changed. I am desperately in need of a spa treatment. It's only Tuesday.

Rebecca's phone lit up. *Ugh, Brody again.* Her charts were for the weekly staff meeting. Every week she goes through the details of the GeneraCur trainwreck. And every week it feels like everyone is taking great pleasure watching her twist in the wind. Except, of course, her boss. Everyone's memory was crystal clear that Rebecca was the one who championed ExpoLytics. "They're the only ones who can handle such a complex case." She was the one who agreed to the contract. "It'll be fine, we don't need to haggle over a performance clause, they'll come through for us." All eyes were on Rebecca as ExpoLytics failed to deliver. *Dedoot!* Another message.

She sat back in her desk chair. *Dedoot!* Brody left a text.

Her boss was planning to use the GeneraCur case to show he could collar the bad guys. Rebecca was letting him down. She wondered if the windows in the meeting room opened. *What's the drop, fifteen floors?* She could land just right, then board a Metro train and ride away. She'd be a legend and in the end, the same unemployed project leader trying to figure out what to write on her résumé about the last three months. Twenty seconds later. *Dedoot!* Brody left a message. She gave in.

You have three new messages and nine saved messages, Message One: Rebecca, it's Brody, I left you a message, like I said, I think I have a solution to the GeneraCur problem. Call me.

She looked out the window at the rain-stained concrete parking structure. *What the hell, I'll call him.*

Brody answered on the first ring, "I knew you couldn't ignore two phone calls."

"Three, plus a text, and a bunch more. I heard you were dead."

"Man, you guys need a better rumor mill."

"You mean you're not dead?"

"Not by my standards. Listen, I heard the GeneraCur case is shit."

"Thanks USA Today, I'll write that down."

"I think I can fix it."

"Are you insane?"

"Yes, but I'm working through it, thanks for asking. But I need you to do something. It's a little out there, I need you to get access to about a thousand desktop PCs. More if you can manage."

"I don't even know what that means."

"Password access to the routers they're on and screen sharing access."

"Hashtag impossible, way above my paygrade."

"No, seriously, if you can get me access to a bunch of computers, it'll break the logjam."

"How?"

"We're going to do an end run around Pittsburgh."

"Why didn't ExpoLytics tell me?"

"Because they don't know anything about it. It's a bit unorthodox but—"

"This doesn't sound like a tight plan. Oh and, unorthodox is kinda frowned upon at SEC… and the FBI, and I don't—"

"What alternative do you have?"

Rebecca looked at her flaccid charts.

"Access to computers. I don't know Brody, I don't think I can swing it."

"I'll bet that boss of yours could do it. I see his smiling picture on the SEC website. His term is up, and I bet he wants a little more than being reassigned back to the SEC."

"You got that right. He needs to deliver something to the DoJ. Nervous like a thirteen-year-old boy at the spring dance. But this thing of getting access to computers. What's that all about?"

"Well, first, a little wisdom from my father, 'nobody likes a nervous boss when you're the one making him nervous.' Right now, you're making him nervous."

"Career advice from a guy who doesn't have a job. Transcendent."

Brody said, "The only way out of this for you is to get access to massive computing power. If ExpoLytics won't commit the computers, let's get them somewhere else. I can get access to the software to run the analysis and guide someone, maybe Donny, to run point."

"Donny Davino? He's in the Philippines visiting his family."

"What's his family doing in the Philippines?"

"That's where he's from, he's Filipino."

"Damn, I thought he was Italian. I wonder if it bothered him when I greeted him with 'hey paisano' all the time. Hmm, is that racist? But Davino sounds Italian. God I'm an idiot."

"Agreed. You're an idiot. I gotta run. Giving an update on GeneraCur. I'll corner Bruce about these computers after my meeting, a.k.a. ass chewing. He may be desperate enough to do it."

"Bruce?"

"Bruce Donnagin, SEC Commissioner, my boss."

"Oh yeah, I am an idiot. Your meeting sounds like fun, wish I could be there."

"Yeah, you never told me. Why aren't you?"

"Long story. Ciao."

"Paalam."

—ε-ε-ε-ε-ε-ε—

Paul Langevin held the science paper in his hand. It was a reminder of Mme Curie's whimsical spirit. It was also a reminder of the lies that forced her to leave her home. And for what? So small-minded people could please the rich overlords by spreading hate. Paul Langevin is best known for his work in physics and the Langevin equation. His biggest mark on history, though, was organizing resisters to fascism. He was a small part of an overall effort that chipped away at the power of the nazis, but nothing captured his attention like Agustine's theories. He didn't see them as silly. He believed Augustine's assertion that reality could be changed. The equations made sense to him. It became a "thought hobby", mulling it over during idle moments. He wanted to shout it to the world, but discussing her radical ideas would surely bring questions about his soundness of mind. It wasn't the only reason he didn't share her insights with anyone.

He did what was all the rage in 1912, "Gedankenexperiments," little inside-your-head thought experiments, "If we could do this, then that would happen." More and more, his mind crawled through the world of changed reality. It took him to a dark place. If a world leader could change reality, they could disrupt an enemy's social order. In the hands of a dictator, it was the ultimate weapon. Lies could be turned into truth. Authoritarian regimes would have the perfect propaganda. They wouldn't have to go to the trouble of repeating little lies to create a Big Lie, just change reality to make the lies true. Results of elections could be changed, jury verdicts could be reversed or laws altered to jail political opponents. He imagined creating a different set of facts for different sets of people, irreversibly dividing them. A country forced into chaos could easily be overthrown without firing a single shot.

—ε-ε-ε-ε-ε-ε—

Brody sat in his therapist's office, exchanging pleasantries with Kim Dire as if the meeting at Ebenezer's never happened. He sensed she wanted it that way. He palmed his phone, willing Kelso to call him. He wasn't sure what he would say. He tried to make sense of his father's words.

"When all you need is a rock, show them the moon."

It was the only thing he thought about during another insufferable therapy session. He thought better of asking Dr. Matthews, "How do I ask someone to shave a yak so I can get my sanity back?" She had the power to have him committed.

Details were slim as he headed to the Metro.

Step one: Connect on a personal level making it hard to say no.

Step two: Show him the moon and tell him it could all be his, then hand him some rope.

Step three: Let him lasso the moon.

Yes father, but what's the moon?

He found a seat on the Metro. His phone rang. The display flashed, "K Rad." *Yes, a callback!*

Before he could say a word, a strong voice declared, "Make it interesting quick or I hang up. I am not one to suffer fools. It's not productive for me or you."

"I need you to help move reality."

"Does it need moved? It seems to be fine where it is."

"Whoa, are you a yinzer? Sounds like you're from Pittsburgh."

"It doesn't matter where I'm from, or where I am. It is important to respect boundaries in any type of relationship. Keep going, I'm not a patient man."

OK, odd man. "Reality is on a collision course with another reality. Our reality is good for now. But you don't want to find out what it looks like if it crashes into another reality. I've had a peek. You wouldn't like it. Ha ha."

"Wayne said you were prone to fanciful bullshit. It's not a term I use, it is from Wayne."

"I know I sound crazy but there are a lot of people out there like me. We're able to see inside another reality. We need to stop a collision between the two."

Brody detected that Kelso put him on speaker. His voice was distant.

"I will honor your persistence in contacting me, and not hang up. What you say is mildly interesting but ultimately silly. You are really beginning to annoy me and may very well be crazy."

"I've been told I'm prodromal."

"Be careful, I studied psychology so I know what that means. Prodromal is lazy psychiatrist-speak for 'keep an eye on this one.' It is a very incomplete description."

The Metro train went through a bad patch and reception dropped so Brody missed some of that.

He started rambling, parroting Saronda, "I have a set of equations that model reality. They show how it's created, how to change it, how to move it. Think about it, messing with reality itself."

Brody surveyed the train. The only two riders who weren't plugged up with ear buds took notice. He nodded to them. Brody couldn't know but his words set off a series of events inside Kelso's head. Thousands of times a second, deep inside the primal part of his brain, eight carbon atoms, eleven hydrogens, a nitrogen and two oxygens were ripped from an amino acid by the most sophisticated chemical factory in the universe, creating a flood of dopamine molecules that raced from his reptilian complex to his prefrontal cortex, eliciting an involuntary tilting of his head and a rubbing together of the fingers on his left hand. Funny little ticks. Everyone has them, involuntary movements when we're excited or confused... or thinking about how much fun it is to sit at a computer and cause societal chaos. It was the reaction of a power-freak realizing that the moon was right in front of him.

Kelso said, "Change reality?"

"Something like that."

"How do you know it works?"

"I don't. I have equations. I need you to program some code."

Kelso was silent.

Brody's mouth went dry. He tried to sound confident but didn't know if he was just talking to the wind. The background noise of the train made it hard to hear if Kelso was still there. The lack of feedback was chilling and it threw him off his game.

He started winging it. "To change reality, events, things from the past. Stuff like that. I mean I'm just spouting stuff. Hello?"

Brody paused. "Still there Kelso?"

"You were talking about going back in time, which —"

"*No*, it's not going back in time, it's different. I'm talking about moving reality."

Brody hoped Kelso wasn't losing interest. He started shot-gunning, throwing stuff out there, trying to reel in Kelso. "And I guess we could change reality too, not just move it. That would be a little like going back in time, I suppose. Maybe change something from the past, I don't know."

"And you know how to do this?"

A hint of interest.

"Not yet, that's why we need you to write some software to handle the equations."

"Software that changes reality." Kelso paused. "Could be useful."

Changing reality could be "useful?" Brody thought that was a strange conclusion, but if that's what hooked him then, nice. Now to let Kelso lasso the moon. "So what do you think?" Brody put a little lift in his voice.

"It is a proposition. I listened. It could be worth my time."

Time for a presumptive close. "Listen, it's great you want to work on this. We'll get you hundreds, maybe thousands of computers to access. Although it's a long shot right now and I don't have a clue and there's—"

Shut up Brody, stop tripping the customer on the way to the cash register.

"So, anyhow, it's good you're in. I'll be in touch."

Kelso said, "How do we actually change reality?"

"We have to figure it out."

"You represented yourself quite well. Thank you, I'll be going now."

"Wait! So you're in?"

"It is of interest enough to continue the discussion."

Brody disconnected. *One step closer to getting my job back.*

—ε-ε-ε-ε-ε-ε—

"You look shook." Saronda could tell Brody was tense.

Brody stared across the coffee shop at nothing in particular. "I need these things to stop. I walked back last night to my hotel, and, honest to God, it was farmland. No hotel, just a… "

He looked at Saronda. "I'm losing it." He reeked of doom.

"That's messed up. What did you do?"

"I panicked. I thought I was on the wrong street. I ran up past the coffee shop. I was running on a public street. Do you get that? Like friggin' Jimmy Stewart on Christmas Eve. When I went back, the hotel was there again."

Saronda stayed silent.

He ran his fingers through his hair. "This is really getting to me."

Brody fidgeted and made little eye contact. "I think these things may be killing me."

Saronda took his hand. Brody did not resist. She said, "How about we take a walk? Let's not waste this nice weather. We need to find a different place than this coffee shop anyhow now that I don't have a job down here."

They walked across Columbus Circle to Union Station. Brody glanced to his right and sheer terror fell across his face.

He grabbed Saronda's arm. "What happened to the Capitol building?"

Saronda pointed. "It's right there. Looks fine to me. Still full of idiots though."

Brody tried to laugh. His breathing was shallow.

"Dude, you have taken a turn. C'mon we're going to a place with good food and friendly people. It's near where I live."

Brody shuffled onto the train and sat. "You know, I've never asked where you lived."

It was the last thing he said before the fog came.

He was rigid, eyes shut, face frozen as if his muscles were firing all at once. "Oh my God, I can't handle this."

He opened his eyes. They darted wildly, stopping occasionally as if to focus on something.

"Where is it? Where's the fucking train?"

Saronda's voice shook. "Brody, you're on the train."

"There's no train. It's just grass. Moving so fast."

Saronda took his face into her hands. "Brody. C'mon man. Dude. Talk."

Brody slumped. His breathing was unsteady as he opened his eyes.

"Dude, is that what your episodes are like? 'Cuz dayam that was rough."

Brody stared at the floor. "This one was different. I saw a fog. A fog of light."

Saronda's face froze. "That's not good. No. No. That's straight fire bad."

A shroud of terror descended on Saronda. Augustine talked about the fog. It's the lightning that comes before the torrent. Another reality was getting close. Very close. It was mixing, causing swirling pools of an alternate reality where our Whispers don't work. Our Whispers are designed to work only in our reality. Anywhere else, they die. Brody was a canary in a coal mine. And, *there are others.*

Saronda logged into her @MathRonda account and tweeted *#DevilLight "Anyone seeing a fog of lights and a nasty nightmare?"*

She spoke softly, trying to mask her fear, "Brody, the fog of lights you saw. It's not good. Whispers are dying, turning energy into light. The light you saw are the other people's Whispers withering in the face of another reality."

Brody was a raging beacon of what was to come. "I can't go on. I truly will go insane."

"It's going to get worse. As our realities collide, everyone will have these episodes. Despair and confusion will be epidemic."

Brody was panting. "I can't calm down."

Saronda reached into her bag. "Here."

"What is it?"

"It's an edible. A gummy with cannabis. Marijuana."

"You're kidding. Isn't that illegal?"

"Maybe where you live. This is D.C. It's OK. You should try it."

Her voice changed as the horror sunk in. "It'll calm you down."

Brody popped the green gummy in his mouth.

"Dude… I was going to suggest eating half but, this will be interesting."

Brody leaned back against the Metro seat. "Nothing. It did nothing."

"Give it a chance, it will."

"How long?"

"Maybe forty-five minutes."

She was wrong, twenty minutes later Brody was studying the rivets that hold the train together.

—ε-ε-ε-ε-ε-ε—

Paul Langevin couldn't find any flaws of logic in Augustine's paper. It was 1940 and a new world order was being forged by bullies and tyrants. It was a time when only the paranoid survive. He must tell his daughter what he found. Against the backdrop of rising xenophobia and fascism, Paul worried that the paper would fall into the wrong hands. He walked to his daughter's house, mindful that he could be arrested at any moment.

World War I, the "Great War." The war to end all wars was long over, but xenophobia and hatred festered. Marie Curie's experience was but one example of how lies, antisemitism, and twisted facts combine to give bullies power and allow hatred to grow. The war to end all wars may have been over but fascism was just getting started. Fascists used lies to create stories that served to further their power. Paul Langevin watched as they controlled Italy in the 1920s and moved to Germany and Spain. Fascism cast its dark shadow on France, and he knew it was a matter of time before it took root. He risked everything as a strong and very public resister. As France's independence was crushed and Paris was occupied, paranoia drove Dr. Langevin to the point of panic, believing Augustine's paper could be used for evil. Facts could no longer be distinguished from fiction. Wrong would be right, up would be down. A team of nazi-controlled scientists could figure out how, using Augustine's paper as the blueprint.

Hélène Solomon-Langevin waited for the last of the four taps on her door. It was always delayed at least a second, a code set by her father, and she followed it.

Paul Langevin took off his hat and shook off the cold. "These cold nights are starting to bother me. Winter will be here soon."

"Papa, sit near the fire, I will get you some port."

Paul's daughter Hélène and her husband, Jacques, both shared her father's passion for resisting the advance of fascist nazis into France. They had formed an official Resistance group.

She lamented, "I am so disgusted at the lies. They tell such lies about the Jews. Why does anyone believe them?"

Her father explained, "The lies are their biggest weapon. They tell little lies over and over. Repeat them. People start to believe. They use the press to build the little lies into a sinister bigger story. The story is their Big Lie. It is evil. The story becomes 'Jews are bad and cause all the problems.' They call them animals."

"We mustn't let them win. We must communicate the truth. Jacques and I are working hard to stop them. Eventually the truth will win. France must be strong."

Paul sputtered, "But what if they change the truth? What if they change reality so that their lies become the truth. We won't be able to fight that. They will win. The fascists will win, and we will no longer be free."

"Papa, you are talking in circles."

He was animated. "No, I have reason to worry. I have a paper that looks to be based on sound scientific principles. It is possible to change reality, to change the outcome of events, even events in the past. I have studied it. It is well-reasoned. If the nazis find this paper, they will turn it into a weapon of massive proportions. Our basic beliefs would be rendered false. Chaos would reign."

"You sound erratic. This paper, it sounds

outlandish. You are paranoid."

"I am not paranoid. If they control Truth, they control everything."

His shaking hands spilled some port on his shirt.

Jacques said, "Where did you find this paper?"

"It was given to me by Marie, before she left." The words caught in his throat. "I have searched for other work by this writer but found nothing. This paper is a gift to the world. It is written as poetry. I searched for other copies. I wanted to gather them up and hide them but found none. Please God, let this be the only one. It needs to be destroyed yet deserves to stand next to the great papers of other French scholars, ones from Curie, Poincare. To destroy such a thing would be… "

Hélène and Jacques glanced at each other.

Paul was tired. It was getting late. "Thank you, my dear daughter, I should be getting home."

As Paul Langevin headed out into the cold, he turned to his daughter and her husband. "Please be careful. Be awake to what is coming."

He would not see his daughter again until years later.

—ε-ε-ε-ε-ε-ε—

Saronda darted off the train. She needed air. The train wasn't big enough to contain the fear that was building inside her. Brody felt detached and dull as they walked along Michigan Avenue.

She held the door for him as they entered Busboys and Poets, an eclectic neighborhood hangout, equal parts bookstore, coffee shop and diner. The fog of light made it real for Saronda. It cemented the fact that two realities were mixing. Augustine's article, once a joy-filled walk through an intellectual garden of new concepts, was now a foreshadowing of the worst thing she could imagine. It wasn't just a matter of fixing Brody. Soon, everyone would be experiencing these episodes, and nothing would be real. We would be living in two realities. Her new-found confidence was a veil doing a poor job hiding her turmoil.

Brody showed no understanding. "Listen, I've been wanting to tell you. I have a plan. I've got a guy working on code and a woman working on getting us access to computers and—"

"What does that help?" She was curt.

Brody talked slowly as if through a haze. "Well, then we can run the calculations we talked about and get out of this mess. And we all live happily ever after."

His words didn't sit well. She started to speak but then stopped. There was nothing to say. He didn't get it. The world was about to be a chaotic landfill of broken souls and he was in his own little world. *Enjoy your gumdrop, clueless fool.* She looked around the room decorated with art, some playful, some stark. Her eyes were unfocused. She watched the unknowing souls going about their day. She felt a heavy, suffocating fear that kept building. The horrid thought tightened around her with a claustrophobic grip.

"And then what, Brody? What's your plan after that? Have you thought that far? We just somehow turn this other reality around, so it goes the other way? Kick it right in the ass? How're you gonna do that? Huh? Maybe we could ask it to leave. Except, *it can't hear us.*"

She spoke way too loud, with an edge, "Your 'plan' only lets us see what Augustine's equations do. Whoopdi freekin' doo. Just plot them out on a screen. Honestly, Brody. How do we affect reality? Actually affect it, move it? How do we keep it from mixing? Your plan is useless."

They both stared at each other, glare was a better word. She felt desperately alone as the only person on the earth to get it.

Brody deflected. "Do you think we should tell someone? The government, DoD, DHS, FBI pick your part of the alphabet but someone."

"What a brilliant thought. And what would we tell them exactly?"

Her voice trembled. Brody stared at the floor. The way he sat made her wonder if her words had fallen there and he was trying to piece them together.

He spoke after a minute, "Maybe you could teach me more about this collision, what it is, how it works."

Saronda shook her head. "We talked about this. Remember? Balls of reality, colliding?"

"Yep, I knew that, and when you look at these balls, they're a three-dimensional pattern."

Saronda came down from the ledge. "Dude, you have been listening. That's very impressive."

She reinforced his point. "Balls of reality bob around and twist and dance like blobs floating around in a liquid. Like a Lava Lamp. They bob and twist. They ride on a wave. Each ball is a separate reality. When they collide..."

Her voice broke, thinking of the consequences. "Brody, man, the episodes you've had where people's shirts change color? That's child's play compared to what's about to happen. I don't think you understand the gravity of this."

She willed him to understand. "They're going to mix. The two realities. They're going to mix. We'll be living in two realities."

She let out a muffled sigh. She wished she could convey what she was feeling. Unload her sense of doom onto him. Share some common emotions. It would be nice to face the end of the world knowing she wasn't the only one feeling this. Maybe just talk about it. Mentally hold hands.

Brody went right to problem solving. "I know! We'll get it to bob the other way. Keep it from crashing into—"

Saronda practically screamed, "Yes, I know. But *how*?"

They sat some more. Brody withdrew. Saronda stared a hole in an artwork on the wall. It wasn't clear who was more upset. Brody because she was attacking him for trying to solve the problem or Saronda because he wasn't experiencing her dread.

He dialed up a random collection of words. "Odd shaped squishy balls, like rubber duckies in a bathtub."

There was nothing she could say. The annoying sing-songy way he was talking pissed her off. "Two duckies. Get it? Our reality is one rubber duckie, and the other reality is another rubber duckie."

Saronda turned sideways in her seat.

He continued his fixation on ducks, oblivious. "If our rubber duckie bobs this way, right? And the other rubber duckie bobs that way, they would never hit. Just scoot on by."

Saronda's face was stiff. She was disillusioned. To her, his words were like music on an elevator. A pop song played by an orchestra. Vaguely familiar but serving no purpose, just intrusive annoying noise. She turned to face the window. His lack of seriousness made her feel alone.

Brody played out his fantasy. "But you know what would be cool? Make waves in the water to push the ducks apart. They wouldn't hit. Just swoosh with my hand and that duck would move the other way. Bye bye duck."

"Would you just shut up about rubber ducks." She didn't even bother to face him.

He plowed forward. "Don't push the rubber duckie. Push the water. Watch it ride the wave."

Saronda hissed through gritted teeth, "Please, just stop."

Brody rambled on, "Giant lava lamp wave. That'd be so cool. A duck riding a wave."

Saronda shook her head. Minutes went by. Brody was drifting in his own gum drop world when Saronda's face suddenly loosened.

She turned toward Brody and grabbed his arm with both hands. "That's it! I got it! You're right. Move the water. It could work!"

Like when you finally figure out the name of that song playing on the elevator.

—ε-ε-ε-ε-ε-ε—

Paul Langevin was torn. He took a long draw on his brandy. It was the finest from his collection and he rolled it around in his mouth identifying each aromatic note. He had been saving this particular bottle for years and sensed this would be his last chance to enjoy it. The nazi-controlled Vichy Government was rounding up resisters and Paul knew he couldn't hide. He struggled with what to do with Augustine's paper. Burning it would destroy the most complete attempt at a unified theory of the universe. Great minds ranging from Max Planck and Werner Heisenberg to Albert Einstein and Erwin Schrödinger had been grappling with this for decades and showed limited success. In his circle, destroying such a breakthrough would be considered a crime.

But for it to fall into the hands of the nazis would be unthinkable. For them to possess the knowledge to make a weapon that creates unspeakable chaos... Paul couldn't bear the thought. It would tilt the balance of power to regimes that wished to rule through fascism and authoritarianism for generations, if not forever. Paul Langevin considered these thoughts as he enjoyed the rich, headiness of the brandy. He had made his decision. It was time.

He stood at his hearth, sipping the last of the brandy. The fire reflected off his eyeglasses as he watched the last of the burning paper curl and blacken and become consumed. The last fading words to be engulfed and erased forever were those from the scribbled notes that Paul Appell had clipped onto the cover of Science de la Planète on that hot August day more than thirty years prior, "Possible to change reality."

"Not now, not ever, and certainly not by them," he muttered disgustedly.

He hurled his brandy glass at the hearth, shattering it to pieces. He cursed the nazis and the bullies who used lies to gain power. He slumped into a chair and watched the fire die down feeling the warm calm of the brandy. Minutes later, chaos. His door was violently broken down. Uniformed agents marched in, guns drawn. Paul Langevin did not fight back. His role in the demise of such people would come much later.

He was arrested and imprisoned for being part of the Resistance.

—ε-ε-ε-ε-ε-ε—

Saronda was three rapid-fire sentences into an arm waving, woohooing, explanation of how to use computers to change the course of reality and said, "C'mon, let's get out of here. Let me tell you my idea." She led the way out of Busboys and Poets.

Each word was rushed. "My dad, a comm specialist in the Army. He played around with HAM radio. Spent hours at night talking to people. All over the world. He said his voice was a ripple riding on a giant wave. Get it? All the way across the world. That is how we move reality."

She clapped her hands together.

Brody tried to keep up with her fast walking. "I'm gonna have to ask you to say that again."

Saronda spoke with increasing energy, "We make ripples so that the other reality bobs the other way."

She stopped and tapped his forehead. "Hello, you in there? It's like your ducks!"

"My ducks! Go ducks go."

She continued, "Reality is like your ducks. Yes! We'll make a wave in the water. That will push the two realities so they miss each other."

Brody studied her face. "You don't know how to do this, do you?"

"I don't."

"Brody at your service. Maybe my ducks can help, what else do you need to know?"

Saronda said, "How to make a wave in whatever the ducks are swimming in. I remember reading that it responds to electromagnetic radiation."

"Radiation?"

"Radio waves, for one, microwaves… "

"Like the oven?"

"Yes, it's all the same stuff, just different frequencies. We need to figure out what frequency we need and then blast it."

Brody asked, "Blast it with what?" They continued walking.

Brody stopped. "Wireless cards. We'll have access to thousands of computers with wireless cards. They blast out waves when we're surfing the Internet, right? You said it's all the same stuff, just different frequencies, why not tune them to the right frequency and blast away?"

Saronda's eyes asked for more.

Brody replied, "The woman, Rebecca, I told you. Rebecca is getting us thousands of computers. It's part of my plan."

Saronda grabbed Brody's shoulders, making fierce eye contact. "And they all have wireless cards that blast electromagnetic waves. I think that's a great idea."

"All you have to do is ask."

—ε-ε-ε-ε-ε-ε—

Kelso Radovic worked out of a two-room ranch in a location he only revealed as "one of the western states." The walls were stone inside and out, with concrete in between. His house was walled off with a fence using steel posts reaching to eight feet in the air and "sunk a little extra deep."

The decor was consistent throughout, with a primitive minimalist feel. If one had to characterize it, "upscale unabomber" is not too far off. He lived alone. You can do a lot more when there are no prying eyes. He had outbuildings giving the place the look of a compound. The location was perfect, thirty-five miles to the closest sheriff and they never formally decided which town had jurisdiction that far out. Nobody spent much time thinking about it. Kelso knew that when he built the place. He lived on his own island.

Kelso spent the remainder of the night creating a GitHub branch that he had named "Socks" to be as non-descriptive as possible. It was a branch off the core of Brody's Code so he could use the main code and create changes without blowing up the main program. Basic yak shaving. He created a "shadow" branch, accessible only by him with two factor authentication. With all the pieces in place, the code was ready to run. He typed in:

```
SockItToMe
module(sockittome_partial)
export([start/0])
```

He got nothing but errors.

```
Erl_crash.dump
```

Flashing red numerals told him there were eighty-one errors. He needed to sleep.

—ε-ε-ε-ε-ε-ε—

Brody was hoping the sunny morning could pull him out of the funk he was in. The episode the day before left him spent.

He called Rebecca. She answered! Brody said, "How did it go with Bruce?"

"Not great. He had a lot of questions about why ExpoLytics wasn't providing the computers. I'll keep trying but he's right, when we signed on with ExpoLytics, you guys were committed. Why the complete reversal?"

"Drew Waltham. New guy in charge. I'm trying to find out more but I'm kinda persona non grata."

"Yeah." Rebecca hesitated "Do you mind if I ask what that's all about?"

"What's the latest word on the street?"

"I don't know, we've had very little contact with ExpoLytics folks."

"So they've shut you out that much?"

Rebecca said, "Yes, anyhow, are you going to tell me what's up with you and your absence?"

"One version: I'm slowly turning into a psychotic monster because of an unknown mental illness. Another version: the world is about to become a chaotic mess, like end of days kind of stuff and I'm privileged to be watching it in slow motion. It's a toss up."

"God, I never know when you're being serious. Both stories sound interesting. Can I have my choice of which one to hear?"

"How about if we meet somewhere and I'll decide which one to tell you based on whether you get those computers."

"How about we meet at Hamilton's this evening? I'll have an update."

"Deal, except I have a different place in mind. Meet me at Busboys and Poets, the one off Michigan in

Brookland. I may bring a friend."

"You have friends?"

"Just one, see you around seven. And, Rebecca, I haven't been fully upfront with you about these computers. I'll explain when we meet."

"You aren't gaming me, are you?"

"No, well, yes, but it's something we need to talk about face to face."

"God, you're complicated."

They disconnected.

—ε-ε-ε-ε-ε-ε—

The first thing that stands out about Rebecca Standiford is she is tall. The second thing, she's very good at detecting bullshit. If you ever run afoul of the SEC, pray she's not assigned to your case. Her win streak is impressive. She's on the list of fast movers at the agency. The only thing that could slow her down is if she botched a big case. A case like GeneraCur. It's big enough that its demise would drag her boss down along with it. She dwelled on Brody's cute wisdom from his father "nobody likes a nervous boss."

She walked into Busboys and Poets, pulling off her scarf, her copper red hair falling to the side. The place was like the picture on the web. She liked the vibe. Brody was at a table. He stood as she approached.

"Brody, hi, it's been awhile. You look—"

"Like shit, I know. I've been through a lot."

"I was thinking of something more polite. What happened?"

Brody said, "That's what we need to discuss. Have a seat. This is Saronda."

Rebecca studied Brody's stone-like expression for a second and then said to Saronda, "It's so nice to meet you."

Brody cleared his throat. "Rebecca, I want to be right upfront with you. First, I really appreciate you trying to get access to those computers. It will go a long way to getting your case on track. But there's something else. And you can get up and walk out any time you want."

"I kind of assumed that. But, thanks for clarifying."

She paused. "I was trying a little Brody humor."

Brody was expressionless, he said, "The reason I've been absent from ExpoLytics. I'm having episodes. Saronda can explain better. They're getting worse, and reality is going to collide. I've got a guy giving us code. He's out west somewhere. I think."

Rebecca was lost. "Episodes? What code? Like a secret code? Ooh, sounds spooky."

"Computer code, like software. Like an app I guess."

Rebecca said, "Oh good, 'cuz it was sounding a little crazy for a second."

Saronda spoke up, "Brody, why don't we take a step back and explain what's happening. Let's take her through the whole plan."

Saronda told the story of the science article, about mixing chaotic realities. She concluded by saying, "We need your computers so we can move another reality."

Rebecca waved her hand. "Guys, you're killing me here. So, you want me to use government computers to do what now? I'd like to understand, given that I would lose my job. I gotta tell you, I feel used. I don't know what's happening here, but reality is what it is. It just is. It doesn't crash or mix or—"

Saronda said, "The consequences are huge."

"What does getting computers have to do with this?"

Brody said, "We'll use them to prevent the collision."

Rebecca stood to put on her coat. "I don't know what's going on here. You're acting strange and I didn't detect much confidence in your voice."

Brody pleaded, "Please don't go. Give us more time to convince you. We hit you with a lot. Saronda and I have been working on this for what, a month? It took a while, but we're convinced. We need computers to calculate how to direct energy to nudge reality. It's bizarre, silly, stupid, whatever you want to label it. It's all those. But it's also very real."

He stared up at her. "Please, sit. You're our hope. Those computers are our only chance. We don't know where else to go. I promise, when we fix this reality thing, we'll nail the bad guys to the wall. But we have to fix this or else none of that will matter."

"I'm not buying it." Rebecca looked down at him, reading his face. *He's gone through something terrifying. Something that deeply affected him.*

He continued, "Rebecca, this is like in the 14th century trying to explain that the earth goes around the sun. It feels weird, and stupid. This article Saronda found is all we have to go on."

Rebecca studied him. "I can tell you believe this but —"

Saronda said, "There are others. Many others. They're lining up outside psychiatrists' offices looking for answers."

Rebecca set her coat down. *Saronda was measured, confident. She believes this stuff.*

Rebecca said, "You know what? I think I'll get a salad. C'mon Saronda, let's go order. I'm buying. Brody, save the table."

As they walked to the counter, Rebecca asked, "Was I too clumsy, pulling you away like that?"

"Actually, quite smooth. I gotcha."

"I can tell you believe in this paper."

"It's so beautifully written. It makes sense and it's all backed up with equations."

Rebecca turned from the menu. "Equations?"

"Hundreds. Very intense, above my head. They define reality, where it comes from, how we interact with it."

Rebecca looked at the menu. "I have a math degree from Cornell."

Saronda placed a hand on Rebecca's arm. "A math degree? You just might be my new best friend."

"I'm a Financial Analyst. Lots of math."

Saronda said, "Maybe if you looked at these equations, it would convince you. You could really help us."

"Help you with what exactly?"

"Move reality, save the world, basic stuff."

This was outside of Rebecca's comfort zone of black and white financial calculations. Sitting back at the table, she finished her second bite of salad and said, "I didn't expect any of this. But I can't see why you would go to such lengths to make all this up. Maybe Brody is suffering from a mental illness but Saronda, I love your name by the way, you seem so level-headed, I don't see why you would—"

She took another bite, holding eye contact with Saronda. She half-glanced at Brody, willing Saronda to get the message.

Message received. Saronda sat up. "Uh, yeah, Brody, aren't you getting something to eat?"

He went to the counter.

Rebecca waited until Brody was out of earshot. "I wasn't kidding when I said I would lose my job using computers without authority. I can't afford the risk."

Saronda said, "I don't mean to overstep, but maybe think about it this way; from what I've heard, it sounds like your case is major screwed right now. Fix it, make it right, and maybe they won't look so hard at how you did it. Leaving it screwed up gives them a real reason to fire you. I know that's harsh, but if we sat down together, I'll bet us girls could figure out how to solve your problem, and ours."

"Shouldn't it be 'we girls'?"

Saronda smiled. "Ooh, I love you. Grammar's my jam. Dang, though,'we girls' sounds funny. One thing's for sure. I think we'd work well together."

Rebecca set down her fork. "And Brody?"

"I'm sure he'd love working with you too."

Rebecca leaned in. "I meant, you know, you two seem to 'work' well together. I can tell."

"I know what you meant." They laughed.

Brody returned with a sandwich. "What are you guys laughing about?"

Saronda and Rebecca stood up in unison. "Girl stuff."

Brody sat. "Are you leaving? But what about— ?"

Saronda said, "We'll figure it out. Enjoy your sandwich. I'm making a copy of the article for Rebecca. Should I make a copy for your code guy, 'out west somewhere'?"

"What? Uh, no."

—ε-ε-ε-ε-ε-ε—

Rebecca hurried onto the Metro. She had a meeting in less than an hour. She pulled the science paper from her purse and turned to the first page of the article. Ten minutes later, she called to cancel her meeting. With a choice of explaining her dismal case or decamping to her balcony with a glass of wine and Augustine's paper, Augustine won.

There was an order to the equations. They had an

elegance. They told a story. She didn't know where the story led but she was determined to find out.

She grabbed a bottle of white, pulled an old math textbook from a shelf and settled into a chair on her balcony. The crisp air reminded her of her days at Cornell, taking long walks around Beebe Lake, huddling against the chill in the gardens outside Malott Hall. The paper brought back her love of mathematics.

Augustine's novel application of Green's theorem sent a shiver. Fourier Transforms had parameters based on interactions of Fibonacci numbers and Jacobsthal Primes. It was a masterpiece of unification. Playing hooky was every bit as fun as it was when she was younger. She understood why Saronda was so taken by the work.

But what does it mean? The patterns that the equations make must be amazing.

—ε-ε-ε-ε-ε-ε—

Brody sat, wallowing in despair, a half-eaten sandwich in front of him. He wrapped himself in the clatter and bustle of Busboys and Poets. It served as a cocoon while he stressed. His phone chirped.

It was Rebecca. "Where are you right now?"

"Still here."

"You mean you never left that place? Brody, it's been hours."

"I'm depressed. You guys left me."

"Oh, poor baby. Sit tight, I've got something that might cheer you up."

She disconnected.

He took a bite of his cold, dry sandwich.

Rebecca arrived forty-five minutes later. "You didn't finish your sandwich. The bread's probably moldy by now."

"I'm depressed, remember?"

"Quiet down, you'll be fine. Let me show you what I found."

She described in great detail the beauty and refinement. "I had the most magical afternoon with Augustine. And a little wine."

She let out a slight giggle.

Brody asked, "You're able to understand all that scribbling?"

"Yes, I have a Master's in Math."

Brody mouthed an impressed, "Wow." Then, "So you think this paper is legit?"

"It's genius, but what I came here to tell you. I was going to tell you before, but then you hit me with all that crazy talk. I got access to over a thousand computers, but you have to promise—"

"A thousand!" Brody practically came out of his chair. "That's amazing. What about your boss, Bruce?"

Rebecca waved off the comment and pulled a thumb drive from her coat pocket. "Here. This has the credentials in an XML file."

She pulled it back. "But you have to promise we'll finish GeneraC... the case."

Brody eagerly took the thumb drive and put it in his pocket. "What convinced you?"

"Just two girls talking, a little wine, and a deep curiosity about those equations."

Brody added, "And saving my sanity and, you know, societal peace and order, right?"

"Societal peace and order. You're hilarious. Oh, hey, I converted the equations using MathTrac so your code guy can plug them into his code. They're on the thumb drive. Some *change* reality, some *move* reality. Your code guy will need to run some calculations."

Brody hurried back to his hotel. He had a file to send.

—ε-ε-ε-ε-ε-ε—

Kelso leaned back in his chair, frustrated with code bugs. He shaved the yak but the yak wasn't working. The code he copied from the internet had errors he didn't know how to fix. A decent programmer could have fixed them easily, but Kelso didn't have the skills. Maybe if he hadn't been expelled from college. Maybe if he hadn't been driven out by a scandal that was based on a lie. It was years in the past, but to Kelso, it was fresh.

He learned something valuable. Lies can ruin lives. And, they can be "useful."

He faked his way into an entry-level position at Emerson. During the day, he was a second class citizen assisting the "real" programmers. At night, he developed algorithms that searched the darkest corners of the web, down where the slimiest of vermin reside. He boosted conspiracy theories to ensnare the gullible, manipulating whole groups of people into believing anything. Customers lined up. Need a zoning board to rule in your favor or a particular person to win a mayor's race? Kelso could help. He was good, but as good as he was, he could never get more than thirty percent to believe the distorted view of reality he pushed.

By mid-afternoon he was ready to take a break.

He spent the rest of daylight playing with the drone he had been building. It had propellers that folded like origami to make a sleek rocket. He could blast it to twenty-five hundred feet altitude. The propellers unfolded at the apex. He took control with the phone app he wrote and used the propellers to fly it even higher. It broke a few FAA rules. Kelso didn't care. He snapped a few pictures with the self-stabilizing camera. It had enough charge to hover for hours. He liked knowing what's going on around him. He returned to the code.

Five hours, two liters of Mountain Dew and one reheated burrito later he was ready to re-test. It was early evening when he typed in the commands:

```
SockItToMe
module(sockittome_partial)
export([start/0])
```

He looked at the yellow labrador snoozing on the floor. "It might work this time."

His phone lit up. A text from Brody: *Sending a couple equations that should help with the reality project.*

He sent an immediate reply: *Don't be specific in your texts. Sending file is more appropriate. Delete your last text. AND DON'T USE TEXT FOR THIS. I'll send a vpn login.*

—ε-ε-ε-ε-ε-ε—

Rebecca turned off her office light. She stepped into the hallway and stopped. *What about all those military computers at a soon-to-be shuttered military base? Completely unused!*

She typed a text to Brody: *I have an idea. Don't get your hopes up but I think I know where to get more computers. And I doubt anyone will notice.*

She thought better of it and deleted the text. Probably not something to put in writing.

—ε-ε-ε-ε-ε-ε—

Kelso pasted the equations into his Erlang program. The activity meter lit up bright green. The program compiled and ran error-free. After three hours, the computation was at 1.5%. He let it run and called it a day.

"I'm going to bed. Don't stay up late." Kaz barely raised an eyebrow.

At nine the next morning, his self-built, very high-powered behemoth of a computer had only completed about 5% of the job. The two equations from Augustine's paper dragged down what was no doubt the fastest desktop computer in the state. The core temperature was over two hundred degrees, the fan was running at 1800 rpm. All 18 cores were running close to one hundred percent and the calculation was far from complete. This wasn't going to work.

He texted Brody: *Caught a whale. Gonna need a really big boat.*

—ε-ε-ε-ε-ε-ε—

Rebecca went through her morning yoga as the sun streamed through the large glass atrium of her upscale apartment overlooking Kalorama Park in Adams Morgan. She had already made several phone calls about the military computers. There were thousands. They were used for training for a couple months and were sitting idle. She rewarded herself with a french press espresso.

She was excited to tell Brody about the new computers. She didn't have to wait long.

He called. "Is there any way you can get more computers?"

"I'm one step ahead of you, but first, did he get the other ones working?"

"I don't know, he doesn't say much."

"You don't know much about this guy do you? Anyhow, I think I can get my hands on thousands. Give me some time. I'm doing this under the radar."

—ε-ε-ε-ε-ε-ε—

"That appeared to go swimmingly."

Kelso saw that Brody had figured out how to transfer another file through his secure VPN portal. He copied the XML file. Whoa! One thousand and thirty-four computers. A green dot lit up as each computer connected.

"Imagine that Kaz, I'm now controlling a huge network of government computers. Me, of all people."

He typed:

```
SockItToMe_ver1.3
module(sockittome_1.3)
export([start/0])
```

The activity monitor came alive showing a ninety-three percent utilization of each computer. Success!

"Kaz, this is a very important development."

The dog shifted position showing no interest in his scheming roommate. Kelso headed to the kitchen for a fresh Mountain Dew.

"You should be more impressed, Kaz Kropo Kaczynski, old boy. It's important to enjoy the victories."

He cloned some code from GitHub to visualize the patterns made by the equations.

"Snazzy repo. It's amazing the code people give away for free." Kaz did not reflect Kelso's giddy mood.

The visualizer kicked into action. The pattern was like an Etch-A-Sketch, building from one corner and progressing across the screen. Bit by bit the pattern built. Though it was slow, Kelso could tell this was going to be a magnificent, intricate pattern. An early December snowstorm was developing across the valley west of his property.

Better check the generator.

Although it was nice to be far away from prying eyes, it was a pain to be the last on the list to have power restored.

His phone lit up with a text from Brody: *How's the boat?*

He texted back: *Not big enough. Too slow will never get there.*

Kaz turned away. He didn't like lies. The two walked to the side of the house and Kelso brushed the snow off the fuel gauge. A little low but will do. When he got back inside, he saw that the pattern was bigger and even more elaborate.

He texted: *Definitely need more juice. Nothing happening yet.*

—ε-ε-ε-ε-ε-ε—

Paul Langevin was arrested for merely expressing common sense views of fairness and democracy. His views didn't sit well with the bullies who used lies to spread fascism and hate. He spent most of World War II locked up.

A good friend met him the day he was released. "Welcome to freedom."

There was only one thing on his mind. His daughter, Hélène Solomon-Langevin. She had been taken by the nazis. He raced to his daughter's house.

His friend tried to keep pace. "Paul, you have to leave the country. You have no choice. How can I convince you that you are in grave danger?"

"But I must see if it's true, with my own eyes."

"It's true Paul, you must accept this."

"But it's my daughter, dear Hélène, taken to..."

"Auschwitz, yes Paul. We checked as much as we could. It's true."

Paul was breathless when he arrived at his daughter's house. "And Jacques? No doubts?"

"Yes, Paul, firing squad." No dissent was tolerated.

The door was unlocked. It was obvious she had not planned to leave; everything was in its place. Paul Langevin broke down. His daughter and her husband were fighting for the same cause he was. She was sent to a concentration camp, and he was shot, because they fought for the truth. He walked aimlessly from room-to-room. It was as he'd remembered it from three years earlier.

He turned to his friend. "I have to see for myself that they are gone. I have to take a last look at the place they built their life in."

Paul rambled further in stuttering tones, "I don't know. I just thought, if there had been some mistake, some trick of the tale, maybe she would be here with her husband, and they would be preparing for a rally or..."

It was then he spotted an oak box that he hadn't recalled from before. He found inside a note, cryptic and in his daughter's handwriting. "It stands where it deserves to be, hiding in plain sight."

He folded it and placed it in his jacket pocket.

His friend said, "I think it's time to go, get you to a safe place, somewhere that's not France."

"I can't leave France, not while my daughter is—"

"Paul, you need to face the facts. She's not returning. No one does, not from there."

He implored Paul Langevin, "Please, come with me to Switzerland, until it's safe."

"Until it's safe" lasted close to four months. Paul Langevin returned to Paris when it was liberated in August 1944. He was still holding out hope that Hélène would be freed.

—ε-ε-ε-ε-ε-ε—

Kelso woke up to a fresh dusting of snow. A "dusting" that was three feet deep in places. The heavy early December caught Kelso by surprise.

He muttered to Kaz, "Did you see what it's like out there, Kaz? Surely not fun taking a crap today. Would be nice to call UberEats and get us some food. Not easy being off the grid, is it boy?"

He talked to his dog a lot. He used it as practice for the day when he would need to talk to people.

"I know you're concerned, and I admit I'm a little worried too. We'll face winter together, as a team."

The twelve-year-old lab raised one eyebrow.

"So how did I do, delivering bad news? I read it's important to make it a shared experience. Did I soften the impact by showing first, that I understand your fear and indicate clearly that it's normal to be afraid?"

Kelso laughed. Kaz walked away. Neither was going to starve to death. He had enough supplies to last several winters and do it in the protection of a fortified space that could withstand anything short of a nuclear blast. He had calculated the chance of that happening, balanced it with whether the world would be worth living in afterward, and decided not to spend the extra effort on thicker walls and radiation proofing. Inside his twisted mind, it would be fun to drive close to the next hit and watch the world burn.

His phone chirped with a text: *Boat is getting bigger*

Kelso smiled. "I've got him running around God's green Earth pulling together thousands of government computers and giving me access. Can you imagine? This could be a very important step in my long-term capabilities."

His phone lit up with another text: *Tell me when the boats are sailing.*

"When the boats are sailing. How cute."

Truth was, Kelso's code was clicking beautifully. He connected the new batch of computers from Brody. Over twenty-five thousand. He added color and animation to his pattern visualizer.

"Kaz, we have taken some very big steps. We need to recognize the important moments. Are you ready for this?"

He got no answer.

"I was expecting more excitement from you, but you are correct, we must prove success before celebrating."

Click. Each computer connected, twenty-five thousand three hundred and two tiny little green dots reporting for duty.

```
SockItToMe_ver2.0
module(sockittome_2.0)
export([start/0])
```

The screen danced as the pattern slowly built. Then, the screen filled with a giant ball. The pattern was so intricate with so many details that the high-resolution screen couldn't capture the full beauty. Kaz tried to focus on the blurry pattern.

"Looks like I need to zoom in."

He typed in a zoom factor of 1.5.

"Well, that's not enough."

He typed in a zoom factor of 2.5.

Kaz perked up.

"Ahh what the hell, you with me, dog?"

He typed in a zoom factor of 5000. "We're having

so much fun."

They both were motionless, riveted on the screen. The animation kicked in and the pattern started moving.

Kaz looked at Kelso, then back to the screen. He barked.

"Oh my."

—ε-ε-ε-ε-ε-ε—

Wayne Drakauer was in a meeting with his new boss Drew Waltham when his phone rang: KelRad. He silenced it as quickly as he could and then endured the self-righteous glares of everyone in the room, annoyed that they were distracted for several precious seconds.

Gag me, dillrods.

It made Wayne tense, getting a call from a guy like Kelso while sitting among his colleagues. Drew droned on about his thinly veiled plan to slow down the GeneraCur case.

Blipblip Wayne got a text. More glares.

He reached to silence his phone. The text: *pick up.*

He tuned out Drew and shifted in his chair. *C'mon wrap up.* It felt like forever. He bolted when the meeting ended and went to the parking lot.

Kelso didn't bother saying hello. "Are you somewhere you won't be overheard?"

"Yes, but make it quick, it's cold out here."

"Outside, good. No parabolic mics you know about?"

"Jeezus, Kelso."

"No names please. Go log into my VPN."

Wayne went to his office and logged into Kelso's network. There was an encrypted note. He downloaded it onto a thumb drive and then took it over to another computer that had the de-encryption key.

The message: *You need to see what I see. Log on to VPN-406-waco.io tonight. I'll text you the time.*

Wayne left work early. He choked down his dinner and plodded through the 3-factor authorization. Kelso's face appeared on the screen.

Wayne spoke to the screen, "Wow, I'm proud of myself, remembering all those steps to log in. That's a nice fire you got going there. And I love the stone fireplace. Made it yourself?"

"Wayne, please pay attention."

"I thought we were on a 'no names' basis."

"Wayne, VPN-406-waco.io is more secure than the nuclear codes… I checked. I dare anyone to try to get in."

"You are a strange man. Then, names it is, what did you want to show me, Kelso Radovic, the K man, K Rad himself, the Radenator?"

"Please settle yourself. OK, I'm sharing my screen."

"I see it. What is that?"

"That's made with the equations your guy gave me."

"Brody? Brody gave you equations. I'm not sure he knows what an equation is."

"They make a pattern. Now for the strange, when you zoom in, it keeps building and building, the detail is infinite. Watch, I'll zoom in more."

Wayne watched as the code calculated the new pattern. He sat up with a start. "What the crazy pants kind of crap is that? That's wild."

"Be patient. Wait 'til the animation hits."

Then, wham, the screen came alive. Mesmerizing. Twenty minutes later, Kelso broke Wayne's trance.

"Still there Wayne?"

Wayne gathered himself. "Sorry, I've been sitting here watching this thing. How long has it been? I feel high bro."

Staring straight into a pattern that captures all of reality can make a person feel a little trippy.

"Have you tried zoom factors that are like special numbers?"

"Like what?"

"I don't know, primes, pi, forty-two, seventy-three..."

"Those numbers are way too low. I need big numbers, to really zoom in."

"The biggest number I know is Avogadro's number."

"What is it?"

"It's the number of atoms in a—"

Kelso interrupted, "I know what it is. It is important when working with people that you assume they are educated. If they demonstrate otherwise, you gently explain things. Being able to interact with people is very important. I *meant*, what is the number?"

"Oh you forgot? Just how educated are you?"

Total silence. It was an offhand comment. Wayne couldn't have known the impact it had.

"Still there bro?"

It was a long unnatural pause. Wayne said, "Hello?"

Wayne didn't know it but deep inside Kelso a storm was raging.

It was something Kelso kept buried. *Maybe if the*

college president hadn't needed to "clean it up, no matter what it takes." Maybe if the college president hadn't so desperately needed heads on a platter. Maybe—

Wayne said, "Knock knock. We were talking about really big—"

"Wayne, please tell me the number. I'll type it in."

"OK, man. I'll google it. You OK?"

Kelso typed in 6022140857 followed by fourteen zeroes. The screen changed. A dozen seconds later, animation kicked in.

Four hours later, they were still watching how reality was created.

—ε-ε-ε-ε-ε-ε—

The next morning, Wayne called Kelso. "What was that last night?"

"Good morning, Wayne. You should feel very privileged that I answered your call. Get on viper now."

Wayne sat in his shorts and t-shirt and typed the credentials for VPN-406-waco.io into his computer.

He texted work: *Won't be in today. Not feeling well.* Hard to be on top of your game when you stay up all night watching patterns on a screen.

"Oh Wayne, have you recovered from your trance? I sense you were quite taken."

"Bro, that was intense. It shook me to my core."

"If you're ready, I can show you something else. I tried multiples of Avogadro's number. I multiplied it by two then three then four. Nothing special. Then I multiplied it by pi. I will share my screen so you can see."

"Holy crap on a crispy cream cracker, what are those things?"

Wayne tried not to become entranced. "This is so different from last night. Instead of everything knitted together, each line is distinct, unique. They move and vibrate. And those cool spikes. Wow."

"Did you notice, Wayne, they are all different?"

Wayne pushed back from his screen. "Whoa! Dude, did you see that? That spike shot all the way across the screen! Like lightning. That's some rad shit."

Kelso added, "Some are energetic, some just sit there. Whatever these things are, it's incredible to think all this is generated by two equations."

"All you did was zoom in? So these things are what make up that big ball we saw last night?"

"Yes, so Wayne, where did you say Brody got these equations?"

"He never told me. I'll give him a call and ask."

Kelso's tone changed. "I wouldn't do that if I were

you."

Wayne felt his skin tighten.

Kelso's voice was dark. "I don't want your guy to know the code's working, yet. But may I mention something important? I need to inform you that I did a little 'power surfing' the other day and guess what I found? The trading history of one Walter Drane, account number 567-343-09 at TradeWerks for shares of a particular company. GeneraCur."

The words hung in the air.

Wayne's breath left his body. "Whu... but Walter who?"

"Wayne Wayne Wayne. Or should I call you Walter? Or is that only for when you are trading GeneraCur?"

Wayne's mouth went dry, making it hard to talk. "But how did you—"

Kelso took control. "Oh, how did I find out you have a broker account under a fake name? If I can find that out, imagine what else I know about you."

"You hacked me?"

"Hacking is such a crude term, I prefer to say, I did a little research. It's a skill I developed. Sometimes it's useful. In this case, it's very useful. Goodbye, Wayne. I'll be in touch. I suggest you answer immediately when I call. Making people wait shows disrespect. You don't want to disrespect me."

Kelso disconnected. Wayne tried to stave off a panic attack by taking deep breaths. It didn't work. He threw his phone onto the couch and stood. He felt lightheaded so he sat back down. It was probably good that he called in sick.

—ε-ε-ε-ε-ε-ε—

Kelso waited a couple hours to let the panic set in before calling Wayne again.

Wayne answered his phone immediately, "How much do you know about me?"

"Oh good, you answered. You're trainable. Wayne, is that your worried voice I'm hearing? What's wrong? It's important that people who work together understand each other's problems."

"We're not working together."

"That's very hurtful. Especially from someone I know so much about. For one, insider trading with conflict of interest. Enough to get you fired and maybe enough for a nice jail sentence."

"Are you threatening me?"

Kelso became condescending. "Wayne, I'm here to *help* you. Think of me as your best friend. Your decoy fake name account is insufficient when it comes to the Feds. I found it in minutes."

"Where is this headed? You wouldn't be doing this if you didn't want something."

"I understand that these types of calls can be troubling so I'll get right to it. I notice you're buying GeneraCur stock each week. Is that why you're slow walking the project? Delay it enough and the SEC gives up? Buy the stock now when it's low? SEC drops the case. The stock goes up. Good for you, Wayne. Sell, sell, sell. Make a nice stack, take your profits, then fly to an island somewhere and drink mai tais all day. Do I have that right?"

Wayne waited a beat. "I'm not slow walking anything. It's my boss, he's the one slowing things down, I mean—"

Kelso pounced. "Excuses, Wayne. That's all it is. Those words are best saved for the Feds. I am curious though. You asked me to update your software, 'just change the diffs.' Do you remember? That was a very good idea, Wayne. I did as you asked but you never implemented it. Why is that? It would solve your project's problem in an instant. Hmmm. Is it to make a little money, Wayne? Is that what it is?"

Kelso got giddy. "But don't worry, I can set you up so the big bad feds never find out you've been bad. I can make your shady trades go away. I'll skim a little off the top. Not much, just a bit of your ill-gotten profits. No one will ever know."

"Maybe I won't play. Maybe I'll abandon my plan

now. Maybe—"

"Wayne, I'm curious. Do you doubt my abilities? I could make an anonymous tip. Should it be to your employer or the SEC, or both?"

"How do you know I didn't record this call? Extortion is a crime, you know."

"A recording from this phone? First, you would need to prove this phone even exists."

Kelso disconnected.

—ε-ε-ε-ε-ε-ε—

Paul Langevin was an amazing person. Besides being a brilliant mathematician and describing how atoms respond to magnetism, he created a device that detected submarines. He climbed the Eiffel Tower on his fiftieth birthday. The part of his legacy that's never been told is the steps he took to keep Augustine's paper from falling into the hands of fascists. While he was in prison, his daughter was taken to Auschwitz and his son-in-law was executed.

In January 1945, soldiers of the First Ukrainian Front liberated Auschwitz. Paul Langevin's daughter, Hélène, was freed. Remarkably, she became one of the first women elected to Parliament.

On a cool spring morning, Paul Langevin reached into his jacket pocket. "Hélène, do you remember writing this? 'It stands where it deserves to be, hiding in plain sight.'"

"I sure do, it was the day you were arrested."

"What does it mean?"

"Come, I'll show you."

They made their way to the "Centre national de la recherche scientifique" science library in Paris. Hélène pointed to the locked glass case labeled "Papers Of Great Scientific Value." Displayed proudly next to original editions of papers from renowned French scientists such as Marie Curie, Louis Pasteur, Henri Poincare and Pierre-Simon Laplace, was an obscure science magazine that Paul Langevin had worried about to the point of paranoia.

"You were supposed to burn it. That was our plan. You burn the document and I burn the cover notes."

"Yes, but you spoke of it with such high regard. You couldn't bear to see it burn and neither could I."

Paul laughed. "Ahh, but instead it's been 'hiding in plain sight'. Sitting where it deserves. Thank you, Hélène."

Augustine's paper sat proudly, displayed in a glass case, among the works of giants in science. It was on display until the 1970s when an audit discovered the science magazine had no library tracking ID and no one could identify why it was there. It was tossed into a box of discarded books.

—ε-ε-ε-ε-ε-ε—

Kelso noticed he had a text from Brody: *need more boats?*

He squealed, "What a beautiful gift this guy is." Kaz stirred and turned over.

He texted: *Yes. All you can. Might help get this working.*

That should send Brody chasing more computers.

Brody tried again for an update: *How's it going?*

Kelso lied again: *still trying to hitch a ride on these boats. Nothing's working*

Brody tried a more direct approach: *We need to talk, call me*

Kelso lied: *Busy. I'll call you tonight.*

Brody texted: *what time?*

Kelso went back to making soup.

—ε-ε-ε-ε-ε-ε—

The numbers on the clock radio clicked off another minute, a noticeable haze of blue light brightened the sheets on Brody's bed. The room was quiet. The earth rotated through another imperceptible sliver of latitude causing the sun to appear two degrees above the horizon, casting a beam of light directly onto Brody's pillow. Brody wasn't there.

He was two and half miles away leaning against a tree and breathing heavily.

Seven hours prior, Brody went to the workout room. He couldn't sleep. There was a lot on his mind. The workout room was empty. It's not a popular place at a quarter past midnight.

He stepped onto the treadmill. Brody punched the button and it started moving, slowly at first as it always does. He dialed in the speed and started trotting, as he always does. Heart rate 76. Then, without notice, it sped up, like it never does. Brody checked the setting. Same. Heart rate 92. It sped faster. Heart rate 135. Brody was trapped. He tightened his grip on the rails. He couldn't get off and he couldn't keep up. Heart rate 152. He looked down. The treadmill wasn't there. The workout room wasn't there. He was running across a field. The ground was hard under his feet. He fell. Loud insects. Tall weeds. Sticky, clinging seeds. He started walking. A fog of lights drifted closer, wrapping him, twisting him, distorting him into an unrecognizable ball of nothingness, stripped of all emotions. He had no feelings. Something had ripped at his soul. And the pain. He tried to scream but he had no breath. A silent cough caught in his throat, suffocating him. He bent over, trapped in a reality that his Whisper was not built for, unable to connect to the universe. He was less than before, lacking the complex, nuanced feelings that made him human. Empathy, self-worth, love. All were missing.

He leaned back feeling the rough bark of the tree

against his back. He could see a cemetery where the graves were flush to the ground. He found a bench overlooking the Anacostia River.

Rebecca texted: *Call me?*

He used his remaining strength to call her. He was greeted with a barrage of enthusiasm. "These equations are fascinating. They form a Mandelbrot set in twenty dimensions using quaternions and bicomplex numbers. Some have exponents as high as forty-two."

"I wish I could understand that."

She talked excitedly for as long as Brody could muster the strength to listen.

Brody cut her off. "Saronda needs to hear this."

Rebecca talked more. "I don't know for sure but if these are supposed to make a pattern, it'll be a doozy. One giant ball of wonderfulness. Some will have very large spikes shooting out. You know, large exponents."

Brody pushed the pain aside. "OK, but Saronda... Let's meet."

"How about after my update meeting? Say, around two o'clock?"

Brody called for rideshare. He was tired of being tired.

—ε-ε-ε-ε-ε-ε—

Mademoiselle Thérèse Pont was taking a midday

break from running her small shop where she sold collectables and old books. She made another espresso for her friend as they continued one of their favorite activities, making fun of Americans. It was the thing to do in France in the late 1970s. They would talk about how gauche the new American export, McDonald's, was but would still sneak out every now and then and have fries. Mostly, though, they enjoyed needling Americans, with their disco music and bell bottom jeans. They laughed as they leafed through a fashion magazine. "Oh my God, they have their pants up to their ribs."

Her friend said, "I know someone who moved to America. She said it's so tacky over there. The fashion is all earthy brown chevrons and burnt orange. There's actually a guy selling rocks as pets. Can you imagine? But Thérèse, why didn't we do that? Sell rocks! Get rich!"

Thérèse interjected, "French people would never buy a rock. Just pick it up from the ground, done."

She enjoyed these afternoon chats on days when her shop wasn't busy, which was pretty much every day.

Her friend continued, "Oh, and you know what else my friend told me? She said some of the bars line the walls with books to make them look sophisticated. Like they're in the library!"

"Drunk imbécile, tells his wife he's been reading all night!" They laughed.

Thérèse's friend replied, "And people are making money from all this American nonsense. Like the guy with the rock and what about those silly platform shoes? Gullible."

Thérèse had an idea. "You know, if bars want old books, I've got old books and I know where to get more. I could fill a lot of bars in America. French books in America, très sophistiqué!"

"You mean you'd send your precious books to America? But aren't you wanting to sell them to collectors?"

"Surely but, precious is as precious does. Do you see any collectors coming to buy them?" She waved her arms around her shop. It overflowed with unsold books.

"But all your precious books sitting in a smoky bar, Thérèse. How unrefined."

"And how American." They both laughed.

Thérèse's idea was a hit. She packed up old books and sold them to American bar owners. They decorated their watering holes with them. Crazy, and just in time for the 1980s. She would go to libraries all over France collecting their old, discarded books. It was silly, but a franc is a franc. She took pride in her new business, carefully sorting books by size and color, and packing them with care. She placed notes in each box instructing her customers how to arrange them for a pleasing aesthetic. They always came tightly packed, always undamaged. It gave her a great deal of satisfaction. It was a cool autumn afternoon when she packed one box in particular. As she was closing the box, she slid a science magazine between two books, making for a perfect fit.

On that same day, and almost three thousand miles away in an Army hospital in Sierra Leone, Sia Kanu Jackson gave birth to her second baby girl. She named her Saronda Mia.

—ɛ-ɛ-ɛ-ɛ-ɛ-ɛ—

Saronda Mia Jackson and Rebecca Denise Standiford arrived at Busboys and Poets at the same time. They walked in together.

Saronda said, "You seem excited. What's going on?"

"I've been looking at the equations. Oh my God, you are going to die. They're amazing."

Brody came in. "What's amazing?"

Brody had built a fence. Projected onto the fence was an animated version of himself that made him appear normal. Brody was not normal. Behind the fence was a swirling mass of confusion. His Whisper was damaged. The thing that created his feelings, his sense of himself, centering him, defining his place in reality, was broken.

Saronda said, "Guys, I need to tell you something."

She pulled out her phone and pulled up Twitter. "It's growing and it's trending."

Saronda showed her phone. "Hashtag DevilLight. I

don't remember if I told you, but I started a hashtag to see if other people are seeing the fog of lights."

Rebecca glanced at Brody.

Brody said, "It's the nightmare episodes I've been having. They start with a fog of lights. I had a bad one last night, woke up near a river."

Saronda stared a hole in Brody.

He answered her unspoken question, "It was bad, worst one yet. I walked miles in another reality. So, you started a hashtag? What's that all about?"

"I asked my Twitter followers if they are seeing the lights. People are starting to live Brody's nightmare."

Rebecca cast some doubt. "Or they're just saying they did."

Saronda replied, "But they describe the episodes so vividly. They're like Brody's. Look at some of these posts. People are suicidal, they're taking meds."

Brody rubbed his face. "OK. Not good. Rebecca, you have something to show?"

Rebecca spoke in analytical, measured tones. "Let me tell you what I found. I went off the assumption that they create a pattern like you said. If that's true, then the pattern would be a very complex, multi-dimensional structure, a huge sphere composed of smaller patterns. Imagine a large snowball with millions of snowflakes making up a snowball. Each small pattern is different.

But here's the thing, it's strange for a physical system to need so many equations and, like I told Brody earlier, to have such large exponents."

Saronda replied, "You said physical systems."

"Yes."

"This is also a spiritual system. Reality is both physical and spiritual."

All three seemed to retreat into what they heard: the hashtag news, the equations, unique small patterns making a large complex pattern.

Minutes passed when the silence was shattered by a waitress. "Are you guys ready to order? Do you have any questions?"

The trio showed no response. The waitress paused and then said, "OK, let me know when you're ready."

Saronda took what Rebecca had said and bounced it against what Augustine had written. *The entire tapestry of reality, all our emotions, spiritual stirrings, sense of morality, steadfastness of beliefs was in that ball.*

Brody sat behind his manufactured fence, thinking of the other DevilLight warriors and the patients lining up at Dr. Matthews' office.

Rebecca said, "Guys, hate to break the mood, but could there be more than one large ball? The equations say there is more than one ball. And they move."

Saronda said, "That means they can collide. Everything we've been saying is true."

With a sense of urgency, Brody said, "Guys, I'm going to talk to the code guy tonight to light a fire under him."

"Why don't we call now, from here? We're all interested."

"Ehh, he only calls me, I can't call him. We mostly text, and even then we can't use specifics, we text in like a code, things like boats and, ahh it's weird."

Saronda raised an eyebrow. "Does he think someone's watching him? Who is this guy you're working with?"

Brody knew nothing.

He punched in a text to Kelso: *CALL ME.*

"Guys, I think we should meet again tomorrow morning. Same place. I'll let you know what I find out from Kelso."

"Kelso?"

"The code guy."

—ε-ε-ε-ε-ε-ε—

Charles "Winks" Mowhinkle stood with a vacant stare. The large empty room was back to the way it looked when he bought the place except for the layers of spilled beer and splattered cooking grease that had accumulated over three decades. Being a bar owner was quite a trip, making friends and breaking up fights.

He stepped into the sunshine to the pickup truck parked in the alley. "Thank you gentlemen, a term that does not fit you two at all. Here is your one-hundred-fifty dollars as promised."

"Thank *you*, Winks. Hey, we're going to miss the place."

Winks looked at his shoes and kicked a pebble. "Yeah I know, but it's time."

Winks was retiring and shutting down the Bookshelf Bar, a local bar that followed the late seventies trend of lining the walls with shelves of books. The overstuffed furniture gave the place the look of a cigar lounge, but it was basically a watering hole. After a few years of spilled drinks and wayward nachos, the stuffed furniture gave way to long wooden tables and benches, and two pool tables. The books remained and the name never changed but everyone called it "Winks." Winks Mowhinkle put a lot of himself into making this a nice place to gather and it stayed hopping enough to keep the lights on and the family fed. He smiled thinking about how clever he was to use books to cover up a disastrous plaster job that looked like it was done by the three stooges. He wondered how many people ever noticed that all the books were in French. He got them for pennies on the dollar, shipped from France for less than finding them locally. They were the last things remaining to be hauled away. It had taken all morning and most of the afternoon for his two high school buddies to pull down all the books from the oak shelves he had built and haul them to the truck on the way to the dump.

As the truck pulled away, Winks waved wildly and shouted, "Did you get the box in the back?"

The driver responded by taking off his ball cap, waving it in the air, and hootin' and hollerin' as he drove off. Winks thought to himself. "Wow, and he's the smart one."

He trotted back to the storage room and sure enough, the box was still there. It was extra from his last shipment of books from France. It sat in the same spot for most of the thirty-nine- year life of the bar. Never opened.

"Dangit," Winks muttered under his breath, "Place needs to be empty by the end of the week."

"Lookin good!" The voice seemed to come out of nowhere. Winks poked his head out of the storage room and saw a lively woman bubbling with energy.

"Who are you?"

"Oh, I'm Beth. I'm the one buying this place. You must be Charles. I was stopping by to check the place out. It's very exciting."

"Inspection's not 'til Friday. I'll need every minute to—"

"Oh I know, I was nearby and thought I'd—"

Winks asked, "What are you going to do with my place?" It was hard thinking about his place as someone else's.

"A bookstore, I'm opening a bookstore. For old books! That's why I asked that you leave the shelves."

"Old books? I just filled a truck with old books. I think that's called irony."

"Actually, I think that's called coincidence. Irony would be if—"

Winks pulled out his phone. "Excuse me, I need to get the guys to come back and get a box they forgot."

Winks went back inside. Beth hung outside admiring her new purchase. It was a new chapter in her life.

The truck came rambling back and made a dusty stop on the gravel. Billy jumped down from the truck.

He eyed Beth. "You know, you look familiar. Did you go to Saint Tony High?"

He tried desperately to hold his stomach in, but that battle had been lost years ago.

Beth said, "Yes, did you?"

"We both did." Billy motioned to the truck where Stevie was engrossed in a lukewarm tuna melt.

"I'm Billy... Billy Pool and that's Stevie Tallent, although we always say he ain't got none. Get it, Talent?" Billy laughed. Beth didn't.

"Well, I'm Beth Maillon. I think I remember you guys. You made quite a pair."

"Still do, I'm fat and he's ugly." Billy and Stevie laughed way too hard than what was called for.

"So Beth, I figured you moved away, haven't seen you around. What're you up to these days?"

"I'm moving back to the area and opening a bookstore right here." She motioned to the bar.

"A bookstore. Here? What, you think the people around here can read?" The two guys snort-laughed.

Stevie spoke for the first time, "Man if you need books, we've got books, a whole truck full. Right here. Take a look."

He walked to the back of the truck and waved his arm like he was revealing King Tut's tomb. Beth hesitantly looked at the books and picked one up. "It's in French." And then looking through several more. "They're all in French."

"Get outta here. French?" Billy shouted into the bar, "Hey Winks, you in there? Your books are in French! You should get your money back." He laughed and gave a little snort.

Stevie said, "I wanted to burn them in my fireplace, give a little heat, you know. But Billy said I couldn't cuzza glue. He said they got glue."

Billy barked, "They do got glue. If you burn 'em, the glue burns, gives off fumes, it'll kill yer family." Beth was right, they were quite a pair.

"Are you bothering the new owner?" Winks walked out wanting to chase away the two clowns.

"Nah, we're trying to give her all these books. But they're in French!" Billy was pleased to reiterate.

Beth continued to look through the books and tried to figure out how to turn them down.

Winks bailed her out. "Guys, nobody wants these nasty books. She can take the ones in the box I have in storage. They're in much better shape."

He turned to Beth. "It'll be my shop-warming gift to you."

Beth smiled. "That's so nice of you. You can leave them in the back. I'll figure out what to do with them. Maybe a foreign language section."

Winks nodded. "OK, well, I best get back at it. Still have some cleaning to do. And these guys have to make it to the dump before it closes."

Winks walked back into the darkened bar. It was unrecognizable. No more pool tables, no more jukebox, that had been updated from records, to tapes, to CDs, to streaming. No more fake paintings by all the masters displayed proudly in cheap plastic frames, no more neon signs given to him by beer companies. It had been quite a ride, and he had the same thoughts that all people who enter a new phase of life do. Have I had an impact? Winks was the guy who was always there when needed. Cab rides paid with petty cash for patrons who had too much fun, extended family that needed help fixing a truck, or to get out of a financial jam, but mostly, he was the guy who hung out with people when they needed a place to be. He saw that as his life work, hanging out with people, talking to them, being there. He hoped he had made an impact on people's lives. For his community, he donated thousands of dollars to charity from his annual "Boink a Bartender" event where customers would throw a beanbag and hit a target which would "boink" the bartender with a foam rubber mallet. The donations made a difference. But the thing that made the biggest impact on his community and indeed the fate of society was buying one box of books too many from a lady in France.

—ε-ε-ε-ε-ε-ε—

Saronda woke up. Oh God, rent day.

She had barely enough to cover her share. She needed a job, any job. She left a note for Danielle to not forget the rent, again. She ate a nice breakfast while scrolling through the comments on the DevilLight posts. Someone created an account that compiled the stats, rolling averages, projections, and pandemic theory calculations. People were even saying DevilLight was contagious. She was amazed at the number of "experts" there were online. Mostly the same people who the week before were "experts" on the effects of tariffs on global inflation.

The hashtag was growing exponentially. People were taking this seriously. Many posts were about brothers, sisters, parents who were living the nightmare. Paying rent and saving society at the same time can put a person in a mood. She walked into Busboys and Poets. Brody was already there.

He barely acknowledged Saronda. He sat tearing a paper napkin into increasingly smaller pieces.

After a bit, he spoke softly but in a manner that revealed an inner rage, "I can't seem to raise Kelso. He won't respond."

This was not something Saronda wanted to hear. Brody was supposed to be handling this. His anger acted as a feedback loop, drawing out her frustration.

She lit a fuse. "Sounds like either maybe you picked the wrong guy, or you haven't figured out how to… "

Imagine how that sounds to a guy that prides himself on reading people and getting things done. Brody snapped. He picked up a table knife and started stabbing the pile of torn napkins.

His tone of voice was throttled rage. "It's not that simple. OK. OK? It's all about Erlang code and multiple threads. You know what? You wouldn't understand so just..."

Imagine how that sounds to someone who prides herself on understanding things.

Saronda snapped back, "If he knows so much, why isn't his code working?"

"I don't know, Saronda. Maybe your fancy article can tell me. Maybe just one more little tidbit about the cosmos, maybe if we could hear one more Whisper."

Saronda glared. "This guy. This guy that *you* found. Code expert extraordinaire. What do you even know about him anyhow? Huh, can you tell me that? You know, maybe if you would've—"

Brody stood and placed both hands on the table, hovering over Saronda. Water spilled.

"That's not it, OK. You got it yet?"

Saronda turned to the side and exhaled. "Dude, just... sit down. Chill. And good morning to you too. What the hell is this all about?"

Brody felt heat rising up his neck and straight to his temples. "It's just—"

He left, marching past Rebecca as she came in. He pulled out his phone and stepped outside.

Imagine what that looked like to someone who was wondering whether to kill her career to help two crazy people.

Rebecca asked, "What is happening? You look like the last one to be picked for kickball and Brody almost knocked me over without saying hi."

Saronda breathed out some tension. "I don't know. Brody's being a jackass. That and my rent is due."

She became more sanguine. "I'm so down. This started out as this nice little cerebral romp through the mind of a woman from long ago. A beautiful, deep mind. As I read her article, I started to see it all come together. These Whispers, if we let them, they'll weave each of us a beautiful reality. This stuff matters to me, Rebecca."

Rebecca set her purse down and took off her long coat. "I can tell. I can feel your passion."

Saronda continued, "I want people to see. It's the beauty I'm after. If what she said is true, oh my God, the beauty it would bring to the world. Instead we're fighting with a code guy and trying to, hell, I don't know what we're trying to do at this point."

Rebecca sat. "I've never heard you talk like this before. I mean we only just met but everything so far has been doom and gloom and this pesky Armageddon. I half expect four horses to come through those doors."

Saronda said, "That's why I'm so frustrated and why Brody is so angry. We need to save the world. But why us?"

—ε-ε-ε-ε-ε-ε—

Brody stood outside and typed aggressively. *"hey assbag you pos. Y are u gaming me"* And then hit delete. The rage continued to build. The fence he had so meticulously built to keep the world from seeing this was missing a plank.

He started typing again. *Call me now. you and me need to talk ON THE PHONE like people did in the early part of this century U prickly prick prick mfer</.*

He was literally sputtering and hit delete again. He looked off in the distance. He was being played for a fool. He needed to talk, actually talk, to Kelso. About things. Important things, up to and including how to prevent the ruination of society. Texting wouldn't do. He tried to breathe normally but his anger wouldn't let him. He felt pulsing in his temples. He started punching the air in all directions and wanted to throw his phone. He turned his head and saw four eyes staring at him.

Saronda elbowed Rebecca. "Looks like a Tai Chi lesson on fast forward." They laughed.

"Come inside, Rebecca's got some ideas."

He followed them inside.

Rebecca started talking as they sat. "Guys, I'm thinking as a mathematician here so don't beat me up."

Brody said, "Nobody said there'd be math. Ha Ha Ha."

There was no humor in his voice, just robotic muscle memory spitting out a stale joke.

Rebecca said, "OK... So, if I understand correctly, we need to keep two realties from colliding. One of those realities is ours. The other we'll call Reality B. OK? Good? If our reality collides with Reality B we'll be roadkill on Reality Highway. Do I have that right?"

She didn't wait for an answer. "Now, to do this we need to nudge Reality B just enough to avoid *our* reality. Correct?"

Brody huffed. "Good plan. Let us know when you've gotten it done."

Saronda jumped in. "C'mon Brody, be nice. What the hell? A more serious answer is, you're right, we need to blast it with energy. We hope that will cause Reality B to change its course."

Rebecca said, "Good, I looked at that and the equations support that theoretically. The energy would need to be at a certain frequency to set up an interference pattern, and we would need to pulse it. But what kind of energy?"

Saronda replied, "Electromagnetic."

Rebecca pulled up the equations she had saved onto her phone. "Guys, give me some quiet time. I want to study some more."

She moseyed outside, looking at the equations on her phone and then tapped the calculator icon.

Brody turned to Saronda. "Look, I'm sorry I flipped. I mean, it's embarrassing. And that poor napkin. Did they give it a good burial?"

"It's OK, Brody, that's just you. You're intense sometimes. I like that about... I mean, that's good. It's a good thing."

Rebecca came back in, still staring at her phone. "Guys, I think I can use these equations to calculate what we need. But, I'm a little confused on *changing* reality versus *moving* reality. I'll do some noodling on that."

Saronda glared at Brody. "And code, we need code."

The heat in Brody's temples came back and he growled through his teeth, "Dammit I need to get Kelso to *answer my texts.*"

Saronda glanced at her phone. "Oh my God, guys, we made the evening news!"

Her Twitter feed had a sponsored ad: *News4: Watch Tonight as We Dig Into #DevilLight. What is it? What does it mean?*

Brody sat up in his chair. "That's it! That's what I need."

Four eyes stared back.

"I'm going to go chase that little woodchuck prick right out of his hole."

—ε-ε-ε-ε-ε-ε—

Kelso sat at his terminal.

A text lit up his phone: *YOU MADE IT ONTO THE NEWS TONIGHT.*

The fear center of Kelso's brain ignited. People who do the kind of work Kelso does aren't supposed to be in the news. It's a lesson he learned when he orchestrated a smear campaign against the college president who had him expelled. Smear campaigns need to be conducted from deep in the bowels of the system, not in the public eye.

He looked at his dog. "What kind of *all caps* hoodiddle is this? How can I be on the news when I don't exist?" He showed the phone to Kaz.

Kaz climbed off the chair he had commandeered and sauntered away.

Kelso typed an angry text: *PiCK UP YOUr PHOne.*

Kelso was already talking when Brody answered. "What do you mean, on the news?"

"Hashtag DevilLight. Our little project together? Remember? Well, everyone's talking about hashtag DevilLight."

"What is that, Twitter? Facebook?"

"Twitter, you should go on sometime. It's fun."

Kelso shook his head. *If this little twit knew what I've done with Twitter.*

He clicked on his list of computer generated Twitter accounts. They were real accounts and each one tweeted often, but it was all Artificial Intelligence (AI). They detect conspiracy theories and amplify them by creating comments that act as seeds. The seeds rile up online arguments. They then measure sincerity. If the arguments were sincere, the comments were probably true, and the hashtag *wasn't* ripe for conspiracy. But if people respond with cynical half-truths and twisted facts, the bots jump on it and feed the narrative. People start to believe, and a full-blown disinformation campaign is born. Some of these AI-fed campaigns hook a lot of people. Kelso gets paid by the number of believers.

But #DevilLight had been ignored by his bots.

He asked Brody, "What does this hashtag mean?"

"It's the episodes I've been having."

"Oh yes, Mr. Prodromal, how could I forget? How are you? I should have taken the time to ask. I believe it's important to build a connection with those you work with."

Kelso surveyed the screen. Hashtag DevilLight had thousands of comments. None of them were generated by his AI or anyone else's.

He squinted and leaned in. *Why didn't my bots jump on this?*

Kelso said softly, "Sincerity is through the roof."

"Excuse me? You're mumbling."

Kelso said, "I was looking through this hashtag you gave me. This is a very interesting thing you brought to my attention."

"Each of those people are suffering. They hop in and out of another reality."

Kelso tuned him out. DevilLight needed no help from bots. The sincerity was the highest Kelso had ever seen. *This is not a conspiracy.*

He asked a non-sequitur, "How does this hashtag relate to the twenty-five thousand computers?"

"Dammit Kelso, we've been through this." Brody jumbled his words. "We need to use those equations to change reality, move it. We need to move Reality B so it doesn't collide—"

Kelso stopped listening at "change reality."

Brody's voice droned on, "And so if we use what I sent you and plug that into the equations, it should be enough to..."

"Enough to do what?"

Brody's voice dropped to the background. "To move Reality B so it misses ours."

There was a lot going on in Kelso's head. *I've got access to thousands of government computers, trance inducing equations, a viral hashtag based on nonsense, but the bots said, "nope, not nonsense."*

"This is all so very interesting."

Brody exploded. "Dammit Kelso, is it interesting enough to get that fuc— code working? You said you'd have code by now. I'm wondering if you even know what you're doing. And then all this secrecy. Why do we need secrecy if we're trying to save the world?"

"To answer your question, yes this is interesting enough to continue. And I will make progress."

"We need to try out these parameters—"

"Send them to me. The parameters. I'll plug them in."

Kelso disconnected.

—ε-ε-ε-ε-ε-ε—

Brody needed air.

He went into the hallway. He was hit by a fog of light.

But it wasn't fog this time. It was a viscous mass gnawing at his soul gripping him with a spiritual pain. It made a sinewy path deep within him, tearing at his core, leaving him empty. His brain spiraled into a mental discord that left him disoriented.

He was exposed. He willed himself back to his room, away from prying eyes, inquisitive stares.

He was defeated. "Mom, my 98 is not good enough to stop this thing."

He was soulless. He crawled into bed, once again alone. Oh so lonely. His feeling of isolation, of believing he was the only one who could fix this was replaced by doubt. He turned onto his side and stared at the clock on the nightstand watching as the blue numbers changed. *Someone figured out how to light up some blue dots, put it in a box eight thousand miles away, and have it end up on my nightstand just so I could know what time it is, and I can't even get a guy to bang out a few lines of code so I can save the world.* He pulled his knees to his chest, his arms held tightly around his ribs.

"Wrap yourself in confidence until you figure out how to be useful."

"What do I wrap myself in to get this guy to write some code?"

He called Rebecca. "I need the parameters you calculated."

"Brody. It's late."

"I know what time it is. I really need those parameters. Like now. Not later. *Now.*"

"OK. OK. Which ones? I have the ones for changing reality and the ones for moving Reality B."

"Just give me both. I want both. I need to send them to Kelso."

She sounded excited. "Did you talk to him? What did you find out? Is he on the up and up? Do you think it's smart to send him everything? We don't know much about—"

"Just... Please. Send the—"

"Alright, OK, let me double check them and I'll send you a text. Get some rest. Sheesh."

Brody hung up without saying goodbye.

He texted Kelso. *will have parameters soon. CALL ME NOW so we're clear on what we need to do.*

Brody waited. Kelso didn't call.

He texted Kelso again: *???*

Brody waited a long time.

His phone buzzed with a text from Rebecca with the parameters to plug in. He texted them to Kelso.

Immediate reply: *Don't use text for this. VPN next time.*

"Jagoff." He fell into a hollow sleep.

—ε-ε-ε-ε-ε-ε—

Kelso had connected the computers to Brody's Code days earlier. He was an expert at that type of thing. In fact, he was the one who originally wrote that part of Brody's Code for Wayne. But what he was really good at was sending signals through the web without being detected. It's important that the lies not be traceable. It's part of the reason his smear campaign against the college president went so horribly wrong.

Kelso fired up the code.

```
SockItToMe_ver1.32
module(sockittome_1.32)
export([start/0])
```

The computers sprang to life, chewing on the calculations. As the calculations ran, he tackled how to pulse the wireless cards. He logged into a spare computer and started going through the BIOS of the wireless card. He found the setting for frequency but there was no hook into the code that he could use to change it, so he made one.

The calculations finished. Frequency: 213.4 megahertz. Pulse rate: 12 per second. The 12 per second wasn't a problem but the frequency of 213.4 megahertz was thousands of times slower than modern wireless cards.

Kelso looked to his dog for guidance. "What do you think? Can we slow these cards down?"

Kaz did not reply.

"Nice, good thoughts, you useless pile of fur. But while you're listening. If I can get this to work, pulse things just right, I can change reality."

"But first, old boy, I got this whining bastard

griping that reality will cease to exist or something. That could be a real setback."

Kaz moved to the other side of the room. He often reacted that way to Kelso's attempts at humor.

He typed in 213.4 megahertz and fired the wireless card.

Kaz jumped up and ran to the door. He arched his back and dropped his head low and started shaking.

"Whattsa matter, can you hear that? No way, this is way above your range."

Kelso hadn't considered the undertones created by his hack that were in the upper range of dog hearing.

"OK OK, I'll shut it off."

"Let's hope there's no dogs anywhere near those twenty-five thousand computers I'm about to blast. Can you imagine? Twenty-five thousand computers blasting this out all at once."

He made a bologna sandwich with yellow mustard on white bread and watched as all twenty-five thousand three-hundred and two computers came online, complete with the new BIOS.

"Nothing left to do but try it out."

He blasted the pulses into the internet. Nothing happened.

—ε-ε-ε-ε-ε-ε—

Except, something did happen. Twenty-five hundred miles to the east, a little square checkbox on a computer screen lit up red.

Yasmin Roth stared at the 110-inch monitor on the wall. Her eyes darted back and forth. She checked her tablet. She took a sip of coffee. It had gotten cold. She considered pouring a fresh cup, but she couldn't pull herself away. *Yes, the system worked as designed. Yes, the algorithm functioned to protocol. No, it didn't make sense with any of the other data I have. Rats, there's my boss.*

Ray, her boss, walked up behind her.

He pulled up a chair next to Yasmin. "What in God's creation is that?"

The incompleteness of any answer she could possibly give made Yasmin tense.

Yasmin's algorithm routinely created a map of the entire web, watching as information was created and spread around. It compared the information to known facts.

Yasmin said, "I don't know what it is but we need to figure it out quickly. I'm about to issue an RNOT."

"RNOT? Refresh me, no, let me guess. Red Notice—"

Yasmin didn't let him finish. "Yes, Red Notice. High

degree anomaly."

Ray Denmore built his long military career in Field Human Intelligence, or HUMINT, with emphasis on *long*. He started back when pursuing bad guys meant hanging out in seedy parts of the world learning where terrorists lived and how they think. There were only nine others who did what he did, and the job was never listed anywhere. Instead of retiring, Ray built a team to sniff out bad actors who spread lies. He was concerned with the rise in disinformation. He took over a program that no longer existed, the Advanced Aerospace Threat Identification Program (AATIP). Mission: Find UFOs. That's done in other groups now, but Congress passed a law that it had to be funded so Ray converted it to finding people like Kelso who spread conspiracies.

His entire team is Yasmin Roth. Very few know they exist and wouldn't care if they did.

Ray said, "Why RNOT? What's got you spooked?"

"The algorithm detected a mismatch between a Wikipedia page and conventional knowledge."

"So? We see that all the time; people get in there and change things, editors will correct it shortly. What's the big deal with this one?"

Yasmin said, "This one is different. Conventional knowledge says the 1960 World Series was won by the Pittsburgh Pirates. I checked the secure archive, one-hundred percent solid match."

The secure archive is a complete catalog of all accumulated knowledge. It is stored on solid state drives in an underground vault. It's never been online and never will be. It is the closest thing to the pure truth anywhere on Earth. The process to make any changes or additions requires sign-off by a committee.

"1960? You're not going to believe this, but my grandfather went to those games. He talks about it like it was yesterday. Pittsburgh won on a home run in the ninth inning. He tells us the story every time we're together."

"Yes, that's the conventional knowledge stored in the archive, but Wikipedia says the Yankees won."

Yasmin drew Ray's attention to the screen. "Look at this, there were no edits as to the winner of the series. Ever. The Wikipedia page was created in 2002. It started out as a Yankees win, it's still a Yankees win, yet the conventional knowledge archive, and apparently your grandfather, has it as a Pirates win."

"If I follow, someone hacked Wikipedia and deleted all prior edits and time stamps and then changed the facts. That's a hell of a lot of work to change a World Series from what, fifty-five years ago. What's the goal?"

Yasmin continued her analysis. "If you think that's a lot of work, it's not just Wikipedia that says the Yankees won."

"Other sites too?"

"The whole Internet."

Ray pushed his chair back and tried to wrap his mind around this. Hackers change facts on the web, sometimes for fun, sometimes to create conspiracies. Yasmin traces them. She creates a three-dimensional map of how the disinformation got started and how it traveled through the web. For this case, she had nothing, just the fact that the Yankees won a World Series that they lost. There were no changes over time, no controversial discussion groups, no conflicting comments, nothing that would look like seeds of a campaign. And no bad actors.

Ray shifted in his chair. He was about to say something and then stopped. Yasmin read Ray's mind. *One, Two, Three. Let's hold off on the RNOT—*

Ray said, "Hold off on that RNOT, I'm not convinced this is enough to sound an alarm."

Yasmin dropped her shoulders. *OK grandpa.*

—ε-ε-ε-ε-ε-ε—

Brody woke up from an unfulfilling sleep. He texted Kelso: *Call me,* and waited. No response.

Jeez, Kelso, is it too early for you? In a state out west somewhere.

He texted him again and waited. He ordered room service and got in a quick workout at the workout room. His breakfast, and thank God, coffee arrived when he returned. He wondered if Saronda was mad at him for losing his cool and killing a couple napkins.

His phone rang.

"I can't believe you called me back."

"You asked me to."

Brody added this to the things that irked him.

"You know what I want. Is the code working?"

"Yes, of course it is. And I tried some pulsing, nothing happened."

"What do you mean you tried pulsing? Kelso, we have to talk about this first. We're messing with reality here. What exactly did you pulse?"

"I made the calculations and used the frequencies that are supposed to change reality. 213.4 megahertz. Pulse rate 12 with a pattern calculated from those parameters you gave me. It's important, in a working relationship, to give each other independence to try things."

Brody wrote down the numbers. "Change reality? Jeezus, no, we need to use the ones that will keep our reality from colliding. Listen, don't do anything else until we agree, OK?"

"OK. OK, but nothing happened."

Brody tried to remain calm. "It's good that you got the network of computers working but we need to focus on moving Reality B. We have a plan; you need to stick to it. It's dangerous to change reality."

"OK, I'm listening. Tell me what to do. But first, what is Reality B?"

"Maybe you'll get engaged now. Reality B is the other reality that's about to collide with our reality, so we need to... look, we've been through this. You need to make the calculations for moving reality."

"I already did, it's 0.9832 megahertz. Pulse rate 4, with a different pulse pattern. By the way, that's a lot lower than the one to change reality. Does that make sense?"

Brody wrote down the numbers and said with fake authority, "Yes, that makes sense. I want to create this nice gentle wave that will push on Reality B and leave ours alone."

"I will try it."

"But you have to wait until tonight."

"Why?"

Brody was in the zone now. Saronda and Rebecca made great teachers.

He explained to Kelso, "The ionosphere changes at night, it'll let our waves bounce around and travel farther. Do it at two a.m. eastern."

"Two a.m., got it."

The sudden attentiveness of Kelso gave Brody a lift, and some hope. "OK, and all the computers have to pulse at precisely the same time."

"Roger."

"And don't mess around with that other frequency. You don't know what you're doing."

They disconnected. Brody set his phone down and put his head in his hands. He had never been so nervous.

—ε-ε-ε-ε-ε-ε—

Saronda and Rebecca sat at the same table as before. The mid-morning sun streamed through the windows at Busboys and Poets, creating rainbows with their water glasses. Brody was already a half hour late.

Saronda fidgeted. "Come on Brody, where are you? It's not like him to be late."

Rebecca said, "No, he strikes me as someone who is always early. And he's so hyper sometimes."

"Like yesterday." They both laughed.

Saronda said, "God, that was awful. I thought he was going to stab me."

"What? Why?'

"Oh, that was before you got here. He had a knife and was stabbing the bejeezus out of his napkin, I was like, Dude."

Rebecca said, "Yeah, that napkin looked rather beat up when I got here. And wet, was he trying to drown it too?"

Saronda laughed. "I know, right? But I hope he's OK."

"Let's call him."

But Brody couldn't come to the phone right now. It was back, the stifling mass of sinister lights.

Rebecca said, "Huh, no answer. You know I really enjoyed hearing you describe the work by this woman. It sounds like she captured the pulse of the whole human condition."

The fog of lights ensnared him, trapping him in a reality his Whisper wasn't designed for.

Saronda said, "Hmmm, I never thought of it that way, but you're right. The human condition, as you call it, is woven together by our Whispers."

His Whisper was incapable of creating emotions. Emotions require a functioning soul.

"How do our Whispers "know" what to weave?"

He was cut off from the energy of the universe.

Saronda's voice lifted. "There is wisdom in the universe. Our Whispers tap into it making a rich beautiful quilt."

Brody Markovich was smothering in a dark hell able to feel only the most trivial human emotions: anger, spite, rage, hate.

Rebecca said, "I'd love to crawl through the equations to see how it all works. After we fix Brody, and the world, I'd like to work with you on this. The world needs to know it."

Only the darkest parts of his soul had the slightest glowing ember. More planks of the fence fell.

Saronda was jazzed at Rebecca's interest. "Oh, I would love that! We could figure it out together. You with your math skills and me because I can read French!"

"It's more than just reading French, Saronda, you understand this stuff in your bones."

They smiled and clinked water glasses.

"But where the hell is Brody?"

"I'm right here."

It was him but Brody wasn't there.

Saronda said, "You look horrible."

The husk of empty energy representing Brody was wearing a brown shirt, dull orange pants and a blank stare.

"Where did you get those awful clothes?"

He looked down, his already pale face drained to white.

He managed some words. "Must've come over with me."

"Come over?"

Brody's demeanor was cold. "I've been in Reality B."

His eyes were dead, soulless cavities. "The fog of light, it's not light, it's a terrifying, chaotic, smothering mass of—"

Saronda said, "Énergie maléfique."

They both turned to her. "Evil energy. It's when two realities mix."

He sat. "I don't know what it was, but it was like I no longer felt alive, I couldn't feel life. It hurt. It really hurt. There was no beauty."

His voice cracked. "My soul was numb, or not there at all. Something was missing. I couldn't feel—"

Almost under her breath, Saronda said, "Love. You couldn't feel love, love for others, love for yourself, love for life. Your Whisper was in a reality where it wasn't strong enough to weave love."

Saronda continued, "The absence of love. Augustine wrote that the absence of love is not hate. The absence of love is when your conscious mind cannot reconcile with your spirit. You can't temper your basic physical emotions like rage, anger, or hate. It is an angry state where you have no flow, no lightness, no feeling of self-worth, just a deep rage. You are no longer able to see beauty. Grievance is all you have. Without love, your rage at the inherent unfairness of reality suffocates you, it tears at your soul."

They sat for a long time.

Rebecca said, "We're headed for a world without love or beauty or any of the things that make life worth living. We'll be captives of fear and hate."

Brody had nothing to add because Brody had nothing. His spirit was incomplete.

—ε-ε-ε-ε-ε-ε—

Kelso got everything ready for launch. He dialed in the calculated numbers: 0.9832 megahertz with a pulse rate of 4 and loaded in the pulse pattern.

It felt strange trying to save the world, when watching it burn would be so much more fun. But, if you're not the one making it burn, what's the use? He made a dummy test run without firing the wireless cards to make sure everything was set and led his dog out into the night air.

"Kaz, buddy, I think we're onto something. Playing with reality. The possibilities. C'mon finish up, I wanna go back inside. It's cold."

—ε-ε-ε-ε-ε-ε—

Brody was nothing but inner rage and anger. The fence was failing him. *Fuck this reality shit.* The unfairness of it all consumed him. He was a snarling ball of pettiness, fighting like hell to feel normal again. He wanted to lash out at Saronda and Rebecca.

He said, "Look, I've got very little energy. We don't have much time."

Rebecca said, "Did you talk to Kelsey?"

Brody said, "It's Kelso. Yes, he's going to pulse the cards."

Saronda shot upright. "He is? Did you tell him to do it at night?"

"Yes."

Rebecca went staccato. "Did you tell him to pulse each card at exactly the same time? Like truly, precisely, no deviation, but exactly?"

"Yes."

"Did he calculate the frequency and pulse rate?"

"Yes."

"What are they?"

Brody fumbled through his pockets. "Uh, I wrote them down. Maybe they're in my other pants."

"Where are your other pants?"

"Must be in Reality B, but I never took them off so…"

Saronda tried a little Brody humor. "It's never a good sign when you lose your pants."

Brody responded, "I came close once. I got back to my dorm room in college and when I took off my shoes, I was missing a sock."

Rebecca said, "Brody's back!"

He wasn't but the fence was.

—ε-ε-ε-ε-ε-ε—

Kelso and Kaz stepped back inside and shook the snow off. Kelso couldn't stop thinking about what had fallen into his lap. He was good at distorting reality but changing it would be colossal. He made one last check on the launch and then pulled an old computer out of a drawer. He logged into a special portal and went through the three-step authentication which included opening a chat session with a live watchman who generated a six-digit number and sent it to Kelso's phone.

He entered the number, and typed: "Hello Raster, it appears you are on watch tonight."

A document appeared on the screen with the notification "Read Access granted for 12 minutes."

Kelso typed: "Requesting permission to edit." There were only five people on Earth who could edit the document and only under the watchful eyes of the person standing guard. Raster, real name, Yancy Pyotrov, sent another six-digit number to Kelso.

"Write Access granted for 11 minutes."

Kelso scrolled past the title, "Ultimate Lies," and pulled up the appropriate section of the eight page manifesto. He typed: "I am confident we can achieve at least P90. New method for changing facts to be detailed later. Also, found a new source of money. Old acquaintance is sweating about insider trading. Should be able to acquire much capital."

Raster immediately chastised Kelso for putting money talk and identifiers into the manifesto. He removed the offending sentences about the shake down. Kelso logged off.

They would be horrified to know they weren't the only ones with eyes on the document.

—ε-ε-ε-ε-ε-ε—

Yasmin Roth laughed at the elaborate security steps they made Kelso crawl through. Months prior, she had found a backdoor into the manifesto and had been watching ever since. Their plans for using disinformation were well thought out and were as brilliant as they were sinister, but she could never tie them to any overt nefarious activity. She took a few instances to her general counsel, but it was ruled that they fell within First Amendment rights. And even at that, she didn't know who or where they were. She knew four of the five were in an unknown country overseas and one was in the U.S.

She watched their manifesto closely, getting an alert every time they changed something. Kelso's new entry was a game changer. Getting to P90 would be catastrophic. P90 meant ninety percent of a population would ultimately believe a conspiracy theory. The best they can do is P30. While that was enough sometimes to sway an election, cause political unrest, or get someone in authority ousted by a fake scandal, it wasn't enough to overthrow a democracy, at least not quickly. P90 would be devastating to even the strongest democracy. Authoritarianism would win. Yasmin took Kelso's comment seriously.

The manifesto provided very few cues about its origin. It was written in English but much of it was written by someone whose first language was most likely from one of the Balto-Slavic languages. Other parts were written by an American with some western Pennsylvania grammar structure leaving out infinitives or gerunds in calls to action. One stood out to her and still makes her laugh. "This section needs removed." Other than that, not much was known.

She heard Ray Denmore walk in. He threw his jacket over a chair. "Good morning. Anything noteworthy?"

Yasmin crowed, "Manifesto 2015_3 showed activity."

"And?"

"They think they know how to reach P90."

"That would be quite a trick, what's their plan?"

"They think they can change facts."

"Change facts?"

Yasmin chirped, "Like what we saw yesterday with the World Series."

"Is it related?"

She pointed to her summary on the screen. "Yesterday, we got a signal worthy of an RNOT because facts were changed, all the way back to forever, on the entire Internet. Then, a manifesto we've been watching is edited to include… "

Ray scanned the rest of the summary. "P90. Incredible. I'll take it from here, your shift is over, go rest up."

"Should I issue the RNOT?" *Just say yes.*

"No, let's hold off. These things have to be handled delicately."

Yasmin shook her head and left. When she was out of range, she sneered, "These things have to be handled delicately."

Ray studied the data and called an old cohort at the FBI, who answered on the first ring. "This better be important or I'll put a foot so far up your ass you'll get heartburn."

Ray played along. "Are you still the pompous ass you've always been?"

"Are you still a supreme waste of time?"

"Is it a waste of time to save our democracy?"

"Alright dickweed, what's this about?"

Ray Denmore and Greg Laneer spent many years chasing bad guys, saving lives, and occasionally saving each other's ass. Greg was now a senior special agent reporting to the Assistant Director of the Cyber Division, FBI. He still chased bad guys but now it was through the Internet. He had tools Ray didn't have. One was the ability to get subpoenas. Another was the ability to arrest a person of interest. Ray brought him up to speed on what he saw in the data.

"I don't know, Ray, that's all very interesting but these guys are surely using TOR so we would need a warrant."

"But Greg, you must be slipping in your old age. You didn't ask me how I got around TOR to see their manifesto."

The senior agent replied, "You're damn right I didn't ask. How many unlawful search statutes did you violate? Do I even want to know?"

"Settle down, we entered through a backdoor so wide open that we convinced our counsel it was public information!"

"So, these guys are idiots."

"Idiots at security maybe, but these idiots may have stumbled onto something that could bring us to our knees."

"Tell me more, just don't tell me anything I'll have to turn you in for."

"Well, you sure have become buttoned up."

"It's all about surviving 'til retirement, Ray, now fill me in on what I need to know, and nothing more."

—ε-ε-ε-ε-ε-ε—

The day crawled. Waiting until night was the right thing to do technically but emotionally, it was a killer.

Saronda walked into the Union Pub at 1:42 a.m.

Brody was already there. "Tonight's the night I get rid of the fog."

"Yeah, and we get rid of you whinin' about it."

Brody was a bag of adrenaline. "Ha Ha."

"We are going to kick Reality B right in the—"

"Squishy balls."

"You mean boules malléables de forme irrégulière."

"A oui oui."

Their giggles of excited optimism mixed with nervous doubt.

Rebecca walked in and removed her scarf and gloves. "What are you guys laughing about?"

Brody said, "Tonight we get rid of this nightmare."

Rebecca looked over and asked, "What is the clock radio for?"

Brody's nervous system buzzed in his voice.

He grabbed the radio and carried it like a football. "That reminds me, we need to find a place to plug this in."

He trotted to the bar dragging the cord behind him. "Excuse me, where can I plug this in?"

The bartender pointed. Brody swung around, the cord flying. "Where? Here?"

Saronda said, "Brody, settle down, over at the wall."

He skipped over to the table and set it down.

He plugged it in and looked over his shoulder. "Remember I couldn't find the frequencies because they were in my other pants that I lost in Reality B? Well, I found the paper in my room. Must not have put it in my pants. It was an end-of-days miracle! I still haven't found my pants though."

Rebecca looked at Saronda. "He is wired."

Saronda nodded.

The two women high fived.

Brody's entire existence was the remaining scraps of humanity left by the episodes. It was enough to keep the fence propped up and nothing more.

Saronda asked, "But dude, seriously, what's the radio for?"

"I googled the frequency, It's in the middle of the —"

Saronda finished his sentence. "The AM radio spectrum."

Brody piped up, "Yep. We'll be able to hear the pulses on the radio."

Rebecca chimed in, "Pulses on the radio. I danced to that song in the nineties."

Saronda groaned, "Oh no, do we have two Brodys now?"

They double high fived.

"But that's clever with the radio. Way to go Brody. Wished I would have thought of that."

He tuned the radio to 0.9832 Mhz. The closest broadcast to that frequency, TalkRadio 980, was a mess of fuzzy static. It was a late-night sports talk show that drifted in and out. Through the scratchiness they barely made out a heated argument about who won the seventh game of a World Series.

Brody couldn't sit. "Now we wait. Eight minutes, counting down."

At one minute to two the bartender came over and asked if they needed anything. They waved him off. They were staring at the radio listening to horrendous static.

Then, a few seconds after two a.m. EST the radio blasted the most obnoxious growling and pulsing. The bartender barely escaped injury as three people burst into jumping around and dancing like it was the first launch of the space shuttle.

Saronda said matter of factly, "It's happening. Kelso came through. Take that Reality B."

Brody felt a sense of vengeance. He shouted, "Reality B, you're our bitch now."

Rebecca turned down the radio. "Wow, that sound is brutal. I guess that's what it sounds like when you move reality."

It was music to their ears. It was something they had worked on and thought about nonstop for weeks. The sense of relief overwhelmed Brody. He had never felt this way before. He succeeded, fully.

He said, "Mom, I got a hundred."

Saronda gave him a quizzical look.

He said, "One small step for us, one giant leap for reality."

He tried to make it sound like Neil Armstrong, but there was too much lift in his voice.

Saronda filled in the details. "Guys, we changed the course of reality itself. Think about how strange that sounds. A month ago we didn't even know where reality came from and now we just—."

Rebecca couldn't resist. "Kicked its ass."

Saronda laughed. "God, Rebecca, I didn't know you have a sassy side. Somebody needs to keep an eye on you. But you know what, I can't wait to watch that nasty hashtag DevilLight melt away. And Brody, no more episodes, OK?"

"Oh yeah, no more of those, definitely. But I really need to thank you two. Saronda, the way you dug into that article and digested all the weird stuff that lady wrote. Wow, and your passion for the content. I think this is your new calling. Rebecca, your math help with the equations put us over the top in getting this done. Oh, and for putting your neck out at the SEC."

Brody went on. "Tomorrow, after we've rested, I want to get started on the GeneraCur case. Let's use those twenty-five thousand computers you found to get that done. Maybe even salvage our careers."

Saronda looked at Brody. "But Brody, we need to thank you. You're a crazy nut but you drove us. You created the plan and, honestly, how you got Kelso to do the code, dude, you could sell cheese to a Chinese restaurant. How much are you paying him anyhow?"

"Not a dime."

Rebecca chimed in, "What's wrong with you guys? We should be celebrating! We did something that we thought was impossible just a few days ago."

Brody said with fake snark, "Speak for yourself, I knew we had this thing the whole time. No sweat."

Rebecca said, "That's not the tune you were singing earlier. You looked like hell and didn't even know where your pants were." The two ladies laughed.

He got serious. "Yeah, never again. The lightness I feel right now. I never want it to go away."

"Rebecca's right. Let's celebrate!" Saronda noticed they were the only customers in the place.

The bartender was acting busy, putting away glassware, wishing the crazies would leave.

Saronda asked, "Are you closing?"

"Yes, please."

Rebecca threw her arms open wide. "But we just saved humanity from a terrible fate. We saved beauty. We saved love. We need champagne!"

The bartender didn't play along. "Does this look like a place that serves champagne?"

"Got it. We'll come back some day so you can thank us for saving the world!" She waved her arms in the air as her voice boomed.

Brody threw a bunch of cash on the table the way people do when they're feeling on top of the world.

"That should cover it."

"But we didn't order anything."

"I know, I always wanted to do that."

They laughed. It felt good to laugh. They felt close like the cast of a play at the closing night after-party.

The bartender said, "You guys are something else, you've been the funnest closers I've had in a while. Don't forget your radio."

He ushered them out. It was early morning on a cold December Tuesday. A bitter cold that none of them felt. They were too filled with the excitement of what they had done. They didn't want the night to end.

Saronda pulled out her phone. "And, DevilLight is officially... oh shit. Not dropping. Dammit, it's still going up."

The pall that fell over them was immediate and devastating.

Rebecca started talking randomly, "Maybe my parameters were incorrect. I need to go home and check them. But that can't be, everything made sense. Maybe I misunderstood. I feel like..."

Saronda said nothing.

Brody said with half conviction, "It's early, give it a chance."

—ε-ε-ε-ε-ε-ε—

Yasmin added "severe radio frequency interference 02:00AM EST" to her database of unexplained incidents. She conjured up an image of one of her counterparts at the FCC pulling out their presentation on sun flares which they would no doubt be delivering to some high-level director. Sun flares, it's always sun flares.

She stepped outside to watch the sunrise. It was the only perk of working the night shift. That and getting a good parking spot. The cold air perked her up. With renewed energy, she went back inside to finish her proposal to convince her boss to issue an RNOT. She would soon find out her proposal was unnecessary. Ray Denmore had something different in mind. Her proposal was up on the big screen as her boss walked in.

"Good morning, Yasmin. I think I figured out what I'm getting my wife for Christmas, there's this purse, well, it's a giant leather bag... What's that you have on the screen?"

"Ray, this is something I feel strongly about." Her

rehearsed words showed signs of nervousness. "I have taken the initiative to label what these guys wrote in their manifesto as "S,U" serious and urgent. Their high confidence in being able to change facts—"

"Ah, you're wanting an RNOT. I'm way ahead of you. I called the FBI."

"FBI?"

"Yeah, but he doesn't think we have enough to get a warrant. They haven't committed a crime and, you know, saying you can change facts is not probable cause. It's like me saying I can steal the moon."

Yasmin's head was spinning. FBI? This isn't a legal matter, at least not yet. It was more of a matter of national security.

"If we're going to an outside agency, shouldn't it be DHS? FBI has to jump through hoops to do anything, it could take months. By then it could be too late."

Ray countered, "Have you ever seen how long it takes to initiate a counterintelligence probe at DHS? Glacial. Besides, we need the FBI to do searches, arrest these clowns. FBI is trained for this, but they need probable cause."

Yasmin thought through the data. "I don't know if this is anything but there's something I captured before they deleted it. I didn't show you before, but they claim to be extorting someone for money. Isn't that wire fraud or conspiracy or something?"

"Maybe, let's run it up the flagpole. Do you have time to sit on a call with me to my buddy at the FBI?"

It was way past her shift change but what a stupid question. She wouldn't miss it for the world. Ray was finally getting serious about these bad actors.

—ε-ε-ε-ε-ε-ε—

The blast of the wireless cards did nothing.

A heaviness filled Brody. He cringed thinking the fog of lights could come back at any moment. He got to his room and looked out the window. The sun was already coming up.

His phone rang: K Rad.

"Hello Kelso."

"Did I do good?"

"You did what you were supposed to but it didn't work."

"How do you know?"

"Take a look at DevilLight. Growing more than ever. Look, I've been thinking. Are you sure you pulsed the computers all at the same time?"

"Yes, two o'clock."

"I mean precisely at the same time." There was a desperation in Brody's voice.

"Yes, I sent the signal to all the computers at the same time." He was defiant.

All hope left Brody, the theories they were so confident about, the brilliant idea of "hey let's blast it with wireless cards, and nudge it a little," they were fairy tales that made them feel good. He felt naive, not appreciating the complexity. Maybe they should have sounded the alarm, called up MIT or someone. Maybe smarter people would have gone down a different path and could have stopped all this. Maybe one of those people who always got a hundred out of a hundred.

He said dejectedly. "We may be back to the drawing board."

The call disconnected.

"Hello. Hello? What the hell?" Brody fumed. He set his phone down and closed the drapes.

—ε-ε-ε-ε-ε-ε—

Kelso looked at his terminal. "Kaz, my friend. I may have overlooked a detail. I believe I'll run a little test."

He pinged each computer and measured how long it took to get a return signal.

"Kaz, that's amazing, there's a huge lag time until some of these computers get my signal. Some get it right away, others are almost half a second later. It's because of TOR."

TOR is a method for hiding the origin of an internet signal. It bounces the signal through a thousand servers. The path is so mixed up, prying eyes can't trace back to the origin. It's like taking planes, trains and automobiles through Beijing and Paris to get to the grocery store down the block. It adds a lot of travel time but it confuses the hell out of anyone tracing you. He turned off TOR and sent the signals to get a baseline comparison.

"OK dog, now for some math."

Using the data, he calculated how to adjust for lag time so each wireless card would get his signal at precisely the same time.

—ε-ε-ε-ε-ε-ε—

Yasmin sat quietly as Ray and Greg talked through how to justify a warrant. She had presented her idea of using the sentences about extortion to get a warrant. She hesitated because it was a document she shouldn't have been hacking into in the first place, but she was running out of ideas on how to nail these guys.

Greg said, "Look guys, I've been at the FBI for a while now, everything has to be done by the book. If we don't have something specific, this could go sideways if it ever gets to court. Now I'll say one thing, if we knew their location and could tie it to these unexplained incidents. That might get us somewhere."

Ray said, "That would be nice, but we haven't been able to trace them. They are TOR'd up to the max."

Greg said, "How quaint, the FBI cracked TOR a long time ago. But we can't trace through TOR without a warrant. It's protected communication."

Yasmin noticed a notification on her tablet. "What about a signal that doesn't use TOR?"

Greg responded, "That's considered a public display. It's fair game to trace it."

Yasmin showed Ray her tablet. "I just got an open signal that may be related. In fact, sorry, negate that... I have twenty-five-thousand-three-hundred-and-two signals, all coming out of the same location. Hold up, at precisely the same time. I'm sorry, stand by."

Yasmin was starting to ramble. She kicked herself for not waiting until she had firmed up the facts before speaking up. She sensed Ray's impatience.

She quickly scrolled through the data. "It came from... hold on, let me pull up Google Maps."

Yasmin paused to double-check the coordinates. Ray sighed noticeably and she could hear Greg typing on his keyboard.

Come on, computer, hurry up. Oh God, this can't be right.

"It came from, well this is weird, it looks like a small cinder block building on Schenley Drive in Pittsburgh. Let me zoom in."

She consciously calmed her breathing. "Honestly, it looks like a public restroom near a carousel. Let me dig into this."

Greg and Ray proceeded with small talk. *Thank God, they ignored me.*

"Holy shit—" She felt her face flush. "I'm sorry, I usually don't swear. I can't believe I said that."

Ray relieved her awkwardness. "That's alright, I'm prouduvya. What you got?"

Yasmin composed herself. *This is so cool.*

Her voice lifted. "The origin of the signal is where Forbes Field used to be."

Ray sat up. "That's where they played the seventh game of the 1960 World Series."

"Yep!" *I love my job.*

Ray leaned in and surveyed the Google Maps displayed on the big screen. "It looks like a park now. Hard to believe that fifty-five years ago, a guy hit a Series winning home run, like, right there. And now, here we are."

Yasmin spoke with confidence. "That historical event is now under dispute. The committee is being asked to update the conventional knowledge archives."

"Dammit, we need to stop these guys before they change something big like—"

Greg broke in. "Uh, you do know I'm still here, right? Can you tell me what's got you twirling your mustache?"

Ray said, "The winner of the 1960 World Series. That's the changed fact that kicked this whole thing off. Now we have a location for the signal and a direct tie-in."

Greg deadpanned, "Lady and gentleman, am I to believe we are raiding a public restroom?"

"That's my read on it. Let's start the process." Ray ended the call.

Ray mouthed to Yasmin, "Good job," and gave the thumbs up.

Yasmin couldn't believe she was actually helping to chase down bad guys. She also couldn't believe she said shit in front of her boss.

—ε-ε-ε-ε-ε-ε—

The noon sun made a direct hit on Brody's room. He had no idea what time it was. His clock radio was still unplugged from last night and he didn't have the motivation to reach over to his phone. Besides, if he picked up his phone, he wouldn't be able to resist looking at the hashtag stats every ten seconds. It was increasing faster than ever. Reality B was about to make a direct hit. The tormenting spiritual pain was draining. He thought of calling his parents to tell them all was lost and that he had tried. And, that he loved them. But the pain gripped him. He couldn't understand how anything could be so painful and not kill you. His Whisper was giving all it had but couldn't weave a complete pattern. It left out a few things. Like love. And now it seemed, hope.

He thought maybe it was time for some food, but he was exhausted.

He texted Kelso: *Call me* and waited.

Kelso did not respond.

He texted: *Call me, we need to figure out how to fix this.*

Kelso did not respond.

He typed: *WE NEED TO TALK* and then leaned hard on backspace delete until it was gone.

He fell into bed.

—ε-ε-ε-ε-ε-ε—

Kelso marched ahead with his timing test. Little green dots on his screen lit up one by one, a matrix of twenty-five-thousand-three-hundred-and-two little boxes. Each light lit at a slightly different time in proportion to their lag time.

He used a high precision timer app that synced to GPS and his computer. He set it for two a.m. EST.

He texted Brody: *alls well. Will do it again tonight. Two am.*

Smug, dismissive, clueless.

—ε-ε-ε-ε-ε-ε—

Ray answered his phone. "This better be important or I'll put my foot so far up your ass your teeth will get toe fungus."

Greg said, "Ha Ha Ha. Nice try. You never were very good at that sort of thing. But, are you ready to storm a restroom?"

Ray replied, "Tell me."

"The raid is on, six a.m. tomorrow, we are taking that bathroom down, I tell ya. As my son would say, 'It'll be epic.'"

Ray asked, "So do you have to use female agents to do the ladies side? I mean you guys have so many friggin' rules over there."

"You know, actually that's a good question, I'll need to check on that. But hey, there's more. I may be able to shut down their router, if I can show imminent threat."

"You mean take them offline?"

Greg boasted, "More than that, we can fry their equipment."

"Through the Internet?"

Greg admitted, "It's new. We're not allowed to use it, yet. Maybe this will be a first. If this goes through, we shut them down at midnight, no internet for them! Sorry, do not pass go."

Ray signed off. "Sounds great, how can I help?"

—ε-ε-ε-ε-ε-ε—

Brody woke up for the millionth time. He hadn't left his room all day. He made his way to the side table and found his phone. 9:42 p.m. He set an alarm so he wouldn't miss the two a.m. blast. Four hours and eighteen minutes until Kelso said he would try again.

He texted Kelso and waited. No response. Not at all confidence inspiring.

—ε-ε-ε-ε-ε-ε—

"What's taking so long? We're running out of time." Greg glared at Edgar Empecher.

Edgar was the night clerk for DoJ requests. There's a clerk, a judge, and DoJ counsel on call 24/7 to handle emergency filings. It's supposed to be a lightning process if you have all your affairs in order.

Edgar reviewed the request. "Wait just a minute, you know how this goes. I have to check everything before I can send it on, everything by the book, like it's always been."

"Jeezus, you're talking like you're on the *Andy Griffith Show*."

Edgar was old enough to have been a grandfather in that show.

Ray leaned in and said quietly to Greg, "What's the

hurry? If we don't get it by midnight, we'll shut them down at one or two in the morning."

"No, you don't understand, if we don't get it by midnight, it gets kicked into tomorrow's requests, and you know, more eyes than just..."

He nodded toward Edgar who licked his fingers and turned to page two of the filing. He had the air of an expiring sloth.

"The day staff looks at things a lot closer, if you know what I mean, and we'll miss a whole day. I want to get it done tonight. I'll keep at it. Edgar will come through. I'll keep riding him."

"Thanks for doing this, Greg. I appreciate it."

Never has anyone worked so diligently to unknowingly prevent four people from saving the world.

—ε-ε-ε-ε-ε-ε—

If Saronda thought she was going to sleep, she was mistaken. Not a chance. She actually found herself reaching out to Danielle, her roommate, who was flipping through channels.

"Danielle, we haven't seen each other for a while."

"Well, you're never around. Have you found a new job?"

"No, but I need to start looking, not sure where next month's rent is coming from."

She could tell from Danielle's face that she forgot to pay again.

"Really, Danielle, again?"

She started to rant, but then thought, this could be the last day the world is right-side up.

Instead, she said, "Do you want to come with me tonight? My friends and I are having an End-Of-The-World Watch Party Part Two."

Saronda hid her deep depression.

Danielle stared at the TV. "I love parties. It's got a cool name. When do we go?"

"Oh, it's not until late, leave here around one thirty."

Danielle looked at her. "That's a weird time for a party."

"We have to let the ionosphere uncharge first."

Danielle nodded. "Right, yeah."

—ε-ε-ε-ε-ε-ε—

"Dammit Edgar, it's 11:42. What the hell is taking so long?"

Ray said, "Greg, please. There's always tomorrow."

—ε-ε-ε-ε-ε-ε—

Saronda walked briskly in the cold, early morning air.

Danielle tried to catch up. "Where we headed again?"

Saronda said back over her shoulder "It's a place called Union Pub. They're known for their pickle martinis."

Danielle puckered her face. "Eww'"

"Oh yeah, they're nasty."

Danielle said, "I'll bet. I can fake like them if you want. By the way, is it really the end of the world?"

"Could be."

"Nice."

Three stops later, they walked out of the Metro and had a full view of the Capitol all lit up.

Brody and Rebecca were already at Union Pub.

"Hi, this is my roommate Danielle. Danielle, this is Brody and Rebecca."

Brody plugged in the radio. It was already set for the right frequency from the night before. Tonight it was a static filled religious talk show discussing 1 Corinthians 13:13.

"Alright guys, three minutes." They didn't have the same electricity as the previous night.

Rebecca said, "So, all you have is that one text from Kelso that everything would be OK?"

Brody's clenched jaw was his answer.

The young bartender sauntered over and asked Danielle, "So what's supposed to happen?"

Danielle answered, "I don't know. But it might be really cool."

The trio of reality warriors stared at the radio. Danielle and the bartender glanced at each other.

Danielle whispered, "Everyone's so glum."

They all leaned in. Two a.m. Nothing.

—ε-ε-ε-ε-ε-ε—

Kelso stared at the screen. No green dots. Kaz's deep breathing as he slept was the only sign of life.

It hadn't been a good night. Kelso had frantically worked through a series of setbacks. At T minus two hours to blast, his internet went down. His system indicated the fiber optic router he installed two thousand miles to the east inside a loose cinder block of a public restroom was dead, useless. Probably fried.

He scrambled and found another router overseas.

He needed permission to connect.

12:37 a.m. EST

He waited.

12:42 a.m. EST

Kelso huffed, "You rumgumptious fools. Please approve. I'm tired of bowing down to fools just to get access."

He waited.

1:08 a.m. EST

Finally, his screen lit up with approval to connect.

1:17 a.m. EST

Kelso went through a long drawn-out security procedure to connect to the new router.

1:43 a.m. EST

As he connected, a checkbox on Yasmin's tablet lit up red. He ran his lag time test again. More lights lit up on Yasmin's tablet.

1:54 a.m. EST.

The test finished.

1:57 a.m. EST.

"Three minutes to blast." Kaz shifted in his sleep.

The timer counted down to exactly 2:00 a.m. EST.

Nothing. No green dots.

Kelso frantically reviewed his terminal. Everything was set. Code was active. Ports were active and matched. Timer was set to go off at exactly...

"Shit."

The part of Idaho he was in is Pacific Time. The timer he downloaded assumed the entire state was mountain time. Details. The timer had another hour left to go. He quickly reset it to go off in one minute. Smooth as silk.

—ε-ε-ε-ε-ε-ε—

2:05 a.m. EST.

They stared at the radio. Just scratchy obnoxious static, every once in a while some words would drift through. "...but the greatest..."

Danielle said, "Why is everybody so bummed? I thought this was a party."

Brody's ears were pinned back, his chest felt heavy. The thought of being consumed by that hateful fog of light again was unbearable. Being let down by Kelso was a punch to the gut.

2:07 a.m. EST. The radio resonated with a harmonious collection of tones and pulses. No one reached to turn it down because it was beautiful, ethereal.

—Ɛ-Ɛ-Ɛ-Ɛ-Ɛ-Ɛ—

Yasmin's tablet lit up.

Twenty-five-thousand-three-hundred-and-two incidents. This time they weren't all at precisely the same time.

Another screen showed a notification: "severe radio frequency interference 2:07AM EST"

—Ɛ-Ɛ-Ɛ-Ɛ-Ɛ-Ɛ—

Kelso sighed, "Whew, time zones." Kaz shifted, yeesh.

—Ɛ-Ɛ-Ɛ-Ɛ-Ɛ-Ɛ—

Danielle and the bartender asked a lot of questions with their eyes as the trio sat quietly, hovering over Saronda's phone for what seemed an eternity.

Danielle turned to the bartender. "Strangest party ever."

Then, Saronda jumped up. "Shout it, guys. Wait for it. We have downtrend, I repeat, we have downtrend."

Rebecca shouted, "Hold your phone still, let me see."

Saronda turned her phone toward everyone.

Brody and Rebecca in unison. "Yes, it's trending down!"

Danielle broke in. "Is down good?"

"Down is very good. DevilLight is going down, Reality B has left the building."

Saronda was up and dancing. Rebecca was up and dancing.

"I feel like singing."

"We need a band." Rebecca kept dancing.

Brody bragged, "I played a little drums in my day. I could beat on the table."

Rebecca looked over. "Really, I played the harp."

"The harp? I've never known anyone who played the harp. Why the harp?"

"So my parents wouldn't make me join marching band."

She was giddy. "Ever tune a harp? A harp is like half a piano turned sideways. 47 strings. Not like those guitar guys who sit on a little stool and twist a few knobs. No, a harp is like you're reaching up and then you're down on all fours."

Saronda caught the giddiness. "I can see you, climbing all over that thing, plucking and turning little knobs and shit and the crowd is like, 'Play us some Dave

Matthews.'"

Brody screwed up his face. "You played harp in a band?"

The trio laughed.

Danielle kicked in; she raised an arm. "Free Bird." The bartender looked at her like she was from another era.

Rebecca continued the vibe. "Not as cool as a guitar."

Brody deadpanned, "I guess that's why guitar players get the girls."

The bartender looked at Danielle. "Are these people high?"

"I think they're fun. I've never seen my roommate like this. She's usually pretty dull."

They were experiencing what it felt like to pull together as a team. They hadn't just hit a home run, they hit a home run through a knot hole in the fence. It felt good to be giddy. Fear and doubt and anger melted away and the pure joy of accomplishment released all at once. Reality B was gone, long live reality. Our reality, the one that our Whispers were meant for.

Rebecca said loudly, "What about the lead singer? I thought they got all the girls."

She looked at Saronda with a knowing look.

Brody went into a thickly accented bit, "Well the lead singer is out front, ya see. Yeah, he's right out in front of all de other clahns on stage. So when da girls start gettin rilly silly drunk, 'nat, they can't see so good, so they just pick da one that's closest. Know whuddah mean? Get it? They're looking at the stage… And they take the one that's da closest."

Saronda and Rebecca were laughing hysterically now.

Rebecca snorted, "Ooh I just peed a little." Then through her laughter, "So do you really think girls do that? Just pick one and let's go!"

Brody gave up the accent. "In my rock and roll fantasy they do."

Danielle came to life. "Huh, my dad always blasts that song. I'm like, 'turn it down boomer' and he's like 'it's all part… of my rock and roll fantasy'."

Danielle sang it with a surprisingly good singing voice.

Saronda said, "You've got a beautiful voice, Danielle Sközy. What song is that?"

"It's by Bad Company. I'm an expert on ancient music. My dad was always blasting music and we would both sing to it, whole songs. We learned all the words. I know a million."

Saronda said, "I've never heard you sing. Why don't

you sing more often?"

"I used to sing a lot and thought about recording some stuff, but I don't know... "

The bartender said, "I'll make you a SoundCloud. I'm in a band with some buddies."

Rebecca looked at Brody. "What are you going to do now that big bad Reality B is out of your life."

"I was thinking we'd nail some bad guys."

They high fived.

The bartender spoke up, "Guys, I need to close up. I don't want this place to lose its liquor license. I need the job and I'm late on my rent."

Saronda and Danielle looked at each other and laughed.

—ε-ε-ε-ε-ε-ε—

Three people saved the world. They were heads back and arms up. They stopped an unknowable tragedy.

The chemical factory inside their brains shifted to overdrive. Three ecstasy chemicals: dopamine, norepinephrine, and serotonin, flooded their system. They surged, creating a rush of ecstasy. In the right balance, life is normal. Experience a life-changing event and the factory comes alive. Experience a world-saving event like Saronda, Brody and Rebecca just had and the factory blows its top.

They danced. They sang. They were on a gambler's high. They had beaten the odds, deciphering secrets from a paper they had no reason to believe were true other than they entered their lives as if by destiny. But euphoria doesn't last forever. The brain slowly balances the chemicals and we feel normal again. Except Brody. There was a battle going on inside him. The episodes changed him. The euphoria was but a temporary shield from something desperately wrong.

For now, he was on top of the world and life was good. He bounced into his room, carrying a handheld steamer he borrowed from the front desk. He was pumped. He plugged in the steamer. The red safety light glowed. He took his suit coat from the closet and skipped over to the window, pulling the drapes closed with a healthy swish. He turned quickly to check the steamer, then turned back on his heel and opened the drapes a crack to use the morning sun as a backup alarm clock. He smiled as if pleased with himself, and moonwalked to the bed. If the chemicals surging in his cortex could be bottled, they would end sadness. But…

Things hit differently when your Whisper is dying.

He sat on the bed tapping his foot, staring at the steamer, waiting for the ready signal. In the vault-like stillness of the room, unnoticed at first, a feeling of dread descended on him. He tried to focus. The steamer's light turned green. Brody did not move. Fifteen minutes later, a red light flashed three times and the steamer shut off. It creaked and ticked as the hot surfaces cooled. The unused steam condensed and ran down the inner surfaces. His tailored suit jacket was a nondescript shape on the side chair. The merry-go-round had stopped. The chemicals of euphoria gave way to the first tattle of the slow death of his soul.

Saving the world took a lot out of him. It was more than anyone could know.

—ε-ε-ε-ε-ε-ε—

Many things can cause a human brain to fire up the chemical factory and start spitting out euphoria chemicals. Doing something you have no idea how to do, and then realizing just how useful it could be is one of those things.

Kelso fidgeted about the room, walking, then practically skipping. He stopped and stood akimbo at his computer; #DevilLight was dropping to nothing. *Incredible.* A random phone call from someone spouting nonsense about changing reality had enabled him to do something he'd been trying to do for years, change the course of a Twitter conspiracy in mere hours.

He glanced again at the screen. *Like it fell from above.* He was saturated with the same chemicals. But...

Things hit differently when you're a sociopath obsessed with the idea that Earth could use a change in management.

He rocked back and forth, rubbing his fingers together. Changing reality would allow him to bypass months of repeating lies, drumming them into the minds of the gullible and laboriously spreading them to the righteously concerned. Unlike with the college president, there would be no inconsistencies. No chance that a few sloppy comments would cause it to come crashing down. No public humiliation. No disappearing into the dark web. *I'll do it all in broad daylight. It won't be me. It will be the new me.*

—ε-ε-ε-ε-ε-ε—

Yasmin stared at her monitor considering multiple scenarios. Her algorithm detected thousands of open signals with the same profile as before, but from a different location, somewhere overseas. It detected no changes in facts. She wanted a buttoned-up explanation before Ray arrived. No such luck.

She said, "You're in early."

Ray hung up his jacket. "Lots happening today. The raid, and we shut down their internet last night."

"When?"

"11:58, just in time."

"But I got another set of signals from these guys. Seven minutes after two."

"Same guys? Are you sure?"

"Profile's the same, different location. Same number twenty-five-thousand-three-hundred-and-two."

"They outsmarted us."

Yasmin said, "And something else, these signals look like they were sent to government computers."

"U.S. Government? Where?"

Yasmin didn't look up from the screen. "Everywhere. Domestic, overseas, I'm still compiling the list."

Ray became impatient. "If this involves government computers, we need to know now. Where they are, what they're being used for, and more importantly, who the hell in our government is working with these guys. We need to know now. Jump on this."

No shit, Sherlock. Yasmin continued typing. "Yes sir."

Ray's phone rang, it was Greg. "They completed the raid. They were confused but they did it."

"And?"

"Nothing, except they did take away a lifetime supply of toilet paper. No urinals were hurt."

Ray looked at Yasmin. "Greg, give me a minute."

He put Greg on hold. "Are you sure about that location?"

Yasmin felt her coffee rising in her throat. "Yes, I checked it thoroughly. I'm confident in our—"

"OK, wait up."

He took Greg off hold. "Can you get someone up there to tear that place apart? We've been chasing these guys a long time and I don't want to lose them now. There's gotta be something there."

Whew. Her analysis was being taken seriously, but the focus on this was unnerving.

Greg said, "I'll drive up there myself if you're confident I'll find something."

Ray made strong eye contact with Yasmin. She nodded. She felt her heart pounding.

"OK, do it."

He hung up and turned to Yasmin. "Tell me more about these government computers. If there's an inside person working with these guys, they're gonna wish they stayed in their mommy's basement."

—ε-ε-ε-ε-ε-ε—

Wayne Drakauer was up early. He logged into his fake brokerage account and scheduled an order to buy another fourteen thousand shares of GeneraCur the instant the market opened. The stock had dropped sixty-seven percent since the SEC investigation was leaked. This final purchase not only drained his entire nest egg, he actually took out an unsecured loan at a very high interest rate. Unconfirmed rumors about an indictment made the stock toxic. No one was buying it. No one except Wayne and his cohort Drew Waltham. Together they had come up with excuse after excuse, why the project couldn't move forward. The technically challenged executive team at ExpoLytics didn't understand the software enough to push back and with Brody out of the loop there was no one to cry foul. Drew convinced the board to pull out of the contract with the SEC. The announcement was scheduled for one week before Christmas. Wayne planned to sit in his office and watch the stock soar as investors learned the case was dropped. He had a spreadsheet ready to calculate his profits.

He took a bite of his egg sandwich and clicked the purchase button. *Merry Christmas to me.* He was happy they were at the tail end of the scheme, but he fretted about his "Kelso problem." Sharing his stash with an extortionist wasn't in the plan.

—ε-ε-ε-ε-ε-ε—

The morning sun blasted through the opening in the curtains of Brody's room. He dragged himself from the shower and leaned on the bathroom vanity not bothering to towel off. Euphoria gone. The summer's tan was gone, making his gray eyes look flaccid and pale. He managed enough energy to fix his hair. He leaned close to the mirror. *Decision time.* Did he have the courage to tell Saronda what was on his mind? Did he have the energy?

He practiced his words. "I'm thinking there might be something between us, you and—"

His voice was lifeless. He wasn't feeling it the way he did. He wasn't feeling anything the way he did. He tried to focus. His mind switched to a different matter. *I should call Wayne.*

"Hey Wayne, it's Brody."

"I know, phones have caller ID now."

"I wanted to thank you for finding Kelso for me. It worked out great."

Wayne said, "What did you need him for again?"

"He got Brody's code working on over twenty thousand computers, and hey, when I downloaded the GitHub I noticed you put that checksum idea in there. Anyhow, I think we'll be able to knock out that GeneraCur stuff in no time."

Wayne sputtered, "What? No. Are you working again?"

"Not yet. I meet with HR next week. I'm sure they'll reinstate me. We'll be working together again! Like old times. I'm sure that's just the news you were looking for today. But thanks again."

—ε-ε-ε-ε-ε-ε—

Wayne disconnected and immediately dialed Drew. "We've got a problem."

Two sentences later, Drew interrupted him."Yeah.

Yeah. I got it. Calm down. I'll have HR stop him in his tracks. I'll contact the SEC that he should have no access. By the way, where are we with the, you know, transactions?"

Wayne choked out, "All complete."

—ε-ε-ε-ε-ε-ε—

Rebecca went to her office early, eager to get started on over twenty terabytes of data from GeneraCur. It was every financial transaction from the past ten years. Twenty minutes later, it was still being read into memory.

—ε-ε-ε-ε-ε-ε—

Brody texted Rebecca: *Everything set?*

She texted back: *Taking longer than expected. Patience please!*

His phone lit up with a text from Helen HR.

His face stiffened as he read the text.

He called Brooster. "What the hell Brooster?"

"What are you talking abaht? First, it's nice to hear from you. How're things goin'?"

Brody scoffed, "I'm fine. Things are fine. Reality is safe. But what's with this 'urgent mandatory drug test'?"

He leaned on the wall. "Why did Helen Ramsey, HR Gestapo woman... Here, I'll read it verbatim, 'Critical

Urgent Mandatory Drug Clearance Test'."

Brody was required to meet with HR by nine o'clock that morning or risk termination.

Brooster replied, "Kid! Ever heard of small talk? What have you been up to? I guess you're still alive, that's good."

"Yes, and the world as we know it is still here, you're welcome. But what's with this test?"

"I dunno anything abaht it. Same old paranoid Brody. Good to hear you're back to your old self. You'll be fine. I gotta go, emergency staff meeting. Drew is spittin' bullets alla sudden. Never seen 'im this tense."

Brody hung up and then realized he hadn't asked Brooster what he found out about Drew's takeover of software. He dragged his luggage to the front desk and checked out.

Ed, the doorman, said, "Looking fine young man. All cleaned up. Sharply dressed. Fine fitting suit. I'll bet it's that lady isn't it?"

Brody said, "Hold my luggage." And left.

—ε-ε-ε-ε-ε-ε—

Brody tapped his foot as he waited in Helen Ramsey's perfectly arranged office. Everything was still in perfect alignment. He reached over and tilted one of the pictures on the wall.

It was humiliating, peeing in a cup. He glanced down at the slip they gave him: "Remove everything from your pockets and place it in the box. Do not flush when you are done. Leave the sample on the tray. A nurse will be right outside the door." *Jeezus, 'Right outside the door' I'm not a criminal.*

The door opened and Helen rushed in. "Thank you for waiting, we have the results."

"You have results already? It's been like ten minutes."

As she sat down, she noticed the crooked picture.

She gave Brody a look. "Yes, we do, Mr. Markovich. You are positive for marijuana use."

Helen Himmler Ramsey radiated authority like she had brought down a crime syndicate.

"Well, that can't be because I've never— "

And then he remembered the gummy and the metro ride.

"Well, it was only… should I get a lawyer?"

Brody thought about confessing to the crooked picture if it would get him a lighter sentence. He knew he wasn't taking this seriously enough but screw it.

"You can get a lawyer, yes. It won't do any good. Anyone working on government projects must be totally drug free, zero tolerance. Did you not read the document you signed on your first day at SEC?"

"You mean that War and Peace, thick, like huge, ahh you know what… just—"

He looked at the floor. *No way this was random. It was a set up. Test results take longer than that.* He thought for a second then stood, and maintaining eye contact, slowly turned one of the pictures on her desk. He paused, glared, then turned on his heel and left. He didn't want to give Helen Gaufϋhrer Ramsey the glory of firing him to his face.

And he had an urgent call to make.

—ε-ε-ε-ε-ε-ε—

He rushed to the hallway and was already out of breath. He struggled down three flights of stairs. On the street, he was about to call Rebecca when he noticed a text from her: *Analysis complete. These guys are toast. Like burnt toast. Burnt toast in the trash on pick up day. Toasted beyond recognition. They are ex-bread.*

He walked around the corner and ducked into the doorway of an empty store. He sat down, his back sliding down the painted door.

He clicked on her name and waited for her to answer. "Get it to Donny and file it fast. Get a judge to stamp it. Someone doesn't want us working on this. Make sure Donny doesn't tell anyone."

"Are you out of breath? What's going on?"

"Just a suspicion about the people I work with."

He disconnected. He didn't want to tell her about getting the ax. She might get suspicious and not pull the trigger on the filing. He could feel his heart pounding and tried to calm down.

—ε-ε-ε-ε-ε-ε—

The pleasant-sounding bell rang as she entered, as it had weeks earlier. This time the space was different, brighter, organized and inviting. Saronda was different now too. She was confident and knew what she wanted to do with her life. She had a new energy. It showed in the way she carried herself. The space was filled with books and interspersed with comfortable chairs. To her, it looked like a great place to spend an afternoon. But Saronda hadn't come to browse. She needed a job.

Beth Maillon greeted her, "Welcome to 'Corner Books', is there something in particular I can help you find?"

Saronda took in the "cadre magnifique" of the bookstore. It brought back the feeling of exploring shelf upon shelf of old books. Something she hadn't done since becoming obsessed with saving humanity. "Wow, this place is amazing. A step up from the bar that was here."

"Yes, it was a lot of work, but my husband and I are finally getting organized."

"Yes, how is he? I met him before you were open. He was unpacking boxes."

"Oh, OK. Well, if there's anything I can help you with—"

"Actually, I was wondering. I'm here to see if you are hiring. I love old books, very passionate about them."

"We could use someone to open in the morning. We open at nine."

"I'd love that. I got laid off from the Postal Museum. I'm great at helping people."

"OK then, let me get you the web address for the application and we'll take it from there."

"Thank you so much. By the way, where did you put the French books?"

Beth shook her head. "French books? You mean the ones that were in the bar? Oh they're—"

"No, they were in boxes. I helped unload some boxes with your husband and there were books in French."

Beth looked quizzical and then remembered the "shop-warming" gift from Winks. "Oh those boxes. I tossed them."

"Huh, because I bought a magazine that was in one of the boxes. I was your first customer!"

"So you're the one. Alex told me about that." Beth pointed to the framed dollar hanging on the wall. They laughed.

"Good thing you didn't throw that magazine away, it taught me a lot about reality."

Beth showed no inkling of understanding. "I'll get the link to the application. Better yet, you seem like a fit, why don't you hang around, get a feel for the place."

"I think I'll do that. Thank you. I've got a few minutes before meeting a friend."

—ε-ε-ε-ε-ε-ε—

Brody climbed the Metro escalator as it screeched its annoying song. He fixed his hair as he fast-walked to Busboys and Poets. Saronda was sitting at an outdoor table under the warm glow of a heat lamp.

He took a deep breath. "Wooh, weird day. Sorry I'm late."

He noticed her hair was different and she had on a touch more makeup.

He also noticed she was checking him out. She touched the side of her face. "Wow, nothing like a man in a suit. You cut a mean silhouette. But? I thought this was a simple lunch."

Brody sat. "My father set up an interview for a job this afternoon. He wants me to see what else is out there. Probably a good thing. ExpoLytics is firing me."

"Are you serious? They still think you're crazy?"

"Nope. Taken out by a gumdrop."

"No way. You mean... dude. You must hate me for giving you that. You don't seem upset."

"Eh, Even Steven. That's me."

Saronda laughed. "Have you ever been around yourself?"

Brody felt energized being around Saronda, but he couldn't feel the spark.

He smoothed his napkin. "Just one of those things. The fun starts when I tell my father."

"Will he be pissed?"

Brody looked away. There was a catch in his throat. "He has high expectations. But hey, we're here to celebrate. By the way, GeneraCur is about to be spanked. Their stock dropped like thirty percent today after a certain court filing. Someone's losing their shirt."

"I don't understand, is that what you were working on with Rebecca?"

"Yeah, she nailed those guys."

There was a beautiful light snow falling. Bits of tinsel had fallen from the street decorations and stuck to the pavement. A leaf danced along the ground and for the briefest of moments, hesitated on Saronda's foot. She reached to brush it away, catching Brody's attention. He looked down.

Her shoes were blue. *They're back.*

An instant crushing vertigo overcame him. *Wait a minute...*

He caught a glimpse of the broad smile on Saronda's face.

Saronda raised her water glass. "Clink me jackass."

Brody sputtered, "Oh, you beast. You... "

They both laughed. "Dude, I got you good. I bought them a while ago, waiting for the day when I could yank your chain."

"Consider it yanked. I was about to walk in front of a truck. I can't go through it again. God, what we've been through."

He leaned in. "So, did you get the job?"

"Yep, at the bookstore and I signed up for a class too. Oh, and I'm going to complete the translation of Augustine's paper. You know, I never read the whole thing."

She was animated, talking about what she was going to do next. It was a tale of enthusiasm and determination. He noticed she painted her nails.

Her voice drifted back in. "So that's me, I guess your future is a little hazy."

No response.

Saronda filled the gap. "But you've got time to

figure things out. It's just great that Reality B is bygones and never to be mentioned again."

"I mean, Brody, saving reality was kinda big."

"Yes, yes it was, and we did it together. As my father said, 'When the world gives you lemons, solve the damn problem.'"

He looked directly at Saronda. "Listen, there's something I want to... I'm glad we have this chance to talk. There's something I want to, well you and me, we've been—"

"It's I."

"What?"

She twirled her hair and raised the heel of her right foot, subconsciously smoothing her napkin.

She said softly, "It's 'you and I' Dude, learn to talk."

"OK, 'you and I' have been through a lot together and I was thinking maybe—"

A shadow fell across the table. "Excuse me, Mr. Markovich? Sir, are you Brody Markovich?"

Two men in shiny dark blue jackets hovered at his shoulder.

"Yes."

"Mr. Markovich I'm agent Patrick Shell and this is agent Mark Rice of the FBI. We'd like to ask you some questions about someone you recently worked with."

There was a black SUV parked along the street, another agent standing next to it. The back door was open.

"Now?"

"It concerns an urgent matter."

"Uh, is there some other time—"

"Sir, please."

They led him to the car. He peeked back over his shoulder. Saronda had both eyebrows raised. Brody got in the car.

WHAT HAPPENED NEXT

The SUV snaked through the streets of D.C. Brody fidgeted in the back seat. He was a dithery mix of emotions. The anxiety of the episodes propped him up, releasing a low-grade drip of adrenaline. But it was gone. Talking to Saronda boosted him but spending time in an alternate reality ripped him apart. The only thing left was a twisted mess of self-pity and emptiness. And a fence he built to keep the outside from seeing in, but mostly to keep what's inside from getting out.

Brody drummed his fingers on the armrest. He craved interaction. It happens when your soul is dying.

"So you may think this is the most bizarre thing that happened to me, being dragged away by the FBI."

The two agents gave each other a glance.

Brody leaned back. "I mean, yesterday, we actually moved reality. The whole thing. We pulsed some computers and kept our reality from crashing head-on into another reality."

"Mr. Markovich, I need to be very clear, you should only answer questions. Anything incriminating you say can be used against you."

"Incriminating? But that's only for people who have done something wrong. We actually saved the world from a lot of anguish. I should be celebrating."

"It is highly recommended that you not talk. Wait until we are at the facility and then only answer the questions presented to you. You can get counsel if you wish."

Brody leaned on the front seat. "Am I under suspicion for something? What's this about?"

"We are not at liberty to say. You will be communicated with at the facility."

Brody sat back. "Facility makes it sound like an interrogation or something."

"Mr. Markovich, please, it is in your interest to stay silent."

It was good advice that Brody did not take.

—ε-ε-ε-ε-ε-ε—

Yasmin put her tablet down in front of Ray. "Look."

Ray studied the tablet. "Idaho?"

"The signals. They were using a remote router in

Pittsburgh, but you shut it down. They moved to a router in Belarus. When they did, they leaked a connection signal on an open port. Our sniffer snagged it. Boundary County, Idaho. Thirty-six miles north of Bonners Ferry."

"I can safely say I've never been."

"Do you know there's a Good Grief, Idaho? Fun but not relevant, sorry for the diversion."

"Are you sure it's our guy?"

"Signal profile, timing, everything matches. Only thing is, they didn't change any facts."

Ray called Greg and barely let him answer. "Cancel your trip to Pittsburgh, we need to talk about Idaho."

—ɛ-ɛ-ɛ-ɛ-ɛ-ɛ—

It started with a low buzz, then pop!

"What the?" Kelso scanned the room. Kaz ran to the kitchen.

His phone buzzed. *You've been detected. Air gap and run. Commencing remote shutdown.*

Kelso shouted, "Raster, you bastard."

He sprinted outside and launched his drone rocket camera set to surveillance mode.

As he came back inside, his phone was blaring its emergency alarm.

"I am simply not leaving until I compile this code."

He texted: *I order you to stop the shutdown.*

He knew his order was laughable. He knew they would not stop. He had been detected. His entire value hinged on being anonymous, of not existing.

—ε-ε-ε-ε-ε-ε—

According to the transcript, Brody talked for forty-eight minutes and thirty-five seconds. He spilled everything to the FBI. Everything. The FBI agents sat quietly. Their list of questions on a yellow legal pad sat unused on the table. Brody told them about pulsing computers, colliding realities, hundreds of mathematical equations. He talked about how Whispers reach out into the universe and weave reality.

" ...and it was all spelled out by this lady, Augustine Chalamet." He took a breath.

The agents looked at each other. "Mr. Markovich, that is quite a story. Um, but that is not why we asked you here."

Agent Dawson said, "Please answer the following questions. Do you know Rebecca Standiford? Have you recently worked with her as part of a case at the Securities and Exchange Commission?"

—ε-ε-ε-ε-ε—

Every few minutes, a low buzz and then pop! A

cloud of thin blue smoke bore witness as electronic components met their death. Kelso tried to calm himself but his brain sparked like a shorted out electrical panel. He continued organizing files that had become fragmented in the frenzy of saving the world, but each pop brought with it a wave of euphoria.

"Go ahead, destroy everything."

Around him, his world was being destroyed with a series of timed commands issued from a thousand miles away. The "Proboys," his compatriots, no longer trusted him, no longer needed him.

A loud whirring signaled a hard drive revving well beyond what it could withstand, followed by a disturbing screech as the read head was purposely jammed onto the spinning surface, destroying any chance of data recovery. Kaz was increasingly agitated, his eyes watery from the smoke.

"They really think this will destroy me. What do you make of that, dog." His voice dripped with acid.

He continued compiling the code. Everything Brody gave him was methodically being condensed to one neat package small enough to fit on a thumb drive. The code that had been used to save the world was being repurposed. It was a pocketful of irony.

"And I don't need those guys."

He hated that they treated him like just another team member. They were always "you're not the one driving the train" and "just do your part, ignore everything else" and "be a team player." Kelso is not a big fan of teams. Not since he was forced to sit as his parents were scolded by overbearing school nazis. He remembered their words. *Kelso does not work and play well with others.* There were so many parent/student conferences. His parents would stare down at him like he was fresh gum on the sidewalk. Sometimes they didn't show up at all. "Lost child. Why bother?"

Another loud pop from a server across the room and then a telltale puff of smoke as silicon and epoxy exploded into worthless ash. The acrid haze thickened.

They were erasing him, frying his equipment, washing away an embarrassing stain. It had been that way his whole life. *He should maybe try a different school, a fresh start, where the other kids don't know his, shall we say, history.*

The words were embedded, deep. They had become part of him. But now he had something big. And it all fit in his pocket.

"Blow up all the shit you want. Bastards aren't getting your hands on my new plaything."

He typed 'git push clone thumb_drive master' and watched as each file arranged into folders.

He peered through the corrosive smoke. "Already 18 gigabytes. I've been a busy busy boy." He glanced at his phone, still no activity on the highway.

Pop! The adrenaline surged. Another piece of equipment fried. Kelso chuckled. "Losers."

Oh shit. His phone buzzed with an activity alert, an SUV was headed up US95. It was in a hurry. He pulled the thumb drive from the computer.

The dog paced the room trying to avoid the smoke. Another piece of equipment buzzed then popped as voltage spikes rendered another server useless. Kelso took one last look at the smoldering equipment. *That's not how you destroy something.*

"This is how you destroy something."

He punched a button on the wall. It would be exactly 15 minutes before its light flashed, another 1 minute until it sounded a warning.

Kaz watched as Kelso left. He was carrying only a go bag. And a thumb drive.

—ε-ε-ε-ε-ε-ε—

Field Officer Bart Youngman turned onto County Road 42 in northern Idaho. Claiming it as a road took a lot of confidence. It was basically a twelve-foot wide clearing in the trees with snow covered gravel. Special Agent Ken Hart held on tightly to the passenger side armrest.

They did not speak.

—ε-ε-ε-ε-ε-ε—

Kelso raced to the outbuilding. Judging the snow depth, he chose the snowmobile over the ATV. Both were gassed and ready to go. With a well-practiced twist of shoulder and hips, he unfurled the protective tarp. It was go time and Kelso had his route memorized.

The snowmobile sputtered to life and he sped across the open field. The sky burned yellow and orange, painted by a winter sunset, casting long shadows of the towering pines onto the virgin snow. He raced on, focusing not on the beauty around him but on admitting to himself that he had been detected, igniting a malignant rancor.

Kelso didn't know he was detected; he was *told* he was detected. People in his business can't tell when they've been detected, it requires a lot of effort, so they buy a service from the Syndicate. The Syndicate is the knower of everything that happens on the Internet, dark web included. Kelso and his fellow Proboys pay them to keep watch. A faraway dirt dwelling web worm noticed a slightly odd signal in the complex chatter of the internet, one thing led to another, and Kelso was detected. Creatures who do nothing more than scan the web for strange signals get paid for finding people who don't exist.

He squinted as he turned west into the setting sun, squeezing a little more speed from the humming beast between his legs, hanging on as the winds of a winter storm picked up. Being Kelso Radovic, the fugitive, requires a different set of skills than being Kelso Radovic the hacker.

—ε-ε-ε-ε-ε-ε—

Ray looked blankly at the screen. "Still nothing?"

Yasmin fidgeted, willing the screen to report a status. "This is intense. There's so much riding on this."

Yasmin's nervousness was punctuated by unsought career advice from Ray. "If you're going to survive this type of work, you need to learn to smooth out the mountains and valleys."

Yasmin had no desire to tame her emotions at the moment. Today was not a day for personal improvement. Today was all about catching Kelso. Her dark brown eyes darted from one part of the screen to another.

Ray leaned back and took out a stick of gum. "I used to do this all the time, in the real world, huddled in cars or bunkers, listening to scratchy radio traffic. We'd go hours with nothing, sometimes days."

Yasmin pulled her eyes from the screen. "Must've felt great when you nailed someone. I want this guy. I want to interrogate him. Probe him. Find out why he thinks he can reach P90. I can't believe he wrote it all in a document. Yikes!"

"I guess that's what these nuts do when they think no one's watching."

"I hope he hasn't left by now."

Ray leaned back farther and put his feet on the desk. "Why would he leave? He doesn't know we're coming. Sonofabitch thinks he's a ghost. No, he'll be there. Let's hope it goes peacefully and he's not some maniac wanting to blow things up."

—ε-ε-ε-ε-ε-ε—

Field Officer Bart Youngman drove up to a large metal gate two-hundred feet from the specified GPS coordinates. Agent Hart ran to the gate. It was not locked. Intuition told him this was not good. They approached the stone house with caution. Agent Hart knocked twice and burst through the door, his semi-automatic weapon trained on a shaking yellow labrador. Kaz ran to the fireplace and started barking. The sharp, acrid smoke of blown circuit cards hung thick in the air of the two-room building.

Barking.

Officer Youngman gave the clear signal and Agent Hart lowered his rifle.

Barking.

"It's OK boy, we're just going to have a look around. Where's your owner?"

Kaz was very agitated, pacing back and forth near the stone fireplace.

More barking.

The sight was astounding. Walls were lined with

computer servers and terminals. There was comms equipment. The equipment smoldered, with soot stains at every opening, telltale signs of high voltage spikes. A notebook computer was the only thing functioning. In the corner of its screen was a message, 'Disk Not Ejected Properly - Socks1_copy_prvt.'

Barking.

Kaz pawed at one of the stones. Youngman called out that the mortar was a slightly different color. He kicked the stone. It was loose.

Kaz ran to the door.

Barking. Pawing the door. Frantic.

Youngman pulled back the stone. Wires. And a gray box.

"Get out. Evac now. Immediate action. Bomb."

Hart opened the door. Kaz led the two men, running frantically to the SUV. Hart opened the car door and Kaz hopped in. Youngman was close behind and jumped in the driver's side. He maneuvered the SUV in a 180 degree turn he had trained for. He had never done it in twelve inches of fresh snow. One of the back wheels skidded off the driveway and got stuck. He revved the engine, but it only dug deeper.

"Back off the gas."

"I know I know."

He feathered the gas pedal and the SUV crawled out of the ditch. He gunned it and they fishtailed their way down the drive. The SUV righted itself and they drove off. They got far enough away so that in his side mirror Hart saw the explosion before he heard it.

—ε-ε-ε-ε-ε-ε—

Kelso felt the explosion. It was a work of art. Sixteen simultaneous explosions, timed to within a hundredth of a second, each bouncing off well-placed boilerplate, directing the full force of the explosion inward, focusing an inferno at the center of the cabin, incinerating everything. The shockwave blasted up the stone chimney plastering the sky with fire and ash that could be seen for miles. Everything he had built was now dust. Terabytes gone. None of it was backed up. Nothing saved in the cloud. Nothing for vile insects to rummage through or resell to the highest bidder. Kelso Radovic was erased.

—ε-ε-ε-ε-ε-ε—

It was dark when Brody left FBI headquarters.

He looked around to find "the yellow X not the blue one" on the sidewalk. He wanted to be sure to stand exactly where they told him for the car to pick him up. He didn't want to break any rules, not when standing outside FBI headquarters. A black town car pulled up fifteen feet from Brody, precisely in front of the blue X. The driver rolled down the passenger side window and called out "Markovich?"

Brody shrugged. "I was told you were picking me up at the yellow X."

The driver pulled up to the yellow X. Brody jumped in the back.

Brody wasn't impressed. "Poor operational precision. I'll need to bring this up to my new best buds at the Bureau."

The driver looked in the rearview mirror. "Where are we going this evening?"

"Home."

"And where would that be?"

"Pittsburgh."

The driver glanced over his shoulder. "They didn't tell me this was a long-distance run."

"Oh hell, just kidding. I need to go to The George. Bizarre day. Feel like crap. I'm in a weird mood. But I guess a lot of people coming out of there are in a weird mood."

He was right. Interrogated people get a little rattled, but not many of them get into the wrong car.

Brody caught a glimpse of a road sign as they passed an intersection. "This is a strange route, and you didn't even look at the address I gave you."

"Someone wants to talk to you. Don't worry, it's like a surprise party."

Brody took a hard look at the driver. "It feels a lot like a kidnapping."

The car stopped in the parking lot of a WaWa. Brody's window rolled down. Brooster was there.

"Jeezus, Brooster, what the hell is this? First, you set me up on a fake drug test and now you have me kidnapped? You're like the worst former boss ever."

"Settle dahn, nobody's getting kidnapped."

"I already was."

Hank "Brooster" Drucker had driven to D.C. from Pittsburgh, in a hurry. His office assistant got a call from the FBI asking where they could find Brody Markovich. That sent up enough alarm bells for the entire executive team of ExpoLytics to convene. They decided Brooster needed to get to D.C.

Brooster was direct. "Listen, I need to know what you told those guys."

"What guys?"

Brooster looked over the car and then to the side. "The Feds."

"The Feds? It was two guys and a clip board. Why do you care?"

Brooster leaned in and lowered his voice. "Because this thing could affect the whole company. All the company bigs are pissin' on zinc right now. And me, all

I got is ExpoLytics stock. If that goes in the crapper, I'm toast."

"OK start over, what thing are you talking about?"

"Don't play that way. We know you know everything. Now tell me what you told them."

The fence was coming down. "OK, in addition to you talking like a mobster, you're pissing me off. I don't have a clue what you're talking about. But what I do know is that what just happened here is a tad illegal, coercing a witness or something, and kidnapping... Look, it's late and I've had a day. Can you have your cosplay goon take me to my hotel."

"You really don't know what I'm talking about, do you? So, what did the FBI want then?"

"Jeezus Brooster."

Brooster got in the front passenger seat and turned around. He pointed to the driver. "I'd like you to meet my son."

Brody said, "We've met before. At your house, Christmas party. I remember him."

Brooster looked at his son. "Seriously? You met him before?"

The driver nodded. Brooster turned to Brody. "But you called him a goon."

"I played along. But seriously, you staged the worst

kidnapping."

Brooster said, "I'll bet you're hungry. Let me take you to Plume."

Brody said, "You can't get in at Plume."

Brooster bragged, "When you have more money than God, you get things."

Brody sat numbly. Normally, Brooster's puffery would have triggered a burning desire to get what Brooster has. Snap your fingers, get things. He was all about having it all, but then the episodes came. He wanted to know about the scandal at ExpoLytics, but the desire never materialized.

"Uh, guys, I don't feel great. Can you take me to my hotel so I can get my car? I need to drive back to Pittsburgh tonight."

Brooster turned around to face Brody. "Don't be crazy, you can't drive back tonight. Stay in tahn."

Brody replied, "I don't have a room."

"I'll getcha a room."

They drove Brody to "The George" hotel, the same hotel he had spent almost two months in. Brooster walked to the front desk, said a few hushed words, and just like that, a room freed up. Brooster was all smiles. Brody couldn't decide if he should thank him or punch him in the neck. Or if he had the strength to do either.

—ε-ε-ε-ε-ε-ε—

Rebecca Standiford's day was similar to Brody's, but without the kidnapping. She sat for two hours with the FBI and said exactly nothing. She understood the value of the Fifth Amendment.

—ε-ε-ε-ε-ε-ε—

Brody entered his room, and the familiar smell and color scheme brought a surge of dark memories. He pulled his phone out of the inside breast pocket of his nicely tailored suit jacket.

Suit jacket. Shit.

He had totally forgotten the interview that his father set up. Brody sat at the edge of the bed and rubbed his face, then his eyes, causing a dance of little spots. His phone went through its start-up routine and then chirped maniacally with notifications of texts and phonemail.

He typed "f" and pressed "Father."

His father answered immediately, "*I thought you were dead.*"

"Feel dead. Would it be better if I was?"

"It's the only thing that can keep me from killing you. I had you all set up, a huge opportunity Brody, and then you're a no show. Brody what the h—"

"Father, I got kidnapped... after I was questioned

by the FBI."

Arthur Markovich was a smart guy and an excellent businessman. Brody knew he was clicking through a series of responses.

All that came out was, "What?"

Brody said, "I don't know where to start. Can this wait until tomorrow? I'm not feeling well."

"I don't know, Brody, it sounds like you're into something serious. The FBI? I mean, come on."

"It does kinda take the thunder out of my kidnapping story."

Arthur's tone got firm. "At any rate, I'll set up another job interview for you."

Brody dropped his shoulders. "I'm not sure I want to. I'm not sure about that job. I'm a little overwhelmed right now."

He waited through the silence. He heard disappointment and a touch of anger in his father's voice. "Look, take some time. Rest up. Think about it. You need to figure this out, whatever it is. I'll hold off for now."

Brody Markovich was a hollow husk of his former self

—ε-ε-ε-ε-ε-ε—

There are many things that are underappreciated about our universe. One, it is big. Really big. In relation, we are not. Another underappreciated thing about the universe is that it's been around for a long time. We have not. But the most underappreciated thing about the universe is that it's made of some pretty cool things. The universe beat very steep odds to make those things. At one time, the universe was a cauldron of atoms colliding with each other in a random frenzy. Sometimes, the atoms stuck together making molecules. Some of the molecules collided and became plants and animals and rocks and planets. Everything had to collide just right. A few collisions go a different way and none of the cool things would exist. Neither would we. And yet here we are. Something must have wanted it this way.

People collide with people. Sometimes they do cool things like save the world from insanity. Saronda Jackson, Rebecca Standiford and Brody Markovich collided. Purely by chance. Together they saved the world. On the surface, that's a good thing. Surely, the universe would not have wanted its most precious creation to wallow in despair with broken Whispers.

Augustine Chalamet wrote a science paper about it. Brody, Saronda, and Rebecca thought they understood it.

—ε-ε-ε-ε-ε-ε—

Kelso didn't take the time to lock up. That was smart. It gave him more time to get away. It may seem that blowing up your place and all that you had worked for would occupy one's mind. But Kelso had something else on his mind. He was now verified to exist. He wasn't just a microcode bot winding its way through the web leaving comments on people's social media. He was a real live person with an identity. Live persons can be charged with crimes, or forced to testify, or tortured for information, or any number of things, depending on who's doing the charging or the torturing or worse. The people he does business with don't like people who exist even though he was the best in the business, the dude of the dark web. He was good, he got the job done, and no one ever heard of him. When you're anonymous, you can do all the nasty you want. You can devour people's reputations, twist the truth, and get paid handsomely. Just don't get detected.

Kelso wasn't like the other slime worm gunslingers out to make a buck. He was rancid acrimony with a manifesto and he had big goals. His manifesto had some things in it that a couple people in Washington D.C. would love to chat about, which puts him in a very odd spot. His business associates want nothing to do with him and the Feds can't wait to get their hands on him.

It's like having a scarlet letter on your chest and a target on your back.

His current situation, though, was to get the hell out of Dodge. He had an escape plan; get to an access road and go to the first barn, pick up a stashed car, and drive baby drive. He grabbed everything he cared about, set the timer on the explosives, and bolted. He practiced the route and knew every turn, every treeline, every fence post and hazard. He created little phrases and sang them out loud.

"Around this fence then it's straight for a quarter, straight for a quarter, straight for a quarter, I'll go."

A bit childish but it's a twenty-seven-mile route through fields, barbed wire fences, trees, and deep gullies. If he knew about the people in Washington, he may have had more fear, but he was mostly pissed at the lack of loyalty among his fellow dirt dwellers. Bastards. He was the smartest guy he knew and now he was literally riding off into the sunset. He didn't usually push it this hard, but the adrenaline was flowing.

He needed to get to that access road. There was a lot at stake.

The sun adhered to a celestial clock billions of years old, racing to the horizon, creating textured colors in the gathering storm clouds. He cranked the snowmobile faster.

—ε-ε-ε-ε-ε-ε—

Yasmin Roth was way ahead of the Syndicate. She knew a lot about Kelso long before he had been detected. She knew he wasn't just an artificial intelligence wet dream. He was a live person, and he had plans. She knew this because she had been reading his manifesto. She knew his goals, his innermost thoughts. She didn't have a psych degree, but it was obvious he was more than a bit off.

Ray Denmore stood behind Yasmin. "Still nothin'?"

Yasmin tapped on the keys for no other reason

than to calm her nerves. "I'm glad you came in tonight. I could use some reassurance. Is this the way these things normally go?"

Ray poured coffee for both of them. "Yep. Long periods of nothing followed by a firehose. Hopefully all good news. Greg tells me you were able to place this guy within plus or minus a few feet."

"Yes, it's the new satellite data sharing program. You pushed for it so thank you."

Ray swirled his coffee cup. "Satellite data. So different now. Internet, wiz kids like you. All we had was shoe leather. Waiting, praying for zero casualties."

Ray sat and leaned back. "With all the places to hide now, I'm impressed you found this guy."

"Actually, I give credit to the web sniffer. It picked up the non-conforming signal."

"Yasmin, you need to take credit for this. When we bring this guy in, the feather will go in *your* cap. Take all the feathers you can get. They're few and far between around here."

"Well, let's start by catching this guy."

Yasmin could have toasted Kelso months ago, along with other slime. With what she built, she could swoop in and decommission dozens of bad actors and "disinformation farms" that sow conspiracy theories. But working for the U.S. Government meant she had to respect their rights; little things like privacy, free speech, and the right to hide from prying eyes. Certain signals were off-limits. She could detect them. She just couldn't act on them.

Ray said, "Refresh me on this guy, how long have you been watching him?"

"Officially, the warrant says two and a half years, unofficially it goes back—"

"Wait, don't tell me anymore, two and half years is the answer. It was the manifesto that got us the warrant, right?"

"Yes." Yasmin chuckled. "Remember, this is the guy we were laughing at because he had a three-step security protocol to log in to his precious document. One of the steps… "

Nerves took their toll and she cracked herself up.

After an embarrassing snort, "Oh my, he had to contact a live human being who was assigned to watch over the document at all times."

A ripple of nervousness made her giddy. "Think about that, they had a live person watching the front door, meanwhile I'm walking right through the *back* door, hello, don't mind me, oh my… Whoo. Sorry, that gets me every time."

She reached for a tissue to wipe her eyes.

Ray watched her recompose herself. "It's nice to see

you're in an upbeat mood about this."

"I'm not, I'm a raw bundle of nerves. I get like this when... "

She forced herself to yawn to loosen her face which felt tight and flushed.

Ray filled the silence, "That back door got us a warrant which gave Greg a ticket to the guy's house. Nice work."

—ε-ε-ε-ε-ε-ε—

Anyone who's ever done something for the first time knows it's hard to predict the consequences. Saronda, Brody and Rebecca kept the world from becoming a very dark place filled with miserable people who don't have an ounce of empathy and can't see beauty. People who hate everything because they can love nothing. In other words, perpetually whining piss ants. Everyone. Not just the perpetually whining piss ants already walking around.

Brody was one of those piss ants, at least for brief periods of time when his Whisper drifted into a different reality. He hasn't turned into a snarling piss ant since. It was a wildly cosmic bonding experience, and the three became close friends. Saving the world together does that.

But there were consequences.

—ε-ε-ε-ε-ε-ε—

Saronda knocked and then opened the door to Shay's condo.

Shay said with mock surprise, "Girl, you need to wait a sec before you go barging into people's places. I coulda shot you."

"That's so sad. I texted ahead so I'm not barging into 'people's places.' You're not a 'people', you're my sister and you knew I was coming."

"Ha ha, you have a reply for everything, don't you."

"I miss my friends."

"Are those the two friends you've been talking about?"

Saronda said, "Yes. I am so exhausted. Someday I need to tell you what I've been through."

The two sisters hugged.

Shay squeezed a little harder. "Wait. Is this that guy you told me about at Thanksgiving?"

"Yes, same guy."

"Ooh, he's a long-timer by your standards. Color me intrigued."

Saronda shrugged. "He's just a guy I met at a coffee shop."

Shay leaned toward Saronda. "Sounds like he

captured your attention."

"He thought I was wearing blue shoes."

Shay smirked. "Blues shoes? You?"

Saronda said, "He was seeing a different reality. He was having episodes. And he lost his job."

Shay asked, "Are you sure he's not one of my exes? But episodes?"

"He was going crazy. The episodes got bad, but we fixed them. And now I don't know where he is."

"Honestly Roni, this is much more interesting than your usual stuff."

Saronda said, "Shay, I'd like to be called Saronda now, remember? I never liked Roni."

—ε-ε-ε-ε-ε-ε—

About ten billion years before Kelso blew up all his stuff, stardust coalesced to form giant rocks. One of those rocks flew aimlessly through the universe with no particular destination in mind. Fate was its only guide. The rock traveled for a couple billion years, blazing a ramrod straight course through vast open darkness. For a billion years it was a molten hot mess, but it slowly cooled into a nice hard globe. It seemed like its destiny was to fly forever, but it got irresistibly pulled into an orbit around a nice warming star. It went around the star in a never ending orbit. It sounds like a nice life for a rock, but it was constantly battered by other rocks, sometimes getting hit straight on, sometimes at an angle. This caused the rock to wobble, listing to the right then to the left.

Getting battered changes a rock. According to math invented billions of years later by Isaac Newton, each time it got battered, the rock's orbit changed. There was no way to predict how the little pinball was going to end up. Blow after blow pounded the rock until one last glancing shot tilted the rock at an odd angle. A few billion years went by, and someone named it Earth. Along the way, it acquired some creatures.

One of those creatures was Kelso. As fate would have it, Earth tilted at just the right angle so that at exactly forty-six seconds after 4:51 on the evening of any given December 7, the sun disappeared below the horizon, producing the one small detail that Kelso left out of his escape plan; darkness.

It was a special kind of darkness.

Black, total black, as in no light, not even light from a gas station sign reflecting off the clouds. There was no up or down. Kelso was in a black cube, way north in Idaho, up where there's nothing. A mere twenty-nine miles farther north and he'd be in Canada, surrounded by beavers and hockey players. Where he was, he was surrounded by nothing. Earth is tilted, so yeah, it's dark at five o'clock in the winter. He was racing in total darkness, alone, across a very frozen part of a once lonely rock.

Normally the feeling of isolation and lack of preparedness would have overwhelmed Kelso, but he was busy fumbling for the headlight switch.

—ε-ε-ε-ε-ε-ε—

The sisters laughed. Saronda wearing blue shoes. Not a chance. It started out as a full-hearted laugh but, for Saronda, it ended with a nervous titter.

Shay tried to puzzle it out. "So was it you in a different reality? A reality where you wear blue shoes."

"Yeah, it's something like that. He was able to see into another reality. Another reality where I, Saronda Jackson, wore blue shoes."

"I'll bet you looked hot."

Saronda pushed her hair behind her ear. "Actually, blue shoes are hot. I bought a pair and showed Brody."

"Uh oh, girl, buying shoes to impress a guy. Sounds serious. Did you show him? What did he say?"

"I bought them as a joke."

Shay asked, "Ohhh, an inside joke? Huh. Is he cute?"

Saronda said a little too quickly, "Yes."

"Yes, he's cute? Or yes, it's an inside joke."

Saronda stayed silent.

Shay gave Saronda a sideways knowing glance. "I think I'm feeling something here."

Saronda said, "OK, maybe he's a little cute, but that's not what's important about this story."

"OK, but I'll need to know more."

"No you don't. But I haven't seen him since... since we changed the course of reality. That's what I want to tell you."

Shay's eyes narrowed. "I'd rather hear about this cutie at the coffee shop—"

"Shay. Stop."

Shay said, "Alright, fine. Bring on the crazy. But this sounds like something we need wine for. Maybe start with those episodes Brady was having."

Shay headed to the kitchen.

"Brody."

"What?"

"His name is Brody."

Shay walked back to the living room with two bottles and two wine glasses. The distinctive clinking signaled it was time for two sisters to have a chat.

Saronda raised an eyebrow. "Two bottles?"

Shay poured the wine. "I don't wanna get up in the middle of this."

—ε-ε-ε-ε-ε-ε—

Kelso was struck by how little of the road was lit up by the headlight. He estimated maybe fifty feet ahead. Could have been more but not much. There could be a dead moose in the road and he wouldn't see it until he was skewering it with the snowmobile runners. He thought back to the manual and the section on headlight adjustment that he skipped over; "Warning: Vertical aim of headlight is pre-set to shipping config." Kelso wondered if he'd given enough respect to night driving, but he was juicing on the rage he felt about being discarded. He patted the pocket with the most precious thing in his life right now, a thumb drive. He felt a pulse of adrenaline and gave a slight twist of the wrist to nudge the snowmobile faster, darkness be damned. To Kelso, the tradeoff was worth it. Blow up an entire life's work, leave with a weapon of mass destruction. *First, you get them to believe nothing, then they will believe anything.*

—ε-ε-ε-ε-ε-ε—

Ray's phone came to life. "Hey Greg, speak to me."

"Not great. Our guys are OK."

Ray asked, "And the guy?"

Greg said, "Gone when we got there. The agents were lucky to escape before it blew."

Ray said, "They were inside?"

"Yeah, place was empty except a buncha computers and electronics... and a dog. Plus a timed charge."

They disconnected.

Ray said, "I can't believe he left his dog."

Yasmin said, "Not a surprise, the guy is a psycho. I mean, you read his manifesto."

Ray's face was blank. "Well, I have to admit... "

Yasmin exploded. "What? You never read the manifesto? Surely you read my psychoanalysis."

Ray looked at his shoes. "I skimmed it."

"Ray! C'mon. I put a lot of work into that. I ran an algorithm on his manifesto. The words he used, the goals he outlined. Ray, he scored a thirty-four."

"Thirty-four doesn't sound too bad."

"The scale only goes to forty. Normal people score less than ten."

"So, anger issues."

"No. Manipulation issues. Lack of empathy issues. Pathological lying issues. He'll lie to get his way. He doesn't care about consequences. He doesn't care if people suffer as long as he can work his plan."

"Sounds like a psychopath."

Bingo.

—ε-ε-ε-ε-ε-ε—

Shay plopped down on the couch. "So where do we start?"

Saronda said, "I thought you said we start with the episodes."

"I meant, red or white?"

Saronda said, "Shay, I gotta thank you."

"For what?"

"For listening. For being interested. For not thinking I'm crazy. Mom wouldn't let me get past the first sentence."

Shay put up her hand. "Let's not talk about mom. Let's hear your story and more about this cute guy. Oh, and, girl, you've always been crazy. Love ya, Sis. Keep going."

Saronda got serious. "About six weeks ago, I'm getting coffee and this guy, Brody, insists I own blue shoes. I brush him off cuz he might be whack. But he's not whack, he was nice. I feel bad about dissin' him. I avoid him. But he's persistent. He hits me up the next day."

"He liked you."

"Maybe, who knows, but he really thought he saw me wearing blue shoes but it was because he was seeing a different reality than me... or mine. Me or mine? I'm not sure which one is—"

"It's mine, now go on, you're killing me. How did you know he was seeing a different world than you?"

Saronda said, "Not a different world, a different reality. Same world, two different realities."

Shay exhaled after a long sip of wine. "Girl, that's some shit."

"It happened."

"I wanna believe you but you're saying a guy sees you wearing shoes you don't own, and then he gets fired because he's seeing things, and you miss him? Sounds like you dodged a bullet if you ask me."

Saronda said, "It's not like that, we fixed him."

"Girl, I've been trying to fix guys all my life."

"Shay, we used information from a hundred-ten year old science paper and blasted pulses into space."

Shay raised both eyebrows and set her glass down. "Science and outer space. Uh huh. More wine?"

—ε-ε-ε-ε-ε-ε—

The snow picked up, adding an animated star field in the darkness, nightwind swirling left, then right.

Kelso strained to keep his eyes on the bouncing reflection of the headlight, focusing, straining to find the break in the tree line. He barely saw it. It looked different in the dark. It was the only break that would allow him access to the road. It had taken weeks to find it. He slowed the snowmobile through the break, tilting his body first to the left then quickly to the right to compensate for the uneven ground, a maneuver he had memorized. Smooth as silk he eased the quarter ton machine over the snow that had drifted beside the road, then down a small but steep gully. He gunned the engine to lift him out to the other side of the gully. He caught some air as usual. Any less power and he would have slid back into the gully. He knew his momentum would carry him across the road, so he cut hard to the left. Snowmobiles don't fishtail so Kelso needed to cut hard right and then delicately settle into a nice steady straight line. It took a lot of practice, but he got good at it. He breathed easier now that he was on the road. He added more speed. It was virgin snow, no tire tracks, no ruts, just clean sailing from here on. The beam from the maladjusted headlight was nothing more than a bright cauldron of blowing snow.

He fixated on the hypnotic pattern, his peripheral vision sensed the tall trees that lined the road, using them as guideposts. The nervous pit in his gut pushed aside all thoughts of his grandiose plan. Beyond his headlight, the road was a black hole, an infinite inkiness swallowing the snowmobile as it rocketed along. His ride was now an act of faith that the road was clear. The hissy roar of the air rushing past his ears, muffled by a winter hat, and the relentless hum of the horsepower he clung to had a cocooning effect. The sound reflected off the trees as he passed one tree then another, then another and another, so that the relentless drone became a throbbing polyrhythmic heartbeat. The brown-white noise lined up with the pulsing roar creating an ethereal evolving chord. The isolation was numbing. He settled into a trance-like focus. And then, nothing.

The dead man switch killed the engine less than a second after the snowmobile plunged headlong into a ditch. Total silence.

The only light was the fading taillight and the gauzy glow of the headlight buried in the snow.

—ε-ε-ε-ε-ε-ε—

Aduco Lim was one of the fortunate few who were able to turn a quirky hobby into a money making business. It wasn't illegal but it was rancid. If the current lawmakers understood it, they would surely do something because the lawmakers of tomorrow won't be allowed to. Aduco wasn't even one of the unsavory ones. He was just a low-level player feeding the monster, funneling information into the Syndicate. On a whim, Aduco started scouring the dark corners of the Internet, collecting unrelated scraps of information. He was elated to find that the Syndicate paid decent money for some of his scraps. They combined it with scraps from other freelancers. In Kelso's case, the Syndicate cross referenced Aduco's information with what they already had and status update; Kelso was not a random web bot, but rather a real live scheming human being. It was extortion really. The Syndicate told Kelso he was exposed. He could pay a fee and they would bury the information. Kelso would be undetected again. No thanks, with what Kelso had in his pocket, they would be paying him soon. But for now, Mr. Ego Pants was lying in a heap, beside a frozen road, in the dark.

Also in the dark, five-thousand-two-hundred-and-thirty-six miles away, Aduco Lim rolled over in bed to check his phone that was on a small table in the rented room he shares with one wife and two dogs at 63 Vicolo Fratelli Scotti in Treviso, Italy. After a quick look, he turned off his phone and went back to sleep. Like clockwork, the Syndicate had paid him at precisely 4:20 a.m. local time, like they always did.

Kelso didn't know anything about Aduco. Remarkably, neither did Yasmin Roth or Ray Denmore.

—ε-ε-ε-ε-ε-ε—

A portable humidifier turned on. Its soft click was the only sound. Saronda had poured out her soul nonstop for close to an hour. All the crazy stuff. She left out no detail.

Shay finished the last of the wine. She slurred, "Yeah, I really enjoy that humidifier you got me last Christmas."

"You don't believe me."

"What makes you say that?"

Saronda glared. "Take your pick. Either your total

silence or your declaring a deep love for a humidifier. By the way, Mom gave you the humidifier."

"You sher?"

"Yes, who gives their sister a humidifier? Anyhow you're dodging the question."

Shay struggled to focus. "What? You're really asking me if I believe you. Think about it, Roni poo, it's a crazy story. And I... "

Saronda nudged her. "Hey, wake up so you can go to bed. Don't sleep on the couch. Go upstairs, I'll clean up and wash the glasses."

Shay monster-walked to the stairs, gripped the railing and studied the staircase as if it were the first time she'd seen such a thing. She called out, "Oh, hey, Roni, I hope Brady comes back. He sounds nice."

The words hit Saronda as she rinsed a glass. He wasn't gone. Was he? With the sound of the running water as background, Saronda reflected on how the ambience is so different from the tiny kitchen that she shares with Danielle. Maybe it's because of the type of countertop or the position of the sink or maybe the size. She had read a book on room acoustics once and...

"Come on, girl, snap out of it, you're avoiding the truth."

"What truth?"

Saronda almost dropped a wine glass, she was so

startled. Shay was standing behind her, using the wall for support.

"Shay. Dammit!" Saronda raised her shoulders and shook her arms. "You scared the livin— I thought you were in bed."

"Sorry, wee ooh I got you good. Didn't mean to girl but, whoa. I came down to say a proper ganight and make sure— you know, that you and me, we leave good."

"It's 'I.' 'You and I.' Ah, never mind. Go to bed. We're good. And you're drunk. But, thank you, you made me think. Like you always do."

—ε-ε-ε-ε-ε-ε—

It wasn't bad, as snowmobile crashes go.

There was no flipping, no explosion, just a garden variety high-speed impact straight into some drainage rocks that, helpfully, had been covered in a couple feet of fluffy drifted snow. The snowmobile was unusable and Kelso's right leg nearly so, but good luck had prevailed. He had barely missed hitting a large rock. He wasn't dead but his escape plan was now plan B. Unfortunately for Kelso, he didn't have a plan B. He crawled to the rock and slept in the only position he could find where his leg didn't scream with pain.

Clearly, sleeping on a rock wasn't part of his plan. He had to get to an abandoned farm with a barn where he stashed everything he needed. The road is used by workers maintaining the large power lines that bring electricity from natural gas fired plants in Alberta, Canada. It was as far away from prying eyes as he could get and still be somewhere. The first light of the morning woke him up. After a few tries, he was able to stand and walk. He took ten steps in the deep snow and stopped. He thought his chest would explode, taking large gulps of cold dry air. Years in a cabin hunched over a computer is a horrible way to stay in shape.

—ε-ε-ε-ε-ε-ε—

Saronda approached the registration desk. "I'm hoping you can help me. I signed up for a psychology class. I've been switched to History 107, but I don't want a history class."

The clerk looked at her computer, "OK, let's take a look. Yes ma'am, you've been switched to History 107. It happens to Provisionals."

"But I'm taking this class so I can qualify to be a Junior next year. I need the credits."

"History 107 will provide that for you."

"It sounds downright boring. Useless."

The registration clerk gave a sideways glance at the next counter. "Look I'm not supposed to say this, but that History class needs people. Only five signed up."

"That's cuz it's lame."

"I think it's because it's a new professor. People think he's kooky. He recently left Brown."

"Brown? He's from Brown? Where is that, like New Hampshire or something."

"Rhode Island."

Saronda asked, "What's he doing here at Trinity Wash U?"

"I don't know. Hiding?" The registration clerk let out a nervous chuckle. "Sorry about the change. But maybe the new professor will be good." She lowered her voice. "Even if he is kooky."

"I think I'd better meet him before I commit to this class. Does he have a name?"

"Dr. Axel Mixcertl."

"Mix curdle? Curdle? Like month old milk?"

"So I've been told."

—ε-ε-ε-ε-ε-ε—

Kelso trudged on. The snow had drifted during the night making large tufts of meringue that played with the morning light, giving texture to an otherwise flat road. The sun burned through the morning haze, highlighting tall pines standing proudly with new coats of white cashmere. Kelso cursed the winter wonderland as he sank up to his knees with each step. The deep fluffy snow was exhausting to walk through. Kelso couldn't pull in air fast enough, his heart pounded his chest a hundred-eighty times a minute trying to keep his body supplied with oxygen. The dry air caught in his throat. He put his hands on his knees and bent over. He made it two-hundred feet. Only ten thousand left to go.

The pain in his leg signaled his adrenal glands to produce a shot of adrenaline that enabled him to keep walking. The abysmal situation he found himself in; cold, exhausted, and detected, would trigger fear, doubt and loathing in a normal person. In Kelso, it fed an inner storm of spite and resentment to whoever ratted him out. He knew what a disaster this was for him. Anonymity is crucial when your entire game is spreading lies. It was a lesson he learned from the smear campaign against the college president. No one can attack your credibility if they don't know who you are.

He resolved to march on, two miles from his stuff and a million miles away from what he left behind. He made it another two-hundred feet.

"I can't do this." The words hung as a frozen cloud. He dropped to his knees and took long deep breaths, cursing the pain in his chest.

He squinted at the road ahead, and the freezing death march rolled on.

—ε-ε-ε-ε-ε-ε—

Brody was drifting in a restless numbness when his phone jolted him.

"Brody, this is Rebecca."

"I know, I can see it on my phone, Rebecca SEC." He struggled to put life in his voice.

"You can probably change that to just Rebecca, after what I went through yesterday."

"Yeah?"

"The FBI dragged me to their HQ."

"That sounds like me today."

"Today? You mean yesterday. It's noon. Are you still sleeping? They talked to you too?"

"Yes, right before I was kidnapped."

"Kidnapped? Someone kidnapped you? We need to talk. Come to Busboys tonight."

Rebecca hung up. Brody lay back in bed, his phone resting in his hand. Minutes went by as his screen faded to sleep mode. He had no ambition to workout, shower, or look for a job. The hotel room was suffocating.

Brody called the front desk to bring his car around. He searched the Internet for a realtor in Pittsburgh willing to sell his condo sight unseen and headed to the lobby.

"Your total is five dollars, just one mini-bar charge. Do you want to leave it on the credit card you used at check-in?"

Brody thought about how nice it was for Brooster

to pay for his room, even if he was a kidnapping clown. "No, I'll use cash."

Ed said, "Hey young man. You're back. How'd it go with the lady? I'll bet she loved that suit you were wearing."

He handed Ed the check slip. "Yeah. I need my car."

"Yessir."

- Brody drove to Baltimore.

—ε-ε-ε-ε-ε-ε—

Kelso's life right now was shit. He should have been driving an unregistered 2010 Jeep Wrangler Sahara right now, but Earth is tilted so it got dark early, and a spring rain had washed out a bridge on the road he was on, which he couldn't see because it was dark, and the headlight was a little wonky because he hadn't gone through all the details of owning a snowmobile. He had no choice but to trudge on and hope nothing else went wrong.

"Oh shit."

Kelso turned his face away from the road at the sight of an approaching truck. It was a large truck, probably the only wheeled vehicle that could make it through the drifted snow.

It was stopping. *This is bad. Very bad.*

He mentally scrolled through the section of the

manifesto on loose ends.

Change your dialect, adopt an accent, something to throw off their description.
But most important, eliminate the loose end.

The driver leaned out the window. "Did you see that giant explosion?"

Kelso searched his mind for a story. He hadn't planned on anyone seeing him and certainly not be close enough to identify him. He limped up to the driver's side door, thankful for something to lean on.

He tried to duplicate the driver's accent. It was horrible. "No sir, I didn't see no explosion. Certainly not a giant one." He wasn't lying. He was hauling ass in the opposite direction at the time.

"You don't sound like you're from around here. You gotta touch of the south in your voice."

"Oh I wasn't born here but I've lived in northern Idaho for awhile." *Stop talking before you say something stupid.*

Too late. Nobody from northern Idaho would say they're from *northern* Idaho.

The driver squinted. "Huh. Well I've lived here in *north* Idaho my whole life. I don't recall seeing you before. But the explosion. It was a big one. Last night. Right over there. You can still see the smoke through the trees. I'm going down there. Wanna come? You look cold."

Kelso steadied himself on the large side mirror, the driver tightened his grip on the steering wheel. Kelso looked down the road lined with towering pines. The seriousness of the situation was sinking in fast. He had a sorry ass out-of-shape body, a bum leg, and now, a loose end. That's bad for even the best of fugitives. Loose ends derail plans. In Kelso's tunnel vision mind, derailing the plan is not just a problem, it's an intolerable outcome. He took two steps away from the truck and rubbed the back of his neck.

He took another couple steps. He wrote the section in the manifesto about loose ends. The problem was, he copied and pasted it from a spy novel.

He shook his head. "What a mess."

"Are you talking to me? Because if you are, I can't make out what you're saying."

Kelso glanced over his shoulder. "Oh yeah, I was talking to myself. That ride you offered is most kind."

Kelso limped around the truck using the three inch diameter bull bar on the front to steady himself and then he remembered the washed out bridge. The driver would need to turn around.

He opened the passenger side door. The hinge squealed as metal scraped metal.

"Whoa, that's a loud door."

The driver said, "Yeah, I don't use that door much. It's just me out here."

Nice.

As Kelso was about to step into the truck, he said, "You know, on second thought, I need to be moving on. Why don't you check out the explosion on your own?"

"Suit yourself."

The snow squeaked as the truck pulled away. If he hurried, Kelso could get to the barn in time to find a weapon.

—ε-ε-ε-ε-ε-ε—

Saronda stopped mid-stride and muttered, "What the L. L. Bean is this? Dude's got flannel."

She tapped on the door frame of the open door.

A flannel shirted man in quarry gray chinos turned around quickly, dropping the book he had just pulled from a box.

Saronda felt her cheeks get warm. "Oh my God, I didn't mean to startle you. I assume you're Dr. Mixcertl."

He snarked, "Oh you didn't startle me. I always drop books when people come to my door. Who are you and why are you here? I don't see an appointment in the system, if you can call it that. It's like nineteen-eighty-three around here."

"Uh, OK, I'm taking your class, History... " Saronda

looked at her phone. "Uh, 107."

"Oh so you're the one."

"The one what?"

"The one taking the class."

"They said there were five."

"I was joking. You're right, there are five. Five! Huge. How will I ever be able to teach that many students at once? Five whole people, up to ten eyeballs."

"You sound cynical."

"That's disappointing. I was going for condescending."

He turned to face her directly and leaned forward. "But, you haven't answered my questions, which is very bad for a student."

"What questions?"

"There were only two. Maybe you should have written them down. OK, I'll be nice and repeat myself, although technically I shouldn't have to. Who are you and why are you here?"

"Well, as I said, I am thinking of taking your class and—"

He jumped in. "That's not what you said. You said you were taking my class, not that you were *thinking* of taking my class."

"OK, so I'm taking your class."

"Well if you've already decided, why are you here?"

"Uh, I wanted to see what, you know, what you were like. Look, maybe I shouldn't have..."

"I'm a prick, that's what I'm like."

He intensified his eye contact. "But I'm sure you've been told this or you wouldn't be down here trying to find out how much of a prick I am."

"I feel like we got off to a bad start."

She approached him and extended her hand. "Saronda Jackson."

"No need to shake hands. I trust you have no weapons. My name is Doctor Axel Mixcertl. 'Mixsertle', not whatever the hell *you* said. I'm an MD doctor in addition to the kind of doctors that lurk in these hallways. At least I guess they're PhDs. I haven't had time to talk to them. Or should I say, I've been able to avoid them. By the way, I tell everybody I've got multiple advanced degrees, not just you, so don't think you're special."

Saronda wanted to turn and walk away. Instead, she sat on the arm of a side chair.

Dr. Mixcertl paused. "Oh great, you're staying. Since you've made yourself at home, may I ask, have I answered all your questions? It's only fair, since you've answered mine. Please, have a seat. I mean, you can actually sit in the chair, you don't have to perch on the arm like a…"

He looked at her with what Saronda tried to convince herself was sincerity, but none was showing through the sarcasm. She stood. It was partly to drag the balance of power a little in her direction, but also in case she had to run.

The professor rubbed his beard. "OK, then, I'll sit."

Saronda said, "I guess I'd like to know what the class is about."

The professor threw his hands up. "Ah, good, someone who's done their research and comes prepared with insightful questions. An overwhelming thirst for digging into details beyond what they could find out in five minutes online."

"Professor Mixcertl, I just found out I was assigned to this class."

The professor sized her up. "Very well, in that case, the class is about the methods used by the ruling class throughout history to destroy the middle class and subjugate an entire society."

"That doesn't sound like history—"

He cut her off sharply, "Of course it's history. History is ripe with examples of strongmen taking control of societies, it's important—"

"Isn't it 'rife'?"

"What?"

Saronda parried, "You said 'ripe' but I think 'rife' is a better word, it means abundant, widespread. That is what you meant, right? Not a fruit that's ready to be—"

The professor was clearly taken aback. "Rife, huh. OK OK, history is all about how the powerful few take advantage of societal conditions to take power; fascist tendencies."

"You mean like Hitler and shit?"

"You know, in some circles, I'm considered a rising intellectual. Your unnecessary use of profanity indicates you are either intimidated by my status as a published author, nervous, or amazingly plucky. And that rife thing, I'll have to think about it. But, no, I'm talking about methods more subtle than 'Hitler and shit' as you call it. I do like that term though, kinda captures a whole mood. Hitler's mistake was he wasn't subtle. The world didn't like that. They swarmed him like antibodies. I prefer to talk about subjugation from within, subtle, slithering, for the most part silent, steady, constant, repetitive until... "

Saronda slid into the chair. "Until what?"

He leaned forward. "My my, you are a curious one."

He put his hand to his chest, his back ramrod straight. "The Dark Ages. Oh, to have Chiwetel Ejiofor's voice. That would've come out superb." He deepened his voice and dramatically called out again, "The Dark Ages."

Saronda shook off the non sequitur. "I don't know much about the Dark Ages."

"Watch Monty Python and the Holy Grail, that pretty much sums it up, but, what caused those years of economic and intellectual bankruptcy? An entire society was dismantled bit by bit. What were the factors? Why did an entire society fall apart? Society was thriving, they were building great things, fountains, majestic churches."

Saronda tried to decipher if he was melting down or just rambling like a madman.

He got a little wild-eyed. "They were building domes and giant stone arches." He threw his hands in the air and exalted, "And then, nothing! Nothing got built for centuries. Society went into a hole. Much has been written, hell, I've written a lot. I've been dismissed a lot too. OK, some of my theories are, a polite word they use is, unconventional, or the one I like, non-conforming, but who wants to be conforming?"

He stared at Saronda. "The historians are wrong. I have spent years understanding the factors. I've thought this through, I really have."

Saronda raised her eyebrows. "OK, this is a long way from Psych 103."

His voice deflated. "You wanted to take a

psychology class? Why?"

"I wanna learn what makes people tick."

He rested his arms on his thighs and leaned in close. "Hell, I'll teach you more about what makes people tick than any psych class. I'm talking about what makes people tick on a mass scale." His voice rising.

He held eye contact. "Understand? On a mass scale. Entire societies. Under the control of leaders, if you can call them that. The methods they use to manipulate, control, oppress..."

Then, with a flourish, "And they're doing it today!"

He stood and clapped his hands together. "OK. Enough. You have to leave now. I'll see you in class. Close the door when you leave, I don't want students dropping in without an appointment."

Saronda couldn't get to the hallway fast enough. Apparently, his chumminess had limits.

—ε-ε-ε-ε-ε-ε—

Ray Denmore answered his phone. "OK Greg, give it to me."

Greg summarized, "We found a snowmobile in a ditch. And a truck with a guy inside. He's OK, just a bad bump on his head. He wasn't your guy. The tracks were headed *toward* the cabin. He couldn't remember much. Didn't even know why he was driving out there."

Greg hesitated, then, "Listen, I know you don't want to hear this, but we've taken this as far as we can. I gotta pull the team."

Ray pleaded, "Greg, I know you have your neck out with this, but could you give it a little more time? Poke around some more."

"I'm exposed. I pulled strings to get those agents out there and they were almost killed. Working through the incident reports is gonna be—"

"Yeah I get it. We'll keep listening for this guy. Can I give you a call if something comes up?"

"You got my number. But, Ray, everything by the book, please. Retirement is so close."

They disconnected.

Yasmin stood up quickly. "Wait, he's kidding right? What about a dragnet? Helicopters. Satellites. Throw everything at it."

Ray said, "He wouldn't get approval for something like that. What you heard is just the way things work."

Yasmin fumed on the way back to her desk, mumbling, "What I heard was two guys talking about retirement."

—ε-ε-ε-ε-ε-ε—

"Oh thank God." Kelso fell to his knees as the silhouette of the barn revealed itself through the icy haze. *Please let me get there before that truck comes back.*

The snow had drifted against the barn door. After clearing as much as he could with his foot, he chipped ice from the padlock.

He leaned on the door to catch his breath. His thick gloves made it difficult to use the key as falling snow stung the back of his neck. The large metal door latch clanked open but the deep snow blocked the heavy wooden door from opening all the way. He squeezed through and found a small shovel. *I guess this will have to do.*

Twenty minutes went by as he cleared the snow. The cold, dry air stung the back of his throat as he drew in heavy breaths. None of this was in his plan. None of it was covered in the manifesto. None of it helped with his loose end. He checked for any sign of the truck. *Why is everything so difficult?*

Finally, he was able to open the door. Exhausted. His hands were red and stiff from the cold.

"There she is." He pulled smartly on a large tarp.

This was no used, banged up beater. It was a fully loaded Jeep Wrangler Sahara. It would probably have been better to get something that blends in more, but Kelso wanted to get his fair share of the Common Fund. Every year, his band of anarchists put a portion of the revenue they generated into a pot. They called themselves the "Proboys" because it sounds like the

Russian word for disruption. Kelso knew they would want nothing to do with him now that he's detected.

"Thank you, Proboys. Goodbye and good luck. And thanks for the Jeep."

Still no sign of the truck. He started the Jeep. His buzz of excitement blended with the soft hum of the engine. He had his stuff, a full tank of gas and, most of all, a thumb drive. He also had a loose end, a local, who had gotten a good look at him. He felt panic coming on. He tried to convince himself that leaving the loose end behind was the best course but he also wondered if he was being chicken. There was a hatchet hanging on the wall. *God, what would that even be like?* He ran his hands through his long stringy hair and rested his head on the steering wheel.

He sat for an hour. *Ah, hell.*

He put the Jeep into drive and drove out into the darkening winter landscape.

—ε-ε-ε-ε-ε-ε—

Yasmin combed through the previous twenty-four hours of data. No signals. No signs of where Prairie Dog had run to. Nothing. She set down her tablet and leaned back.

Ray hurried out of his office covering the distance to Yasmin's desk in a strident march.

Ray said, "Holy shit."

"Sir?"

"I just read the manifesto. Holy shit."

Welcome to the party old man.

Ray paced behind her. "We gotta catch this guy."

No shit, sherlock. Was it your years of experience that told you that?

Yasmin said, "I'm nervous saying this but it's very disappointing that you're not pushing harder to catch this guy." *Ooh. I'm getting fired.*

"These things have to be taken one step at a time. That's how the system works."

"Yes, very nice. We're taking steps, working inside the system. He's taking leaps. He doesn't give a sh— flip about the system. He wants to tear down the system. If we don't... "

She was talking to a wall.

—ε-ε-ε-ε-ε-ε—

Rebecca Standiford walked into her boss's office. She noticed that his nameplate had been taken off the door and was sitting on his desk.

"Looks like you're moving up. Congratulations, former SEC Commissioner Bruce Donnagin," she said sincerely.

"Thanks, but we have this little matter we need to clean up. Please, sit."

Rebecca chose the chair in front of his desk. She thought her boss would sit behind his desk like a sane person, but he remained standing, adding to her unease.

She spoke first, "The main thing to understand is, I got the job done. If you remember, ExpoLytics crapped out on us, and we were dead. Our biggest case, the case you hung your career on was DOA. Bruce, no way, if we lost the GeneraCur case, you'd be moving up and no way we could bring charges. I did what needed to be done."

As she talked, he walked around from behind the desk. "But Rebecca, you—"

She regretted sitting. Her boss seemed to grow taller as he hovered over her.

She put up her hand, flashing her palm. "I wasn't finished."

She breathed in, then with a steady voice, "Without acquiring the computers, there is no way we could have finished that analysis."

Her steady eye contact caught him off guard. She stood, making her a little closer to him than she expected.

Her tone remained firm. "What else was I supposed to do when ExpoLytics bailed? Drop one of the biggest, and may I say, highest profile cases we had?"

She was now toe-to-toe with the former SEC Commissioner, soon-to-be boss of the FBI and the entire DoJ.

She paused to let the gravity of the words "highest profile" sink in. "There were a lot of eyes on this."

"But Rebecca, I'm getting reports that these computers you requisitioned without my signature, were used for purposes other than GeneraCur."

Rebecca leaned in close. Her breath grazed his jugular.

"Let's stay focused on what's important, newly appointed, not yet approved, Mr. Attorney General. GeneraCur was the last little check mark on your dance card. Or should I say scandal-free dance card?"

He backed up a step.

Rebecca stepped forward. "So, tell me Bruce, how much do you want to know about what happened? Under *your* watch."

"But, dammit Rebecca, and what did you tell the FBI?"

"I plead the Fifth. I told them nothing."

Rebecca relished the tension for a second and then, "Now, I really thought this meeting was going to be about my much-deserved promotion for closing the case."

Bruce walked to the window. After a minute he said, "OK, I don't think you or the guy, what's his name?"

"Brody."

"OK, you and Brody don't have to worry about the FBI. I'll make sure there aren't any consequences from meeting with them."

Oh, to be so lucky.

—ε-ε-ε-ε-ε-ε—

Saronda fidgeted as she sat alone at a table in Busboys and Poets. Everything was a raw nerve to her. Rebecca was late. Not a peep from Brody. The conversation at the table next to her made her bristle. God, what vapid small talk. Such a waste. People say it every year, "I can't believe it's dark already, only five fifteen!" Saronda felt like leaning over and saying, "Happens every year folks. Can we just post that somewhere and never mention it again?" She shifted in her chair and scratched at the table and waited. She crossed her arms and blankly studied the napkin dispenser. She thought about the hours she spent here with Rebecca and Brody. It was here that she grew close to her two new friends. It was here that they bonded. It was here that she and Brody spent hours talking. She missed him. She leaned back and rubbed some wetness from her eyes. She and Brody talked about everything. It was so easy. They talked about new concepts, where reality came from, what reality is. And Augustine's article, so full of wisdom about the universe, and

Whispers, and how they interact with each other. She believed in Whispers, and she believed hers connected with Brody's, pulled together by the same force that made the stars, the same force driving the universe to its ultimate destiny.

Rebecca strode in, sliding her full-length Burberry coat off her slim figure and setting her calfskin purse down in one smooth motion.

"Sorry I'm late. Wooh, what a day. You don't have a drink yet. Where's Brody?"

Saronda looked at the empty table. "You're right. No drink. Ha ha, what's with that?" Her voice was lifeless.

"Whoa, you're really down. Where *is* Brody? Probably some post celebration lull."

Saronda didn't respond.

Rebecca lifted her voice. "But hey, I've got some good news. First, I'm not fired. Second, they want me to build a data analysis team based on the system we used to help Brody with his episodes. It'll help us catch more fraudsters, maybe even take down some big-time money launderers."

Saronda didn't respond.

Rebecca paused. "But here's the other thing, I have free reign of these computers. I can use them to play with those equations in Augustine's article."

Saronda didn't respond.

Rebecca continued, "I want to understand what they..."

Rebecca lowered her shoulders. "You really are down, aren't you? You were so excited about Augustine's paper and were going to teach the world."

Saronda snapped, "I don't care about any of that stuff."

Rebecca inhaled slowly. "Look, Brody will be here. He went through a lot. He's a guy. He needs—"

"He's a shit. I mean where is he? Before, he was always around, then we fix his sorry ass, and poof, gone."

Rebecca said, "I think we could use some wine. House white?"

Saronda ignored the question. "What happens if he doesn't come back? What does that mean?"

"Saronda, I don't know what to say. Maybe he needs to take care of something we don't know about. There's a million reasons. Why do you assume this is about you?"

Saronda looked at the floor. Her eyes were moist. "Rebecca, I no longer feel a connection with him."

—ε-ε-ε-ε-ε-ε—

Brody was frustrated.

"Look, this is the fourth place I've looked at. It's cold. I'm tired. I don't want to haggle. Your rent is too high. Lower it by ten percent and you have a deal."

The landlord eyed Brody. "I won't be able to include the parking spot at that price."

Brody shook his head. "C'mon, man." He started to plead that he was a cut above the usual addicts and losers but fatigue won out. "Please, just… "

The landlord shook his head. "All right, deal, and you can have the parking spot, but I'd watch that fancy car of yours like a hawk."

Brody looked around the place, let out a sigh, and took the keys. As the landlord left, Brody pulled back the drapes to check out the view. It wasn't exactly the hanging gardens of Babylon, just a parking lot with broken asphalt separating him from a Chinese restaurant. That, and a chain link fence supporting the withered stalks of dormant ragweed. A scrappy sumac with three leaves still clinging since autumn did a poor job hiding the restaurant's dumpster. He tried to decipher the name of the restaurant, but the flickering neon had too many burned out letters. It could've been the Wok Fish or Tok Wisk or any number of combinations that made no sense. He was too tired to play neon Wheel of Fortune and went to bed. It was eight o'clock.

—ε-ε-ε-ε-ε-ε—

The motel desk clerk studied the driver's license and then studied his customer.

"Milo Cuda. Looks like you lost a bit of weight,

congratulations. How'd you do it?"

The comment caught Milo off guard. "Uh, actually I think the beard made me look a little wider in the face, that's all. "Why did you check my ID anyhow? I said I'm paying cash up front."

"Oh, Sheriff Cormick sent a note. There's a guy running loose up in Idaho."

"Running loose?"

"I don't know details. So, that's one night and your total is one-hundred-twenty-five dollars and seventy five cents."

Milo was surprised. "That's rather steep, being way out here."

The clerk said, "Well we need to keep the lights lit. Normally there's an upcharge on race weeks. I charged you regular though. You're not pulling a cart so I figure…"

Milo's face wrinkled with confusion. "That's nice of you, I guess."

He handed the clerk two fifties and two twenties. The bills were wrinkled and torn.

The clerk said, "Haven't seen that in awhile."

"Cash?"

"No, those old style bills, you know, before they started making the faces big."

He gave Milo fifteen dollars in change. "Let's call it an even one twenty-five."

Milo studied the crisp bills before shoving them in his pocket.

"OK, Mr. Cuda, here's your key. Checkout is noon. You don't happen to have a brother named Barry do you? That's a joke. Probably heard it a million times. Sleep well."

Milo was halfway down the hallway when he got the joke and said under his breath, "I guess that's what passes for comedy in… " He glanced at the address on the key tag. "Fernley, Nevada."

He turned around and called out to the clerk, "By any chance is there a liquor store nearby?"

"There's one across the street, but it's closed for repairs."

Milo tilted his head. "Closed for repairs. That's a story. Thanks, I'll make do."

He entered his room and remembered he had a bottle in his musty backpack, at the bottom, past the flashlight, first aid supplies and a long-expired box of Poptarts. He took the plastic wrap off the cheap plastic cup in the bathroom and poured some of the tawny liquid. The stringent notes of the Woodinville rye caught in his throat, and he let out the signature cough of someone who hadn't had liquor in a while.

"Whoa! OK, well, bring on the numb."

He blacked out on the worn, stiff bedspread.

—ε-ε-ε-ε-ε-ε—

Professor Axel Mixcertl, MD, PhD, PriCK, droned on. Five students endured a master class in professorial largesse.

Saronda tried to focus, scribbling an occasional note and willing the clock on the wall to reach two. The class wasn't anything like what the professor had described. It was just a bunch of class rules and self-promotion. Dr. Mixcertl stopped mid-sentence.

His voice showed a touch of drama. "Let's engage, shall we? That's the problem with these elective classes. Everyone tries to just glide through. Well, you will learn something in this class. Trust me."

He paused, took two steps to the left and then turned to face the class. "Consider this. Everyone thinks that history is buttoned up, understood, facts are facts. Historians have it all figured out. We… "

The drama swelled. He paused and softened his tone. "We all think we know history. And the few things we don't know, so what, it's the past. But that's where it gets dangerous. Oh, that bad stuff, don't worry about that. It happened way back then. That doesn't happen anymore. Can't happen. Society is progressing! Always moving forward! 'Getting better all the time' like The Beatles said."

His voice crescendoed. "We think we're smarter now."

He moved to the other side of the room and stretched out his arms. "And we're all so certain about what we know. But tell me this..."

He rubbed his beard and nodded twice. "Yes, let's engage. Can anyone here name even one fact about what led to the Dark Ages?"

He searched the room with serious eyes and paced expectantly. Saronda watched the clock on the wall tick away each excruciating minute wondering why he didn't color the lone patch of gray in his beard.

He paused at Saronda's desk, and tapped it three times "Anyone?"

The indifferent silence appeared to irritate him. "Perhaps many of you are taking this class to meet some arbitrary requirement. Perhaps one or two of you are here because you want to learn from me, the renowned Dr. Axel Mixcertl."

Saronda unconsciously let out a staccato breath that a reasonable person would understand to be a sarcastic snort.

The professor seized on the sound. "Oh, it looks like we have a volunteer to answer the question. But I must ask, do you doubt that there are students in this class for the specific reason that they want to learn history?"

He drew out the word history and continued, "History of the middle ages from one of the most respected authors on the subject?"

Saronda glanced around the room at the blank faces. There were four other people there. "Hard to tell at this point."

"Huh. Well, I suppose you may be correct. But rest assured, you will learn to respect me. And thank you for volunteering to answer my rather simple question."

"Alright, if it will get us out of here today." There was a collective chuckle. "My answer is, the plague."

The professor pounced. "The plague? You are saying that you know for a fact the plague caused an entire society to decline in an economic, cultural and in some cases intellectual tailspin."

"Well, it wasn't the only factor but it certainly was a factor."

He retorted with a strong east coast affect. "Ms. Jackson, perhaps I didn't make it clear at the beginning of class but in this classroom when we state something as a fact, we mean an irrefutable fact backed up by cited studies."

He stared directly at her and asked, "Do you know why you should say something is a fact *only* if you can back it up?"

Saronda raised an eyebrow.

The professor put both hands on Saronda's desk. "Because if you don't, I fail you. End of story. You get an F. So, I want, on my desk, at the start of next week's class, irrefutable evidence that a contributing factor to the Dark Ages, which I hate that term, but it sounds cool..."

He checked the clock and talked a little slower. "You deliver to me, by next class, irrefutable proof that the plague helped bring on the Dark Ages. Don't even think that Wikipedia or some other hack site will get you through this. You have to prove it to me. If you want to have a chance of passing this class, you have to hand me something I would be willing to write 'proved Q.E.D.' on. Good luck. Oh, also, I'm a real bastard about this stuff. And remember, if you present something as fact and can't back it up, I will fail you."

He timed it so his last word came out precisely on the hour. "Clocks ticking, Ms. Jackson."

Saronda's glare was lethal.

—ε-ε-ε-ε-ε-ε—

"Checking out, room 110."

The desk clerk took the key from Milo. "Yes sir, you're all paid up. Anything I can help you with?"

"I'm good. What's the best route to Seattle?"

"Seattle? That's a long way. I'd take eighty west to Reno then north I guess."

Milo said, "Got it."

"Great. Hope you enjoyed your stay. Say, did you have any trouble with the Internet? My nephew said he fixed it and—"

Milo replied, "Oh, I stay away from the Internet. Lotta bad people on there. Have a good day."

Milo jumped in his Jeep with nothing but two changes of clothes, twelve thousand dollars in cash and a bold plan. He stopped at the *Flying J* to fill up gas. It had a casino.

He put three quarters in the old-style slot machine, and it spit out five dollars and twenty-five cents. "Excellent sign."

He headed east.

—ε-ε-ε-ε-ε-ε—

Saronda quickened her steps to catch up to the brown-haired girl who sat in the back row of her class. "That guy's a nut job."

The girl turned around. "Got that right, my brother took his class at Brown. Total jerk."

"Yeah, I heard you say that in the hallway. So why'd you take it?"

"Only choice left when I signed up. My brother laughed his ass off when I told him."

"So is this guy serious about this whack assignment?"

"Yeah, you're screwed."

Saronda implored her to say more.

"He does that every year. My brother told me about it. That's why I sat tight."

"Kinda fed me to the wolf, don't you think."

The girl said, "Man, I need this class so I can declare a major. No way I'm going down in flames on the first day."

"Does he really fail people?"

"Legend has it."

Saronda shook her head. "Has anyone ever passed the assignment?"

"I don't know. Maybe my brother knows."

She gave Saronda her brother's number. "Good luck, gotta run."

His phone went to voicemail.

"Hello, you don't know me but I'm taking a class with Dr. Axel Mixcertl. I understand you had this same class. History of the Dark Ages. I'm wondering if you could call me back, I have a question."

She waited for a callback. There was none.

—ε-ε-ε-ε-ε-ε—

Another wasted afternoon. Brody pulled back the tattered curtain. Just a depressed parking lot and that damn sign for the Asian restaurant. No luck deciphering the name for the tenth time. It would require him to leave his room and walk two-hundred feet across a parking lot. He had no desire to do either.

He plopped onto the bed. "Doldrums. I've got the doldrums."

His desires, urges, yearnings, whatever word best describes that internal drive to plan what you want and then go after it, gone. And Brody had lots of plans, but remembering how they made him feel was just out of reach. He had no sense of initiative. He looked for his phone to call his father but it was on the other side of the bed, so he dozed off.

These were not doldrums.

Whispers weave and humanity dances. Augustine said it. Everything we are and everything we are meant to be is woven by Whispers. They are inside us, reaching out to the universe. When we listen to our Whispers, we move toward our fate, the ultimate thing we're supposed to be. But the universe is a noisy place and Whispers are hard to hear, especially when they're damaged.

Brody's Whisper was broken. It made him feel alone with no desire to connect with anyone.

—ε-ε-ε-ε-ε-ε—

The crimson evening light reflected off wispy clouds. Milo drove on. He felt a heaviness just below the surface. He had to do something he hated, talk to a human. His jaw tightened as the watercolor sky gave way to a monochrome haze. Unlike spreading lies and being nonexistent, humans are messy. They argue. They mock. They're hard to control. They want to be convinced. He read a lot about debating, but blackmail was quicker, and he was very good at it. He knew from experience if you put people in a corner, they become pliable, especially if their freedom is at stake. Milo reached over to the passenger seat and picked up his phone.

He called Wayne Drakauer.

Wayne and Milo go way back. Each has saved each other's butts several times on projects that went sideways. Milo discovered Wayne was a little naughty and did some light insider trading, nothing so big that anyone would notice. Some higher ups at ExpoLytics got wind of his scheme. The CEO, CTO, CMO, and all the other C words should have fired Wayne, but they possessed a dangerous combination of ego, greed, and a broken moral compass. They joined Wayne in his pursuit of riches. Except they went big. It was big enough to draw attention.

Wayne's phone rang for the third time. Wayne had hoped to never get another call from that phone. It was a phone that didn't technically exist. It steals cell phone service between cycles, totally undetected. Only six people on Earth have ever received a call from that phone.

It rang a fourth time. "Kelso, geez, why are you—"

"Let me stop you right there, Wayne. I don't know who you're referring to exactly. This is Milo Cuda. That person you're referring to no longer exists."

Wayne paused. "You mean, he's dead?"

"No, catch on idiot. Do I need to spell it out for you?"

"You mean he's not dead? I was kind of hoping. But, sure, spell it out for me. Why the change? Are you a woman now?"

Milo said, "Careful what you say to me. I can make your life miserable."

"No, that's all over with, the SEC got their list of targets. They're preparing for trial. They're not looking for me."

Milo replied, "And you never really thanked me. Showing gratitude builds bonds. It's part of being a team."

And then, he twisted the knife. "Surely you remember our conversation about no records, no conviction, no problem. Call me tomorrow, see if you're still so confident."

—ε-ε-ε-ε-ε-ε—

Each year Axel Mixcertl got a little better at his schtick. This time he timed it perfectly, finishing precisely at the end of class. Each year he handed out an outrageously impossible task with a touch more arrogance, a little more self-importance. He was tempted to do it in the iconic Sean Connery - James Bond voice. "Clocks ticking, Ms. Jackson. I suggest you move along," but that would give away the game.

The complaints were the same: "It's unfair." "Nothing can be proven for certain."

Professor Mixcertl saw it as a learning experience, life is unfair. That, and he's a prick. He knew they grab the closest friend, partner, sibling, parent, and pee in their ear about their prick professor. He loved musing who the victim of their diatribe was.

—ε-ε-ε-ε-ε-ε—

Shay broke in. "Why'd you volunteer?"

"Well actually I kinda snort laughed and he lasered in on me. Everyone else sat there like scared sheep."

Shay said, "Smooth. Yeah, snorting, the universal sign of respect. So, who is this guy?"

"Dr. Mixcertl."

Shay looked out of the corner of her eye. "Mix what?"

"Mixcertl."

"Girl, you're taking a class from a prescription drug. Ask your doctor if mixasertle is right for you."

Saronda didn't laugh. She clenched her fists. "Lucky me. I'm stuck with this impossible task. Oooh I could just..."

"Why impossible?"

"Oh, come on. Irrefutable proof of something that happened a million years ago? Oh and he's the judge and jury on the whole thing. Thumbs up, thumbs down. Frickin' Caesar. I hate this guy."

Shay became wide-eyed. "Whoa girl, you're talking some shit now. Are you sure there's not something else going on?"

Shay studied her sister. "But you gotta do like you always do, fight through it, get the job done. Figure it out. If other people did it, you can too."

—ε-ε-ε-ε-ε-ε—

Brody was a corpse. Motivation was a distant memory. He needed baby steps. He needed something to make him feel again, a small accomplishment, a minor victory. A shower perhaps.

He willed his legs over the side of the bed and completed the task of standing up. The walk to the shower was a small effort compared to removing his clothes. It wasn't a physical fatigue, it was an emotional dead weight that hung on him like a vine. Brody finished his shower. It would be his biggest accomplishment of the day.

Nothing left to do but take a nap.

—ε-ε-ε-ε-ε-ε—

Saronda stepped out into the cold and pulled out her phone. Her call went directly to voicemail. She left a message. "Hello, again, my name is Saronda Jackson. I called before. Do you know if anyone has ever passed this stupid assignment Professor Mixcertl hands out on the first day?"

A feeling of desperation set in. She felt like her life was total chaos. This assignment was keeping her from translating the last part of Augustine Chalamet's science article from French to English. That and the other significant detail in her life, Brody was missing. But was he missing her? Inner insecurities gnawed at her. She seethed. Bastard. Her phone lit up with the last number she had called. The conversation was short.

"Look, this guy is a prick. Get out of that class if you can. I think only one person ever passed that assignment."

"Oh my God who?"

"Hell I don't know. He wasn't in my class. That jerk professor talked about him, though. Talked about him like he was a legend. Sendrick or Hendricks or something."

Saronda asked, "Do you know what year?"

"No, that's all I know. Good luck."

The phone went dead. She rushed home. Her roommate Danielle was glued to a DVR'd episode of a reality show Saronda had never heard of.

Danielle defocused long enough to acknowledge her. "Hey girl, you're in a hurry."

"I have some online searching to do for a history class assignment."

Danielle looked back to the TV. "Oh I took history, easy peasy."

Saronda walked to her room. It was her cocoon. The scent of a three-year-old, never burned candle mingled with the persistent musk of old books. Subjects ranged from ancient dead languages to quantum mechanics. She had read most of them and understood some of them. There wasn't a single novel among them. Saronda liked factual books, books she could learn from. Each book added bits of knowledge to her sponge-like mind. They were clues to a mystery. Some didn't fit. Those were the ones she took joy in, gaps between logic and reality. This assignment was perfect for that, linking mysteries together, one mystery informing another. She would have seen that way if there wasn't a gun to her head. She dove into ten years' worth of Brown University archives and not a single Sendrick or Hendricks.

"C'mon, princess, figure this out."

She searched more. Her eyes went in and out of focus as she blindly scrolled through the list of graduates. Nothing jumped out at her. She looked up from the screen and realized it was past midnight. She walked across her dark room and opened the blinds. Several stars stood out from the rest but one in particular was brightest of all. She immediately thought of Brody and the day he said she was wearing blue shoes.

"Dammit, Brody, where are you?"

Suddenly nothing else mattered. This assignment. This class. Getting a degree. She felt an all too familiar yearning to lose herself in a random page in a random book. Any subject would do. It didn't matter. It's what she does. It's her refuge.

But she didn't need refuge. She needed to complete this assignment. This stupid meaningless assignment. She stretched and sat down, head in hands. She stared at the screen, trying to focus. She drifted as her computer went to sleep. Then, from a place where thoughts combine and recombine came a spark. She woke up her screen.

"Dang, I was looking right at it."

On the screen, three quarters of the way down, as nondescript as the other hundred names was Cedric Creterjean.

—ε-ε-ε-ε-ε-ε—

Wayne Drakauer pulled into his usual parking

spot. It was easy getting the same spot everyday, now that there were only six cars. He walked into the once bustling ExpoLytics office building, hoping yesterday's phone call from Kelso—now Milo—wouldn't lead to anything.

And then.

"Mr. Drawkooer."

"Drakauer, but yes."

"You are served. Have a nice day."

He had no choice but to take the envelope. He held it at arms-length like it could jump up and eat his face. His nightmare came rushing back, the feeling of being out of control made his breathing shallow.

"Kelso."

He braced himself on the granite counter. "That bastard."

He pulled out his phone and logged into his account. The trading records were back. The naughty ones. The ones Kelso erased weeks ago. The ones with timestamps that proved he was in lockstep with the other fraudsters. A little analysis is all it would take to prove Wayne was the one pulling the strings. They were as guilty as he was, but they had high cotton lawyers that could explain away anything. They were looking for someone to point to, someone to pin it on, someone who couldn't fight back. Wayne would be perfect for that.

Wayne looked up from his phone. He closed his eyes and breathed in. Kelso Radovic, a.k.a Milo Cuda, absolutely owned him.

—ε-ε-ε-ε-ε-ε—

Cedric Creterjean was easy to find. He was a real estate agent in the Miami area and wasn't shy about spreading his number all through social media.

He answered on the first ring, "Never binn a better time to buy or sell, how can I help you to a better life?"

His accent was mesmerizing.

"Hi, this may seem like a weird question, but did you take a class from Axel Mixcertl?"

"Oh mun, many years ago. Like a mix-million years ago." His energetic laugh was more mesmerizing than his accent.

"OK. Well, you sound lively."

"Lively for life, mun. Do you know dee professor?"

"Unfortunately, yes, I'm taking a class from him."

"Unfortunately? No, he's a great guy, mun. Crazy as coconuts but, hey, get to know him outside dee class. Good fun."

"I'll have to think about that. If I survive. I've been told you passed the first day's assignment. Only one ever, according to legend."

"Yah, dat's me."

"So you remember?"

"Oh my Gawd, how could I forget dat? I work my ass off. I really did need dat class to complete my degree. My visa was running out and I was so close, so close, mun."

"So you think he's a nice guy. He seems like a prick."

"Oh. He's a prick. I mean, who fails people in elective class? Face it. And his theories are off dee chain, but he taught me to think, mun. By presenting his theories it caused me to dig in and try to prove him wrong."

"Can you give me any tips for the assignment?"

"Hey, I can give the whole damn thing."

"The proof? You still have it?"

"Oh yah, dat was a proud day for me. I showed my mama. I showed my friends. He wrote, 'PROVED' big letters. And then Q.E.D. Use it as an outline. What is your assignment supposed to prove?"

"That the plague was a factor in causing the Dark Ages."

"No way. Dat wuz mine too." He let out his loud signature laugh. "Use dee whole thing, mun. Turn it in. Ah, I love to see his face."

Saronda was taken aback. "But plagiarism."

Cedric squealed, "Leave my name on it. Don't take credit. Turn it in as is. Did he say *you* had to write it?"

Saronda thought back to the assignment. "Actually, no. Only requirement, 'have it on my desk—'"

"Ah, now you're using dee coconut that Gawd gave you. Oh, take a picture when he sees my name. He'll freak."

"He'll remember you?"

Cedric boasted, "I'm a legend, mun. He luuuvved me."

"I love your laugh. You're a hoot."

Cedric said, "Ahh I like to have fun. Do you need any property in dee south Florida market?"

"No, pretty sure I have all I need."

"Yeah, so how is Rhode Island?"

Saronda was puzzled. "Huh? No, I'm in D.C. He moved to a small university in northeast D.C."

"Oh, D.C., huh? Too many lawyers for me, mun. Hey, give me your address. I'll overnight it. It's a big package. Oh, dis is so much fun. Axel Mixcertl. Name from dee past. Good luck!"

—Ɛ-Ɛ-Ɛ-Ɛ-Ɛ-Ɛ—

Milo had driven all night. He was eager to get to his vacant condo. He was miffed that someone was parked in his designated spot. He took a picture of the license plate and thought how fun it would be hacking into the motor vehicle registration office and ruining this asshole's life. He parked in the only available visitor spot and walked up one flight of stairs. He purchased the condo several years ago with money he earned from a super PAC focused on discrediting windmills. Sounds echoed hollow as he stepped into the stale air of a long vacant room. He turned up the thermostat.

The condo had a convenient rear-facing entrance, and the designated parking spot was around the back, away from prying eyes.

It's unfortunate he wouldn't be using it. He would soon be moving to Washington D.C. All the high-powered friends he hasn't met yet are there. He will take his newly acquired puppet Wayne with him.

—ε-ε-ε-ε-ε-ε—

Wayne Drakauer's sweaty fingers made the paper of the subpoena droop. Reading it for the third time only increased his anxiety. They want everything. They want all his emails. They want all his paper documents. They even want copies of the microcode he wrote while working at ExpoLytics. He will need a lawyer just to handle the records transfer. And, by God, don't leave anything out. That itself is a crime.

His phone rang. "Kelso, Jeezus."

"It's Milo, remember? I don't know who this Kelso is that you mention. I take it you've logged into your account. Isn't it fun to know that those records can disappear and reappear anytime I want? I could erase them again and that subpoena will go smooth as silk."

"How did you know about the subpoena?"

Milo sneered, "Oh look at you believing in coincidence. I call yesterday and a subpoena is served today at, let me look, 8:37 a.m. Oh no wait, that's when the video was logged downtown. The actual timestamp of you receiving the subpoena is 8:12. Does that sound right?"

"Bastard."

"Really Wayne? Is that how you plan to treat your new boss? But cheer up, we're going to have fun together."

Wayne simply wanted to make a quick buck. Instead, he handed a neck cuff to a jackal. That's the trouble with crime, it looks like fun but the consequences can be damnable.

—Ɛ-Ɛ-Ɛ-Ɛ-Ɛ-Ɛ—

Dr. Axel Mixcertl stood like an executioner at the front of the room. He glanced at the clock. Four students waited silently.

"Hmm, we seem to be missing someone. I believe Miss Jackson may be at the registration office dropping this class."

She wasn't. She was hovering outside the door out of view. She wanted to arrive right on time and stroll nonchalantly into class. He did, after all, say to have her assignment "at the start of the next class." The clock ticked to the hour. Her walk was a subtle but noticeable strut. She wore a nice skirt, completed by a cashmere button down that Shay had given her for Christmas. She spent a few extra minutes that morning fixing her hair.

The professor raised his eyebrows. "Well, what do we have here? Was registration closed? Too late to drop?"

Hushed giggles died down as Saronda pulled a thick, bound document from her bag. It had a bold-faced title like the final version of a PhD thesis.

She said nothing as she laid it on the small desk at the front of the room.

She sat, smoothed her skirt, and said nothing.

Professor Mixcertl strode to the desk. "This is not your work, Ms Jackson."

Saronda said, "There is clear attribution on the cover sheet. In addition, permission to use is signed by the author and attached. I believe this addresses what you asked for in every regard."

"What I asked for was—"

Saronda was ready. "Yes, you wanted delivered to you something you would be willing to write 'proved' on.

Pull back the cover sheet."

Handwritten across the page in large letters "PROVED! Q.E.D."

The professor stared out the window as he thought through the criteria he had given. Several students shifted in their seats. Saronda felt her face get hot and her shoulders tense up. Dr. Mixcertl scratched his beard, dwelling on the gray patch.

A very long minute went by. "Very well played, Ms Jackson. So how is Cedric?"

"He's a real estate agent in Boca Raton."

"Oh dear God, I thought he had what it took to do important work. OK, let's go on, shall we? Ms Jackson, please stop by my office after class."

"I'll check my calendar. Also, Cedric wants that back."

Axel squinted slightly and turned to address the rest of the students. Class began.

—ε-ε-ε-ε-ε-ε—

Today was a day for baby steps. With another shower accomplished, Brody planned his next major move. He sat dripping wet and naked on the varnished wooden chair in front of the small desk that came with his piece of shit apartment. His swimmer's body was already showing signs of softness. Atrophy is a bitch for someone who steadfastly stuck to a rigorous workout schedule. His biggest workout these days was getting out of bed, and that was hit or miss. He thought of sitting long enough to dry off, but he needed to get moving. He needed a job, some place to go every day, a routine.

He labored to put his clothes on. He made his way to his car.

—ε-ε-ε-ε-ε-ε—

Professor Axel Mixcertl was deep into it, his voice rising and falling for emphasis. Saronda heard only parts. Her mind was flush with victory. She had faced a dragon and won. She glanced to her right and nodded to the brown-haired girl as the great Axel Mixcertl waxed on.

"And this is the difference between local and global rule. Dictators learned they could control large masses of people easier than small groups. Strongmen set themselves apart, eliciting an air of deification, never admitting mistakes... "

Saronda mindlessly opened Cedric's tome, casually leafing through pages as a respite from whatever the hell Mixcertl was babbling.

He paced the room, stroking his beard. "So you see, many times, society wanted that. They wanted to be ruled with an iron fist. They didn't want to quote 'decide what to do with their lives' unquote. Strict rule was the *people's* desire... "

Saronda's breathing changed. There, on the page, Cedric had used that same phrase.

—ε-ε-ε-ε-ε-ε—

Brody asked, "Is that all there is to it?"

And please, maybe tone down the perkiness.

"Yes. Yes. Yes. Simple and quick. Just go to QwikPage.com and download the app, complete your profile. You'll be done in a jiffy. After that, wait for notifications."

Done in a jiffy?

"When I get a notification what do I do?"

"Go to the baggage claim indicated on the app. You pick up the traveler's misplaced luggage and take it to the address shown."

"Nice, and I can work when I want?"

"Yes, at QwikPage, we pride ourselves on work-time flexibility. When you log in, we receive an alert and send you notifications."

He put his hand on Brody's forearm and leaned in. "We call them pages. You know, as in QwikPage. Good luck, and welcome to the QwikPage team."

It was the perfect job for Brody. Hang in his apartment and wait. When the app chirps, deliver lost luggage.

"Oh and one more thing. We call it *misplaced* luggage. Not lost. Lost is so final. And sad. Very sad. OK!

'QwikPage, we deliver what's missing from your life,' It's our motto."

"Oh, good, I was hoping there was a motto."

The snarky comment was an ember. He walked to his car.

—ε-ε-ε-ε-ε-ε—

Saronda sashayed through Shay's door with head cocked. "Checkmate. Total victory. Yes, it's true. I kicked some professorial ass."

Shay raised her arms. "You passed! I mean you proved that thing."

Saronda gave a single-shoulder raise. "Let's just say yes, yes, I did. Well, he didn't fail me. And guess what? I didn't go to his office after class."

"Whudaya mean?"

Saronda smirked. "He asked me to stop by his office and I totally did *not* stop by his office."

"But... "

Saronda puffed. "That's the way us legends play it."

"Since when did my shy little sister become a badass?"

Saronda got serious. "Shay, I feel like I know what I want to do."

"Ooh, serious face. You mean, like in life?"

"Yes, I beat that professor at his own game and the science paper by Augustine Chalamet gives me mojo. Think about it. A woman wrote down her ideas over a hundred years ago, and she changed the lives of countless people. Girl power!"

Shay flexed. "So is this like 'I am woman, hear me roar?'"

"Oh, it's more than that. Stand back and watch. Don't get in my way. I mean, I slayed the mighty Axel Mixcertl."

Shay replied, "Damn, that dude needs to change his name. But girl, don't forget getting your degree and what about... "

Saronda could tell she held back asking about Brody.

—ε-ε-ε-ε-ε-ε—

Brody drove to his apartment with the name of the QwikPage.com website saved to his phone. He pulled into his numbered parking spot under the Chinese restaurant sign. It was a nice day to get out and do something but that would be too many baby steps in one day.

—ε-ε-ε-ε-ε-ε—

Saronda worked her shift at the bookstore and decided to wait until early evening to see her professor.

She knocked on the frame of the open door. "Excuse me, professor."

He replied sharply, "Do you have an appointment?"

She walked in. "You don't look busy."

He wasn't. He was sitting behind his desk staring at nothing.

The professor said, "Come in. Close the door. I enjoy talking to young bright women."

Saronda didn't close the door.

Axel asked, "What do you want to talk about?"

Saronda said, "I wanted to meet with you because I've read Cedric's paper, and I don't know why you gave him a passing grade. He didn't prove anything. In fact, the more I read, the more questions I have. It's not a complete work."

The professor sounded defensive. "Nonsense, the work is brilliant."

Saronda reacted. "I'm not questioning the work. He comes to some very interesting conclusions, but it can be debated whether he proved anything, but that's not my point."

"Oh dear God, please tell me, what is your point?"

"My point is it had nothing to do with the causes of the Dark Ages. It had more to do with proving that the

Dark Ages were inevitable. Are you feeling OK? You look —"

Axel snapped back, "They weren't inevitable, but they *were* necessary."

"But Cedric said it had to happen."

"I believe he said it was necessary so that society could advance."

Saronda asked, "Advance to what? Are you sure you're OK?"

"To wherever it advances to, in the long run."

Saronda asked, "You mean destiny?"

The professor looked agitated. "I don't like that word and you'll notice it was never used in the text. Not even once."

Saronda picked up on his odd phrasing. "It was never used... by Cedric?"

"Oh come on, I thought you were a bright girl. See through the charade."

Saronda replied sharply, "The charade? You mean Cedric didn't write this, *you* did?"

"Yes! Cedric is a guy who sold a condo of mine in Florida. I took a bath, but he did OK. I asked him to play along with the ruse if anyone ever called him."

"This whole thing was a game?"

"It's not a game, it's history. History isn't about what happened. History is about digging for the truth, learning *why* things happened and asking the question, are the same forces that caused things to happen a long time ago still in place today?"

"You say in the paper that the answer is yes."

"Read it again, it goes deeper than that."

"That's why I think you're talking about destiny. Destiny of society, where it's all headed."

Axel sputtered, "How do you know society even has a destiny? Do you think it's written somewhere? Some master plan that's already been mapped out? And it's recorded."

Saronda said, "It would make things a lot less pointless. Don't you want to believe that all the little things we do, all the people we meet, are part of some grand plan?"

He said, "It's not about what you believe, it's about what the truth is. The thing that's pointless is thinking we can somehow influence the forces that rule us."

Saronda said, "Maybe not influence the forces but change the direction they take. Sometimes meeting someone by chance can have a big influence. Like, meeting you by chance. Even though you are a prick, I've learned a lot from class and from your paper."

"But my meeting you was not random."

This sent a shiver through Saronda.

The professor softened his voice. "Because I came here for you. I left my job at Brown and moved here. I needed to meet you."

Saronda's face stiffened. She gathered her things and power walked to the door, then stopped. Her mind vacillated between wanting to know what this was all about and running.

She spun around, her face hot. "You need to explain yourself. Like. Right now."

—ε-ε-ε-ε-ε-ε—

Brody sat on the bed. His mind was scattered. He felt like throwing something.

Another day had slipped by, and the thick curtains were still drawn. There were no sounds, just a viscous silence. It is in silence that people hear their Whispers. That is, the people who listen for such things. They allow themselves to be guided by the quiet, driving force within them. Brody had no drive. The atrophy of listlessness hollowed him out. He felt nothing. He convinced himself this was his fate.

He was wrong. The universe wasn't done with him.

—ε-ε-ε-ε-ε-ε—

Shay had barely unlocked her door when Saronda burst through.

"Whoa, Shay, why are you standing near your door?"

"I just unlocked it. I didn't want you to break a wrist turning the doorknob. Your texts sounded a little, uh, amped."

Saronda didn't sit. "He's here because of me."

Shay said, "I'm going to need more detail."

Saronda blurted, "Axel Mixcertl. He moved here because of me. He quit his job because of me. He tracked me down, got a job at Trinity U, and somehow made sure I was in his class."

Shay said, "This guy was after you?"

"Yep. Professor Axel MixDickhead. Dude's creepy."

"Stalkers can be that way. But wait, a guy uproots his family, quits his job, and moves here just to meet you?"

"Uh, I'm not sure he brought his family."

Shay held her breath.

Saronda made intense eye contact and said, "Do you want to know why?"

Shay exhaled slightly. "It is on my list."

"He experienced the same episodes as Brody."

Shay exhaled all the way. "Oh, here we go with that again. Girl, you get yourself into some shit, don't you?"

"He saw my tweets about the crap that Brody was going through. I have this account MathRonda. I started a hashtag DevilLight. He tracked me down."

"So, why'd he move here?"

"He no longer feels connected to his family. He's dead inside."

Shay said, "He seemed lively from what you said before."

"They have him on drugs. Makes him normal, but man, when they wear off, he's a downer."

—ε-ε-ε-ε-ε-ε—

There are only three people on Earth who know about the brilliance of Augustine Chalamet. They are the only ones who could teach the world how reality is created. If they studied the paper a little more, they may even be able to figure out the destiny of the universe and answer the question "What's it all about?" But they were otherwise predisposed. None of them had even bothered to read Augustine's paper to the end. There was an entire section they completely skipped over.

—ε-ε-ε-ε-ε-ε—

Saronda paused on her walk to the bookstore. She sat under a tree oblivious to the chorus of spring around her. She was totally engrossed in a document attributed to Cedric Creterjean but written by Axel Mixcertl, a professor who happened to mention he uprooted his life and moved hundreds of miles to meet her. Above her, new fresh leaves were pushing forth, eager to fulfill their season in the sun, taking in the sun's energy, grabbing carbon from the air, making the tree taller, bigger, prouder. Saronda grappled with why masses of people give their freewill to compassionless dictators.

—ε-ε-ε-ε-ε-ε—

Rebecca Standiford tangled with scofflaws. She was on fire at the SEC, building a computer network, breaking up powerful money cabals, bringing down bad guys.

—ε-ε-ε-ε-ε-ε—

Brody mostly just tried to get through the day. Achieving the right balance of hot and cold water in his shower was a triumph.

Three people who had formed a tight connection through the brilliance of Augustine Chalamet were now as far apart as they could possibly be.

That's how the spring went. Summer wasn't any different. Saronda was off chasing new knowledge, Rebecca was off chasing criminals, and Brody was just off.

—ε-ε-ε-ε-ε-ε—

The other thing that was off was Milo's schedule.

This made him very displeased with his team. He had studied books on human behavior and managing teams. He practiced speaking in clear, declarative sentences. Teams need leaders. Leaders talk a certain way. They use specific phrases. He convinced himself he knew all about teams.

His team was Wayne.

Milo burst into Wayne's workstation. "Goody, boxes. Has everything arrived?"

Wayne replied, "Nothing's arrived. I bought these retail."

Milo tensed up. Wayne said, "Don't worry, I used cash. You owe me by the way. The stuff we ordered is still not here."

Milo exploded. "How can it not be here yet?"

The downside of relying on blackmail is it only works to get things started. Day to day details still operate under the rules of give and take, communication. Messy human stuff doesn't always yield to what the book says.

Milo raised his voice. "I've been clear on the importance of schedule, and I distinctly remember asking if you needed anything clarified. You've had ample opportunity to provide meaningful feedback."

Wayne used his height advantage to hover over Milo. "Take a rest, Kelso. You're the one who's slowing things down. It's in that untraceable labyrinth you threw together. God knows where things are."

"My name is Milo. Diss me one more time and I can have you removed from society. And don't use the labyrinth as an excuse. We need it. We can't afford to be detected."

"Blah blah blah. Oh, and who's this guy?" Wayne nodded at a man in his twenties standing behind Milo.

Milo said, "This is Petey. You'll be working with him."

Wayne deadpanned, "Wonderful."

Milo said, "Getting along with co-workers is a sign of high emotional intelligence."

Wayne looked at Petey. "Well, Petey, I don't know what that is. Consider yourself warned. Now if you two gentlemen will excuse me, as in get the hell out of my office, I'll continue basking in the glory of another workday."

—ε-ε-ε-ε-ε-ε—

Brody sat on the plastic chair listening to the indistinct chatter of the other people at the Motor Vehicle Registration office. The small screen flashed: "115 booth 4."

"Yes, finally."

Brody walked to the waiting clerk at booth four.

"How are you today?"

"Reason."

Brody paused. "Oh, reason. Yes, I'm here to get new tags. Mine are expired."

"ID."

He searched through his wallet, noticing a tattered slip of paper. It was a printed summary of his life plan.

"Sir, hello? ID? Please."

"Sorry, right here."

He handed it to the clerk.

"State you're moving from?"

"Uh, Pennsylvania."

While the clerk typed, Brody took out the slip of paper. His plan. His goals. He could tell there was passion there, but he couldn't feel it, no connection.

The clerk's voice broke through. "OK, now the fun part. You get to pick your plates! I've got two to choose from."

"Looks like you enjoy this part."

"Oh, I do. I try to guess which one people choose."

Brody said, "I'll bet it's a rush when you guess right. Let's see, XJ-QXOTE or XJ-TRRTL."

The clerk exclaimed, "Huh, one looks like Quixote and the other looks like turtle."

This brightened the clerk's mood more than it should, but it's that kind of job.

Brody was blank. The clerk hunched his shoulders. "I read a lot. OK, let me guess. Which one are you? Hmm, one is always on a mission and the other crawls into its shell."

Brody picked up a plate, signed his name, and just like that, he was registered in Maryland.

—Ɛ-Ɛ-Ɛ-Ɛ-Ɛ-Ɛ—

Yasmin Roth sat outside enjoying the morning air, scrolling through job listings. She didn't need a job, but she suspected that would change soon. The fugitive she was chasing was a cold case. Prairie dog was but dust in the wind. It had been so long that the guy could have fathered a child by now. Her boss's job and the fate of an entire government project was in peril. Her official job was detecting UFOs. She hadn't found any of those either. Ray Denmore's car pulled into his usual spot.

He walked up. A yellow labrador trotted beside him.

Yasmin shied away. "What's that?"

"It's a dog."

"And?"

Ray said, "They needed a home for this good boy. He's the dog that was in the cabin. What's your codename for the guy? Prairie dog? I told Greg we could take care of him for a while. They named him Phoenix."

Yasmin said, "I don't know anything about dogs." Phoenix leaned against her leg. Yasmin moved. Phoenix leaned farther. Yasmin gave him a stern look. Phoenix showed her his tongue and panted.

She kept an eye on Phoenix. "Ray, I'm down. I don't mind admitting it."

"Oh, I know you're down. But hey, I have a budget meeting tomorrow. Why don't you come with me?"

Yasmin laughed. "Watching puffed up men fighting over budget scraps doesn't sound like much of a pick me up. I think I'll pass."

Ray turned serious. "No, really. I want you there. It's not all men, there are women. Uh, no you're right, it's all men. Anyhow, this isn't a regular budget meeting, it's a one on one with the Colonel."

"And you want me there because he won't shoot you in front of a lady?"

Ray chuckled. "Actually he would, he's probably done worse. But, no, I've got a plan. I'd like your help."

"A plan?"

"I'm going to ask for more money and more

manpower."

"Are you crazy?"

"Go big or go home."

Yasmin stared at the ground. "I have a feeling we'll be going home."

"Nonsense. That's not the way government works. Always use bureaucratic inertia to your advantage. Stopping something that's up and running is hard. Remember Newton? Something in motion stays in motion. Nobody wants to file the paperwork to justify shutting something down. Besides, we have a mandate from Congress."

"Yes, to find UFOs. Remember, little green men in flying saucers?"

"Well, the members of Congress who gave us the funds haven't been in government for a long time. Trust me. Nobody's watching."

Ray started to leave. Yasmin stopped him. "Wait! So, why do you want me at the meeting?"

"To explain this guy's manifesto. You know him. You profiled him. He could be well on his way to playing out his entire manifesto."

Yasmin said, "But you read my reports. If he's working his manifesto, we'll never know. It's undetectable."

Ray lifted his foot to the bench to re-tie his shoelace. "My plan is to get more help so we can detect him, smoke him out and stop his plan."

"Sounds like fun but they won't believe me. Prairie Dog thinks he can change facts. Turn a lie into the truth. Even we're not convinced he can do that."

"He did it once."

"Maybe we were mistaken."

"Alright negative Nellie, you're going to have to sharpen your pitch. Come inside, let's sit down and talk this through."

"Now? My shift is over."

Ray said, "Somehow, I think you'll stay for this."

Phoenix wagged his tail.

—ε-ε-ε-ε-ε-ε—

Milo was furious. "I hired you to help Wayne get this thing working."

Petey Bullard wasn't up to the task. Milo would have known that when he hired him if he had an ounce of people skills.

Petey replied, "I'm trying but a lot of this stuff is new to me."

"Nothing should be new at this point; you've been

working on this for months. The election is two months away. I have tracked your growth. You've made progress in key areas but overall you're not getting the job done."

Petey shifted his weight. "Mr. Cuda, I think you should know, Wayne is always dissing you and shit. The dude straight up don't like you. Got no respect. He laughs at you."

"Petey, I am trying to give you helpful criticism. I am your superior. You need to listen respectfully and internalize what I say. Your attempt to shift this to Wayne's behavior is abhorrent. I will take it into account for your next review."

"Well, I'm just saying. All his negativity bothers me."

Milo stood. "You're not here to be bothered. Instead of prattling on about a team member, maybe you should be completing your work. Where is Wayne anyway?"

Milo opened the homegrown paging app on his phone and clicked on Wayne's name. This was akin to sending voltage to a shock collar. They waited.

A minute later, Wayne walked into the room. "I'm trying to get work done so this better be important."

Milo said, "It's always important when I call. And you took way too long getting here. I expect better. Petey tells me you've missed another milestone."

Wayne glared at Petey and then at Milo.

Milo continued, "We need this now. If we're not fully operational by mid-October there's no way we can throw the election."

Wayne shook his head. "Oh good, now we're saying the treason part out loud. I think vagueness is in order, in front of—"

Milo shot back. "Oh look at Mr. Squeaky Clean worrying about laws all of a sudden. You know I can make you very acquainted with the legal system in a heartbeat."

"Stop with the drama, Milo. It gets old. We're wading through this without a clue as to what you want us to do. Now, would an update make you happy?"

—ε-ε-ε-ε-ε-ε—

The app chirped. Brody headed to the airport. It was a mindless job, but he didn't have to talk to anyone all day. He clipped in his phone and punched the button for XM channel seven.

"God, that's so good. Digging this seventies shit."

He glanced at the screen. "Pink Floyd. Wish You Were Here. Nice."

He arrived at the baggage claim. "Is that it? Just the one bag?"

The clerk nodded. "Just one this time. In the corner."

Brody said, "That little thing? You'd think they would've carried it on."

"You ain't lyin'. If that was my bag, I'd handcuff it to my wrist. Check it out."

Brody looked closer and noticed the fine detailed leather work. It felt luxurious. It had a PRIORITY tag with "first class" handwritten on it. Brody remembered traveling with the elites at his former employer. The ExpoLytics execs traveled first class all the way. A sense of wanting seeped into his thoughts.

Brody picked up the bag. "Must be nice. OK, thank you, Millie."

—ε-ε-ε-ε-ε-ε—

Milo hovered. A dozen monitors flickered and several months' worth of Wayne's toil showed on the screen. There were rotating patterns, color coded, ever changing. Wayne was mapping out reality bit by bit, but there was a lot of guesswork. Put politely, he didn't understand diddly, but the stuff on the screen was dazzling. He did, however, figure a couple things out.

"This is a live trial I ran last night."

Milo exploded. "Wait, you ran a live test without my permission. We talked about this."

Wayne had heard it all before. "Calm down and watch."

Milo did not calm down. "I think you're forgetting

who has the power here."

Wayne said, "I think you're forgetting who knows how to do this shit."

Milo retorted, "You are correct. This is a classic balance of power situation. Please proceed."

Wayne sat for a minute.

Milo fidgeted. "Well, aren't you going to show me?"

"I'm sorry, I thought I was going to get another life lesson. I do cherish them."

Petey chuckled and then looked nervous.

Milo said, "We'll need to circle back. Please proceed."

Wayne pointed to the screen. "I think I was able to change this guy's past."

Petey said, "Cool."

Milo cut him with a glare and then addressed Wayne. "It better be substantial. I already started the rumors about him."

—ε-ε-ε-ε-ε-ε—

Brody exited the freeway, following the directions on the QwikPage app. He was surrounded by large houses with gated driveways.

"Wow, these people have some cheese."

He thought of his parent's house and what a big deal it was to his father, as a sign that he was a success, a self-made man. He parked in front of a huge house. The air smelled of wet earth kept verdant with a built-in sprinkler. The manicured lawn was perfect. Rose bushes and crape myrtles were in their glory. A landscaper was shaping a Japanese maple.

He stopped as Brody walked by. "Good morning, sir. How was your trip?"

Brody was startled. "Oh no, just returning lost, I mean misplaced, luggage."

"Yes sir."

He thinks I live here? That's a rush. The thought filled his head as he rang the doorbell on the elegant double door.

—ε-ε-ε-ε-ε-ε—

Milo was not impressed. "That's it. An image of an old photograph from a newspaper?"

Wayne hunched over in frustration. "Seriously? You're not astonishingly amazed that we were able to change something that happened in the past? Yesterday that thirty-year-old photo had twenty boys and four men. It now has five men. Think about it. I pulled an image from the archives of a newspaper. The picture had four men in it. It now has five. The fifth one is *your guy*. We changed his past. Go to any newspaper clipping, microfiche, frickin' polaroid. That guy will be in the photo. I don't care if it was sitting in a desk drawer the whole time. You can now prove that a guy who was never within fifty miles of that place was actually there. It twists my brain to think of it."

Milo said, "It just doesn't seem like much, changing a photo."

"What is wrong with you? We literally changed history. That has to inspire at least a little awe."

It did not.

Milo blurted out, "It won't get us to P90," and then pulled back like he said too much.

Wayne rubbed his eyes. "Look, I'm tired and you're being a lame ass douche. I'd love to chat. Maybe you tell me about this P90 thing some other time."

Milo said, "In due time. This is a start, but you must learn to control your enthusiasm over halfway goals. It's important to celebrate progress but don't puff yourself up. Think how you can do better next time. It's part of growing professionally and personally."

Wayne said nothing as he walked out. Milo expanded the image. It was clearly a microfiche image from a local newspaper showing attendees at a boys camp on Labor Day Weekend, 1992.

—ε-ε-ε-ε-ε-ε—

Saronda flashed her phone at Shay. "Check it out, check it out. You are looking at a junior in college. And I got every class I wanted."

Shay said, "Way to go! Any more nutjob professors?"

Saronda said, "I hope not. That reminds me, I need to drop off the document I got from Cedric."

"Cedric? Oh, you mean that guy in Florida? It's hard keeping up with you."

"I've been studying that document all summer. You know, it was written by the nutjob professor."

"I remember. The creeper."

"I'm thinking of slipping it under his door. Avoid him. I checked Mixcertl's office hours. He's out today. Did I tell you he didn't go home the entire summer break?"

"He is creepy. And that name. Wow."

—ε-ε-ε-ε-ε-ε—

"No, thank *you*. You're very generous." Brody could tell it was a large tip without looking.

"Well, we made you drive all the way out here." She was wearing workout clothes and smelled nice.

"No worries, it's my job."

Brody turned and walked to his car. "God, that may be the most depressing thing I've ever said. 'It's my job, ma'am, I deliver luggage. It's what I do. Yes, yes, I know, climbing the ladder aren't I?"

Sometimes they would tip. Sometimes they wouldn't. It didn't matter. Brody had no money worries. He had sold his condo. Money was now just a number inside a checking account that paid for the low rent one bedroom on the cheap side of town. Brody got into his car and fiddled with his phone.

"C'mon, what's with this thing?" His XM radio wouldn't connect. He tossed the phone onto the passenger seat and turned on the car radio instead.

...With election day fast approaching, Emerson Randolph is sinking in the polls ever since it was rumored he had an inappropriate relationship with a male minor several decades ago...

"What the? Mr. Randolph? Dude's a perv? God, what a jerk."

His phone rang just as the QwikPage chirped with another notification. Seeing the word "Mom" show on his phone brought on instant homesickness.

"Brody, you answered."

"You called."

"We called before, a lot. You don't answer. We don't even know where you are."

Her voice quavered.

"You could trace my phone if you want to know where I am."

"Brody, I'm not going to hunt you down like you're a lost cat. You're a full-grown adult. Maybe you could at least tell us where you are."

"Why? I don't want to see anyone."

"Brody, that's a horrible attitude, and frankly you're being hurtful, towards us and your friends."

He could tell her words did not come out easily.

"Maybe I'm just going through a phase. Trying to find myself."

"That's not you."

"How do you know it's not me? What do you know about me?"

Her voice sounded choked as she started to say something.

Brody cut her off. "Mom, I'm on the clock so… "

"You have a job?"

"I work as a lost property consultant."

"I don't know what that is."

Brody was short. "I'm returning people's lives back to them. I have to go."

Sylvie rushed to say, "Are you at least staying in touch with friends? What about that girl? You know, the one… "

"You mean Saronda… " His throat tightened, cutting the sentence short.

He changed the subject. "But Mom, what is this about Mr. Randolph?"

"Your father's very upset."

"I just heard it on the radio. Like two seconds ago."

"Just heard? Brody, it's a major scandal."

Brody was curt. "Yeah, I haven't kept up with the news. I didn't even know he won the primary."

"God, Brody." She choked, "It's hard to believe you just heard about this. It's not true. It's just horrible."

Brody sensed the rawness. Emerson Randolph was a longtime family friend.

Sylvie gathered herself. "Your father, it's ripping him apart. This stupid rumor. Brody, we really miss you. We worry."

"Don't… " He felt tears forming.

He forced some words. "I'll be OK. I have to go."

"Brody, we can't live your life for you, but we're here if… Well, maybe if you could reach out more."

Brody disconnected. *God, I miss them.*

—ε-ε-ε-ε-ε-ε—

Saronda turned the corner to Dr. Mixcertl's office and dammit, there he was.

"Saronda, hey. What brings you here?"

Saronda stopped. "Oh, this is unexpected. Uh, just dropping off your document."

Dr. Mixcertl replied, "Oh great. Come in."

Saronda was blunt. "I was hoping not to see you. You creeped me out."

Axel Mixcertl said, "Maybe you can come in and sit and I'll explain."

Saronda said, "Maybe I'll stand at the door while you try."

The professor paused. "Fair enough. But first, you've had my paper for a while now. What do you think of it?"

Saronda said, "That's not why I'm here. But I disagree with most of it. You say authoritarians have used chaos to control people. And eventually they will succeed until the entire world is under their rule. But, dude, look around, democracy's winning."

"Yes, and thank God, but it won't last. Right now, most people see through the chaos. In the Dark Ages, communication was nil, science was infantile. It was easy to convince people that 'dear leader' is the only one who can guide them through the fog. Now, we have better information. We have science. We have mass communication. People can see the truth. But those who want to rule us will eventually fog things up so that no one will be able to see through the chaos."

Saronda said, "In your paper, you conclude that we will be ruled with an iron fist because that's how we are wired. We *want* to be oppressed? That's crap. I believe the universe wants us to have free will."

Axel Mixcertl sputtered, "The universe? Oh that's rich. You're talking about the universe? Like it's got some sort of conscious direction? Like it's headed toward some sort of—"

"Destiny. Yes. I believe the universe has a destiny, a purpose, and it wants us to be free. We're its most precious creation."

Axel snarked, "I wish I had a camera because you are so cute right now."

Saronda shook her head. "You really are a prick. Here's your document. I gotta go."

Axel stopped her. "But you haven't allowed me to explain why I came here."

Saronda replied, "OK. Fine. Tell me."

Axel said, "I thought you could help me. Ever since I had the devil light episodes, I don't feel connected to my family. My family was everything to me, but now I'm not sure I love them."

His throat tightened. "I'm not sure they love *me*."

Saronda said, "OK, but why me?"

Axel answered, "When I read your Twitter hashtag and what all those people were experiencing, it was like they were describing *me*. Their suffering was my suffering. Nothing else matched. Therapy was useless. Devil light stripped me of..."

He couldn't continue. He sat on the edge of his desk.

Saronda tried to detect if this was an act. "So you left."

"I had to. We clashed. Something inside no longer lined up. It was horrible."

"Dr. Mixcertl..."

He continued, "Saronda, it was painful to be with them. The connection was gone. This is my family. My wife. I've known her for thirty-three years. High school sweethearts. She loved me. And now..."

Saronda said softly, "Professor..."

He held up his finger. "Wait. Things changed. I spent a week at home over break..."

He swallowed. "Those were dark days. The people I cared about the most, my kids, my wife. I felt nothing. With friends, things were fine. Normal. But with my family, something happened to me, something broke.

But…"

His voice was weak. "The worst thing is, they don't love me anymore, my kids, my wife. No connection."

Saronda's heart went out. "Professor, that's horrible. But why didn't you talk about this earlier?"

"It's hard, and I didn't know you. I placed my hope in six therapists. They let me down. Your tweet gave me hope but you were just someone from the Internet. I had to—"

Saronda finished his sentence. "You had to know if I was legit. Am I?"

He gave a half-hearted chuckle. "Well, your theories about the universe are practically incoherent, but you're the only one who has a chance of understanding what I'm going through."

—ε-ε-ε-ε-ε-ε—

Brody sat in his car, surrounded by big houses and perfect lawns and gates and all the things that are part of the tattered plan he carried in his pocket. They were a million miles away. His mother's words hit him hard: "We can't live your life for you." He felt a heaviness as the slowly moving shadow of a tall tree ticked off the moments of another lost afternoon. Aimless. Yes, his Whisper was damaged, but Augustine was clear, our Whisper doesn't live life for us. Whispers reach into the universe and weave emotions. What those emotions drive us to do, that's up to us.

It was good Brody felt a heaviness. It was good he felt homesick. It was a step up from feeling nothing. He needed to listen.

—Ɛ-Ɛ-Ɛ-Ɛ-Ɛ-Ɛ—

Saronda texted Shay: *Meet, now*

Shay pulled up the text just as Saronda knocked on her door. "Girl, you need to give more warning, I was about to—"

Saronda cut her off. "I need to see Brody."

"I thought you were over him. You haven't talked about him in—"

"Brody's been hurt bad. Those episodes. I've been so unfair to him. I need to help him."

Shay said, "Do you mind slowing down and explaining?"

"The professor. The episodes broke him. His Whisper needs to heal."

Shay said, "Did you know Mom used to call you Saronda the Wonda? The things you say sometimes. We should make people pay to hear our conversations."

"You think this is funny?"

"No, but dang. What the hell are you talking about?"

Saronda's voice was hurried. "The episodes. Brody.

They killed his love for me. It's bad. But it's good. It means he did love me. But the episodes. His Whisper. It was broken. And now we don't connect, but we need to, to make him well."

—Ɛ-Ɛ-Ɛ-Ɛ-Ɛ-Ɛ—

Augustine described how Whispers create common emotions like joy, anger, grief, etc. But love, whoa. Love is tough. Whispers can't do it on their own. They need help from another Whisper. They need to connect.

—Ɛ-Ɛ-Ɛ-Ɛ-Ɛ-Ɛ—

Augustine wrote a section about love. It's title: "Les Murmures de l'univers se tissent et l'humanité danse" - Whispers weave and humanity dances.

Saronda hadn't read it, but she was about to. She couldn't wait to dive into Augustine's thoughts on broken Whispers. Her walk had a slight skip to it as she made her way home. As she turned the corner onto Michigan Avenue it struck her. She stopped suddenly.

She muttered, "Oh my God. I need to get Axel's document back."

—Ɛ-Ɛ-Ɛ-Ɛ-Ɛ-Ɛ—

Brody pulled out of the large winding driveway and headed back to the airport. He exited the freeway and took a wrong turn.

"Dammit, what did I do? Go this way a million

times and still screw it up."

The nearest turnaround was the parking lot of Vinny's Cafe on Holabird Avenue. He pulled into a spot under a tree. He was filled with thoughts, the landscaper's comment, his mom's voice, and Saronda. Everything was confusing. And there was the scandal. Emerson Randolph was everything you'd want in a candidate, if character was near the top of your list. He was ex-military, rugged, but with a common man vibe. He was your everyday guy, and smart. Arthur Markovich and "uncle" Emerson go way back. They grew up together and both went on to have highly successful careers.

He couldn't reconcile the scandal with the guy he had heard his dad talk about. He turned off his car and went into the cafe.

—ε-ε-ε-ε-ε-ε—

Saronda burst into Axel Mixcertl's office. "Oh thank God you're still here. I need your paper back."

Axel said, "Saronda, you're out of breath. What's so important?"

"The people. In the Dark Ages. They stayed away from each other because of the plague. They couldn't be with the ones they loved. Their Whispers started dying. I need to —"

Axel said, "Wait. Slow down. You can have the paper, but I don't see how it relates to— "

Saronda cut in. "Your Whisper, your family's

Whispers. They need to connect again. They need time. Think about it, the people in the Dark Ages. They stayed away from loved ones. No communication. Their Whispers got weak. Everyone. As a society. Whispers need to connect. You cut yourself off. So did Brody. That's how they controlled society."

Axel wasn't catching on. "Controlled society? Listen, you're a little disjointed. Why don't you take the paper and firm up your thoughts? Come back, especially if you think you can help me and whoever Brody is."

"He had the episodes."

"One of the devil light people? Were you close?"

"Yes."

He looked at her with hope. "And now?"

Saronda shifted her weight. "I don't know, but I have an idea."

—ε-ε-ε-ε-ε-ε—

Vinny's Cafe was flush with the aroma of baking bread. Brody ordered the Chicken Cheese Steak and a sweet tea.

"Your number is eighty-seven."

He took the slip and sat down on the bench next to a mother with a baby.

Brody said, "Hi, I didn't take someone's seat did I?"

"No, you're fine."

"Number eighty-five!" The cashier called.

The baby squirmed and let out a whimper, then a louder cry. It crescendoed into a full scream. Customers took notice. The mother looked distressed.

Brody called out above the crying. "How old?"

The mother stood and rocked the child. "Thirteen months."

He looked at the baby. "Hey, little man, it's OK. Thirteen months. That's young to be feeling rotten."

Brody continued in a soft voice. "It's OK. I feel like that sometimes too. But I'm old, I'm not allowed to cry. I just hold it in."

He looked sideways like he was sharing a secret, his voice barely above the din of the cafe. "Sometimes, when I'm feeling down, I want to scream too. Sometimes I do… when no one is around."

He looked directly at the baby. "But you know what, little fella? It doesn't make me feel better."

He lowered his eyes. "But I do it anyway."

Brody paused. The baby got louder.

He connected with soft eye contact as the baby cried. "The only thing that makes me feel better is to laugh. But…"

The baby looked away. Brody raised his voice a notch, "Hey, little dude. You know what?"

Brody waited until the baby turned back toward him. "It only makes me feel better if I can laugh with someone else. Wanna try?"

He puffed out his cheeks and made a face. The baby's cry softened slightly, and he coughed, then blubbered. His face was red and covered in tears. He was a mess.

"The only thing crying gets you is attention, but laughter brings joy. You know, I was thinking... "

His voice was slow and inviting. "I haven't laughed in a while. Wanna laugh with me? I'd really like someone to laugh with me. I really would."

He leaned closer as the baby peered down at him. Brody's voice was but a whisper. The baby was fixated on Brody with wide tear-filled eyes. His crying slowed as he sucked in air and chewed on his finger.

Brody stuck out his tongue and puckered his lips. The baby was mesmerized.

"Let's laugh." Brody threw back his head and let out a big fake laugh.

The baby looked at his mom and then back at Brody and made a crooked grin. Brody smiled big and faked another laugh. The baby giggled, a bubble sprouted from a nostril.

"That feels a lot better, doesn't it, little man? I wish I could feel good like that too. Just once. Again. Like before." He ran his fingers through his hair, wishing away the darkness, trying to feel something.

The mother bounced the baby who was full on laughing.

"Did you hear that, little man? That came from inside you. It's called joy. Grab it with both hands and don't let go. You'll learn that from your mom. She won't say it. You'll have to listen for it. But you'll hear it someday. Remember that. For me. OK?"

"Number eighty-six. Order up."

The mother said, "That's my number. Thank you, my baby loves you."

"Number eighty-seven. Eighty-seven."

Brody was already out the door. Halfway to his car, the sun reflected off his new license plate, XJ-QXOTE. He deleted QwikPage.com from his phone. He had made his last delivery.

—ε-ε-ε-ε-ε-ε—

Petey Bullard watched as Milo harangued Wayne. It happened every day. Do better. Work faster.

Petey came to Wayne's defense. "Mr. Cuda, I think it's pretty cool what Wayne did, changing a photo like that, from, like before I was born."

Milo said, "Thank you for that constructive observation. But this is about Wayne. Everyone must decide what type of employee they want to be. Wayne, do you wish to be a high achiever?"

Wayne puffed out his cheeks and let out a breath he knew he was holding for a moment like this. "That's a tough one."

Milo continued, "Because to be a high achiever you need to dedicate yourself to the task at hand. We are a long way from where we need to be. Does that not bother you?"

Wayne said, "I'm not your employee, I'm a trapped slave. I'm a warm body forcing numbers into equations I don't understand. A chimpanzee in overalls could do this shit. Anyhow, I'm not sure what the task at hand is."

Milo said, "For you, the task is simple, fulfill my wishes. My role is much harder. I am strategically mapping out the plan. It requires higher level thinking."

"The plan? There's a plan?"

"Yes, but that is for me to worry about. I am the manager. You are not. Everything goes better when people stay within their role in order to maintain a healthy manager-employee relationship."

"Thank you, wise one. I will do better now that you've taught me that."

"Very good, you're making progress. Don't get

down on yourself."

It was late. Wayne wanted to retreat to his twelve-by-twelve living quarters in a cinder block windowless room. Anything but this.

Milo said, "But I must add, it's hard to see any progress lately and our schedule is in tatters."

Wayne walked to his room snarling, "Tatters. I tell ya. The schedule is in tatters. Bite me."

—ε-ε-ε-ε-ε-ε—

"Be there in a sec."

Sylvie Markovich dried her hands on a dish towel and walked to the front door, expecting to sign for a delivery.

She turned on the porch light and opened the door. "Boy, when you guys say delivery by eight you really—Brody."

Brody said, "I thought about what you said."

She hugged him. He let the hug linger.

"Can I come in?"

She called out, "Arthur. It's Brody!"

Arthur looked up from the remote video session. "Guys, I gotta go. Handle this. I'll call in later."

He walked, actually trotted, to the front foyer and

greeted Brody with two observations, "You have bags. Your hair is long."

"I want to stay with you guys, do you mind?"

Sylvie and Arthur exchanged glances and said in unison, "Are you kidding?"

Sylvie asked, "Did you drive here? Do you need food?"

"Screw the food. Brody, where have you been? What the hell have you been doing?"

"Arthur, not so fast, let him catch his breath."

"He oughtta be catching hell. Honestly, what the hell, we had no idea—"

"Arthur, stop. Brody, we're happy you're here. Now come in. Let's talk. And Arthur, get his bags and take them upstairs. We need to get his room ready."

Arthur did as he was told.

—ε-ε-ε-ε-ε-ε—

Saronda pulled up her class notes.

"OK, just me, myself, and I. Let's study. Mechanical Engineering 401. Yay."

Beside her computer, Mixcertl's thick document with its strange take on the plague. In a drawer, Augustine's paper with keys to the universe. Inside her head, thoughts of Brody.

She closed her laptop. "This is torture."

—ε-ε-ε-ε-ε-ε—

Brody sat in his room, his overstuffed bags at his feet. His parents' Australian Shepherd Sydney sat outside the door with intense eyes asking if she could come in.

"C'mon, I could use a friend." Sydney sat on his feet.

All the things he planned to say to his parents, all the carefully orchestrated thoughts he had while driving up, were replaced with overwhelming doubts. His thoughts were incomplete and lacking, because he was incomplete and lacking.

Sylvie and Arthur sat in the large living room. Sylvie wanted to hug her son. Arthur wanted to strangle him.

"Arthur, we need to give him a chance to explain. He's very fragile right now. Obviously he's been through something we don't understand."

"We've all been through things, Sylvie. He's an adult. He burned me with the job interview. He wouldn't tell us where he was for months. Months. And now he just shows up, out of the —"

Sylvie cut in, "He's our son. He's not one of your he-man business associates. Let's listen to him."

"He's weak. We didn't raise him to be weak."

"Oh hush, you're so emotional. Doesn't that make you the weak one? He's coming down from his room. Let's listen. OK?"

Brody entered and stopped halfway across the room. "You probably think I'm a schmuck."

Sylvie fixated on his wrinkled shirt. Arthur huffed out a sigh.

Sylvie touched Arthur's forearm. "Maybe if you could tell us—"

Brody didn't wait for her to finish. "I've been through a lot. I can't explain it. The problem is, even if I could, you would never understand."

Arthur pulled away from Sylvie. "Aye yi yi."

Sylvie said, "Maybe one step at a time. We were... are very worried about you."

"I'm worried about me too. I can't seem to care about anything."

Arthur couldn't hold back. "Oh if that doesn't take the prize."

Brody stood firm. "Father, our reality almost crashed into another reality. Ever since then, it felt like my soul..."

His parents looked at each other and Brody stopped talking.

He abandoned his rehearsed lines. "You're right, Mom. One step at a time would be better."

It's every parent's dilemma; when to hug their kids and when to wring their necks. Brody had disappeared for months, burned bridges, put his life on hold and ignored all outreach.

Arthur tried sorting this out. "Is this that cosmic bullshit you hit us with at Thanksgiving? I'm surprised you let yourself be pulled in so deep. I mean what were you—"

"Yes, it's that cosmic bull— Look, you don't have to believe me but, another reality almost crashed into ours. Saronda and Rebecca and I stopped it. Ever since, for me, it's been dark."

Arthur held his tongue. Sylvie studied the floor.

Brody reverted to his rehearsed lines. "I came downstairs to tell you I love you and I think you love me. I ask that you accept what I say at face value."

He turned to go upstairs. "I'm going to bed."

Arthur looked at Sylvie. "He's going to bed at nine?"

He sat on the bed in his room, immersed in the darkness. He turned out the light and fell asleep, not bothering to change clothes.

—ε-ε-ε-ε-ε-ε—

It was late. Mechanical Engineering 401: Collisions

in Dynamic Systems lost out to Augustine's description of "Collisions amoureuses." "Collisions of love."

It was all there. When two Whispers are meant to be together, they *need* to be together. It's the way the universe is designed. If one of the Whispers is damaged, neither can feel love. The connection is incomplete.

—ε-ε-ε-ε-ε-ε—

The aroma of a Sylvie-prepared breakfast filled Brody with a sense of home like nothing else could. He knew she did that on purpose.

"I'll bet you don't cook like this every morning."

Sylvie turned from the stove. "We don't always have the prodigal son returning."

Brody mused, "Let me try to remember. That story turned out OK for the guy, right?"

Arthur arrived from his office. "Maybe, but the parents were pissed."

"Arthur, please. The prodigal son was welcomed home."

Arthur said, "I'll bet they put him through hell first. Ah, I'm just busting his chops. I'm sure Brody didn't expect anything less. How are you this morning champ? Up for some golf?"

Brody said, "Golf? So you do want to put me through hell, don't you?"

On the surface, the familial ribbing was just a family reuniting, choosing not to talk about the huge holes in their hearts, leaving that for later. Augustine had a deeper view. Sure, they were talking, but the real communication was between their Whispers. Augustine had equations that proved it. Their Whispers were reaching out, finding patterns that fit, weaving them together. Brody hadn't felt like this for months.

Brody kept the lightness going. "I appreciate your willingness to be that close to a crazy person with clubs."

"I'll never be too far from a golf cart."

"I bet I could outrun it."

"It would be fun watching you try."

Brody thought golf might be a good thing. "But yeah, if you have an opening, I guess I could give it a whirl. Haven't swung a stick in a long time. Is that what you golfers say?"

"It'll do. But yeah, we always have a spot to fill. Emerson pulled out ever since… "

Brody finished the sentence. "The scandal?"

"I was going to say ever since the primaries started."

"So you think the scandal is true?"

Sylvie focused on the skillet she was washing, scraping a little harder.

Arthur bristled. "Look, I've known Emerson for a long time. He's not a pervert."

Sylvie shut off the water. "Let's talk about something else. How about figuring out how to get Brody ready for golf."

—ε-ε-ε-ε-ε-ε—

Petey sat listlessly at the computer. "Wayne, I don't know how to do any of this."

Wayne said, "Don't tell dear leader, but neither do I. He's all over the place on what he wants."

"No, I mean, programming. I feel like I'm in the way. Maybe you could show me some things."

Wayne said, "In the way? That is a great idea. Petey, let's try something. It's called pair programming. We each type in code at the same time adding what we know." *That should slow things down nicely.*

Petey replied, "Sounds like fun."

Wayne muttered, "and slow."

—ε-ε-ε-ε-ε-ε—

Brody hopped in the golf cart. "I can tell you're upset about what they're doing to Mr. Randolph. But why are you so sure it's not true? You can't always tell if someone is lying, even if you're close."

"Because I was with him that whole weekend. He

sure as hell wasn't at some boys camp doing God knows what. We were camping. September seventh, Labor Day, that's how I remember that I was with him. It was a weekend camping trip, just a guys thing. Three of us. Steve Montgomery, me and Emerson."

Arthur was clearly upset. "We were camping, end of story." His first tee shot hooked badly to the left. It was one of his better shots that day.

—ε-ε-ε-ε-ε-ε—

Milo was alone, seething. His rumors about Emerson Randolph had a three-day life cycle. It was salacious but with no victims coming forward, the story faded. If he released the photo now, it would land with a thud.

He went to where Wayne and Petey were working. "Dammit, you two. Do better."

He turned and walked out. Wayne and Petey laughed.

—ε-ε-ε-ε-ε-ε—

"You went on a camping trip with Steve Montgomery, who's now the Comptroller for the commonwealth of Pennsylvania and Emerson Randolph who is now a candidate for leader of the free world?"

"Yes."

"That's incredible. Tell me the story. Do you remember anything from it?"

"I remember everything. We survived a thunderstorm by running to the lowest spot we could find. By the way, once you start running down a steep hill, you're committed. You gotta stick with it to the bitter end."

"Oh so that's where that comes from."

"Where what comes from?"

"It's one of your idioms."

"I have idioms?"

"You must know you have idioms."

"You make it sound like a rash."

"If idioms were a rash, you'd be dead from scratching. But yeah, you always said, 'running downhill sounds easy but once you start, you're committed'."

Arthur reflected for a moment. "Ha Ha, that's a nice idiom."

"Not your best but I like it."

Arthur and Brody's Whispers were getting along nicely.

"What else do you remember?"

Arthur leaned on the cart's steering wheel. "Oh my God. The hamburger. So, we're out in the woods, see, I mean deep, deep in the woods."

Brody soaked it in.

"And Steve, he was such a clown, really wanted a hamburger. I did too, to be honest. But we hadn't brought anything to make hamburgers, no meat, no buns, no—"

Brody jabbed, "I can see you guys, sitting around a fire, hankering for a burger. Hope it didn't ruin your trip. Poor guys, have to eat spam."

"Oh we got a hamburger."

"Oh?"

"Yeah, yeah, the best burger ever. It had sun dried tomatoes, bacon, the wide, thick smoked kind, not maple, I hate maple bacon, and an egg. It had an egg, sunny side up, perched right on the patty, which was seared to perfection."

"You guys made this on a campfire, with no ingredients?"

Arthur shook his head. "Oh and a giant toothpick holding it all together, but it was ever so slightly off to the side, so it didn't puncture the egg yolk. Magnificent. Uh, campfire? No campfire needed. We got the burger at a place that Steve said was nearby. So, here's our choices: build a fire and heat up some pasty stew or hike back to the car and find this burger joint."

Brody was engrossed. "Real back to nature."

"Hey, when a man wants red meat, a man gets

red meat. We hoof it to the car. It was getting dark. We couldn't see two feet in front of us. But anyway, here's the thing. This place wasn't nearby. Steve's such a blowhard. It was at least eighty miles, winding roads, smelly guys in camping clothes, bumping down these roads, God it was a riot."

"That's quite a scene, you three hot shots piled into a car to get a burger in the woods."

"Well, we weren't hotshots back then. But, and I'll never forget this; we get to the place, hungry, tired. We were shoehorned in that car for hours. And, Emerson, you know he used to play basketball. How his six-foot eight carcass survived all those turns folded into that car, I'll never know."

—ε-ε-ε-ε-ε-ε—

The clock ticked past noon. Saronda bounded out of the bookstore. She usually hung around a little after her shift, instead, she trotted to the college.

Saronda said, "Oh good you're here. I don't have an appointment but so what. No one ever meets with you."

Professor Mixcertl said, "Thanks for the boost. I think I see you more now than when you took my class."

Saronda said, "You need to go home. Go to your family. You need to be around them, let your Whispers re-connect, grow your love again."

"I told you, they don't love me anymore."

Saronda said, "But they *can* love you again if you allow your Whisper to build itself back. It was damaged during the episodes."

"Thank you so much, I'll think about it. Your crazy stuff is always fascinating and fun to toy with."

Saronda said, "Congratulations, you're almost condescending. Very close."

Axel said, "It's a work in progress."

Saronda said, "That's all I came for. Oh, by the way, you said in your document that autocrats use propaganda which is well known, but you also said there was a guy who said they could use altered facts. What is that?"

"Huh, no, I think I mentioned there was a guy after World War II who was convinced the nazis were going to actually change facts. Nutty. I ran across it during my research. He even wrote a paper about it. I tracked it down once. It's around here somewhere."

Axel rummaged through some drawers. "Ah, here it is, Paul Langevin. A guy from France, listen to this, 'by employing these equations in an ordered manner, a hostile force could render society chaotic, causing great mental stress. Society would not hold up against constantly changing facts orchestrated under autocratic rule.' He put facts in quotes because he said they would change. This guy was serious. Look, he had equations!"

Saronda's head snapped back when she saw the

document. The equations were familiar. They were Augustine's.

"Oh my God, can I have that?"

"Sure, I've got no use for it. Just another crazy thing to come out of the war."

I need to have Rebecca check this out.

—ε-ε-ε-ε-ε-ε—

Brody sat in a large oak chair in the clubhouse. "You didn't finish your story."

"Yeah, well, I would have if we hadn't spent so much time looking for your tee shots in the weeds."

"Ha ha ha. OK, you were talking about the long ride in the woods."

Arthur took a draw of scotch. "Right. So, there we were. Gravel parking lot, house with a small front porch, one light on above the door, a single lightbulb with a wire cage. Moths and bugs flying around it. Crickets chirping. We slog up to the door, and the place is closed."

"Closed?"

"The place is closed! Labor Day. That's how I remember the date. I looked it up, September 7, a Monday. And a holiday."

"And Judge Randolph was with you?"

Brody wanted to trust his father, but the rumors

were so specific.

"That's right! He was there. One hundred percent."

Arthur took a deep draw of scotch and motioned for another. "So how do you like this scotch?"

"It's earthy."

Arthur explained, "Brody, that's peat."

Brody held his drink high. "Pleased to meet you, Pete."

"Please tell me you're not that dense."

"OK, I'm not that dense. So, go on, if the place was closed, how did you get the hamburgers?"

Arthur thanked the waiter. "OK, here's where it gets good."

He took a sip and let the smoke from a peat bog a thousand miles away fill his head.

He set down his glass. "We were on a mission. We wanted those burgers. We, oh man, we were such idiots. We started banging on that door. I mean, banging. My hands were getting sore, so much banging. I may have done some long-term nerve damage. Anyhow. We were laughing and faking outrage, putting on a real act, ya know. Buncha clowns. 'We demand a burger now, hurrah' we cried. We weren't mad, just putting on a show."

Brody could tell there was more. "And… "

Arthur leaned forward like he was sharing a secret. "Then, the door opens and this tiny little older woman pokes her head out, 'We're closed. Go away.' Well, I start pleading our case, 'We're hungry to the point of starving, kind and wonderful older woman, who I heard makes an awesome burger. We drove hours to get here. By car through mountain roads.' The whole bit. 'If you could be so kind and... ' I mean it was different than that, but you get the idea."

"And she bought it?"

"Not at first but as I really got into my bit, I could tell she was softening. You know, I read people pretty good." He took a sip and let it linger before letting it drift down his throat.

Brody said, "She didn't stand a chance. The mighty Arthur Markovich was a good negotiator even back then."

"No, not really. I didn't know it, but Steve was behind me waving around a stack of fifties."

They both laughed.

Arthur mused, "1992. I was your age."

"Old enough to judge a burger. How was it?"

Arthur leaned back. "Well, first of all, we sat in the kitchen, not the dining area. This was like a converted house. The kitchen was the kitchen and the other rooms had tables and chairs so that people could sit and have a meal. Family operation I assume. Very cozy."

"Quaint."

"Yes, quaint. But anyhow, we had the best time. The old woman was a hoot. I think she enjoyed us being there, and I tell ya, she was well compensated. We got up to leave and started throwing money on the table. Fifties, twenties... God we were so full of ourselves."

Brody said, "Wow, my age and already hanging out with future power brokers, throwing money around."

"Money we couldn't afford to throw around, I might add. We were your age for sure, but we were broke. Hell, those may have been the last dollars your mother and I—"

"But you went on. You survived. You thrived. How did you hold it together?"

"Because I always knew I was going to make it."

Brody felt a flame inside of him. "How did you have so much confidence?"

"Confidence is everything, Brody. Build a wall of confidence that the doubters can't knock down."

Brody said, "Yeah, I just need some bricks right now."

"You'll get there."

—ε-ε-ε-ε-ε-ε—

Brody slept well. It was a deep sleep. Playing golf with his father lifted Brody. What was happening on the surface was a fraction of what was taking place inside their Whispers, each seeking out the unique pattern that makes family bonds so strong. Brody's Whisper was getting stronger. He walked to the kitchen. No amazing aromas this morning.

Arthur walked out of his office. "Well, there he is. Good thing you're not a farmer."

Brody rubbed his eyes and reached for a coffee cup. "Why's that?"

"I don't know. Don't farmers always get started early?"

Brody poured a cup. "Yeah, do we know why?"

Arthur said, "I've actually never thought about it."

Brody sat. "Speaking of thinking about something. I have a thought. Why don't you go to bat for Judge Randolph? Get together with Mr. Montgomery and make a public statement that the two of you were with him on Labor Day that year."

Arthur paused. "You mean like a press conference?"

"No, start online. Make a video, try to get attention."

Arthur looked nervous. "I stay out of politics."

"C'mon. This is about right and wrong, falsehoods versus rumors. If anything, helping a friend. If they can do this to Emerson Randolph, they can do this to anybody."

—ε-ε-ε-ε-ε-ε—

It was like the text came out of the blue, a ghost from the past. Rebecca stared at her phone. *You need to see this.* It was from Saronda.

Rebecca walked the length of Columbia Road in Adams Morgan, past the stately four story manors, proudly showing off their turn of the century grandeur. She hoped to one day own one of them. She met Saronda at the DuPont Circle Metro.

"Hey stranger. It's been a while. Have you seen Brody?"

Saronda looked rushed. "No, I don't know where he is but I have an idea what he's going through. That's not why I texted. You need to see this."

Saronda and Rebecca leafed through Paul Langevin's paper.

Rebecca was astonished. "Oh my God, those equations look very similar to Augustine's from what I remember. That's amazing."

A guy named Paul Langevin had copied Augustine's equations and tried to warn the world that they could be used as a weapon. Saronda hadn't finished translating, but the only attribution to Augustine's work was a reference to a footnote in Augustine's paper. Paul Langevin wrote his paper forty-one years after Augustine wrote hers.

Rebecca said, "Let me know when you get done translating. But Saronda, how are you? Have you had any contact with Brody?"

Saronda looked away.

—ε-ε-ε-ε-ε-ε—

Brody bided his time, wishing he could hear what his father was talking about in his office. He hoped he called Steve Montgomery like he said he would. The door opened.

Arthur came out. "OK, we're going to do it. I talked to Steve. We're going to issue a statement that we were with Emerson on the day in question."

Brody brightened. "That's great news. Why the change of heart?"

Arthur said, "Because it's the right thing to do. Emerson and I go way back. We've both gotten each other out of jams in the past."

Brody responded, "I think you're doing the right thing. When you make your statement, you need to be sure of all the facts. Details matter. There will be questions. I can help you go through the details. You know one of your idioms, 'no one will buy your house if a few bricks are missing'."

Brody and Arthur combed through the details of the camping trip. Brody grilled his father about details, imploring him to remember. They called the Randolph campaign but couldn't get through to Emerson Randolph, he was too occupied trying to become the most powerful man in the world. The campaign staff was incredibly busy too, trying to counteract the firehouse of questions from reporters trying to get some new tidbit they could blow up into a story. It was sad having to fend off rumors. As candidates go, Emerson had everything. He was a ramrod straight military veteran with an impeccable record of service. He graduated top of his class in law school and went on to become a respected judge known for his fairness and toughness.

Brody scoured the notes. "It looks like you're ready to go, Father."

Arthur knew this would expose him to the raw world of politics. The scandal was growing. Today's facts clashed with yesterday's facts. Sources were anonymous and no victims ever came forward. That didn't matter. The rumors were enough. Denials were boring compared to the salacious rumors about a man who was everyone's grandpa. Arthur Markovich and Steve Montgomery dropped their statement into the vortex and the piranhas turned their attention to the fresh meat.

Cute headlines like "Burger or Boys Camp?" popped up.

—ε-ε-ε-ε-ε-ε—

Milo burst into Wayne's work area and shut the door behind him.

"Wayne, do you want to hear something wonderful?"

"Yes, your words are my oxygen. Breathe into me."

Milo considered whether that was sarcasm. "Very well, I've got good news. Randolph's friends are saying he was never at that camp."

"Yeah, probably cuz he wasn't."

Milo chortled, "They say he was with them that whole weekend. But we have proof that he wasn't."

Wayne corrected him. "We have a photo. That's all we have. We didn't change his friends' memory."

Milo's shoulders slumped. "I thought we actually changed the event."

"We changed all *accounts* of an event that never happened. His friends' lives didn't change. They still remember where they were, what they did. We didn't actually access their brains."

Milo said nothing, then, "But we need to. We'll have to find another way."

Wayne said, "If it's any consolation to your twisted brain, everyone will think those guys are liars. Their reputations are shot."

Milo brightened. "Ooh, that's it! That's beautiful. Brilliant! Wayne, thank you for brainstorming with me. Open and honest discourse like this is what leads to breakthroughs. I may consider adding you to my consult team someday. The pieces are falling into place."

Milo opened the door. "But first, I've got a photo to publish."

Wayne looked blankly at his shoes.

—ε-ε-ε-ε-ε-ε—

Arthur had no idea what was about to hit. The doorbell rang. It was Steve Montgomery.

"Hi Sylvie. It's so nice to see you. Is Arthur here? His phone's off."

She walked him to Arthur's office. Steve was breathless. "Arthur, have you seen? There's a photograph. Emerson, at that boys' camp, on that weekend. Look."

Arthur focused on Steve's phone. "Oh c'mon, a sixteen-year-old with photoshop could have whipped that up. Politics."

Steve said, "News folks are breathlessly claiming they checked it out. This isn't going away, Arthur. What does this say about us? I'm the Comptroller. I never should have done this. Now I'm political."

"Hey, I've got clients that trust and respect me. I

can't have it that I'm a liar."

Brody was in the kitchen with Sylvie. "What the hell is this all about? Father's story is so convincing. Could he have been wrong about the year, the date? Something? Is he just an outright liar?"

Sylvie tried to answer. Her throat managed only a muffled cough.

Brody hugged her. "We'll get through this. There's gotta be an explanation. We'll figure it out. I need to go to D.C. and see my friends."

—ε-ε-ε-ε-ε-ε—

Petey and Milo stood silently as if concentrating.

Wayne said, "Is there something I can help you guys with? You've been here for like ten minutes and haven't said anything."

Milo tilted his head. "I'm listening for the first notes of chaos."

Wayne asked, "Chaos makes a sound?"

Milo said, "I was waxing poetic."

Wayne said, "Oh, is this the part of this travesty where you grow a personality?"

Milo said, "I'm talking about the ruckus that photo makes in the information sphere. It's a beautiful thing."

Wayne was annoyed. "Nice. I'm busy. Do you need

something? Besides poetry lessons."

Milo said, "Actually, Wayne, I was also thinking what your next step should be. This photo is going to send the race for president into a frenzy. First, we win the election. Next, we own President-elect Finchman."

Petey was wide-eyed.

Wayne lost it. "Own the President. That's what I love about this place, there's a new kind of crazy every day, where treason is just a warm-up act. If this is where we're headed I need more than just unpainted block walls and cracked concrete. You know those cracks are letting in invisible radioactive gas that's slowly killing us. Everyday, I sit here breathing it in."

Milo said, "Wayne, are you concerned about radioactive gas?"

Wayne's voice sounded of menace and rage. "I'm concerned it's not killing me fast enough. It's not exactly my childhood dream to grow up and throw an election by tearing apart a man's reputation. And now, I'm presented with the opportunity to own the President. Boy will my résumé look impressive."

He drew close to Milo, clenching his fist.

Petey said, "Wayne, are you OK?"

Wayne got louder. "Oh, yeah, just peachy. I spend 12 hours a day watching patterns on screens looking for some clue as to what the fuck I'm doing. You know what? I don't understand shit. We got lucky and we changed one tiny thing in the infinite universe of history and this guy thinks we're going to own the President."

Milo tilted his head. "Your admission that you don't know what you're doing is very disturbing. I will take that into account at your next review. Now, concerning your next step—"

Wayne leaned into Milo. "I want fast food."

Milo took a step back. "What?"

Wayne leaned in more. "I want fast food."

Milo sputtered, "You are way off track. We need to discuss your next step, not some random food hankering."

Wayne got very close. "I said I want fast food."

Milo sighed, "OK, Wayne, we'll get you fast food. But first—"

"*NOW.*"

Milo looked at Petey. "Petey, can you please go get Wayne some fast food? Get one of everything. Go. Scoot."

Wayne slumped in a chair.

Milo closed the door. "Now that you are calmed down, I need you to ruin someone's life."

Wayne said, "Oh, like we did with Emerson Randolph and his two friends?"

Milo said, "Oh dear God, that was just a start. We'll discuss later."

Wayne studied a spot on the floor as he listened to Milo's footsteps fade down the hall. "I'm getting a cheeseburger. Good day so far."

Petey returned carrying four bags of food. Wayne sat up and looked in the bags. "Oooh, two kinds of fries. You're a good man Petey. We should hang out together in hell. Be sure to look me up."

—ε-ε-ε-ε-ε-ε—

The past few days gave Brody the urge to reunite with his friends. Brody selected the news channel on his XM account and put his phone in the dashboard mount.

...Today on Race To the White House 2016 we'll touch on each candidate's thoughts on how to improve the dismal job numbers but first we have an expert on altered photographs followed by noted psychologist Mildred Lang on why people blatantly lie to help a friend...

He turned it off.

He hated leaving his parents in such a chaotic state, but this was their problem to work through. More than that, he was drawn to D.C. Driving gave him a chance to think through how he was going to reunite with his friends.

—ε-ε-ε-ε-ε-ε—

Petey and Wayne were enjoying their

cheeseburgers.

Petey asked Wayne, "Why do you talk like that to Mr. Cuda? He's your boss."

"Petey, listen, there's a lot you don't know. This is not a well man. He's dangerous and possibly insane. He's also annoying. He's a walking, talking manager's manual. Pisses me off. But the thing you need to understand—"

Milo walked up behind them. "What? What does Petey need to understand?"

Wayne spun around. "That this is a hell of a milkshake. I was telling him he did a great job getting the fast food."

Milo paused. "Yes, he did a good job getting the fast food. Hmm, OK, now, are you ready to hear what we do after we defeat Emerson Randolph?"

Wayne said, "Go to jail?"

Milo said, "Petey, I need to talk to Wayne. Please leave. And shut the door."

Milo shifted nervously. "Please don't talk about jail in front of—"

"Am I scaring the child?"

Milo tilted his head. "Wayne, like I said earlier, I need you to destroy someone's life."

Wayne said, "We're doing that with the photo. Those poor saps. Forever known as liars."

Milo snapped, "No, not good enough. It needs to be a complete annihilation. Total devastation. The people I need to control have no shame. Calling them a liar isn't enough. I want to ruin lives. I want constant misery with no escape. Let them wallow in a pitiful reality."

The capillaries feeding Wayne's internal organs expanded, delivering more oxygen. His heart raced. His breathing was rapid and shallow.

Milo was dead-eyed as he rubbed the fingers of his left hand together. "I want nightmares to haunt their dreams, night after night, so sleep is not a refuge. Nightmares about unbearable things. Things that make their life worthless. And when they wake up? The nightmare is real. They can't escape the reality we create for them."

There was a heavy silence. Neither one blinked.

Wayne consciously slowed his breathing. "Isn't that kinda drastic?"

Milo's voice lowered. "Oh, that's not drastic. It's just a little calling card that says, 'If I can destroy that guy's life, I can do it to you.' The ultimate blackmail. And nothing can be proven."

Wayne said, "Brutal. And in broad daylight. Not only do you do it but then you brag about it. "

Milo became very serious. "It's not bragging, it's selective communication. Wayne, I think I trust you enough that I can share something with you. Ruining someone's life is just one step. It's a parlor trick to get attention. I need a neutron bomb. I want total control of reality."

"I wish you luck."

Milo said, "But we need to ruin a life. It needs to be someone without a hint of scandal. Clean, but not a saint. When we get that done, I'll show you my neutron bomb. No one on Earth has seen it. You'll be the first."

Wayne said, "Awwwh, the first. I'm starting to feel special. But why me?"

Milo turned to go. "Because you're going to build it."

Milo's footsteps faded down the hall. Petey walked in.

Wayne said, "Man, those were good fries."

Petey said, "Yeah."

—ε-ε-ε-ε-ε-ε—

Saronda walked to Busboys and Poets.

It had been a little more than a year since Brody "introduced" himself, more like inserted himself into her life. Today, he was coming back. From where she didn't know, a darkness she could never fully appreciate.

Rebecca was sitting at a table..

Saronda pulled up a chair. "Oh, thank God you got

here early. We need to talk."

"Yes, early. The line for voting was short. But, hey you, wow, you are looking good. Have you lost weight?"

"Oh, girl, you're the best for noticing. I haven't worn these jeans in years. Couldn't get in them. But I think they're just the right amount of snug, if you know what I mean."

Rebecca said, "I'll say."

"Rebecca, I'm a bundle of nerves. What do I say to him? Or do I just strangle him and get it over with?"

"Strangling may be a little harsh. I'd go more subtle like let him talk and then kick him in the nuts."

Saronda snorted. Rebecca giggled.

"But honestly, Rebecca, I'm pissed and joyful at the same time."

"Let him talk. There's always an explanation."

Saronda said, "I've been reading Augustine's paper. There's a whole section on how the Whisper inside each of us interacts with the Whisper in other people." Her throat tightened. "But I can't talk about that right now."

Rebecca looked over Saronda's shoulder and saw Brody enter. "Oh my God, he looks like hell. I'm so sorry, I shouldn't have said that. It just kinda came out."

Saronda turned around. "Oh my God, he looks like hell."

"Hey guys." Brody stood beside the table. "Can I sit?"

Saronda wanted to hug him. Rebecca wanted to cut his hair.

Brody kicked off the reunion. "Should we get drinks, or should I start telling my awful tale?"

Saronda tried to control the mix of emotions welling up inside her. "God... Brody."

It was harder than she thought.

Rebecca filled in. "Brody, we have been wondering. No, we have been worrying. Ah hell, spill it. Why did you leave?"

Brody had rehearsed a new set of words. "I went into a hole. Something inside me broke and I couldn't deal with whatever it was. I don't know where to start."

Rebecca looked at Saronda and then at Brody. "Maybe start with an apology?"

Brody said, "I don't know what to apologize for."

Saronda crossed her arms.

Brody got the hint. "OK, you're right. I was an ass. I left. I created a lot of hurt. Not just you guys but with my parents. I was dead."

Silence.

Rebecca stepped up again. "Did you get a new job? Did you move in with your parents? Where were you these last eight months?"

"Baltimore."

Saronda looked at him. "Baltimore? What the?"

"And yes, I got a job. I delivered lost, excuse me, misplaced luggage."

Silence.

Saronda said, "Sounds exhilarating. What did you do the other twenty hours a day?"

"Slept."

They looked at him. Brody said, "I'm serious. Pretty much slept. That and planning out how to take a shower and get dressed."

Rebecce said, "You're making this up."

"Something's wrong with me. But I'm trying and I'm getting better."

Saronda started sobbing. Rebecca said, "Can't you see? You broke her heart."

Saronda said, "That's not why I'm crying. Your Whisper broke. That's why my professor left his family. It's just like Augustine said. I'm so happy."

Rebecca and Brody looked at each other in total

confusion. They mouthed the word "happy."

Rebecca said, "You're happy? That's something I gotta hear. I'm thinking white wine for this."

—ε-ε-ε-ε-ε-ε—

Milo was livid. "Why can't you get this done? I want to be able to show this to soon-to-be President Finchman. I told you this. We established clear requirements."

Wayne said calmly, "You can shout all you want. Use every managerial cliche in that head of yours, but we are working as hard as we can. This shit doesn't come easy. We have miles to go. Now let us work."

Milo turned, looked at Petey, and stormed out.

Petey said just above a whisper, "But we know how to do this. Why did you tell Mr. Cuda we couldn't?"

Wayne stood up and closed the door. "Look, I told you. This guy is dangerous. He's ruining a guy's life so he can use it as blackmail against people. Important people. People with power."

Petey was wide eyed. "But he's been so helpful to my career."

"Oh grow up. This isn't a career, it's a sentence. The only reason I haven't walked out is that we need to slow him down. Stop him. It's called slow-walking. I'm a programmer. I'm good at it."

Petey displayed a dull, dairy cow stare and then, "If you feel he's doing something wrong, why not report him?"

"To who? And exactly what do we say? 'Hey! We changed a photo by altering reality. We can't prove it cuz, ya know, we changed reality.'"

Petey added his insight, "They would think we were crazy."

"Yer catchin' on, Petey, yer catchin' on."

He opened the door. Milo was about to barge in. "Aren't you going to listen to us win an election?"

Milo's plan was simple. Use his blackmail machine to become the right-hand man of a newly elected President Gerhard Finchman. Then, after a little of this and a little of that, own humanity.

He just has to keep the snowmobile out of the ditch. He increased the volume on his phone.

...And we're back with election night coverage, Race to the White House 2016. These are certainly surprising early returns. Too close to call in six key states. Emerson Randolph is very close in states that Gerhard Finchman was expected to win easily. What do you make of it, Eloise?...

Milo was livid. "Wayne, the photo doesn't appear to have worked."

Wayne said, "Damn. Scandals aren't what they

used to be."

Milo thought back eleven months and one name change ago when he was broken, lying on a rock beside a dead snowmobile miles from where he needed to be. And the years before that, failing to take out a college president. Learning and honing his craft of spreading disinformation. Planning, scheming, waiting. Waiting for pieces to fall in place. Waiting for the one idea, the one trick, that would get him to P90. Oh, the power of P90. But, he knew, to be the most powerful man in the world he must first *own* the most powerful man in the world.

He listened again to the election results coming in, waiting for the person he picked, the person he needed to be President, the person he did everything he could to make sure he won, including changing reality. Without the right president his plan crumbles.

...Back to our coverage of election night. Folks, Emerson Randolph was just declared the winner of two more key states. This is definitely a good sign if you're a Randolph supporter. Not a good night so far for Gerhard Finchman...

Wayne set down the election night drink Milo let them have, sat back, and watched the eruption.

Milo threw his phone across the room and kicked his chair. "Good sign? Shut up. It's hopeless."

Yes, Emerson Randolph, the guy who is in a picture at a boys camp he was never at with boys he was never with, will soon be the most powerful man in the world. Wayne smiled briefly and then wondered what fresh hell this would bring. He walked to his cinder block room.

He shouted to the air, "I wouldn't mind a little insulation on these bricks. Frickin cold in here."

Winter was coming.

—ε-ε-ε-ε-ε-ε—

Brody knew this wasn't going to be easy.

Saronda said, "Guys, Augustine wrote about this. It's the section about love."

Brody shifted in his chair and was drawn in as Saronda told the most wonderful story about how two people who are destined for each other fall in love. She described how Whispers reach out to another person, how they span the universe, seeking wisdom and depth from distant places that we will never see. They merge, feed off each other, and link as they weave love. Love created by the universe.

He felt her intensity.

He took Saronda's hand, trying to connect, but her voice was distant, as if through a cloud.

"When two people are meant for each other, their Whispers combine. Each Whisper draws energy from the far reaches of the universe. The pattern they weave transcends all others. It's unique, true to itself. Their Whispers just... they just fit. They're open to the will of the universe. To what was meant for them."

Her voice was tight. "We had that. My professor

had that with his family."

She paused, "And now, it's not there."

Brody let go of her hand. "I'm so sorry."

Rebecca sobbed.

Brody said, "I just don't feel anything for you."

Rebecca searched in her purse for a tissue. "Oh my God, this is so sad. Saronda, your heart. It must be… you're sitting there, and Brody feels nothing."

Saronda looked away. "I don't feel anything either."

Rebecca wiped her eyes.

Saronda took Brody's hand. "That's why I'm happy. It means my Whisper is meant for you. It can't feel you right now because you're broken. But it will heal. When your Whisper gets stronger, we'll connect."

Rebecca pulled out a second tissue and excused herself. "I'm going to go clean up. I'm a mess."

Brody pulled away and put his head in his hands. "This is heavy."

—ε-ε-ε-ε-ε-ε—

Milo said, "Wayne, I'm sure you know how much it pains me when you fail."

Wayne replied, "Sharing our pain is a bond we will

forever share. Your pain is my pain, my pain is your pain."

Milo tilted his head. "That may be true, but it doesn't compare to the disappointment I feel about not being able to get the result I wanted in the presidential election."

Wayne said, "Yeah, sedition is hard. But hey, we gave it our best."

"I have a new plan. We need to convince President-elect Emerson Randolph to work with us."

Wayne said, "Seriously? I thought we should pack it in. Do a captured learning post-mortem Venn diagram or whatever your manager's guide calls for. But hey, if you want to march over to the White House, I am sure he'll be open to ideas from a complete stranger who tried to throw the election against him."

Milo said, "That's exactly what I plan to do. It's not about who you want to win. This is about what all leaders want. Power."

Wayne said, "I'm pretty sure he's on a really cool power trip already. He was elected President of the United States."

"That power is messy, too much give and take. The kind of power I'm talking about is absolute. It's having society bend to your will. It's the neutron bomb you're going to build for me. But first we need to capture President Randolph's attention. We are going to ruin someone's life right before his eyes. Like we talked about.

We'll let Randolph watch as it happens."

Wayne said, "I don't feel comfortable doing this. I've decided I want out. I've lost my motivation. Bye bye."

"Wayne, that's a horrible thing to say. We are on the cusp of creating societal change the world has never seen."

"Well, could you let me in a little? What is this neutron bomb?"

"You know it is best that you just do the things I tell you to and not worry about such things but I will share a little."

Wayne leaned in. Milo became animated. "Imagine this. Let's say you want to bring back slavery. With my neutron bomb we could change who won the Civil War. We could change reality so that the south won."

"Uh, you do know that would fuck up a lot of things."

"Yes it would. But here's the thing Wayne," His eyes narrowed, "That's not how we're going to do it. We don't want to tear society apart, we want to control it, shape it, bit by bit, into what we want, into what it should be."

"Exactly how do we do that?"

"Drip... Drip... Drip..."

Wayne leaned back. "That's it? Drip drip drip?"

Milo walked slowly back to his office.

—ε-ε-ε-ε-ε-ε—

Saronda stared at Brody, one eyebrow raised, "You think this is heavy? Think about what *I've* been through. You disappeared off the face of the earth. For all I knew, you were dead. You need to hear this. I'm about to lay out the heavy shit."

"Hey, what I'm going through isn't pleasant. It is real."

"I know it is, but you need to power through. It's go time. The only way you're going to get better is if we fix that Whisper of yours. To do that, you need me. And Rebecca. And Augustine. But mostly, you need to be around people. Around us. Our Whispers will get you back on track."

Rebecca trotted back. "Sorry, what I miss?"

Saronda said, "I was about to talk about the destiny of the universe, how our individual reality is created, and how to fix Brody's broken Whisper so we can fall in love."

Rebecca's eyes widened.

Brody looked up at her. "Love? Really? Can we just get me back to normal first?"

Saronda said, "To do that, we need to fill in some holes in your pattern so the universe can do its work. Augustine has a section that describes how Whispers span the universe, connecting everything to everything. They form a network. They communicate through the universe 'Plus rapide que la lumière du soleil', *faster than light from the sun*. This is why no one ever heard of Augustine."

Rebecca said, "I don't follow."

Saronda explained, "Guys, 1905 was not the right time to be saying something goes faster than light. Einstein was king. He said there's nothing faster than light. End of story. You know, all that E equals MC squared and relativity stuff. If Einstein said it. It must be true."

Rebecca said, "Whoa, Augustine defying Einstein, in real time. Badass woman."

Saronda said, "Girl power! Think about it. When our Whispers weave our reality, they are accessing wisdom from the entire freaking universe. Our reality is created the same way the universe was created. Amazing stuff!"

Brody looked at the floor. "How's all that gonna make me not feel like shit?"

"Because it's not your destiny to feel like shit."

Brody said, "Well I wish destiny would hurry the fu—"

"Brody, you are meant to love me. If the universe wants something, it will get it."

Saronda then laid down the facts. "You will love me because the universe wants it that way."

Rebecca purred, "Awwhh."

Brody squirmed. "Can we take it one step at a time?"

"You need to let me show you. I have a plan."

Brody shook his head. "You have a plan for how we're going to fall in love? Kinda mechanical don't you think?"

Saronda said, "No, it's destiny."

"How do you know this?"

"Because our Whispers. Right now, yours is broken. We need to fix it. Then we'll fall in love."

Brody said, "Just like that?"

Saronda said, "Just like that."

Rebecca's head snapped back. "Whoa! I feel like I have a front row seat to the weirdest courtship ever."

Saronda admitted, "Yeah, it's gotten a bit odd. I'm going to need your help in understanding the equations."

Rebecca said, "Love among the equations. I can't wait to help. This is fascinating."

Brody looked at both of them. "What is happening?"

—ɛ-ɛ-ɛ-ɛ-ɛ-ɛ—

Milo walked in and closed the door. "Wayne, I found the person whose life we need to ruin."

Wayne replied, "I hope it's not me or Petey, we got work to do."

Milo asked, "How is he doing? I noticed you are working with him. I appreciate the initiative you've shown in helping his career growth."

Wayne said, "We're doing pair programming. It's had the right effect on speed, and it makes a good impression of effort."

He finished the sentence in his head. *By slowing us down to a snail's pace, while looking busy.*

Milo said, "Very good. OK. Here's our guy. Damien Matthews. Got filthy rich day-trading. All online. He made a couple lucky trades. Miserable record since."

Wayne asked, "How do you know all this? Oh, I know, you hacked him. So, you're going to do to him what you did to me."

Milo's eyes went dead. He rubbed the fingers of his left hand together. "Oh no, Wayne. This is different. I control you through fear. We're going to make this guy insane and show him off like a trophy."

His eyes gave Wayne a shiver.

"Wayne, do you understand me? Insane. A raving, intolerable lunatic."

Wayne said, "Wow, it got chilly in here. I may need a jacket."

Milo's voice was straight ahead steady. "We will change reality so he never made those trades. The paper trail will not exist. No archived records. No account with his name. No windfall. He was never rich. He's living high right now but we'll make it so he never had anything. Just memories of being rich, of being somebody. Of having friends who believed him."

"You are serious about this, aren't you?"

Milo's voice filled with pride. "His friends will remember his bragging about the great trades he made. The banks will remember all the money he borrowed. He will remember the feeling of waking up every day as a rich man. But it will no longer be real."

Wayne said, "This is pure evil. His whole life will have been a lie. But he knows it wasn't. He'll melt down."

Milo said, "Not evil, just a necessary step. Now get to work. I need to prepare to meet the newly elected president."

—ε-ε-ε-ε-ε-ε—

Rebecca said, "Saronda, your professor had

episodes?"

Saronda replied, "Yes, he went through what Brody went through."

Brody asked, "Does he feel like shit?"

Saronda said, "He did. Still does. He left his family. Didn't go back."

Rebecca said, "Left his family? Because of the episodes?"

Saronda said, "His Whisper was damaged. Just like Brody's. He lost his capacity to love. Their Whispers couldn't connect to his."

Rebecca said, "That's great news!"

Brody said, "This guy left his family, lost his ability to love them, and that's great news?"

Rebecca answered, "Yes, I get it now. His Whisper is damaged. Your Whisper is damaged. He lost his love for his family. You lost your love for Saronda."

Saronda broke in. "That means as your Whisper gets stronger, you'll be in love with me."

Rebecca said, "Best love story ever!"

Brody said, "I feel like a seventh grade science fair project. You guys act like love is just two Whispers linking."

Saronda said, "It is! And when two Whispers are meant for each other, it's destiny."

Rebecca said, "I can't wait to see what the equations say. This is way more interesting than anything I'm doing. Putting fat cats in jail is fun but it's just my day job."

Brody said, "Does that mean you weren't fired for getting those computers?"

Rebecca answered, "I got promoted. My boss wanted to fire me, but I explained things to him in terms he could understand."

—ε-ε-ε-ε-ε-ε—

Wayne threw a loud fake tantrum. "Coffee pot broke. And damn do I need caffeine."

He took a step back. "Oh never mind, I fixed it."

He looked at Petey. "You could have told me it wasn't plugged in. I wasted like five minutes. That's going to affect my productivity rating."

They chuckled.

Wayne was running out of ideas on how to ruin someone's life. He didn't have much to work with: a few parameters that Brody gave Milo many months prior, a chair to sit in, and Petey. The most useful thing was the chair.

"How does this code look, Wayne? I wrote it this

morning."

Wayne tried to be nice. "It's truly amazing. It's amazing it made it through the auto test."

Petey replied, "Oh I turned that off, it kept giving error messages."

Operation Slowdown was in full swing.

—ε-ε-ε-ε-ε-ε—

Milo sat alone, exhausted. He had spent the morning doing something that sucked the energy from him, talking to people. He was buoyed only by the fact that he wormed his way into working on President-elect Randolph's inauguration. It was a low-level task of getting flyers printed.

Wayne walked past Milo's office and saw him sitting alone. "Hey boss, missed you this morning. I almost couldn't function without hearing one of your engaging life tips."

"Hello Wayne, that's nice to hear. I did something very important today. Where is Petey? I need to tell the two of you."

Wayne called down the hallway and Petey trotted over.

Milo said, "I landed a position on President Randolph's transition team."

Petey said, "Whoa, that's big."

Milo said, "Yes, it is. I will use my new position as a way to meet President Randolph."

Petey looked at Wayne. "Did you hear that? The President."

Wayne said, "Knock me over with a feather."

Milo said, "I will need you two to speed up what you're doing. We need to demo our capability for the incoming president."

Petey said, "That is so cool."

—ε-ε-ε-ε-ε-ε—

Emerson Randolph was just what the country wanted. His speeches were a blend of rainbows and butterflies with enough detail to make you believe in unicorns. After his military service, he was an attorney who worked hard for his clients, often using clever arguments to get acquittals. He was also an idealist and felt his talents would better serve society as a prosecutor and then as a judge. He won the presidency on a vision of making society better for everyone.

Milo spent weeks studying him, analyzing every utterance, looking for clues to what motivated him. Underneath the rhetoric, Milo saw a man driven to get things done. "Cutting through the D.C. mud" was his calling card. He also saw a man who didn't have a clue how Washington worked, and his military training didn't leave a lot of room for give and take. He was very much a man who believed in top-down control. Do what you think is right, if not always in the right way. To Milo, this was an opening. He looked past the goody two shoes ideology. Underneath the happy talk, Milo saw a burning thirst for power. Milo planned to attract him with a little light fascism.

—ε-ε-ε-ε-ε-ε—

It was a big day at transition HQ. The big man was stopping for a visit to meet the troops.

Milo was all smiles and handshakes. "Congratulations, Mr. Randolph, or should we call you Mr. President?" He strained a smile.

The barrel-chested Randolph replied, "And you are?"

"Oh, allow me to introduce myself. I am Milo Cuda. I serve on your transition team. I've been a supporter of yours for a long time. I was so happy when you decided to run. I would love to meet with you, share some ideas."

Emerson did the typical brush off. "See Hari Blanek, he controls my calendar. It was nice meeting you."

As he walked away, Milo called out, "I know where that photo came from."

Emerson glanced over his shoulder but kept walking.

—ε-ε-ε-ε-ε-ε—

Wayne had hoped to get through a cup of coffee before the crazy started.

His hope was dashed. "Good morning, boss. So how are you going to get a meeting with the new president?"

"I already planted a seed. I've been studying him."

Milo pulled out a tablet. "Look at his bookcase in this campaign video."

Wayne said, "OK, I see Art of War, The Prince, The Campaigns of Alexander, Civil War books. Lots of war stuff."

Milo expanded the screen. "But look at this one. You can hardly read the title, it's been opened so much. It's about Genghis Khan. Genghis Khan treated war as a science. He defeated enemies before they even knew they were at war. Annihilate the poor saps before they see you coming. We have just the weapon for that. I think the new president will like that."

Wayne said, "This will come in handy for our defense. They can't put you in jail if the dude has war books on his shelf."

—ε-ε-ε-ε-ε-ε—

Emerson Randolph was direct with Hari Blanek. "The Congress creatures are pathetic. All they want to do is stall."

Hari Blanek sat back with his drink of choice, a Manhattan. "They aren't known as bastions of productivity. It'll take a little convincing, some horse trading."

As he spoke, his phone bleeped with a text notification. Hari said, "There are a lot of clowns in this world. I think this guy texted like four times. Says you asked to meet with him."

"Does he say what he wants?"

"Yeah, he says he can tell us where that photo of you at the boys camp came from. Says he's on your transition team. Doesn't give a name."

"There was a fella in the meet and greet today. Said the same thing."

Hari texted back: *Make yourself known. What do you want? We have no recollection of you.*

An immediate text came back: *I can make myself very memorable. Best not dismiss*

Emerson didn't like the sound of that. "He sounds like a nut but we gotta nip it. Give him a ten minute time slot, we'll be eight minutes late. We'll dress him down and never hear from him again."

Hari warned, "I think we should stand clear."

Emerson said, "We need to see if he's trouble."

—ε-ε-ε-ε-ε-ε—

Saronda pulled a chair into the sun. "First, thank you for meeting with me. I love these fall days when it's warm."

Axel Mixcertl replied, "Yes, Indian summer."

Saronda asked, "Are we still allowed to call it that? We need a new term."

Axel replied, "OK, global warming. Let's order a drink."

Saronda said, "It's like three in the afternoon."

Axel said, "You're right, it's getting late. Where is that waitress? I go to bed at eight."

He waved his hand. "Excuse me, a whiskey sour for me and…"

Saronda said, "Ice tea. I stay up 'til midnight so…"

Axel said, "I still get exhausted. These episodes nailed me."

Saronda said, "That's what I want to talk about. Brody came back. He's still not well but I'm convinced we're destined for each other, and you're destined to be with your family. It's the way the universe wants it."

The professor sat up in his chair and turned to face Saronda. "Are you talking that destiny crap again? This is why I'm glad I'm a prick. For these exact moments when someone brings up something so illogical that saying it's asinine does a disservice to the word asinine. If only there were a stronger word than asinine to fully capture —"

Saronda cut him off. "Dunderheaded. Dunderheaded feels stronger to me. Lots of percussive consonants. But I get it, seems like you're a little dug in on the destiny thing. Can I present a different view?"

"A different view? Like there's two sides to this? I would love to hear your theory. Fire away, there's nothing I'd rather be doing right now, other than sipping a whiskey sour and putting a bullet in my brain."

Saronda parried, "The waitress is bringing you the drink. I'm sure there are a lot of people who would help you out with the bullet. Seriously, there's a lot riding on the answer, including your family life."

Axel said, "Think about it. We're insignificant. Even if we assume the universe has a conscience, how would it even know we exist? It's a million light years across."

Saronda replied, "Current estimates say over twenty billion light years across. That's not important right now. But yes, the universe has a conscience and we're its ultimate creation."

Axel said, "That's religion. Talk to a theologian. Now, where is that drink?"

Saronda said, "No it's history. Think about how many times tyrants have tried to rule us and the improbable events that defeated them. The destiny of the universe is to protect us and let us live in freedom."

Axel shifted in his seat. "Nonsense, the universe

doesn't think and if it did we're not the thing it wants to protect."

"The universe doesn't have to think, everything's already written. In the Whispers. You're destined to be with your family. Now, settle down and let me tell you how Whispers work. Are you ready to listen?"

Apparently, he was.

As the ice melted in his drink, Professor Axel Mixcertl, a proud prick, listened, enraptured. He went home the next day.

—ε-ε-ε-ε-ε-ε—

The administrative assistant to the next President of the United States carefully touched her finger to the security button under her desk. "Please sir, if you could step back from my desk."

Milo apologized, "I am so sorry if I alarmed you. But this is my time slot. I was told very specifically that I would have ten minutes. I arrived early fully expecting to have to wait, but it is now seven minutes past my time slot."

"Sir, please sit. They'll be with you shortly."

Milo sat. "OK, I am now sitting but there are three minutes left in my time slot. Will I still be able to… "

Just then the door opened, and Milo was ushered in. "Hello, I'm Hari Blanek. I'm sure you know who this is." He pointed to Randolph.

Milo scurried in. "Will I still get my ten minutes?"

Hari said, "These aren't your minutes. Tell us what this is about."

Milo hurried through his carefully written script. "I have something you will be greatly interested in. I know where the boys camp photo came from. I created it by altering reality. I can do the same, tailor made to your purposes. I have prepared a website. I will send the link. I have also made a video. Please watch it. I will sit quietly until the video is over."

Hari and Emerson looked at each other. Milo sat with his hands in his lap, perfectly still, looking at nothing in particular.

Hari looked up from the video. "Are we supposed to know this fella?"

"No, he's very average. His name is Damien Matthews. He made a few good trades and got rich. Now he brags. Facebook, Twitter, but mostly Instagram. Everyday, 'My boat looks like this. Look how big my house is.' That's all about to change. I will be very direct with you because your time is important. In six weeks, I will contact you. During that time, watch his Instagram account, don't follow it, that will seem strange to him. You will see a man melt down."

Emerson was livid. "I don't know if this is a threat, or an admission to crime, but I feel you've exposed me to something that I shouldn't have knowledge of. I'm the next President of the United States of America. I am asking you to leave."

Milo said, "Very well. I expected that. You are a man of high integrity. I can tell that from the extensive research I've done. But as the next President of the United States of America, you need to think about this not just in terms of America but other countries as well. OK, gentlemen. Six weeks. I believe I've ended on time."

Milo walked out. Emerson looked at Hari and laughed. "This is how it's going to be isn't it? Everyday a new nut."

Hari sighed, "I advised you not to give this guy a meeting. But honestly, it went as well as your meeting with the Senate leader."

They laughed.

—ε-ε-ε-ε-ε-ε—

Wayne was aghast. Petey about fainted.

Milo said, "Yes. I did. I met with Emerson Randolph and his future chief of staff. That's not public but I saw a placard sitting on the secretary's desk with his name and new title."

Wayne said, "You are a god among men. You just walked in there and said, 'I need to see the freaking President of the United States of America and they said, 'come right in'."

Milo said, "I made an appointment."

Wayne asked, "They're taking appointments? Like a nail salon?"

Milo said, "Well they don't meet with just anyone, I had to make them interested in me. I told them I knew where that photo came from."

Petey's jaw dropped. "The balls."

Wayne said, "Are you sure that was a good idea? Ah, hell, I don't know what a good idea is anymore. I'm just a simple, country programmer from a lower tier school. But, man, we committed fraud and you're telling the leader of the free world."

Milo said, "And his chief of staff. Wayne, there's no way they can prove we changed the photo. That's the beauty."

Wayne's voice got screechy. "But you told the *President!*"

Milo said, "I had to get their attention."

Wayne rubbed his neck. "OK, well we need to get back to work. I'm sure you're going to promise them something."

"Oh, I already did. We're going to destroy a man's life over the next six weeks and they're going to watch."

—ε-ε-ε-ε-ε-ε—

Wayne sat alone in his room staring at the wall. He chose a black marker and slid it out of its vinyl sleeve. A set of markers was one of the few indulgences Milo allowed in from the outside world. He pressed the marker against the cinder block wall, wiggling it to create a jagged line, the veins of a leaf on a tree he started months ago. The scene he was drawing was taking shape, the only accomplishment he was proud of since the day he got a subpoena. His phone exploded with a sound that most people would describe as pleasant. To Wayne, it was nails on a chalkboard. Milo needed to see him.

"Wayne, thank you so much for coming to see me. There is something we need to discuss."

Wayne said, "It's late. I thought we established that this is my time."

Milo didn't acknowledge the comment. "I logged into your workstation. I don't do it often. We must respect boundaries in the workplace, but there is a lot of working code you haven't told me about."

Wayne said, "It hasn't been tested."

"I ran some models, it works fine."

Wayne said, "Yeah, the later versions show promise. But I wouldn't— "

Milo said, "You've had this code for months. We could have used it to destroy Randolph before the election and he never would've won. Now I have to get cozy with that yay hoo and convince him to work with us. This has made my job very difficult."

Wayne knew he had held Milo off as long as he could. "Look, I can have Petey speed up the testing. Even so, we'll have to use some untested code if we want to hit your six-week target."

Milo erupted. "It's not a target Wayne, it's a deadline. If that deadline is not met, there will be severe consequences."

—ε-ε-ε-ε-ε-ε—

Wayne rousted Petey from his sleep. "Get up, come look at this."

Wayne pointed to a pattern on his screen.

Petey rubbed sleep from his eyes. "I don't know what to look for."

"Check out this part of the pattern. See how it changed? I don't know if it will work in the real world. It's totally untested. I'm debating. Do we blast this thing? Ruin a life."

Petey said, "I think we should because it would be cool."

Wayne said, "You're right it would be cool, but it could be bad."

"We changed that photo. Same thing, right?"

"We got lucky. This time we have to be precise. Otherwise... Ah, hell, I don't know what to do."

They stared at each other. Petey shrugged.

Wayne said, "You're right. Let's do it." He texted Milo: *blast. yes/no?*

He got a quick reply: *yes*

Wayne told Petey, "Always get it in writing from the boss when you're about to do something stupid. Here goes. OWAN away!"

He clicked the button. Petey asked, "What's OWAN?"

Wayne said, "OWAN. Operating without a net."

"Nice."

—ε-ε-ε-ε-ε-ε—

Damien "soon to be emasculated" Matthews poured another cognac. "Pissed me off. Jethro's down the street ran out of the Looey. Like, who else fucking buys it but me? At five grand I don't think any of the jugheads around here do."

The conspicuous mention of Louis XIII cognac was not lost on his friend Jake.

Jake asked, "Jethro's? You mean Jeter's Fine Liquors?"

"Ah, yeah, I call him Jethro cuz he's, ya know, a Jethro. No offense to all the other Jethros out there." Damien belly laughed as he took a puff on his cigar. "Oh hey, lemme show ya what I got installed last week. Hey

Stanley, island mood."

The lights around the pool changed colors and soft calypso music played. Cylinders rose out of the deck and unfurled into fake palm trees.

Damien said, "Isn't that something? I had to give it a name. I named it Stanley. You know Stanley Company. That was my first big market win."

First and only big win. And he actually bought stock in the wrong Stanley company. He clicked on the second one down the list instead of the third. Months later, when he noticed his mistake, he was already rich. The stock had skyrocketed. That was the extent of his prowess at trading stock.

Damien poured another cognac. "All we're missing are a couple of island girls. Maybe some of those fufu drinks with the umbrellas."

Jake replied, "Makes this cognac kinda awkward. Can you turn this place into a bistro?"

"Hell, I can try."

Presto, cobblestones were projected onto the deck while accordion music played.

"So, Damien, how's the trading?"

"Ahh, ya know, hits and misses. Market's been hard to figure."

"You're always saying that. I'll bet you're hitting

it out of the park. I mean, look at all this, the house, beautiful wife, pool that turns into a bistro. We're hitting pretty good too. Market's been kind, showing us its hand. Easy money amirite?"

Jake was right, the market had been kind but not for Damien. He hadn't made decent money for a long time. His funds were drying up. He was living off borrowed money. Milo's perfect mark.

—ε-ε-ε-ε-ε-ε—

"Oh my God, I should *not* be feeling happy about this." Wayne scrolled through the details.

Milo's skin tingled. "This is amazing. The Stanley trade is not there. It's like the trade never happened!"

Wayne's voice revealed some nerdish pride. "That means we got the location right. Now we have to erase the *account*, like it never existed."

Petey couldn't stop giggling. Wayne looked over. "Petey, my man. You alright over there?"

Petey squirmed in his chair. "This is so cool. Do it. Erase the account. Don't you think so Mr. Cuda? Just do it? I wanna see it."

Wayne said, "We can't just do it. We need to calculate the energy. Get that wrong, and the whole brokerage may disappear. We need to peel off reality one thin layer at a time."

Milo was silent, thinking, and then, "Thank you, Wayne. I'll take note of that. Petey, there's something I need to discuss with Wayne. Leave."

Milo shut the door and then listened to hear if Petey had walked away. "Wayne, this is not to be shared with Petey. By the way, is he on drugs? He acts strange sometimes."

"No drugs. Just Petey. You have him on such a short leash. Maybe he needs to get out more. See some friends."

"That's a terrifying thought. What if he tells someone what we're doing here?"

"Why does it matter? You said none of this can be detected."

"Our plan depends on the element of surprise. They must never see us coming. It's why I never invested any time in deep fakes. Everyone knows about them. Only stupid people will believe them."

"Milo, who is 'they'? It sounds like you're targeting, what, a race? religion?"

"Wayne, I am targeting all conscious and semi-conscious human beings. I want them all. For centuries, people have been divided up, pitting one group against another. Hasn't worked. We need everyone."

Wayne had never heard anyone talk like this.

Milo continued, "But that's not who 'they' are. I'm talking about the seventy percent of humanity who refuse to be captured."

The words sounded angry. He calmed his voice. "People who refuse to be captured by conspiracy theories, people who—"

"You mean people who sort through facts and see through the lies?"

Milo's voice filled with derision. "Yes. No matter what we did, only thirty percent came along. We need to go higher. Ninety percent. P90."

Milo paused for a second, then calmly said, "We will discuss that at a later date. For now, I want to talk about what you said. You said 'peel off reality one layer at a time.' It gave me an idea so thank you for sharing your thoughts."

"Always glad to help."

"As we peel off layers of someone's reality, we can control the level of a person's sanity. We can build custom-made nervous breakdowns."

"You little teaser. Tell me more."

Milo said, "Think this through with me. If we change small facts about a person's life, they suffer annoying memory gaps, something like insisting their first car was a Pinto."

"I don't think anyone would insist on people knowing that."

"Wayne, you're off the point."

Wayne cut in. "No, I get it. If we change enough facts about a person's life, like who they married or how many kids they have, oh man, total insanity. Their heads would be nothing but chaos. They'd be thrown into an asylum."

"Yes Wayne, I believe you're catching on. And I do like your use of the word chaos. We will continue this discussion. But there's something I want to tell you. After what I saw the last couple days, you have gained my trust. I believe in your skills to a degree that I am going to let you do a little strategizing with me. We will meet tomorrow. Please be prepared to map out next steps. Ruining lives is a good first step. But we need to take this to the next level and I trust you are the person to do it."

Milo walked to his office. He told Petey he could return.

Petey pulled a chair over to Wayne. "So what did he want?"

"Petey, I can't tell you his exact words but what I think he said is, shit's about to get real."

—ε-ε-ε-ε-ε-ε—

It had been ten days since Emerson Randolph met with Milo, and ten days since he gave it a single thought.

Hari was wrapping up the daily debrief. "So, that's where we are. I doubt we can move Congress on this until after the midterms. Oh, I've been checking that guy's Instagram."

"Who are you talking about?"

"The guy whose life we're going to see crumble, Damien Matthews."

"Don't bother me with that stuff. Now get out of here."

"Eh, it's just a little fun. Thank you, Mr. President."

—ε-ε-ε-ε-ε-ε—

Milo said, "Wayne, have you thought about next steps? I think we need to turn the screw. Take away his bank loans."

"Milo, that's his only source of money. He's living on fumes."

"Exactly why I picked him."

"But don't you think it's unfair to randomly pick a guy and ruin his life?"

"It's a necessary step. We need a demo. The President needs to understand the power of this. He can use this to control people by showing what he can do to them. It's amazing the things you can get people to do when you play on their sense of self-preservation."

Wayne could relate.

—ε-ε-ε-ε-ε-ε—

Damien Matthews sat on the balcony overlooking his sculpture garden. His ample belly hung over his striped boxers, his bare feet soaking up the first warming rays of a Costa Rican morning sun.

He poured another shot of Jameson Whiskey into his coffee. "Hey, babe, I gotta check something at the bank today. I got a notification that my margin account bounced."

"But you promised you'd drop me at the spa."

"Oh I can, babe. Get ready to go."

Damien will not like what he learns this morning. It's not a matter of a transfer not going through. It's a matter of there being no bank account. Never was. The bank manager will not be pleased with the language this unknown person uses. Security and then the police will be called.

That will not be the end of Damien's nightmare. His lawyer, the one who helped him navigate arcane tax laws to optimize his fortune, will ask him to kindly leave his office because there never was a fortune.

Poor Bebe, his young wife will arrive at the spa for an appointment that doesn't exist. They will not recognize her. Sure, she'd been there before. She was the cashier from the shop down the street, not the ranting woman with the grotesquely overinflated lips and breasts that defy gravity. Their day will be as confusing as it is terrifying. They will look back and regard it as one of their better days.

—ε-ε-ε-ε-ε-ε—

Petey looked at the pattern on the screen. "You're getting good at this, Wayne. Why do you keep trying to slow things down?"

"Petey, we're in survival mode. We need to make sure we come out of this alive. There are only two ways this can go. Milo fails and we turn evidence or Milo wins and we end up with a nicely feathered nest. I need to figure out how to turn this into a money machine. Do you know how much coin we could make with this?"

"No."

Wayne paused. "Uh, Petey it's… rhetorical."

Petey said, "Sounds like a lot. Righteous."

Wayne shook his head. "Yeah, something like that. But back to work. I'm now able to peel back layers of reality. Have you finished running the energy calcs?"

Petey was excited. "Yes, it looks like we can remove his house purchase. The dude will have no way to prove he owns his house. He'll be homeless!"

Wayne said, "You said that with glee."

Petey said, "It is kinda fun, don't you think?"

Milo came bounding in. "What's fun?"

Petey said, "Ruining a guy's life."

Milo said, "It is a beautiful thing. What's the status?"

—ε-ε-ε-ε-ε-ε—

Damien wanted to sue the bank where he never had an account. Same with the brokerage. He wanted to sue the mortgage company who never gave him a loan. No lawyers will take his case. "I'll represent myself," he screamed at no one as his chins wiggled. The only thing he accomplished was drawing attention to himself. It wasn't flattering. Convincing the state's psychiatry board he's not crazy will become a full time job. Bebe didn't see any reason to hang around. It was the complete dismantling of a human being. Killing him would take away his future. This was worse. It took away his past, leaving him as an empty zombie. Milo watched it all on Instagram. It was the highlight of his life, and things were only getting better.

—ε-ε-ε-ε-ε-ε—

Milo took deep even breaths and then walked into the Office of the President. He made eye contact as he had practiced. "Were you gentlemen sufficiently entertained?"

Hari Blanek, soon to be chief of staff, stared back. "You destroyed a man's life. That's illegal what you did."

Milo took a breath. "No, not when you look at the details. Damien Matthews never made those trades. They are nowhere to be found. Never happened."

"And yet he did make those trades. He got rich and had a great life."

Milo said, "You need to adjust your thinking. Allow me to frame it this way. His life wasn't ruined. He never had that life. You can't destroy something that never existed."

Hari said, "That's twisted. Look at his Instagram. In his mind, he got rich."

Milo looked at Emerson and said with confidence, "Yes, that's the beauty. It only happened in his mind."

Hari's face was red. "You took his sanity."

Milo preened and held eye contact with President Emerson Randolph. "Exactly. And I can do it to anyone. Anyone."

He let the word linger. "Thank you for recognizing the benefit. If you can provide me with a list of people that need to be controlled, we'll ruin some, others we threaten. I suggest you take your time and be strategic. It is not to be overused. Think of this as a rifle not a flamethrower."

Hari stammered, "Provide you with a list? Mr. Cuda, we should have you arrested."

Milo continued holding Emerson's eye. "If that's the way you want to use your time then I greatly underestimated you. Now, I am sure President Randolph here, being a student of history, knows that when a new weapon comes along you can't afford to let it get in the hands of your enemies."

Hari spoke to the side of Milo's head, "Is that a threat?"

Milo turned to face Hari. "Goodness no, but if I'm ever going to be able to... let me explain, the world's out of control. Would you like to be the ones to fix it, or should that be left up to someone else?"

Hari stared at Milo. "Mr. Cuda, may we have the room?"

Milo turned to the President. "Certainly, if there is anything I failed to cover sufficiently or if you have any questions... "

Hari motioned for him to leave.

As Milo was leaving, the President spoke for the first time, "Uh Mr. Cuda you wouldn't be able to do what? You said if we didn't do this you wouldn't ever be able to... "

Milo tilted his head and said, "My plan. Thank you, Mr. President."

He walked out.

Emerson turned to Hari. "Whatta we got here? Evaluate this for me. I mean what is this?"

Hari said, "When we figure that out, the bigger question is do we kill it or hope it goes away?"

The President intoned, "Or do we use it? Two things. One, he's got the weapon of our time. He doesn't care who gets it. He's no ideologue. Two, if we don't work with him, he will destroy us. You remember Johnson 'it's better to have them inside the tent pissing out than outside the tent pissing in?' We need him inside the tent."

"Seems we get wet either way."

Randolph was tired of dancing around the issue. "Hari, dammit, I wish you weren't making me have to say this. I want the weapon. I want to use it. I want to blow through a few senators. Soften up a couple holdouts in Congress."

They called Milo back into the room. Only Hari spoke, "We'll be in touch."

Milo tilted his head. Hari motioned him to leave and walked him to the door.

Hari stopped him and nodded toward the President. "Aren't you forgetting something?"

Milo stood frozen, then, "Thank you, Mr. President."

Hari closed the door. "Emerson, this is a slippery slope. Didn't one of your friends say 'once you start running down a hill, you're committed'?"

Emerson clenched his jaw and swallowed. He thought of his friend Arthur and what that photo did to him. His stone cold stare signaled the meeting was over.

"Thank you, Mr. President." Hari left.

—ε-ε-ε-ε-ε-ε—

Brody was enjoying his egg and cheddar sandwich at Busboys and Poets. Saronda and Rebecca huddled around Paul Langevin's paper.

Rebecca said, "Thanks for translating this. I messed around with it last night. It's amazing those equations are identical to Augustine's."

She leaned over to whisper in Rebecca's ear, "Paul Langevin was Madame Curie's lover."

Rebecca squealed, "Scandalous! Positively radioactive!"

They laughed. Brody asked, "C'mon tell me. What's going on."

Rebecca said, "Saronda got a paper from her professor that uses Augustine's equations. Written by a guy who was afraid the nazis were going to use them to take over the world."

Saronda said, "Yeah, this guy Paul Langevin wrote it. He was a big deal in France. Mathematician. Inventor. He and Madame Curie, well, they kinda had a thing..."

Rebecca said, "You know, he left out some things. He left out a parameter, Epsilon. And the reference to Augustine is to a footnote in her paper that says, 'Epsilon can be negative'. It's odd that he refers to something that he took out. Just for fun, I made Epsilon a negative number, and wow! Whole sections of the pattern collapsed."

Saronda asked, "They disappeared?"

"No, they went into chaos."

Saronda said, "That's what he was saying in his paper. He warned that the nazis would use chaos to rule the world. What bothers me is he laid it all out for the world to see."

Rebecca said, "Except, he left out Epsilon."

—ε-ε-ε-ε-ε-ε—

Milo drummed his finger on the desk. He closed his computer. "Aduco Lim. So, he's the one who detected me. I'll need to have a word with the Syndicate about him." He tilted his head. *Doesn't explain why he talked to the agency looking for flying objects.*

Wayne knocked on the door frame. "You busy?"

"Wayne, you scared me. I was deep in thought. Please announce yourself first."

Wayne said, "That's what the knock was for. Anyhow, Petey and I have been talking. We'd like to spruce the place up a bit. We're doing productive work and I think we deserve better."

"What do you mean?"

"Some paint, really cool furniture, neat lighting, a pool table, wet bar."

"Goodness, are you not happy here?"

"You're kidding, right? I couldn't be happier if I was eating a bag of hair. I just think if we're trapped here, we should have nice things. I know you've got the money. You shook down half the banking system for chrissakes."

Milo said, "I guess that wouldn't be out of the question."

"Good, I'll have Petey start right away. Have you seen his latest video package? I bet your presidential friend will love it. It's everything we know about strategic persuasion."

Milo said, "I'll need to look at that. Please use the term 'strategic persuasion 2.0' to highlight our new ability to micro-layer reality."

"Wow, look at you, Mr. Marketing."

"Tell Petey not to make the video specific to the United States. I'd like everything we present to be generic. These guys think they have an exclusive. That may change."

Wayne said, "Sinister."

"Oh, and Wayne, I won't be here tomorrow. I'm meeting with some folks who track down UFOs."

"Curious."

"Yes, very."

—ε-ε-ε-ε-ε-ε—

Yasmin was about to leave when she got the email. "Seriously? Here?"

She pounced on Ray the second he arrived. "He's coming here?"

"What's going on?"

"Milo Cuda is coming here."

Ray said, "I don't know anything about—"

Yasmin thrust her phone with a full extension of her arm. "Look."

Ray shook his head. "What does he want with us?"

"Ray, he's a member of the National Security Council."

Ray said, "I know. When? Today?"

"Not today. *Now!*"

Yasmin filled the dog's water bowl and started preparing for the meeting. Her email lit up. She was not on the list of attendees.

She marched to Ray's office. "Why am I not on the list? Milo Cuda, the President's lead on everything having to do with cybercrime, the dark web, these guys we're chasing, is coming here today and you want me to sit at my desk."

Ray said, "Isn't your shift over?"

Yasmin put her hands on her hips and used the full force of her fiery dark eyes.

Ray Denmore explained, "Look, my hands are tied. They want to keep the room to a minimum. Keep the discussion flowing."

"You mean keeping me from correcting the higher ups."

Ray's face tightened. "Don't take this as meaning anything, it's just the way things are. Oh, it looks like he's here. Gotta go." He trotted off.

Yasmin fumed at her desk. "This is so stupid, Phoenix. I should be in there." The yellow lab felt her pain and laid his wet chin on her lap.

The dog perked his head up. Yasmin turned and looked, "Wow, this guy doesn't travel light. Is that security?"

The entourage disappeared into the conference room. The yellow lab looked at her and barked and then ran to the meeting room.

"Phoenix, come back here." He looked in through the glass wall.

Yasmin pulled him by his collar. "Come on, if I'm not invited, you certainly aren't."

No way she was leaving, she wanted an update as soon as the meeting broke up so she played busy at her computer.

"Excuse me, office girl, will you please direct me to the restroom?" It was Milo Cuda, three feet from her desk. She froze.

"Yes, um, hi, Mr. Cuda. uh the restroom—"

Her sentence was interrupted when Phoenix jumped up, wiggling and bowing and jumping on Milo Cuda. Yasmin had never seen him so excited. He danced and twisted, tail beating furiously. Milo looked panicked. Yasmin was shocked..

"Um, I am so sorry about this dog. He's normally very calm."

Milo squirmed. "Please, dear God, get this mutt off of me."

"Phoenix, down. So sorry. Restroom is down the hall to the left. Phoenix, stop."

She paused and stared at Milo. "He's such a loose end."

Milo's face froze as Phoenix pawed at his leg.

"Uh, don't you mean loose cannon or loose wheel or..."

"Oh, so sorry, sometimes I mix up. Silly me. Excuse me now." She grabbed Phoenix by the collar and walked quickly, taking tiny steps. Phoenix stared back at Milo as he was dragged.

Once she was around the corner, Yasmin took long strides and exhaled for the first time.

She burst into Ray's office, shutting the door behind her. She sent him a text: *Your office now. Can't wait. This is big.*

She peeked through the blinds in Ray's office as Ray huffed out of the meeting.

He was spitting nails. "What the hell? If Mr. Cuda wasn't in the crapper—"

Yasmin hyperventilated, her arms stiff at her side. "It's him. Milo is him. It's Milo. Milo is Prairie Dog. Prairie Dog is Milo."

Phoenix agreed.

"Yasmin, come on, that's crazy talk. Milo is a top aide to POTUS. He's not some fugitive."

"It's him. The dog. Phoenix. He went nuts. He stared at Milo when he got here and then went nuts, jumping all over him. This dog doesn't get excited about anything but food. The wet kind, hates the dry."

Her eyes burned a hole in Ray. Every word was punctuated with shallow breaths. "*That* is our fugitive and *this* is his dog."

Ray minimized. "Yasmin, settle. Just because a dog

gets a little excited doesn't—"

"I tested him. I used a phrase he was hung up on in the manifesto, loose end."

Ray said, "Hell of a case you built there."

"We have to arrest him. He needs to be stopped."

"Be reasonable. That's silly talk. He's part of the President's inner circle."

Yasmin said, "That's why we have to stop him."

Ray asked, "From doing what?"

Yasmin peeked through the blinds again as Milo returned to the meeting room. "That's what we need to find out."

—ε-ε-ε-ε-ε-ε—

Milo got out of the town car and brushed off dog hair as he walked the hallway to his office. He stopped. "Whoa." His eyes darted back and forth. "My, my, my. I don't recognize the place."

Petey was smiling so hard it hurt to look at him. "Yeah. It's cool, isn't it, Mr. Cuda? Wayne said I could go out and buy stuff. What do you think?"

Milo said, "Air hockey. I thought you were getting a pool table?"

Petey blurted, "We did! It's in the other room with the bar. We thought air hockey would be too noisy to be close to the theater. Wanna see?"

Milo said, "No, I need to talk to Wayne about something. Don't let these new toys affect your productivity."

Petey skipped away. "I won't, Mr. Cuda."

Wayne walked up. "Sweet crib, don't you think?"

Milo had more urgent matters on his mind. "Progress has stalled. We aren't where we need to be."

Wayne said, "Aren't you gonna tell me about your visit? Are they holding little green men in embryonic saline tanks?"

"What? No, the visit was uneventful. Now, back to your lack of progress. We need to move faster, before... Listen closely, I will have to put your promotion on indefinite hold if you—"

"Stop it Milo. Just stop. You're just edgy about something. How can you say we're not making progress? We have the entire government in a twist. Shit's all messed up. We've produced so many compromised judges and DoJ agents they're afraid of their shadow. They couldn't convict Charles Manson if they had video and a public confession."

Milo said, "It is wonderful isn't it? I am so glad to see you take pride in it. That is healthy, but we have made no progress towards P90. That should be your every waking thought. P90. P90. P90." He rubbed his fingers together, his face stiffened. "We have done very well convincing people that everyone in government is corrupt. But they move on. They take their kids to soccer. They focus on their jobs. Government corruption has become nothing more than entertainment."

"Milo, they have lives. And you do know you're the one who screwed everything up. 'Designed Reality 1.0.' Remember that?"

Milo said, "We need to keep pushing until nothing is believed because nothing *can* be believed. Everything will have two sides. Even science."

Milo became animated. "I've explained this three times. We need to get to P90. Please pay attention, it's when ninety percent of people believe something that is clearly false. I am very good at getting to P30, but thirty percent isn't enough to dictate the course of society. It always fails."

Wayne shook his head. "Yeah, OK. I get it. But that thirty percent you brag about, they like being lied to. Easy picken'."

Milo got upset. His life work had been attacked. "Wayne, it's not that easy. Now let's focus on the sixty percent that we need to—"

Wayne leaned in. "Sixty? What about the other ten percent? Shoot them?"

Milo shot out of his chair and paced. "Dissidents, every last one of them. There will always be dissidents.

They will be dealt with in due course. They are not your concern. Your job is getting people to think nothing is real. Nothing is true. Real facts are fake. Fake facts are real. We'll make something true one day and false the next. They won't know what to believe. They'll give up. They will believe nothing."

Wayne asked, "But why? Why do this?"

Milo sat down and looked at Wayne straight on. "When people believe nothing, you can make them believe anything."

"Well, good luck with that."

Milo said, "Where are you going? Why are you walking away?"

Wayne stopped. "I have to pee. We've been through this. We don't have the tools. We plug numbers into the same two equations. It's reached its limits. When you were best buds with Brody, did he tell you anything else that might help?"

Milo said, "I will check my notes but Wayne, this is totally on you to figure out. I fully expect— "

"Quiet. I get it. Maybe give me your notes so I can search through them."

"I will think about that but maybe you should call Brody and ask *him*."

Wayne threw his hands up. "Oh, that's cool. 'Hi, we're trying to take over the world, can you do a brother a solid and tell us how?'"

"Wayne, I am starting to detect some sarcasm from you. Now, I think you can figure out how to ask your friend. Please prepare a plan for how you're going to do that."

Wayne said, "In the meantime, can you give me your notes? I will cherish them in a fashion worthy of their author."

—ε-ε-ε-ε-ε-ε—

Wayne soaked in the quietness of the cinder block room that had become his refuge from the madness. He selected a green marker, the fat one, from the vinyl sleeve. He methodically filled in the outline of a leaf on the tree he was making. The tree would become the most prominent part of the tapestry. He set down the green marker and picked up the black fine tip to add texture to the gnarled tree trunk.

He muttered the line from Milo, "When people believe nothing, you can make them believe anything." *What does that even mean?*

Wayne knew what it meant. He just couldn't bring himself to admit that he was a part of it.

The tree was elaborate, growing in a distant field as seen through an imaginary window. He'd been at it for months. When they find his bunker, they will be impressed. Each detail he added was a reminder of the daily reports he got from Milo of another life ruined or another powerful person squirming, worried they could be next. Senators cried in public, "I never met that woman, I don't know anything about those hotel receipts."

Or money showing up in bank accounts with a tangled string of deposits from bad people.

Milo's plan was sinister. Even the President of the United States, the most powerful man in the world, bowed to the wishes of the pathetic cloistered weasel. America was becoming a democracy in name only.

He shook the marker pen. "Damn, another one dried up."

Wayne knew he needed a solid exit plan. He needed to change a few lines of code, funnel huge sums of money into his bank account and send damning evidence to the Feds that would tie up Milo in court for the rest of his life, without Milo catching on.

He needed a little cooperation from Brody.

—ε-ε-ε-ε-ε-ε—

Yasmin heard the same answer each time. "No. No. And no."

Ray bounced a tennis ball off the wall of his office. "We've been through this. We can't spy on the President's right-hand man based on a barking dog."

"He didn't bark. He wagged his tail. And it's not spying. I just want to do a location history match."

"That's spying."

"Your words not mine." Yasmin knew Ray was right.

She also knew that the brick wall was insurmountable and wondered why locking up people like Milo is so friggin' hard. In her mind, she used the real F word. She had seen enough.

She thanked Ray for his time. "OK then. That's that. I guess that's it... then. So... should I close your door when I leave? Wouldn't want the ball to get loose. He he. Bye." *OK, walk as you normally do. Oh God, I can feel him staring at me.*

She turned the corner and exhaled. *I'll take my case somewhere else.*

—ε-ε-ε-ε-ε-ε—

Wayne could see Milo's silhouette reflected in his monitor. "I know you're back there, Milo, I can feel the micromanagement oozing out of you."

Milo stepped forward. "Now that I gave you my notes, have you called Brody?"

"I can't just call up Brody and ask him about this stuff. Have you not seen the news? It's all about fact checking and no one agrees. If I start asking about how to change facts, he'll put two and two together."

"He will not. He's not that smart."

"But he is mildly sentient. When people get calls out of the blue asking for weird shit, they get suspicious."

Milo turned on his heel to leave and bumped into the air hockey table. "Clutter."

Wayne knew he couldn't hold him off much longer.

—ε-ε-ε-ε-ε-ε—

Days passed. Wayne ran simulations and tests but was getting nowhere. The atmosphere was one of despondent misery.

Milo walked up behind Wayne. "Who is Augustine Chalamet?"

"Dammit Milo, you scared the shit out of... who?"

"Augustine Chalamet. I need to know."

"Let me guess, a rising starlet from the forties. Died in a fiery crash well before her fame."

"You are incorrect. It is a woman that Brody knows."

"Brody? What the hell is this all about?"

Milo said, "I was going through some files, and I found her name."

"Files? What files?"

"It doesn't matter."

"Does too. What files?"

"FBI files, now who is she?"

"You hacked the FBI?"

"Didn't need to. I have privileges with the President."

"Privileges. Interesting word for having someone by the balls. I never heard of that woman."

"Well, you need to find her. She knows how to do what you're trying to do."

Milo leaned over and typed a link to a transcript of everything Brody told the FBI.

Milo said, "I highlighted some sections. I'll leave you to it. Have an answer by this afternoon."

Wayne looked at the screen as Milo disappeared. "Answer to what?"

—ε-ε-ε-ε-ε-ε—

The legato rhythm of Phoenix's breathing while he slept contrasted with the creaking of the coffee pot as it heated up. It was the night shift. Yasmin time. Time when she could explore and create and connect things. Basically, a time when she could do the things that let her understand how the Internet works. How, in the dark recesses of the darkest of webs, lurks an entire ecosystem of people and bots whose sole purpose is to get you to believe lies.

And now, one of those worms lives inside the ear of the President of the United States...

Yasmin slumped in her chair. Minutes went by. Then, in an aggressive, catapulting move, jumped out of the chair. She screamed. Loudly. Phoenix almost pulled a hamstring trying to run away on the slippery floor. She did not apologize.

"Arrrgghh."

"Lock tight case you got there." She repeated it. This time, giving it the mocking twisted whiny face treatment. "Lock tight case you got there, little missy. Run along and look for spacemen. Beepboop beepboop."

The night shift was also a time when she carefully, over time, developed trusted relationships with those that had access to the inner sanctum of the dark web.

She woke her computer up and started sorting through the list of the trusted soil dwellers.

—ɛ-ɛ-ɛ-ɛ-ɛ-ɛ—

Brody's phone lit up. He looked at Saronda and Rebecca and mouthed, "Whuu?"

It was Wayne.

Brody turned away. "Well as I live and breathe."

Wayne was direct. "I need to know about

Augustine Chalamet."

Brody's head snapped back. His mind raced trying to remember if he told Wayne about Augustine.

"Who?"

"The lady who told you about all that reality shit you were messing with."

Brody was lightheaded. He convinced himself he never told Wayne. Who else? Kelso? No, not him either. There was no connection.

Brody's breathing became shallow. "Wayne, hey, can I call you back? I gotta, well, I gotta go."

He disconnected.

Brody looked over at Saronda.

Saronda said, "You look upset."

Brody said, "The guy from ExpoLytics who put me in touch with our code guy is asking me about Augustine."

Brody ran his fingers through his hair. "What is he working on that he needs to know about Augustine?"

Saronda asked, "How does he even know her name?"

Rebecca said, "You need to call him back."

He put his phone on speaker, and called Wayne.

"Wayne, dude. Sorry I had to... Anyhow, what's happening? What have you been doing these days? Still at ExpoLytics?"

Wayne cut off the chit chat. "I'm working for a very important person now. I need to know how to contact this lady."

Brody put his phone on mute. "He thinks she's still alive."

He reengaged with Wayne. "I'm not sure who that is. What's her name again?"

"Brody, don't mess around. The guy I'm working for is Milo Cuda. Heard of him?"

They inhaled. Right hand man to the President.

"Uh, yeah, I guess I've seen his name. What does he do?"

"He advises the fucking President. He's on the National Security Council. I work directly for him. The degree of separation between me and the prez is breathtakingly small."

"Whoa, uh, congratulations. I wish I could help you."

Wayne said, "This isn't over. You need to tell me where I can find her. I'll call you back when your memory is better, hopefully before your life is ruined."

He disconnected.

The three of them sat motionless. Brody thought through every possible explanation.

Saronda broke the silence. "What does he know about what we did?"

Brody talked with staccato angst. "Nothing. I didn't talk to Wayne about it. Our code guy, Kelso, of course. But not about Augustine. I didn't even tell him about you guys. I told my parents. Not about Augustine. Did you guys talk to anyone?"

Saronda said, "My sister. And Danielle was there that night."

Brody said, "But he asked specifically about Augustine. I told no one. I mean why would I?"

They looked at Rebecca. "Me? Who was I going to tell? I was interrogated by the FBI and I didn't even tell—"

Brody said, "Oh shit."

Rebecca looked at him. "What? You told them. Why in the world… ?"

Saronda asked, "Brody, the FBI? Augustine? Changing reality?"

"It may have come up."

Rebecca asked, "But how would your friend know what you told the FBI?"

Brody asked, "And why does Wayne care?"

Rebecca said, "Let's put on our detective hats. Who knows what at this point? Your code guy, does he know about Augustine?"

Brody said, "No, all I gave him are parameters and some equations. The ones you gave me. He needed them to set the pulses."

"But did you give them to Wayne?"

"No, there was no reason to."

"So we're back to how did Wayne hear about Augustine?"

Brody said, "Must have been from Kelso. That means Kelso's involved in this. But why did Wayne call me? Why didn't Kelso?"

Saronda said, "Forget Kelso. Why is Wayne even a part of this?"

Rebecca said, "I'm thinking the same thing. What did Wayne sound like on the phone? Jovial? Old friends catching up?"

Brody said, "More like a robotic monotone."

Rebecca said, "Like 'tired' monotone or 'hostage tape' monotone?"

Saronda asked, "What are you thinking, Rebecca?"

"Maybe Wayne's not doing this by choice."

—ε-ε-ε-ε-ε-ε—

When Milo was Kelso he tried to destroy a college president with rumors. Rumors he made up. He planted "facts" and implications, innuendos, accusations. He blitzed the media. Each TV and radio station had different pieces of the story, so people "can draw their own conclusions." They hear a snippet here and a snippet there. "I'm hearing it from all corners and it seems to all tie together." He did a masterful job. But he failed. He failed because he pumped the whole thing in a single day, hoping for shock and awe. He learned that's not how lies work. Lies work by becoming progressively absurd, over time, building a story based on innuendo. Small falsehoods at the beginning become established facts, which must mean the next lie is true. And then it's drip, drip, drip with "new shocking allegations."

Shock and awe wasn't the only thing he did wrong. He let the world trace the disinformation back to him. He was discredited when he could offer no proof. Never have a single source that can be traced. The story died. He was a laughingstock. Kelso dropped off the planet. He failed, the world laughed. It was like at school. He studied, worked hard, and still would be dragged into an office for an update meeting with his parents who mostly didn't bother to show up. It was always the same, "Kelso doesn't fit in," which, in French, translates to "Le garçon doesn't belong here." He never forgot the feeling. It wasn't just the school people. It was everyone.

It's been a path of destruction ever since. He doesn't like to fail.

—ε-ε-ε-ε-ε-ε—

"Wayne, it is very disappointing that you are unable to find this woman. If he wouldn't recognize my voice, I'd call Brody myself."

"I'll keep working on Brody."

"We don't have time. Tell him we'll ruin him."

"He won't believe me."

"Show him the demo."

"Don't you think that might give up the game?"

"Wayne—"

"—Milo."

Milo ground his teeth and rubbed his fingers together.

Wayne said, "Can I work my way into a negotiation for half a minute before we go nuclear? He'll come around. Why are you so agitated today?"

Milo took three huffing breaths, turned and walked out.

—ε-ε-ε-ε-ε-ε—

Wayne called Brody. "Bro, you need to listen. Don't mess around with this guy. His thirst for painful retribution is far stronger than his ability to handle rejection."

"Wayne, what the hell is going on? You're talking like he's a Bond villain."

"Look, I'm doing my best to slow this guy down but if I told you what's going on, you wouldn't believe me. Get me anything, anything to show progress. I'm trying to check a box here and get him off my back. And give you the chance to live out your life in peace."

"I don't think I have anything to offer."

"Think harder."

"You sound desperate. What is so urgent? You're working for the government. It doesn't seem like anything is urgent there."

"I'm not part of the government."

"But Milo Cuda..."

"Neither is he."

"Wayne, tell me what's going on or I'll hang up."

"Milo Cuda is not who people think he is. He has a plan. I'm resisting but I can't hold him off. This dude ruins lives by changing facts. We started by changing a photo. We altered reality. Totally fooled everyone."

Silence, and then, "What photo?"

"It was that photo of Randolph at the boys camp. During the election. You must have heard about it. And those two saps who looked like fools."

"Yeah, I heard about it." His voice was rough from the acid that had crawled up his throat. "One of those saps is my father."

"Brody, I didn't know. Man, that's rough. I'm sorry."

"Yeah, it is rough. My father's pretty messed up right now. His clients dried up. His business was all about trust. Now—"

"Brody, I get it."

"Do you? Then why'd you do it? Screw you."

He disconnected.

—ε-ε-ε-ε-ε-ε—

President Emerson Randolph looked at his calendar: Call with Arthur Markovich, private.

Emerson picked up the phone. "Hey Arthur, how's the swing these days? Wish I had time for a round. So, what did you want to chat about?"

"Emerson, thank you so much for speaking to me. I know your time is important, so I'll get right to it. You're going to think I'm crazy, but you know I would never lie to you, about anything other than golf."

"You sound serious."

Arthur was direct. "Emerson. Milo Cuda is a rogue. He created that photo you were in at that boys camp. Made it from thin air."

Emerson Randolph, the most powerful man in the world, struggled to hold the phone. He tried to speak. It was just as well he couldn't because he had no idea what to say.

Arthur said, "Listen, I can tell you have other things going on there, so I'll leave you to it. But you should keep your eye on that guy."

The President tried to sound strong and jovial. "Thank you, Arthur. Let's schedule some golf. Bye now."

He exploded. He knocked the phone off the desk and strode across the Oval Office and flung open the door with a force proving he was still navy strong. "Where the hell is… Hari, get in here now."

Closing the door, Hari asked, "What the—?"

"That little Rainman piece of shit told Arthur Markovich about our little toy."

He flung his arm and knocked some papers off the desk.

He walked right up to Hari. "Arthur Markovich called. Out of the blue. Tells me I got a guy in my shop that's gone Red October. Calls him by name. 'Milo Cuda made that photo'."

Hari Blanek, Chief of Staff, whose job description reads "never be stunned," was stunned.

In an even voice Hari asked, "Emerson, listen to

me. How much can you trust Arthur?"

"We go way back. Why?"

Hari replied, "You need to call him and tell him not to spread this. Finesse it. And ask, where did he hear about this?"

Emerson said, "In the meantime, get that little asshat in here."

"Thank you, Mr. President."

—ε-ε-ε-ε-ε-ε—

Milo smiled as he sat in the limo. Being summoned to meet with the President of the United States, especially one that you own, makes for an exciting day, whether you're evil or not.

Milo gave the administrative assistant a friendly nod, "Good day, Miss Kathy, you are looking refreshed after a nice weekend off."

"Miss Kathy" deadpanned, "I work weekends, in fact, I work every day. Thank you. They are waiting for you."

Milo waltzed into the Oval Office, straight into a smothering silence. Emerson Randolph's eye contact was intense. Hari's stare was just out of view but palpable. The tension was thick enough that even Milo could tell something was off.

The President spoke first, his deep voice striking a

menacing tone, "How did Arthur Markovich know about the photo?"

Milo didn't so much as blink as he ran through several scenarios in his head and, after a long pause, sniffed, "Yes, apparently we have encountered a non-optimum information path. I think we'll come to find it was during an effort to procure knowledge that will increase our capabilities exponentially."

The President stood up, his hulking frame casting a shadow on Milo. "Let me be very clear. No more of this 'persuasion.' We're done. We're shutting you down. Now go."

Milo said, "Thank you, Mr. President."

He walked slowly to the door, and with his back to the President, tilted his head and said, "Have I ever told you gentlemen about my neutron bomb?"

—ε-ε-ε-ε-ε-ε—

Wayne stormed into the work area after leaving Milo's office.

"Petey, can you just, like leave. I have a call to make."

He punched Brody's name. "Brody, there's some shit going down. They found out your father knows about the photo. I assume you told him. That wasn't smart. They're going to threaten him not to say anything. Their threats are real, and they are severe."

"Bullshit, he has every right to clear his name. He's planning to—"

"Tell him to stop. Whatever it is. You don't know who you're messing with."

"Emerson Randolph will protect my father. They're buds."

"You don't know the guy as well as you think you do. The President is in on it."

"In on what? This is all bullshit."

"I don't know how to get through to you. They will destroy your father. They will destroy you. They will destroy anyone their fetid minds think is getting in their way. I suggest he play along and let it go."

"Play along? Let it go?"

"It's the only way out. Look, I don't have much time to talk, Milo tracks my call history. I'll make this brief. At this point, the only way to prevent this is if we work together."

"What are we preventing exactly?"

"The total rearrangement of society so that we're controlled by only a few. It's happening and it's happening fast. Your dad has to let this go and you have to get me something that explains these equations. There is no other way."

"You said we had to work together?"

Brody's subconscious ignited. Something Wayne said.

Wayne lowered his voice. "Yes, I have a plan. Ah shit, can I call you back? Bye."

"Milo, what do you want? I can't possibly have any more ass left for you to chew."

"We have something very important to discuss."

"Is it more important than squeezing Brody, 'cuz I'm kinda up to my eyeballs in that right now."

"Oh, maybe. I need you to know that I promised my neutron bomb to the President. Oh, and Wayne, what was that plan you were talking to Brody about? Just now on the phone."

"Whu? No, it was just. God. It's a plan on how to… Can you please leave me to it."

"Uh huh. Sure. OK." Milo slinked away

—ε-ε-ε-ε-ε-ε—

Brody sat with his phone in his lap. Something Wayne said raised every hair on his body.

His subconscious mind was screaming. His phone rang. It was Wayne. "Wayne, I've been thinking, you need to open up if you want to work together, whatever that means."

"OK, you do know that I have the power here 'cuz I can ruin…"

He tuned out Wayne. He replayed every word from before, re-running the conversation. *Equations! Wayne said he has the equations. There is only one source: Kelso.*

Brody gathered himself. "Sorry, I kinda lost focus for a second. Tell me this. Is Kelso involved?"

"Kelso no longer exists."

Brody's subconscious was screaming again. Wayne replied too quickly. Odd phrasing. *It was a prepared answer.*

"Did you kill him?"

"Don't be stupid. He had a motorcycle accident."

Wayne disconnected.

—ε-ε-ε-ε-ε-ε—

Yasmin sat in the stillness of the night shift, the echoes of her outburst long faded. Phoenix was settled and sleeping.

She wrote an email that she was sure would get attention. She debated each sentence, "Milo Cuda is the biggest threat facing our country today" or "Resources must be applied to understand the true nature of the threat posed by Milo Cuda."

An hour later, she was confident that it said

everything it needed to say. The coffee pot finished a fresh pot. She poured a cup, walked back to her desk, and deleted the email.

"It's all bullshit." Phoenix started. "Oh, sorry buddy. I swear when I get pissed. I'll probably be pissed a lot from now on so get used to it."

She pulled up her list of trusted contacts and drummed her fingers on the desk. She considered each name on the list. There were only four. The one she chose, Aduco Lim.

"Some things are best handled by yourself. Right dog?"

—Ɛ-Ɛ-Ɛ-Ɛ-Ɛ-Ɛ—

Rebecca rushed into Busboys and Poets. "What's so urgent? I thought you guys were on a hot date tonight."

Saronda said, "Oh, we're still going out. I'm not letting Brody off the hook that easily, but he learned some things we should talk about."

Brody said, "Wayne has the equations and said Kelso no longer exists."

Rebecca asked, "He's dead?"

"How else does someone not exist?"

Saronda said, "OK, so, Wayne is trapped by Milo and wants out. Kelso gave him the equations and is dead."

Rebecca was incredulous. "Wayne got the

equations from Kelso, killed him, and is now reluctantly doing everything Milo asks?"

Brody said, "Wayne's not a killer."

Rebecca said, "So, Milo killed him? But Kelso knew more about this than Wayne. Again, why is Wayne involved?"

Saronda said, "Maybe Wayne's the mastermind behind all this."

Brody said, "Wayne? Wayne's a cynical code guy that worked in the basement. He'd rather play Minecraft and drink beer than take over the world. Besides, he sounds like a scared puppy on the phone."

Rebecca said, "Milo trapped Wayne, got rid of Kelso, and sent Wayne to find out what Kelso already knew. Makes no sense."

They sat awhile and Rebecca said, "Well, you guys need to get going. Enjoy your date. I'm so glad Brody is getting better and your Whispers are you know... You two make a wonderful couple. Have fun! And don't think about this stuff."

Saronda asked, "With all this going on?"

Rebecca replied, "'Tis love, that midst chaos' tumult thrives."

"Shakespeare?"

Rebecca giggled. "No. Me."

—ε-ε-ε-ε-ε-ε—

They sat in the movie theater, Brody's arm around Saronda, Saronda's head on Brody's shoulder. If Augustine were to describe it, she would say their Whispers were connecting quite nicely. While their Whispers were going at it, their minds spent the movie trying to figure out what the hell was going on with Wayne.

They stepped out into the night air. Brody whispered in her ear, "Wanna go to the park and make out under the cherry blossoms? It would be romantic."

"Jackass. It's freezing. How about a drink instead?"

"Yes! Union Pub, with their famous pickle martinis!"

They rushed in from the cold. They sat at the table where almost eighteen months prior they had huddled around a clock radio waiting to hear the signal that Kelso had done his job. It was a heady time. As a team, they divined wisdom from an ancient text and moved reality. They celebrated, filled with confidence that they alone knew the inner workings of the universe.

Neither touched their drinks. Brody tried to remember what was so appealing about a pickle martini.

Saronda said, "You got quiet all of a sudden."

Brody swirled his martini glass. "Do you think Milo is Kelso?"

"And there goes Brody, deep into left field again. Back, back and it is—"

"Think about it. Kelso didn't want anything to do with me until I told him we were messing with reality. Then, he was downright eager to help. He never asked to be paid. Strange because he didn't seem the humanitarian type."

"And from that you think Milo is Kelso? That's quite a leap."

"Just my brain spitting out weird stuff."

It got late. They stepped outside. Saronda said, "I can't believe I have to ride that damn Metro."

Brody stretched and said, "I can't believe how cold it got. I thought it was spring. I mean, look, the cherry blossoms are shivering. Here, put my coat over you."

Saronda said, "Then *you'll* freeze."

"I'll be fine. My hotel is right up the street."

Saronda then made a nonsensical argument that made total sense to both of them.

"Keep your coat. I'll walk to your hotel. You can give me your coat there and I'll walk to the Metro and be on my way after that."

They got to Brody's hotel.

"This is where you stayed for months?"

"Yeah, it's nice. Come see my room."

They rode the elevator in silence. It was the type of silence with no awkwardness, no urge to fill it, just two people enjoying the fact that they were with each other. It was a large elevator, but they stood with their shoulders touching.

Saronda said, "What would happen if I stayed here tonight?"

Brody paused. "Uh, there's only one bed."

She leaned over and kissed him. A soft kiss on the lips.

Brody drew back and said, "Whoa, I did not expect that to happen."

"Yes you did."

"Yes, I did."

What happened over the next twelve minutes and thirty-two seconds was so cosmic that to describe it requires sentences that are parodies of themselves. Anything else would violate their privacy. They moved with a restrained urgency as their Whispers merged and soft contours collided with firm smooth skin, urged on by forces set in motion over billions of years. It was no longer him and her, just a gauzy illusion, a blending. Their Whispers surged, reaching into the universe, weaving a glorious pattern as they harmonized and peaked until the passion could no longer be contained.

Glory!

Neither one spoke, immersed in silence and darkness. Their energized Whispers reached out to the farthest parts of the universe, drawing upon, and merging with the innate beauty of a pattern woven by countless collisions over billions of years.

They soaked for long minutes in the rapture as their Whispers aligned with each other's, weaving a destiny meant only for them.

Other than that, it was pretty standard stuff.

Brody broke the spell. "Thoughts?"

Saronda said, "I think you should straight up ask him if Milo is Kelso."

Brody said, "I have a slightly different take."

He rolled onto his side to face Saronda. "I need to treat this like my father would. As a negotiation. He would say *asking* shows weakness. I'm going to force his hand and say we *know* Milo is Kelso. See how he reacts. And then lay out my plan. Boom."

Saronda purred, "Ooh, strong. Wanna make out?"

"Well I have an early morning, so... "

"You're such a Jackassshhh, whoa, OK."

—ε-ε-ε-ε-ε-ε—

The night shift was when Yasmin allowed the

frustration to fester. Her mind dwelled on the fact that there was someone who was nothing more than a nerdish web thug advising the President of the United States. He was a parasite convincing leaders to carry out plans that ultimately would lead to their destruction.

The night shift. There was no one around to question her every idea. No one to remind her about the First Amendment or privacy rights. No one to tell her to stand down. She had to know if Milo was Prairie Dog.

She walked to the women's locker room. There were no cameras there. She reached into locker 42, the one with the false back. She pried open a hidden chamber, one big enough to hold a burner phone.

She pressed the second button and typed a text to Aduco Lim: *Avail4wrk?*

Aduco: *depends*

Yasmin: *I need info*

Aduco: *Do you have $?*

Yasmin: *I need everything you can find on Milo Cuda*

Aduco: *Not enough $$ in the world*

Yasmin: *Take care*

This told Yasmin what she needed to know. The price is cheap if the question is about a nobody. It's unaffordable if the question is about the guy who has a death grip on the fate of the world. It's deadly if you ask the question to the wrong person.

Aduco forwarded the request to his new boss, Milo Cuda.

—ε-ε-ε-ε-ε-ε—

Rebecca inquired, "So, you two, how was your date last night?"

They glanced at each other and smiled.

Rebecca bubbled, "Ooh goosebumps. Tell me all about it... actually no, don't tell me all about it. OK, sorry. Enough of that. Looks like it went well."

She bit her lower lip and changed the subject. "What are we doing about Wayne and this whole mess?"

Saronda said, "Brody has a plan."

Rebecca said, "I'm all ears."

Brody said, "First, I need to call Wayne."

Wayne answered on the first ring, "You had better have something for me."

Brody said, "I know Milo is Kelso. You need to tell me exactly what's going on."

Wayne paused. "That's ridiculous. I need you to stop messing around and tell me how you knew how to change facts. Was it straight from God, Youtube, fucking late night infomercial?"

Brody heard a tightening in Wayne's voice. *Nervousness? Desperation?*

"Wayne, now is a very good time to tell me what's going on. If you are really trying to slow this guy down, and he's as evil as you say, maybe I can help."

Wayne paused for a long time. "OK, listen, this guy is using your little trick of changing facts. He blackmails people, powerful people, but he wants to take it further, into a very dark place. He's relentless. If you don't tell me something, very bad things will happen to you."

Brody said, "You're going to need to give me more than that. Why are you so desperate? You already know how to change facts."

Wayne said, "Because we don't know how to create mass chaos, OK? Oh, and, I'll give you more, Milo is Kelso. Now that we've opened up with each other, maybe you can share—"

Brody disconnected.

—ε-ε-ε-ε-ε-ε—

Brody set the phone down. "I was right, Milo is Kelso."

Rebecca asked, "So they know how to change facts, but they want more? Why?"

Saronda said, "I get it now. They want chaos. They want a world where truth is fluid, on a grand scale. This guy is like all the other tyrants. People can't handle chaos, so they give up. That's when we become their sheep, our freewill destroyed. It's a cycle. 'Chaos then numbness then acquiescence'. Tyrants, fascists, kings, emperors, they tried for centuries. My professor said it over and over, 'chaos then numbness then acquiescence'. Milo thinks we know something that will help him create chaos."

Rebecca said, "Augustine's paper won't help with that. The equations that I've played with create beautiful patterns. Never chaos. It's not how nature works. Everything tends toward order and beauty."

Saronda said, "That's what Einstein said, 'God does not throw dice.'"

Brody asked, "Did he mention anything about the devil?"

—ε-ε-ε-ε-ε-ε—

Milo scowled, "I'm losing patience. Your work product is lacking. You have not learned anything from that man. I am preparing a plan to use persuasion on Brody. It will be my most vengeful persuasion so far. I will have that to you this afternoon. We will start tomorrow. Enough!"

He stormed out. Wayne's phone rang. It was Brody.

Wayne answered, "Hi Brody, we were just talking about you." Wayne's tone contained no lightness.

"I have an idea. I'll send a paper with more equations, but you have to let me work with you on shutting down Milo."

Wayne said, "What paper? Where'd you get it?"

"What, you want my life story?"

"Fine. Play it that way if you want. Get me the paper and we'll talk."

"Wayne, we're saving each other's butts here. Don't double cross me. I think you know your long term prospects aren't good. Once he gets what he wants, you'll be discarded onto a very unpleasant compost pile."

"The possibility has crossed my mind, but worry about yourself."

"I'll send the paper. That should keep your man-baby happy for a few days."

—ε-ε-ε-ε-ε-ε—

Rebecca shouted, "You're sending him the paper? That's nuts."

Brody said, "Saronda has a plan."

Saronda said, "Right, remember the paper by Paul Langevin, Marie Curie's lover? That's the paper we'll give him."

Brody said, "OK, full disclosure. I told Saronda I think this is risky because you guys said it had a recipe for chaos."

Rebecca's eyes lit up. "A recipe, but not the ingredients. I like it. Paul Langevin left out Epsilon. Without that, Wayne can't create chaos."

Saronda and Rebecca high-fived.

Brody said, "So this guy wrote a paper telling fascists how to create chaos and left out the most important part? Such a tease."

Saronda said, "It will drive Milo crazy."

Brody said, "And allow Wayne to slow things down."

Rebecca said, "But it wasn't written by Augustine. How does Wayne explain that to Milo?"

Saronda said, "It refers to a footnote in Augustine's paper. He can say Brody was confused."

Brody said, "So, we're giving the dice to the devil but he won't know how to roll them. I like it. And, we're relying on them thinking I'm an idiot."

Saronda smiled. "An easy sell. I think it works."

Rebecca said, "Not to be a downer, Ms. Curie's lover may have left out Epsilon, but he left in a way to calculate it."

Saronda said, "Do you think Milo's smart enough to see it?"

Rebecca said, "It may not matter. He'd have to do matrix math on, hmmm, billions of variables. His computers would buckle under the weight of the calculations."

Saronda chimed in. "Paul Langevin gave evildoers a recipe for chaos knowing they would never be able to calculate the key ingredient. A brilliant way to send them on a wild goose chase."

Brody said, "I'll bet they did nazi that coming."

—ε-ε-ε-ε-ε-ε—

Wayne saw right away what Brody gave him was nothing more than a delay tactic. Just what he needed.

He put on a great act. "Great news! Brody buckled. I hard-balled him, and he gave in. Gave me a whole damn paper. It's exactly what we need. It looks like our computers aren't powerful enough so we will need to acquire more. That could take some time, maybe months. And then the calculations will take a long time. I know that's not what you want to hear, but we'll get started right away. We are months away so we'll... "

Wayne paused and looked at Milo. "Are you OK? You're practically dancing. I was not expecting that reaction."

Petey said, "You sure are happy, Mr. Cuda."

Milo said, "Oh, I've never been happier. Gather round my little codesters. I have really good news. A while back, I got access to a quantum computer. DARPA has one that they mothballed because Congress cut its budget. I didn't want to tell you, because I didn't want to slow down progress. But if we need computing power, we got it! I'll need to thank my favorite President."

He practically skipped back to his office.

Wayne looked at Petey. "Oh boy, yay, a quantum computer." And then put his head in his hands. He had lost control of the monster. Operation Slowdown was dead.

Petey asked, "What just happened?"

"A quantum computer is about ten million times faster than what we have. Literally."

"Whoa, that means you can do all those calculations you wanted. Awesome."

"Petey, did you ever get one of those tension headaches right between your eyes, like if you looked in the mirror and saw a bullet hole, you wouldn't be surprised and then you kinda wish it *was* a bullet hole?"

"No, I don't think so."

"Well, you're young. You still have time."

—ε-ε-ε-ε-ε-ε—

"It's tough to be a hero if you don't get the details right." —Arthur Markovich.

Rebecca was worried. "Guys, our plan. I was thinking. We need to think long term. All we're doing is slowing him down. Eventually, he's going to figure this out. He'll keep trying until he gets what he wants."

Saronda said, "We have to put our faith in the

destiny of the universe. The universe doesn't want evil to rule us. Augustine said the universe gets what it wants. Surely, it doesn't want us to be ruled by a madman. We're meant to be free. We are the universe's most prized creation. We're not destined to be trampled by this idiot."

Rebecca said, "I've looked at the equations, I've read your translation. She never said we're some sort of treasured pet. There are other nice things. Like quokkas."

Brody googled quokkas. "Oh my God, what a happy little guy."

Rebecca said, "Pictures of quokkas are my stress relief. Hard to have a bad day looking at those fellas."

Saronda said, "Yeah, quokkas are cute but we're special. We love. We think. "

Rebecca said, "As much as I enjoy romping in this metaphysical meadow, we need to figure out what to do. One thing I'm sure of, I don't think that evil toad should ever get the ability to change facts. We need to stop him, not just slow him down."

Brody asked, "You know how to do that?"

"Not yet. We have work to do."

—ε-ε-ε-ε-ε-ε—

It was late. Wayne and Petey had worked all day running trials with the quantum computer.

Petey said, "This is so awesome. This new building

is cool. That computer is... you click the button, and it finishes the calculation before the screen can refresh."

Wayne refilled the liquid nitrogen cooling tank. "Yeah, this is the most fun I've had in forever. Even neater, it made a three-dimensional graph of reality. That's what's on that screen over there."

They walked over to the screen. "Look at this. I loaded the matrix and made it calculate one-hundred-thousand scenarios. Theoretically, our old computers would've taken ten thousand years. This bad boy, six minutes."

Petey said, "Whoa."

Wayne said, "Check this out. When I subtract this matrix from this matrix, it's usually a positive number. But sometimes the number is *negative* and... "

A voice came from behind them. "And what?"

Wayne turned around. "Milo, I didn't know you were back there. Welcome to our new playground."

Milo asked, "What happens when it's negative?"

Wayne said, "Uh, nothing."

Milo said, "No, you were about to tell Petey. Tell me."

Wayne looked at the floor. "Reality falls into chaos." He instantly regretted saying chaos.

Milo said, "Well, that's very good. That's what we

want. You discovered a secret. You are to be commended, but can you do it just a little bit? Can you cause just a little chaos?"

Wayne said, "Are you going soft?"

Milo said, "It's so they can't see us coming. The plan mustn't be revealed. We do it slowly, so they don't feel it, until—"

Petey snorted, "Oh, I get it. Screw with people a little at a time so they don't notice. Smart, Mr. Cuda. That's real smart."

—ε-ε-ε-ε-ε-ε—

The key card light turned green and they bounded into Brody's room, eager to figure this thing out.

Rebecca said, "Before we start, where's your restroom?"

Saronda answered quickly, "It's around the corner, kinda hidden."

Brody's room became a war room. The credenza was cleared. The TV was unplugged and set on the floor. Hours went by as they sent test after test to Rebecca's array of old government computers. They scoured the patterns on the screen, looking for clues. Discarded pizza crusts and stale coffee turned the room into a church basement after a father/son fellowship. They worked into the night. Each added their ideas, searching for solutions, determining what to try next. Rebecca drew up a designed test matrix and each of them had a role in trying different parameters. It was not going well. Tensions rose.

Rebecca let out a frustrated sigh. "I can't find the right combination of factors. These equations aren't going to get us there. Maybe we should use equations from a different section of the paper."

Saronda snapped, "You're the one who chose the equations."

Rebecca's eyes were intense. "I *'chose'* the equations based on what made sense from *your* translation."

Saronda looked away, pressing her lips together. It was three o'clock in the morning and the room was stone cold silent.

Saronda said, "I'm not sure I care for the negative vibe. We're going to figure this out. We were brought together to stop Milo. If we don't, we will all live without liberty. That is *not* our destiny. That is *not* what the universe—"

Rebecca stood up. She was clearly miffed. "Alright. Look, sorry I snapped but we need to keep going through this *logically*. We don't have time for your—"

Saronda added an edge to her voice. "My what? You think the equations are the only place the clues are? 'Cuz, if you would've read my translation you'd hardly think the universe would create us and give us feelings, emotions, love, and then let a weasel like Milo destroy us. Huh uh, no way. That's a special kind of crazy. Why would it create such a precious thing and then have Milo destroy it?"

Brody yearned for levity. He said, "Especially when humans are doing a great job destroying it already."

"Jackass."

"No, seriously, maybe the universe wants—"

Rebecca cut him off. "Guys. Guys. Can you tone down the philosophy talk and get practical? We're not getting anywhere."

She hovered over the equations, flipping through the translated paper. "Saronda, I read your translation. That's what guided me on what equations to try. But, we need to create a counter-pattern and none of the sections talk about that."

Brody asked, "What the hell is a counter-pattern?"

Rebecca said, "A pattern that goes opposite of what Wayne is doing. A wrinkly set of waves in the opposite direction of Wayne's artificial reality. I can't see how to do that. We've tried equations from about every section of the paper. Twice. Three times. We're spinning our wheels."

She slumped down in a chair. "I'm tired of dead ends. I'm tired of this room and you guys are talking like cosmic hippies."

Saronda muttered under her breath, "That was harsh."

Rebecca let out a caustic sigh. "Well, what do you recommend? How would *you* create a wrinkle in the pattern? There are only two sections we haven't tried. The section on love and the section on rides, whatever the hell that is. I'm ready to give up. Maybe the "universe" can get what it wants from somebody else."

Saronda scoffed, "What are you talking about with rides? What rides?"

Rebecca slid the translated paper over to Saronda and pointed. "See for yourself." Her demeanor was tense.

Saronda grabbed the paper. She took out the original paper and flipped through the pages, shaking her head.

Her face froze. She turned away. "Oh shi— dammit. The French is 'Comment créer une ride dans la réalité'."

Her voice quavered. "I translated it to 'how to create a ride in reality'. The French word 'ride' is wrinkle."

Rebecca stood up, exasperated. "What? Let me get this straight. It should be 'how to create a wrinkle in reality?'"

The fatigue, the frustration, the failed attempts descended on her.

Rebecca lost it. "Are you effing kidding me?"

She looked at Brody. "Did you hear that? It's supposed to be 'how to create a wrinkle in reality'. Makes you wonder why the universe picked us, we can't even—"

Saronda choked. "Yes, sorry. My brain skipped over—"

Rebecca reacted. "I need air. This is bullshit. All this time, it was ride. How could you be so—"

Rebecca stormed out. It put Saronda in tears.

Brody looked at Saronda. She said, "Don't just stand there. Go get her."

He trotted to the hallway and found her seething. "Look, Rebecca. We're all tired. Let's take a break. Mistakes were made. It's time to get back at it."

"All this time. I'm tired, my clothes smell like pepperoni, we're no closer than when we started."

"I guess I should have ordered the salad."

"Stop it Brody. I don't need cheering up. I need to just…"

Brody said, "Maybe this is good news. Maybe the wrinkle equations will help us, you know, create a wrinkle…"

"Yes, Brody, I know, creating a wrinkle might do it, but it will take time to understand what's in that section and I'm not sure I want to go through…"

Brody said, "It was a simple mistake. The universe isn't going to let a simple mistake stop us."

Rebecca's face was stiff, red. "Oh here we go with the destiny thing again. Maybe the universe didn't factor in stupidity."

She took a breath. "OK, I need to calm down. Let's go see if we can create a wrinkle so that evil Dr. Dipshit never gets those equations. But first I need to apologize to Saronda."

Brody said, "Oh, look, the new pizza's here."

Rebecca glared. Brody said, "Hey, there's no pepperoni this time."

They worked through the night. Brody wrote out the plan on the last remaining square foot of space on the bathroom mirror.

Create a wrinkle
Reset reality so that Kelso never gets Augustine's or Paul Langevin's paper. No paper. No evil plan.

Brody pulled back the curtains. The rising sun cast its beam on quite a scene. Pizza boxes. A half-filled coffee pot. Crumpled paper. Mirrors filled with scribbles of long abandoned ideas.

Brody said, "We should try it. See what happens."

Saronda said, "We can't just be throwing stuff out there."

Rebecca said, "No, I think that might be good. We'll use low energy pulses, enough to see if it works but not enough to change anything."

She typed a few commands. The clock radio hummed with a harmonious sound.

Rebecca smiled. "I think that's it. It's gonna work. Let's call Wayne."

Wayne answered on the first ring. "What did you decide?"

Brody looked at his two teammates and replied, "You send your pulse, we'll send ours to counteract yours."

Wayne hesitated, then, "OK. But we need to make sure all your computers fire at the same time as mine. I mean precisely. I will give you a locking code that will sync us together."

"What do I need to do?"

"You need to type the code into your system. It's called a global unique identifier."

He looked at Rebecca who gave an affirmative nod.

"OK, send it."

"No, I can't send it. Milo took control of the Syndicate. The Syndicate owns the Internet. They know everything that happens. They'll see us and report back to Milo."

"Well then, read it to me. Sounds easy enough."

A global unique identifier is a number that is 32 characters long.

Wayne pulled up the code on his screen: *a0e140aa-62de-4c43-bccc-fe09de9dce6a*

Wayne started reading. Brody stopped him. "OK, wait, ay, oh, e, one, four, oh. Is that zero or oh? OK what's next? Ay ay, dash sixty-two What? I don't need the dash? Got it, keep going."

Wayne said, "OK, ay ay sixty-two."

"Is that another ay ay sixty-two or the one I got already?"

"Brody, this has to be exact."

Brody chewed on a stale pizza crust, "I know, I got it. Keep going."

Saronda and Rebecca paced, making no eye contact.

Rebecca shuffled through some notes, rechecking her calculations, while Saronda flipped through some of the pages she hadn't read yet.

Brody's voice was a backdrop. "Was that three cee's or three c?"

When he had finished, he looked up from what he had written. "OK, let's type this in and then, time for breakfast!"

—ε-ε-ε-ε-ε-ε—

They drifted into Union Pub with the morning breakfast crowd and sat at a table near the door. The fatigue of the all-nighter evident in their faces.

Brody stopped. "Dammit, I didn't bring the radio."

Saronda opened her arms. "That's OK. C'mon guys. Get up. Let's hug. Let's go through this together. Rebecca, we good?"

They stood in the back corner of a mostly empty bar holding each other for support.

—ε-ε-ε-ε-ε-ε—

Milo hovered behind Wayne, rocking back and forth, his moving silhouette reflected on the screen. For years, he was alone in a stone cabin, and, as luck would have it, ended up at the right hand of the most powerful man in the world. As luck would also have it, he learned a secret to the universe, a secret that landed in his lap as if hand delivered.

The fingers on his left hand made their distinctive sound as he rubbed them together, inches from Wayne's right ear. It was loud enough to be annoying, unpleasant.

Petey coughed. Milo scolded, "Petey, quiet. I want total silence."

Then, with a voice barely louder than the soft

hum of the idling quantum computer, he said, "Click it, Wayne! Click. It."

Wayne's eyes narrowed. *Click.* Eleven seconds and counting.

Wayne knew the exact amount of time it would take for his code to lock with Brody's. Both signals would blast at the same precise moment, canceling each other. When that happens, a discrete checkbox on Wayne's screen will light up indicating Milo's plan will be nothing but a pile of evidence, each detail recorded on a thumb drive. No one will come to Milo's defense. He will be an island and the nightmare will be over.

Wayne leaned in. His eyes on the checkbox.

Milo rubbed his fingers together faster. Nothing was happening.

Wayne sensed the tension. He lied, "It's spinning up the subroutines. Patience."

Three seconds. Two seconds. One second. Wayne looked away. The checkbox didn't light up. The codes didn't lock. The quantum computer sprang to life making the calculations that would alter society forever.

Wayne dropped his shoulders and looked at the floor.

Milo's voice dripped with sick triumph. "Oh, it launched. Did it? Yes! It did!"

Wayne's face and neck felt clammy from sweat.

He stood up, hoping the air was better than the stifling, crushing atmosphere that came crashing down on him. He needed relief. He walked stridently down the hall. The walls twisted and contorted, bringing on vertigo. He stopped, hand against the wall, wheezing. One big, deep breath and he turned around.

He walked right up to Milo, gritting his teeth. "Do you know what you've just done?"

A normal person's ears would have melted from the acidic derisive bile dripping from the comment. Milo stared coldly at the screen. "Oh, I do. You can see it right there on the screen."

The screen showed the emerging pattern of a twisted, chaotic reality. In the corner of the screen was a message: Checksum mismatch. Subroutine failure. Code not locked.

He mused, "Soon they will wallow in a mist of lies. They will be trapped. Pathological believers."

"Milo, that's a cult."

"No, Wayne. It can't be a cult if everyone's in it."

Wayne slumped into a chair and pushed back from the desk.

Milo said, "Now, you two hard workers, it is important to celebrate milestones. Be proud of what we've done here, as a team. No more work today. Enjoy your theater room or pool table. Go all out. I'll even allow you to turn up the music. Tomorrow, we begin the next step."

Milo went to his office to watch the spark that will become the flame that will become the inferno that will turn freewill to ash.

Wayne slapped his knee. "Petey, I'm thinking a little AC/DC. What about you? I have a doobie I've been saving. It's just the right blend to take the edge off but not make you paranoid."

Petey was jazzed. "I'd like that."

"We'll sit back, listen to tunes, and cling to the hope that by the end of this, our souls will be so damaged even hell won't want us."

—ε-ε-ε-ε-ε-ε—

This was no harmless app they launched. It was a series of timed charges, each set to go off at precise moments. But they were decoys, drawing attention away from what was really happening. Milo's neutron bomb was set to destroy all meaning of the word "truth." It wasn't an explosion, it was a slowly evolving cauldron of shifting facts. Milo learned when trying to smear a college president, you don't hit them all at once. Instead, it's drip, drip, drip. First, it will be small things to give people something to banter about. Does Woody in "*Toy Story*" say "There's a snake in my boot?" Or was it boots? Milo changes it in one part of the movie, leaving it alone in another. Oh, the lively conversations and senseless arguments that will be had. The issues will get more serious. Agreeing to disagree about a movie is one thing, but as time goes by the issues will be too important. When facts get fluid on important issues, people dig in. There will be no reliable authorities. When facts change, institutions can never be right, constantly explaining how they got it so wrong. We'll be damned if we'll listen to someone who can't keep their facts straight. One day it's "do this," the next it's "we have new information." Nothing will be trusted.

The plan pits one group against another, dividing them, then pits subgroups against each other, dividing them, constantly dividing. Then it's friend against friend and family member against family member. News shows become nothing more than anger farms. People give up. Nobody wants to fight all the time. Holding up your hand and saying "ATD" will become the universal sign of "agree to disagree." It will be the only way to socialize. All subjects of conversation will be controversial.

Eventually, people will choose to believe nothing. Then they will believe anything.

—ε-ε-ε-ε-ε-ε—

"When you're the one flying the rocket, don't screw up." —Arthur Markovich

Saronda asked, "Did our wrinkle work?"

Rebecca answered, "I don't know. We have to wait to see what changes. Could be a long long time."

Brody motioned for the check. He said,

"Everything seems normal, so I guess Rebecca's calculations worked."

He looked at Saronda. "What did you mean when you said 'it's written in the Whispers.'?"

"Whispers hold the key to reality. Everything that happens, everything we see. Everything we feel. Whispers weave according to the universe's plan. That's why I knew it would work. It's the way the universe wants it."

Rebecca asked, "What does that say about freewill? Look at Milo. Was he acting according to the Whispers? Can people go off script? Mess up the pattern? How do you reconcile freewill with the universe's plan?"

Saronda responded, "Milo was free to try but the universe brought us together to stop him. Milo did as he was designed to do. But so were we. Don't you see? The Whispers brought us together to stop him. The universe wasn't going to let its most precious creation be ruled by that guy."

Brody finished paying. He stood up to leave.

Barely above the din of the cafe, Rebecca said, "But what if *we* aren't the most precious creation? What if it's a lie we tell ourselves?"

The eye contact between Saronda and Rebecca was mind melding.

Neither one moved.

Saronda spoke first, "It would mean that everything we did wasn't to protect *us*."

Brody shook his head. "Guys guys, our wrinkle worked OK. Now, c'mon, we all need rest."

WHAT HAPPENED AFTER THAT

But it didn't work. Milo achieved P90. It took time. Season by season, drip...drip...drip, Milo's plan played out. Ninety percent of humanity believed pretty much anything they were told. Milo made facts fluid, people got numb, they gave up. It was easier than arguing all the time. It was easier than "But what about... ?" They gave in. Acquiescence became a beautiful drug.

Milo ruled. He wasn't the "official" leader. The people with titles were in charge, but Milo ruled. He was well on his way to "owning" Earth itself, managing things so Earth survived, just like the universe wanted. When you own something, you protect it from bad things. Nuclear weapons. Gone. A warming climate affecting coastlines. Work on it, do what it takes to reverse it. He systematically eliminated anything that could harm Earth and the precious world that enjoyed its bounties.

—ε-ε-ε-ε-ε-ε—

On Saronda's bed in the apartment she shares with Danielle Sközy, Augustine's paper sat open to the last page Saronda had translated. Two pages further, pages left for later, scribbled in the margin, Augustine wrote:

"L'univers conserve sa création la plus précieuse."

The universe preserves its most precious creation.

It was her deepest fear.

—ε-ε-ε-ε-ε-ε—

Milo won. Plain and simple. He controls reality. But, it's not like his winning was based on merit. The universe wants cool things, it gets cool things. The universe wants to reign in a wayward creation, Milo reigns in a wayward creation. The universe gets what the universe wants. Ninety percent of humanity follows Milo around like a puppy dog. The other ten percent didn't take the bait. Some were like Wayne, learned to play the game, and got rich. They were patsies who did Milo's bidding. Some hid under a shell of fake acquiescence.

Others didn't play along. They didn't fit in. Milo looked at them like they were fresh gum on the sidewalk and were dealt with.

—ε-ε-ε-ε-ε-ε—

"Knock knock, Miss Yasmin. Happy New Year 2048. I have a surprise for you." Nurse Shelly was all sunshine and daisies.

She sat beside Yasmin. "It's a new year and today is your release day! We didn't give you any pills this morning. You're going to start feeling yourself again.

Yay!"

The nurse leaned over and looked closely into Yasmin's eyes, "I think I see someone in there. How are you, Miss Yasmin? Do you understand? No more Posilac. It takes a while for it to wear off. You've been on it for, let me look, oh my, *twenty years*. You must have been one of the early ones. I've only been working here for five. Daddy was smart, making me go to school to learn dissident care. I can get a job anywhere."

Yasmin blinked and looked around the room she had been in for two decades. It was sparse. The Government didn't want her to have much. Not that she needed it. A couple pills a day and she was happy and oblivious, the way the Government likes their people. People who get along, like nurse Shelly.

Nurse Shelly said, "You're all set. We got your clearance from the Government. There's a copy in your portal. Oh, you won't know how to use your portal. I'll show you later. You won't remember much if I showed you now. It's easy once you learn to connect your mind to it."

Yasmin closed her eyes.

"Shall I roll you to the window so you can watch the trees grow? It's a sunny day. You like sunny days."

Nurse Shelly bubbled out of the room.

Drug them. That was the option Milo chose for dissidents. It was a neat and tidy way to deal with people who refused to give up their freewill, to take away their desire to fight. Yasmin's life melted away like a warm summer day.

—ε-ε-ε-ε-ε-ε—

Decades went by and Milo made a neat and tidy world, selling reality bit by bit to the highest bidders. If you can afford it, reality can be a wonderful thing. The only thing that could crash the party was the truth. The actual truth, not the one Milo created. For those who knew their freewill was stripped away so others could prosper, reality was hell.

Brody looked out the window of the bungalow he was permitted to share with Saronda in one of the nicer inter-racial sectors. "We've been through this. We can't let the world go on like this."

Saronda's eyes turned to fire. "Why not? People are happy. They talk about nice things, the flowers, the clouds. You were happy. And then all these thoughts about the future that might have been. It's not a bad life we have."

Brody shot back. "I'm not into 'not bad.' I want the future we were supposed to have. I want kids. I don't want to be told the only way to have a baby is to move to sector 27. I want to live here with you, raise a child. I need to make this right. Like my father said, 'Live everyday like what you do matters and one day it will.' I want my life to matter."

Saronda looked away. "It matters to me."

Rebecca said, "Guys, if we don't want to do this, we don't have to."

They spent years creating a plan to change things back to the way they were.

Saronda said, "There is no way we should do this. Not with this new information."

Rebecca regretted ever suggesting the plan. Augustine's theories supported the plan. But there was a problem. The plan involved using Brody's Whisper to erase the current reality and replace it with the way things used to be, before Milo was Milo. Brody latched onto the plan like it was inevitable, it had to be done.

Saronda glared at Rebecca. "I can't believe you're just now finding out how risky it is. You should have known."

Brody jumped in. "Saronda, be fair to Rebecca. We all knew this calculation would take time. What's it been, fifteen years?"

"Seventeen, we started in 2031. When the government put more limits on public computing power, I had to scale back the calculations."

Brody held Saronda. "It's OK. We always knew it was risky."

Saronda pulled away. "I won't let you do something that has a sixty percent chance of killing you."

Rebecca spoke up, "Sixty three percent. Brody, there's a sixty three percent chance that if we reset reality, you could die. That's what the calculation says. I'm with Saronda, we shouldn't do this."

—ε-ε-ε-ε-ε-ε—

Yasmin sat in her wheelchair, Posilac slowly losing its iron grip on her once hyperactive brain. The day passed. And another. And another.

—ε-ε-ε-ε-ε-ε—

It took three decades to plan the details. Rebecca's plan was brilliant. Use Brody's unique Whisper, the one that can reach into other realities, to reset reality to before Milo learned to change facts. Reset reality to what's in Yasmin's archive. Brody jumped on this as a way to regain freewill and get their future back. The one where he and Saronda go on to do important work while raising interracial kids and living wherever the hell they want. Screw Milo and his ethnic population balancing.

A recently discovered detail, Brody has a sixty-three percent chance of dying.

—ε-ε-ε-ε-ε-ε—

"Knock knock, Miss Yasmin. You have a visitor. I told him you were still not one-hundred percent but I can't legally restrict visitors anymore. Shall I ask him to leave?"

Yasmin stared blankly.

"He says his name is Brody Markovich."

Yasmin motioned for him to come in.

"Ms. Roth, thank you for seeing me. We need your help. A lot has changed in the decades you've been in chemical prison. The government controls everything. They tell us what to think, where we can live, everything, unless you can buy the reality you want. The sad thing is, people laid down their freedom without even a whimper. We have a president, Milo Cuda, who is basically a world dictator. He's built a worldwide network of people who do his bidding. He owns them. He owns us. He does it by manipulating reality."

An interesting thing about Posilac, it works by shutting out the world but it doesn't take away your memories. It's like waking up in the morning after a long sleep.

Yasmin labored to say, "P90. Prairie dog. Milo Cuda."

"You knew Milo Cuda was going to manipulate reality?"

"He put it in a manifesto. I didn't know he figured out how to do it. I wasn't allowed to investigate him."

She wheeled to her bookcase and took out a thumb drive. She laid it on the table. "That's his manifesto. He had a plan. People thought I was crazy. 'His lies will never work' they said. 'Not with smart people'."

Brody looked at it. "Haven't seen one of those in a long time. It looks like it has a port for a physical cable. Is that USB? Hilarious. Anyhow, I didn't come here for a manifesto, I came for the archive. I should say I came to find out if there is a back-up for the archive. Milo destroyed the original."

"He didn't destroy it."

"He made an announcement about it. Said it was false history."

"He must have been bluffing. He couldn't destroy it because there is no way he found it."

She turned her wheelchair. "You see that bird in the tree? It's a penduline tit. It built that elaborate nest, the thing that looks like a hanging basket. The nest is in plain sight for all to see. Everybody knows there are defenseless babies in there. The basket has a door to keep the babies safe. But the bird is smart. It built two doors. A hidden one that leads to the babies and an obvious one that leads to nowhere. The bird knew that one day the snakes would come, and when they did, they would try the obvious door, the one that leads to nowhere. Frustrated, they leave. Trust me, the archive is safe."

She could see Brody's reflection in the window. He shifted his weight from one foot to the other.

"Take the thumb drive. It doesn't have the archive, but it will help you find the door."

—ε-ε-ε-ε-ε-ε—

Saronda's stiff face spoke volumes, every muscle holding back tears.

Brody said, "I know it's risky. I'm doing this. I need to do this."

He sat on the floor. "Rebecca's got the archive loaded, wrinkle is programmed, we're locked in. You'll have a constant view of my vitals. We're ready. I'm ready. Let's go."

Brody looked at Rebecca. "Click it, Rebecca, click it."

Rebecca glanced at Saronda. Saronda said, "Whatever, go ahead."

—ε-ε-ε-ε-ε-ε—

Wayne Drakauer's mind-portal lit up with a notification. Petey had detected an anomaly in the pattern.

Wayne reviewed the data. Yes, an anomaly. Possibly an attack, usually some dissident throwing himself on a digital bonfire trying to change the world. But this was different.

Wayne walked to his kitchen. *bing!* His mind-link disconnected and then *doop!* It reconnected in the other room. He could upgrade to a longer-range device. Though they told people it didn't cause brain cancer, Wayne saw the data before it was changed during a routine reality update to version 12.7.2.

He mind-linked to Petey and responded. "Anomaly type 10. Access to a restricted area. Good catch. Go ahead and zap them."

Wayne knew the perfect place in the organization for Petey. Petey would detect intruders in the reality algorithm. It was usually people messing with something they shouldn't. He would wait for approval to take them out, with malice. He'd hunt them down and then, zap! He would change their reality and their lives would crumble with soul crushing pain.

Petey sent another mind-message. "They're attacking an unknown access point."

It was the archive. The archive that was supposed to no longer exist. It was the archive Yasmin lorded over, saving for eternity everything agreed to be factual through 2016, before Milo started his shenanigans. Wayne told Milo he destroyed it so Milo could make one of his grand announcements: "The world is now rid of all facts that don't match reality." It was a cleansing of history. It also happened to clean up any evidence of Milo's scheme. But Wayne couldn't find the door to get access. And now, someone was walking through it.

He rubbed his eyes. "How the hell did they know that door was there?"

It didn't take him long to guess that the person who knew about the door was the person who put it there.

"That woman who built the archive. What was her name?"

He input the question into his mind-portal.

"Ahh. Yasmin Roth. Junior staffer. Milo's little dog problem."

He pulled up her full record. Chemical confinement status: released.

He focused his portal back to the archive.

"Oh shit."

Reality was, bit by bit, being reset to the archive, back to a time when Milo was Kelso and Wayne got paid decent coin at ExpoLytics to work on cool stuff with smart people.

"This can't be. A lowly analyst three days off Posilac… " *No way she knew how to change reality.*

Inside Wayne's brain, one hundred trillion neural connections worked in tandem with his government-issued AI bot running on the newest generation of quark tunneling processor cores. Working together, they combined to make the most sophisticated computing device in the universe.

Wayne drew himself a glass of water and raised it to his lips. He set the glass down without drinking.

"That little shit. He's resetting reality."

—ε-ε-ε-ε-ε-ε—

Resetting reality sent Brody on a tailspin straight into hell. From outside appearances, he was calm. Deep down where his soul resides was a war zone. His Whisper was inside two different realities, rapidly losing strength. He'd been down this path half a lifetime before. Every negative part of human existence rose up. All the parts we keep safely tucked away. Rage replaced hope. Despair fed on the rage igniting an inferno of fear. Fear that he wasn't good enough. Fear that he wasn't loved. Fear that he wouldn't be missed. Fear that he was a failure in the eyes of those who loved him. A disappointment.

Brody fought the dissonance. *This will not be another 98 out of a 100.* But the bravado was engulfed by an unraveling will to live. Sixty three percent chance of dying. Something didn't want this happening. Brody was fighting the whole damn universe. A universe where a lot of things had to go just right so that Milo could learn a couple secrets from an ancient science paper and put the world under his thumb.

—ε-ε-ε-ε-ε-ε—

Wayne switched off his portal. He didn't want his thoughts to be recorded, a privilege few enjoyed. He sized up what was happening. If reality is reset to the archive, everything Milo did would be overwritten. His plan will have never existed. Brody was systematically erasing Milo, taking everything back to the way it used to be.

Wayne watched as more of the archive was woven

into the current reality. "How does a jagoff like that come up with a plan like this?"

He raised his glass high. "Brody, my man. Not sure how you're doing this but it's fucking brilliant."

He switched on his portal and connected to Petey. "Let me know the minute you find him. Stand down the zap order. I'm going to handle this one personally. And Petey, good luck in whatever the past holds for you."

For decades, Wayne lived in fear of being exposed as the one who could've stopped Milo. He lived in fear that if the world knew what they did, he would be gutted and everything he had would be taken away. He had a lot: cars, houses, free hypersonic transportation to anywhere he wanted, but getting rich wasn't the comfort zone he thought it would be.

—ε-ε-ε-ε-ε-ε—

Brody was at the most critical point, overlaying the wrinkle Rebecca had prepared. The wrinkle will ensure Brody never contacts Kelso. Milo would never be unleashed, and history wouldn't repeat. The forces against him grew stronger. Brody was fading. His Whisper was in three realities, the one created by Milo, the new one he was creating, and the archive meticulously maintained by Yasmin long ago. The archive was a reality created by the universe using one hundred percent natural ingredients. It had all the incongruities, paradoxes, deadends, pitfalls, heartaches, that reality used to have. It had all the wonderfully messy things that make for interesting lives well-lived, a contrast to the polyester pile of saccharin Milo created.

The strain on his Whisper was painful and debilitating, with every bit of energy from every part of his body working to complete the plan. Any energy left over was rationed to bare essentials like a heartbeat and breathing. One by one, each system in his body was shutting down. He was dying.

Maybe if he knew how close he was to succeeding, he'd give one last push, but he was drowning in a viscous sea of dark chaos. It doesn't matter how close you are if you can't see the shore. His last wave of consciousness was a vision of what he was fighting for: Saronda and their future, with kids this time. He thought of right versus wrong, freedom to live as we want, to pursue our goals. He thought of his father, and expectations. The internal pep talk didn't matter.

Brody Markovich gave himself permission to die.

—ε-ε-ε-ε-ε-ε—

Saronda was hunched over, on the floor, in a corner. She was sobbing. She had never felt this way. The only thing that mattered to her, the only thing that made it all make sense, was being ripped away. She had been with Brody for thirty-two years. Their love built a life. Yes, the world is horrible. The haves got more and the have nots got screwed. But…

She wiped her face. "We were together. That's what mattered."

Rebecca sat on the floor next to her, holding her hand.

Brody was slouched against a wall fighting for the "future they should have had."

Saronda took in an uneven breath. "I never could convince him we *have* a future. It's right here in front of us. Don't go chasing what might have been."

Brody's wrist band shattered the silence. *Skreet. Skreet.* His vitals were crashing. His head fell to one side at a grotesque angle, mouth open, skin pale. Saronda rushed over and held his face. "Brody, wake up."

Rebecca pulled her away. "He can't have any outside stimulation like that."

They held each other. *Skreet. Skreet.* The alarm continued.

"His face was cold, Rebecca, his... it's not fair."

Saronda's tears stained the light-colored silk of Rebecca's blouse. *Skreet. Skreet.* The alarm seemed louder, angrier.

A guilt descended on Rebecca for suggesting the plan. Minutes went by. Nothing but the sound of the alarm and Saronda's sobbing.

And then it stopped. Silence.

They pulled away from each other, empty, with

nothing to say.

The next and only sound was two people inhaling as if preparing to say, "Oh my God."

—ε-ε-ε-ε-ε-ε—

Charles "Winks" Mowhinkle pulled his truck into the library parking lot. The radio told him something he already knew.

"...Welcome back D.C. It's cold out there. In fact, record cold. It hasn't been this cold in October since 2005. That's right, you'd have to go back ten years to feel this cold, this early. Can you believe this weather Charlie?

Ken, I can't believe it's been ten years since 2005, alright next we have..."

Winks stepped out of the truck. "Hello, Missus K, how are you?"

"Winks! I heard you sold your bar. Congratulations."

"Yeah, cleaned it out, just this one box of books left. I'm donating it to the library."

"Well, you came on the right day. It's our annual donation day. The two volunteers inside can help you. It's Roni and her sister Shay."

Winks carried the heavy box through the double doors and set it on the front desk.

He squinted to see the name tag. "So, you're Roni. Is

that short for something?"

"Saronda. How can I help?"

"I'm donating these books."

"Cool, let's see what you got."

Winks pulled out a pocket knife and cut the box open.

Roni squealed, "Ohh they're French. Let's see. Hmm, tight fit." She pulled out a book. A magazine dragged along with it and fell on the desk.

Winks asked, "Is French OK?"

"Yeah, it's great. I love French books. Especially old ones."

"OK, great."

Winks picked up the magazine. "Do you have a place to throw this away? Must have been used for packing. Oh, you know what. It looks like science fiction, uh, from 1905, no less. I'm visiting my nephew in Idaho next spring. He loves science fiction. Thirty years old and still reads this stuff. Huh, French science fiction. It'll be like a joke."

Roni was engrossed in one of the new French books. "Huh? Sure."

"OK, uh, can I get a receipt? You know taxes."

"Huh? Yeah, here's a slip. You can fill it out.

Thanks."

She went back to reading the book. It was French poetry, her latest passion.

Roni watched as Winks walked out, the magazine dangling from his pocket.

Shay said, "C'mon girl, it's time to party like it's 1999."

"Well, I have to study like it's 2015. I have a Mechanical Engineering test next week. Besides, I want to look at this book of French poetry that guy dropped off."

"Boring. How you gonna find a guy when you're readin' all the time?"

They pushed through the doors into the cold air.

Roni said, "It'll happen. I know it." She took a few steps. "Oh no look, he dropped that magazine. I'll take it back inside."

"Girl, they locked up already."

Roni picked up the magazine. "You're right. I'll throw it away at home."

A car pulled into the parking lot. The driver pulled around the two women so the setting sun wouldn't be in his eyes. "Excuse me, enny yunz guys know where The George is at? I'm staying there… 'nat."

Shay cocked her head. "Is that English?"

Roni stepped forward. "Don't listen to her. I know where The George is. It's next to a coffee shop I go to. Type in Union Station. It'll get you close."

"Thank you. That was very helpful. See ya."

He drove off. Shay said, "Cute. Nice hair."

Roni replied, "I saw."

As they started walking home, Roni stopped. "Why are you looking at me like that?"

"I'm just sayin', I didn't see no ring on that young man's finger."

"Zip it, Sis."

—ε-ε-ε-ε-ε-ε—

She never studied for that midterm exam. In fact, she never took it. Mechanical Engineering? She lost interest. And be precise what you call her. It's Dr. Saronda Jackson. She earned a PhD in Theoretical Physics and stays up late one night a year waiting to see if she wins the Nobel Prize for her paper, "Proof that Whispers Go Faster Than Light Using a Mass Array Wormhole Lens." She's well-known for another paper, "Dark Matter Doesn't Exist, Never Existed and was a Silly Idea in the First Place." Bigger than that, she has two amazingly curious children who bring light into the world with their deeply sensitive Whispers.

Mr. Brody Markovich-Jackson went on to become a VP with an impressive sounding title. Bigger than that, he is Saronda's husband. He lives in a nicely appointed house with Saronda and their two interracial kids.

As for the SEC, Rebecca Standiford ran the whole damn thing for a while and then became one hell of a President of the United States.

After ExpoLytics folded, Wayne Drakauer made some decent coin as a freelancer until the javascript framework he was using stopped supporting quantum tunnels and he said screw it.

WHAT HAPPENED IN BETWEEN

A lot. Danielle Sközy is the only one who knows.

The End

*To learn more about reality go
to QwikPage.com:*

QWIKPAGE.COM

ABOUT THE AUTHOR

Matthew Kevan Zimmer

Matthew Kevan Zimmer holds two science degrees and studied music composition for decades. He has a deep curiosity about how the world works and enjoys riding his bike up hills when it's warm and skiing down hills when it's cold. He spent the first eighteen years of his life exploring the hills of western Pennsylvania when the Steelers, Penguins and Pirates dominated. He experienced the emotional rollercoaster of the Immaculate Reception followed a few days later by the tragic death of Roberto Clemente. He and his wife have a daughter and a grand-dog Australian Shepherd.

STAY IN TOUCH

Website: twistedrealitybooks.com
Facebook: facebook.com/mist.of.lies
Twitter (X): twitter.com/MathRonda
SoundCloud: soundcloud.com/danielleskozy

QwikPage.com   Access Kelso's VPN

QWIKPAGE.COM   vpn-406-waco.io

ALSO BY THE AUTHOR

Mist Of Lies: The Dog's Diary (Coming soon)

Mist Of Lies: Quest of a Parasite (Coming soon)

Stories I Tell Myself

Made in the USA
Monee, IL
08 May 2024